elp us Rate this book...
ut your initials on the
ft side and your rating
on the right side.
1 = Didn't care for
2 = It was O.K.
3 = It was <u>great</u>

			DATE DUE		
			11/22		
E 2. M	1 2 3	JAN 0 3 2022			
	1 2 3				
	1 2 3				
	1 2 3				
	1 2 3				
	1 2 3				
	1 2 3				
	1 2 3				
	1 2 3				
	1 2 3				
	1 2 3				
	1 2 3				
	1 2 3				
	1 2 3				
	1 2 3				

PRINTED IN U.S.A.

DEVIL'S
RIDE
WEST

Center Point
Large Print

Also by David Nix and available from
Center Point Large Print:

Dead Man's Hand

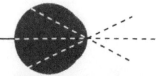

**This Large Print Book carries the
Seal of Approval of N.A.V.H.**

DEVIL'S RIDE WEST

David Nix

CENTER POINT LARGE PRINT
THORNDIKE, MAINE

To Mr. Charlie Patton,
my ninth-grade English teacher,
who was the first to tell me,
"You should become a writer."

CHAPTER ONE

July 1869, Wyoming Territory

Inner demons starved of air never die for good. Jake Paynter's demons returned with a vengeance when a pair of Texas Rangers came for his head. Jake scanned the sweeping expanse of blue sky overhead to find a hawk circling the broken hills of sandstone and sage that walled him on three sides. Satisfied, he turned back to the task of setting a rabbit snare. Perhaps the bird knew what he was doing and hoped to jump his claim. Disregarding his potential rival, Jake shoved a stick into a soft patch of clover two handspans away from the skirt of a juniper bush.

With deft movements, he tied a length of sinewy twine between the bush and the stick, leaving a large loop suspended above the clover. With luck, a jackrabbit in search of a tempting meal would wander through the loop until the twine tightened around its furry neck. As he stood, Jake brushed away mild guilt over condemning an innocent creature to the same fate he'd escaped the previous September. After all, a man had to eat. And the driven hunter remained, the last vestiges of the inner wolf he'd only lately laid to rest.

Jake moved along the ridge of earth that followed a creek until he found another lush outcropping of clover. His mind soon drifted while he set another snare, content to inhabit solitude for a time. Nature conspired to dull his senses. The pleasant touch of an early summer breeze. The warmth of the unobstructed sun. The scattered trill of birds drowning out distant calls of children at play somewhere near the village. Perhaps that was why he didn't sense them coming until it was too late.

"Stretch yer hands, Paynter. Slow-like."

The drawling voice from ten feet behind him snapped Jake back to reality. He didn't bother reaching for his revolver, which he'd irresponsibly left at the village. The knife in his hand wouldn't do him much good with a bullet in his head. Out of options, he did as commanded and raised his hands skyward.

"Stand and pivot," said a second voice with similar intonation.

Jake rose slowly and turned to face the strangers. Two men, both at least five years north of fifty and solid as stretched wire, faced him with confident wariness. One stood a head taller than the other. Matching mustaches framed straight-lipped determination. Twin Remington forty-fours gripped in steady outstretched hands targeted his chest. The shorter man lifted his chin.

"You gonna drop the knife, son? Or we gotta do this the hard way?"

Something in their aspect informed Jake that his run was over. That he was dealing with professionals who weren't likely to make a mistake. The sudden and unwelcome realization was what undoubtedly resurrected his demons for the first time in nearly a year. The taller man seemed to sense what was coming because his eyebrows lifted with uncertainty. Too late, though. Jake flung himself from the ridge headfirst down the embankment and into the creek. His body bounced up from the rocky creek bed, and his legs were in motion when his feet found soil.

"Dog blast it!" one of the men swore.

Without sparing a backward glance, Jake knew that to stop running was to die. The splashing of boots in the creek behind him gave evidence that one man had taken to the water. The other raced along the embankment above him, no doubt. Jake dodged right as a blue screamer whipped past his ear. He clung to the narrow border between the water and the flaring embankment as it bent slowly to the right. Shouted conversation from behind and above identified the locations of both pursuers.

Left to his own devices, Jake might've run all day until one of the men got off a clean shot. His deepest instincts, however, had different plans. Without much forethought or so much as a glimpse at his adversaries, Jake scrambled up the embankment like a treed cat and launched himself at the startled man. A shot went wide beneath Jake's arm as he bear-hugged the taller pursuer and dragged him back over the embankment to land atop the second man in a pile of arms, legs, and desperation.

"Holy hell!"

The shout from the shorter man as he splayed face-first into the shallow creek spurred Jake into a frenzy of advantage. As he flung the tall man away, he came away with his revolver. When the shorter fellow rolled over to face him, Jake liberated his weapon as well, even as the man squeezed his abruptly missing trigger. With a Remington pointed between each set of eyes, Jake stood over the shocked men lying side by side on their backs in six inches of water and sand. Dark whispers urged him to end them, and quick, with a narrow tunnel through each forehead. While he was considering the advice, the shorter one leveled a glare at his partner.

"Dammit, Hyde. I done told you he was a runner. Didn't I say one of us should watch the creek?"

Hyde's forehead creased with disagreement. "Go to Hades, Chancellor. If you'd a' just shot him instead of chattin', we'd not be bathin' in this damn creek, now, would we?"

"Ain't never shot a man with his hands raised and never will."

"And you think I would?"

"Didn't say that. I know you wouldn't either."

"Damn right. Might've changed my mind, though, had I known I'd be lookin' at the wrong end of my own firearm."

"Can't say I disagree." Chancellor expelled a heavy sigh. "Can't believe it's come to this after thirty years."

Jake's predatory gaze faded into a pair of blinks when Hyde extended his left hand toward his partner. "It's been the time of my life, Chancellor."

Chancellor reached across his body to shake the hand. "A hog-killin' time, Hyde. The finest."

The warming display of well-worn camaraderie had the effect of beating back the darkness. Of freeing Jake's reason. A parade of shining faces slipped uninvited through his consciousness, calling to him. Gus Rivers. Stacy Blue. The Emshoffs, the Robersons, and others who had extended a hand of friendship at their own peril. And brightest among them, Rosalyn Ashley, the kindhearted sister of a man who wished him dead. With the emergence of mental quiet, Jake recovered long enough to study the men before him and to see what he'd missed before. Knee-high, pointed-toed boots. Holsters mounted high on the hips instead of slung low, for drawing while riding. Wide-brimmed vaquero-style hats. Beaten leather chaps. The familiar drawls. His brow drew down with recognition.

"You're Texas Rangers."

Hyde lifted an eyebrow. "We are. What of it?"

"Why'd you come for me? I ain't wanted in Texas."

Chancellor sat up slowly, showing both hands to Jake. "Fair question, son. I suppose it's just a matter of serendipity."

"Come again?"

Hyde sat up as well. "We're headed from down Austin way up to the Powder River in the Montanas, gunnin' for a rip who's wanted in Texas. The boys over at Fort Laramie mentioned you, and we thought, 'Heck, why not make a side trip?' "

Chancellor snorted. "Not our best decision. Shoulda never let you talk me into this."

"You only needed three words of convincin'. You wanted to come."

"Yeah. Probably." Chancellor glanced up at Jake. "You gonna shoot us? 'Cause if not, I'd like to lift my hind parts outta this creek. It's a mite frigid."

Jake stepped back two paces. "All right. But tell me, how'd you know where to look and then slip past four thousand Shoshone to find me?"

As the men stood, Hyde shrugged. "Been doin' this a long time. Findin' things that're lost or hidin'. It's what we do."

"But why come so far out of your way on a lark?"

When the Rangers raised eyebrows at each other, Jake knew he was in for a surprise. He hated surprises.

"He don't know," said Hyde.

"Know what?"

"About the bounty on your head."

"Bounty?"

Chancellor retrieved his soaked hat from the creek and began wringing water from it. "A thousand dollars. Five hundred from the government, matched by some feller . . . What was his name?"

Hyde scratched his chin. "Asher, or Ashton, or . . ."

"Ashley," growled Jake. "Lucien Ashley."

Chancellor grinned. "I see you know the man. But more to the point, you're a valuable commodity right about now. Every lawman, detective, bounty hunter, glory hound, desperado, and lowlife west of the Mississippi is comin' for you. And every one of 'em aimin' to bring you in, dead or alive. A thousand dollars is five years' earnings for most of that ilk."

The Ranger's pronouncement struck Jake like a fist. No. Not now. Not when he'd finally found a bubble of peace after nearly a decade of conflict. "I just want to be left alone."

Chancellor's eyes softened. "I understand,

13

son. Been there myself. But you don't have that luxury anymore. Eventually, they'll find ya. They'll keep comin' 'til you're dead or they are. I'm sorry to be the one to tell you."

"Why'd you do it, anyway?" said Hyde. "Kill your captain."

The disastrous incident above the Green River burned through Jake's brain in a flash of anger and resistance. "He ordered the slaughter of Arapaho women and children. I refused, so he tried to kill me. And I don't take kindly to being murdered."

"Don't have to tell us that." Hyde laughed and shook his head. "Women and children, you say?"

"Two hundred, give or take."

Silence fell until the whir of a nearby locust dominated the conversation. Chancellor scratched his gray-grizzled chin and turned to his partner. "Whadda you say, Hyde? Should we leave this man to his lonesome?"

Hyde peered at his revolver in Jake's hand and pursed his lips. "Seems prudent. 'Sides. We gotta fetch that bushwhacker off the Powder River and get him back to Texas before the captain docks our pay. Again."

Without much forethought, Jake dunked the pair of Remingtons in the creek before returning them to the Rangers. "Powder's wet now. You'll need to reload and then catch me again down the creek a ways. There's a thousand Shoshone

14

that direction who'll likely respond to further gunshots. It won't go well if they do, I'm thinkin'."

"We won't shoot ya," said Chancellor as he holstered his soggy gun. "You have my word as a Ranger. One Texan to another. Come on, Hyde."

As they walked back along the creek to wherever they'd stashed their horses, Hyde looked over a shoulder. "Best of luck, Paynter. If we found you so quick, you can be sure a horde will be comin' after us, and right soon. Keep a revolver on yer hip, for the love of Betsy."

The advice proved superfluous for Jake. He knew a storm was coming, and everyone he cared about would suffer from his proximity. More certainly, he knew his old mentor, Ambrose Blackburn, would track him down sooner or later. Vengeance was a powerful motivator. When fueled by the promise of riches, it became a poisonous crusade.

CHAPTER TWO

"And then what happened?"

Beah Nooki asked the question calmly, as if unconcerned that Jake had nearly been killed by a pair of crusty old Rangers. That was his way, though. One did not become a Shoshone elder through overt displays of panic or consternation. Jake scanned the skyline where the men had departed before he'd returned to the village. The Little Wind River cut through a wide, green watershed backed by snowcapped mountains that held up the edge of the sky on natural pillars of granite and time. The murmur of the river tumbling by the bank matched the tranquility of Beah Nooki's tone.

"I chucked them into the creek and took their guns."

The old man nodded slowly, frowning. "Where are the bodies?"

It was an appropriate question. Jake's history of finishing fights usually included lifeless husks bleeding in the dirt. He expelled a sigh. "No bodies. I let 'em go."

Beah Nooki's eyes widened in a rare display of emotion. "Is that so?"

"Yes."

He placed a hand on Jake's shoulder. "That fills me with pride for you."

The show of fatherly affection drew forth a shudder from Jake that passed as quickly as his miserable childhood had. Degradation he could understand. Condemnation he could accept. Slaps, punches, and kicks he could tolerate. But kindness left him uneasy and wallowing in his dead father's proclamations of his utter unworthiness. He stepped away from the well-intentioned gesture without trying to appear as if he was rejecting it.

"Figured if I killed 'em, I'd have more Rangers on my trail. I was just trying to be smart, given that others will be comin' for me."

Beah Nooki smiled slyly, clearly seeing through the lie. "Tell me about these others."

Jake told him what Chancellor and Hyde had said. About the steep price on his head, compliments of the government and Lucien Ashley. About the cavalcade of steely and desperate men determined to claim a piece of him. About his desire to be left in peace. Beah Nooki listened in silence, letting it drag for a time after Jake had run out of words.

"We protect our guests."

The simple response seemed the end of the matter as far as Beah Nooki was concerned. The Shoshone nation could mount a thousand warriors armed with rifles, bows, and war lances at a moment's notice. Stray bands of man hunters seemed little more than a nuisance against such a force. Jake flicked the back of his hand toward the elder.

"I know. And I am grateful. But I don't wish to put anyone in danger. No one should fight on my account. No one should die for my sins."

"So what will you do?"

Another good question. An answer had begun forming even as he was leaving the Rangers in his fading footsteps. When he'd escaped hanging at Fort Bridger three seasons earlier, his initial target had been the Yellowstone country. Everyone who'd traveled there had claimed a man could lose himself for a lifetime in such a place and pass from the notice of mankind forever. The agony and relief of such isolation called to him. Circumstance had cut short his intentions, propelling him instead into the Wind River country and winter shelter with the Shoshone. The arrival of summer, though, had reopened the door of his original plan.

"Tell me about the Yellowstone, Beah Nooki."

The old man chuckled, likely guessing Jake's thoughts. "What can I say? A land of mountains rising like walls to circle the world. A place of forests too thick with timber to pass through. A realm of the Spirit, who blows fountains of water into the sky and sets snares of boiling pools to capture man and beast alike."

"But you've been to that place?"

"Many times, in my youth."

"Will you take me there?"

Beah Nooki gazed at Jake for the space of a dozen breaths, as if seeking to weigh Jake's soul but finding it absent. "No. I will not take you there."

"Why not?"

Beah Nooki chuckled again when Jake frowned. "Because you are the saddest of creatures. You seek solitude with all your strength, but solitude poisons you like foul waters. I will not help you die, Paynter. If you wish to stop living, then you must do so alone."

Jake hung his head, stung by the assessment. He couldn't disagree, though. "I understand."

"What about the woman?" said Beah Nooki. "The one you left at Fort Bridger?"

Rosalyn. Sweet Rosalyn. Too good for him by a country mile. As far from his reach as the stars in the heavens. "I don't even know where she is. She and her brother were headed for Boise. She's five hundred miles west of here by now. And a long way from the Yellowstone country."

"And you do not wish to see her again?"

"I do. But I can't. Not ever."

Beah Nooki nodded. He squatted to inspect the grass at his feet and followed the progress of a black beetle as it beat a path through the forest of blades. When he stood again, he slapped his hands together and leveled an iron gaze at Jake. "You will stay here for now. You will find your thoughts. The days will show you wisdom."

With that, Beah Nooki turned to walk away, having made an elder's proclamation. Though Jake wasn't subject to the decision the way a young Shoshone would be, he couldn't muster the disrespect to ignore it. Beah Nooki had afforded him great kindness and patience. He had shown more fatherhood to Jake in a short time than his real father had in the ten years before he died. Unlike Beah Nooki, his father had been cruel and uncaring of Jake and had molded Jake's older brothers in his image. Perhaps that was why he'd hated Jake so much. Because he wouldn't conform. The stray thoughts dredged up an unwelcome memory of the day his father had said as much.

• • •

Six-year-old Jake stood invisible to one side as his father ambled toward the woman on the main street of town. Jake recognized her. He'd seen her at church, and once she'd come to the plantation with other visitors for a meal. She was pretty, but the beauty faded at her eyes. They were cold and wary as Jake's father approached her. Like a raccoon trapped in a corn crib. His father tipped his hat and began a conversation in low tones that Jake failed to hear. She mumbled a response, and he slipped closer to touch her elbow.

She flinched and spoke again, this time with a sharp edge to the inaudible whisper. He leaned toward one of her ears, his mouth moving in near silence, a half smile twisting it. Her eyes flew wide, and she stumbled back from him, yanking her elbow from his grip. She laced his cheek with the flat of her palm before fleeing as fast as she could in her billowing skirt. Jake's father stood rooted to the earth for a few seconds and an eternity, his chest heaving and fists clenching. When he turned, Jake knew that pain was about to visit.

His father yanked him by the arm and tossed him onto the seat of the buckboard before bounding up beside Jake. With a curse, the man set the horse in motion toward the plantation. Jake tried to make no eye contact while his father fumed a foot away. When the wagon had barely cleared the confines of the village, his father abruptly belted Jake from the seat to sprawl headlong into the dirt of the road. Jake rolled over and rubbed the sting from his jaw.

"What'd I do?"

"You look too damn much like your mother." His father snapped the reins. "Git on!"

Jake watched in disbelief as the wagon rolled away. When it became lost to sight among the East Texas pines, he stood, dusted off his shirt, and began walking. Fear gripped him. Did he know the way home? Would his father beat him again when he arrived? Somewhere along the road, though, something stirred in Jake. Something new. Something wild. Whatever the thing was, it lent him determination and resolve.

It was dark before he'd covered the five miles to the entrance of his father's sugar cane plantation. He lingered outside the house until all voices inside had ceased and all lanterns had been snuffed. Then, silent as a vapor, he slipped upstairs to his bed, disrobed, and crawled beneath the covers. The cicadas singing outside his window serenaded him into sleep, but not before he realized just how alone he'd become in his own family.

CHAPTER THREE

Jake knew the world was about to change the moment he opened his eyes. Flares of light chased shadows across the roof of his cramped lean-to, followed by the murmurs of a thousand whispered voices. He donned his breeches and boots before rolling from his shelter beyond the edge of the Shoshone village. Torches moved among the lodges, not aggressively but with purpose. The collective voices of excited children, chattering adults, and reluctant horses told the tale. The village was packing up for the first time in months, ready to move. Only three things would prompt such an undertaking— enemies, changing weather, or the promise of buffalo. Given the hopeful energy, Jake guessed the third. He pulled on his shirt, strapped his Kerr to a hip, and strode toward the village with hat in hand. A man wearing a blue cavalry coat met him on the way. Jake nodded.

"Follows the Wind."

"Paynter."

As an army scout, Darwin Follows the Wind had borne witness to the events above the Green River that fateful day now nearly two years past. When Jake had fled for his life, it was Follows

25

the Wind who had sent him to the Shoshone for shelter with his grandfather, Beah Nooki. Fate had returned him for refuge a second time. He and Follows the Wind had come to an understanding that transcended the need to speak of what had happened in the past. Jake pressed his weathered hat onto his head.

"Buffalo?"

Follows the Wind grinned and fell into step beside Jake as they entered the village. "Maybe five thousand head, up range toward the pass."

"Where you burned grasslands last summer?"

"That's right." Follows the Wind handed him a braided loop of rawhide. "Go find your horse. Pack your lean-to. Bring your rifle."

Jake separated from Follows the Wind to approach the mass of horses milling and circling along the far side of the village, held in check by two dozen young men with switches and raw determination. When he'd drawn within a hundred feet of the equine mass, Jake put two fingers between his teeth and gave a sharp whistle, followed by another. Within seconds, the herd spit forth a sleek mare who made a beeline for Jake. She tossed her head as she high-stepped toward him, simultaneously communicating pleasure and disdain at his presence. When she reached him, he looped the tether over her head despite her huffed complaint. He pressed a cheek to her muzzle and patted a massive jawbone.

"That's a good girl. Did you miss me?"

She snorted in reply, as was her nature. Jake led her back to his lean-to and packed his worldly possessions, all of which fit in a roll of hide behind the mare's saddle. He'd once lived in a fine house on a sugar plantation, the son of privilege and wealth. He wouldn't trade his meager possessions for the whole lot of it now, the hellhole that it was. Finished with his packing, Jake watched in fascination as three hundred towering lodges disappeared into bundles of buffalo hide and lodgepoles to be strapped to horses, dogs, and people for the thirty-mile journey. They'd cover the daunting distance in a single day.

The sun hadn't quite cleared the hills to the east when the village lurched into motion. Fifteen hundred men, women, and children, along with hundreds of horses, followed the great Chief Washakie west by northwest toward the foot of the pass where the buffalo grazed. Beah Nooki rode alongside his oldest friend at the front of the procession, while Follows the Wind joined a band of riders armed for the coming hunt.

Without prompting, Jake rode alone to one side, telling himself that he was watching for threats, escaping the dust. That wasn't quite the truth of it. Though the Shoshone had shown him hospitality, he only counted a few as friends. Others displayed open animosity to the interloper. Most, however, didn't much care. He was a curiosity. Beah Nooki's odd little project. The white man who had killed a white chief to preserve a village belonging to an adversary of the Shoshone. He would leave in time. They always did.

The procession moved at an astonishing pace away from the Little Wind River to intercept the Wind River proper, the children covering twice the distance of the adults as they chased one another in playful circles for thirty miles while burning up the endless reservoir of energy unique to youth. When Chief Washakie called a halt, the sun had already dipped behind the Wind River Mountains to cast behemoth shadows that swallowed the sprawling landscape. Jake found a place away from the bustle and dined on antelope jerky, dried gooseberries, and isolation.

"Wake up, Paynter."

Jake sprang awake in darkness, ready for a death match before realizing the voice belonged to Beah Nooki. "What's going on?"

"Come."

Without further question, Jake dressed, gathered the mare and his weapons, and followed the old man toward a gathering of shadows. As he drew closer, the vague forms resolved into a host of hunters on horseback, armed with bows and spears. Most of the rifles had been left in camp, it seemed. A trill of excitement rose within Jake.

Was he to hunt buffalo with the Shoshone this day? As if sensing those thoughts, Beah Nooki gripped Jake's shoulder with a gentle hand.

"You may not hunt today. This is only for Shoshone. You may watch, though. And when the hunt finishes, you will help slaughter buffalo. Is your knife at hand?"

"Yes. It is." Jake must have failed to keep the disappointment from his voice, because Beah Nooki laughed.

"You will find blood soon enough, Paynter."

Within minutes, the small army set out behind Washakie, perhaps four hundred strong, all mounted bareback and tense with anticipation. Two hundred more followed on foot, mostly women and young boys, dragging travois for hauling meat and brandishing an assortment of blades for separating hide from flesh, bone from sinew. Despite his prestige, Beah Nooki chose to ride alongside Jake, who appreciated the gesture. Beah Nooki appeared to understand Jake's need for silence and gave him liberal doses of it.

"We draw near now," said Beah Nooki after a few miles. "I smell them on the wind."

Jake could too. It was not so much the odor of the animals as it was the musk of churned earth and bleeding grass. He watched the hunters draw into groups of fifty or a hundred under the direction of the older men, counting their arrows and checking their spears as they did so.

"Why no rifles?" The question had been plaguing Jake for an hour.

"Too hard to reload on a running horse," said Beah Nooki. "And each hunter puts his mark on his arrows. The mark tells who killed the buffalo."

Jake nodded with understanding. He who brought down a buffalo had first rights to the hide and the choicest cuts of meat. Marked arrows would prevent ugly disagreements. These thoughts were still in his head when the party topped a ridge and halted. Jake inhaled an awed breath. Below him, thousands of buffalo filled a valley like a lush, brown carpet, rippling with slow movements, drawn by the tender green shoots that had grown in the wake of a burning.

"Watch now," said Beah Nooki. "Today, I hunt buffalo."

As Jake settled back into his saddle to observe, scores of women and boys flowed around him to find vantage points on the hilltop, blissfully disregarding his presence. The line of hunters on horseback descended the ridge in three directions, flanking the herd. When the first hunters were nearly upon the buffalo, Jake expected the animals to stampede. However, they simply eyed the approaching horses and snorted a few half-hearted warnings. When Washakie waved a spear overhead in a sweeping arc, the hunters drew bows as one and sent arrows into the unlucky creatures ringing the herd. Initially, nearby buffalo wandered toward their fallen comrades with seeming concern, oblivious to the fact that death was upon them.

Only when the second wave of arrows penetrated hide did the herd react the way Jake had expected. A large bull charged one of the horses, only to stagger beneath a pair of well-aimed projectiles. It pressed forward with sheer momentum before falling at the feet of a dancing horse as the rider thrust a spear into the buffalo's neck. As if cued by the bull's collapse, the nearest animals turned and barreled toward the center of the herd. Within seconds, the ripple of panic propelled the entire population into flight.

With sharp cries and pumping fists, the hunters burst after the animals. Working alone or in pairs, the men isolated outliers and shot or speared the fleeing creatures behind the ribs in an attempt to puncture the lungs or heart. A dozen buffalo fell, then a dozen more as dust rose to engulf the valley. The blur of men on horseback raced through the murk, shouting over the bawls of angry or dying buffalo. A flash of white hair that might have belonged to Beah Nooki or Washakie flew by—old warriors, made young again by the ritual of the hunt that seemed embedded in the souls of men.

For a moment, the urge to wade into the midst of the slaughter welled up inside Jake. Before he could act, though, before he could disgrace himself, memories crowded into his head of smoking battlefields churned with mud and blood and filled with a dark symphony of the rage and anguish of men intent on destroying one another. He looked away from the carnage to gather his reeling senses, slowing his rapid breathing. When he dared to look again, the hunt had all but finished. The herd had moved on in a rush, leaving perhaps three hundred dead in their wake. The hunters circled the kills, shouting with joy and bloodlust. It had been a good hunt. The people would eat well for a long time.

The women and boys had begun moving down the hillside toward the kills before Jake realized he'd been left behind. He nudged the mare after them and struck out across the valley toward the carcass of the large bull who had dared challenge the attackers on behalf of his herd. Jake wanted to be the one to care for him in death, to honor his futile fight. Empathy was a fickle thing, springing up in the oddest of moments to remind a killer that a candle of humanity still flickered inside.

CHAPTER FOUR

Jake was up to his elbows in buffalo gore when the triumphant hunter returned. As the man slid from his horse and stepped toward him, Jake recalled his name. Big Elk. He was middle-aged, going gray but still powerfully built. His persistent glare rested somewhere between granite and ice.

"This is my kill, *dyvoe*."

After two different stays and nearly a year among the Shoshone, Jake had begun to comprehend more than just their language. He'd come to understand the nuance of tone and intent. Big Elk was challenging Jake to refute him, perhaps wishing for it. He had even used the tribal term for "white man," which sounded remarkably like "devil." Jake lifted his chin and returned the steady gaze.

"It was a good kill. I saw you make it." He extended the pair of arrows he had extracted from the bull toward the man. "These are your marks."

Big Elk frowned and accepted the arrows. "Did you pray over the bull?"

Jake ducked his eyes, cursing himself silently for his mistake. "No. Forgive my disrespect. I am a fool."

33

Big Elk's frown faded and he shrugged, seemingly appeased by Jake's groveling. He began praying over the slain buffalo, speaking too fast for Jake to follow every word. However, what he recognized and what he knew were enough. Big Elk was giving thanks to the bull for sacrificing his life to sustain the lives of his people, as was the custom with every kill. On finishing his prayer, Big Elk produced a long knife, moved to the opposite side of the animal, and began separating hide from flesh with steady but energetic strokes. His butchering skills shone all the brighter for Jake's relative inexperience. Sure, Jake had skinned a hundred animals, but never one this large and bloody. The hunter swiftly surpassed Jake before rounding the carcass to stand beside him. He watched Jake's efforts briefly before nudging him aside and making short, sharp sawing motions over the hide with his hand.

"Not this way." He engaged Jake's eyes as if checking for attention, and then moved his hand across the hide with long sweeps aligning with muscle striations. "This way. Yank the hide behind the cut."

Jake watched Big Elk's technique as he squatted and peeled back two feet of hide in four cuts. Then the hunter stood. "Now, you try."

Jake knelt and performed his best imitation of what Big Elk had done. His strokes were less even, his yanking of the hide less effective. However, he immediately doubled his former progress. "I'll be damned."

After overseeing several mostly effective slices of Jake's knife, Big Elk grunted mild approval and began carving out the liver. He and Jake worked together in silent solidarity, removing the hide and carving the great bull into slabs of red meat and piles of bone. As the giant disintegrated before his eyes, Jake took comfort in the fact that the animal's death would sustain a family for months and warm their bodies for years during the cruelest onslaughts of winter. By the time they finished the butchering, blood plastered Jake's shirt to his body. He laid the last hunk of flesh on the steaming pile and removed his hat to mop his brow with the back of his arm, forgetting the blood soaking his sleeve until it was too late. He grimaced and replaced his hat.

"Do not stand like a dead tree," said Big Elk. He motioned over Jake's shoulder. "Go help the women."

Jake followed the hand wave to find a pair of young women striding away from the kill zone, armed with long knives and intention. He questioned the hunter with a frown.

Big Elk expelled an impatient breath. "One fell beyond that hill, also my kill. Help carve and carry the meat."

Jake nodded and followed the hunter's

instructions without further question. As the women climbed the low roll of land, he closed the distance until he trailed them by no more than twenty paces. When one noticed him following, her eyes grew wide and she nudged the other. Their uncertainty grew palpable, sticky and occluding in the cool air of morning. He mustered his best Shoshone accent before calling out.

"Big Elk sent me. I will help cut and carry."

The young women exchanged a long glance before continuing their journey. Jake lagged intentionally, acutely aware of his outsider status. They were right to fear him, though. If they knew the truth of his past deeds, they would flee him like rabbits before a wind-whipped prairie fire. Upon crowning the ridge, he spotted Big Elk's kill—a cow who'd collapsed on the far side of a small creek that hugged the low ground between rolls of adjacent hills. As he descended and crossed the creek, all trace of the hunting party fell away until only he, the two women, and the dead buffalo remained in all the world. As the women stood over the carcass in prayer, Jake stopped to remove his hat, bowed his head, and tried to remember how to pray. When the women finished offering thanks, they began removing the hide from the rump without waiting for Jake to join them. When he had paused too long, one looked up with an impatient smirk.

"Remove the entrails, Niineeni' howouuyooniit."

The use of the name given him by the Arapaho surprised him but gave way to a grimace. Removing the entrails was the foulest job, reserved for the most junior of the group. He waited for them to roll the hide past the midsection before going after the stomach with his knife. The young women pretended to ignore his presence even while whispering about him with grins and suppressed laughter. He took no offense. The snatches of conversation proved mostly flattering. They liked his new beard, anyway. And maybe the revolver at his hip. Jake returned the favor by pretending to understand nothing of what they said, despite his inability to release their feminine forms from the corner of his vision. If only he'd known his sidelong interest would get one of the women killed, he would've paid less attention to them.

"Turn around slow, Paynter."

The gruff voice at his back dripped menace and triumph. His arms filled with entrails, Jake stood and slowly pivoted in place to find five grubby men at his back leveling an assortment of revolvers and long guns at his chest. Bounty hunters. They flashed black and yellow smiles, clearly pleased with their capture of the wanted fugitive. When one of the women tried to slip away, a burly man with twin trails of tobacco juice staining his beard seized her arm and shoved a blade beneath her throat.

"Where you goin', missy?" He pulled her ear up to his mouth. "Keep quiet now."

"Do not call out," Jake said in Shoshone. "They want me. They may let you go."

He knew the words to be a lie, but a cry from either of the women would lead to immediate carnage that would surely claim them all. Besides, he needed a moment to decide how he would kill these men.

"Don't speak that savage filth," said the man nearest Jake. "You're comin' with us now. And these little girls. They make a sound, and we'll put a bullet in yer skull."

"A thousand dollars!" whispered another man, his eyes shining with greed and glory.

Jake nodded with false compliance, even while feeling the weight of the revolver on his hip. His Kerr single-action carried five shots in the chamber. One for each bounty hunter hoping to take him. In his mind's eye, he saw how the coming seconds would play out. Throw the entrails at the men in front of him. Liberate the brains of the burly man restraining the young woman. Put a knife through the throat of the nearest man. Drop to the dirt with the falling dead man and squeeze off three shots in three seconds to take down the others. And hope the inevitable slugs that found his body wouldn't prove fatal. That was how he saw it. But that wasn't what happened.

"Damn!" shouted the burly man as his captive tore skin from his wrist with bared teeth. As he pulled away from the woman, he sliced her throat half through and let her drop. In the heartbeat that followed, Jake's darkness poured forth like the angel of death. He charged the other four men, hurling entrails, stabbing, and pulling his Kerr all at once. One attacker fell beneath his knife and another from his first bullet. Before he could launch a second shot, a fist found the side of his head. He rolled away to regain his feet, intending to kill the burly man who'd hit him, but was too late. The second woman plunged her skinning knife between the bounty hunter's spine and right shoulder blade, stopping his heart. The man's eyes flashed surprise as he tumbled forward.

Jake turned to find the two survivors busting tail over the adjacent hill. He took aim, but the lever slipped from his thumb, encased as it was with buffalo innards. By the time he recovered his grip, his prey had disappeared over the rise. Before his feral instincts could propel him on a deadly hunt, an anguished cry froze him. He turned to find the standing woman staring in disbelief at her fallen sister, both hands covering her mouth. Jake fought a brief war between vengeance and humanity before the latter scored a narrow victory. He knelt beside the downed woman, whose dead eyes examined the sky for the rescue that would never come. Her long, black braid, so reminiscent of Stacy's, drifted beside her head as if unaware of its owner's passing. Gently, he slid his arms beneath the woman, gathered her to his chest, and stood. Blood drained from her neck to mingle with the buffalo gore on his arms, a panorama of death painted upon the canvas of his shirt.

How long he stood watch over the fallen woman, he wasn't certain. The pounding of hooves finally drew his eyes upward to find a dozen mounted Shoshone racing over the ridge, led by Big Elk.

"What happened?"

Big Elk's rage filled the tiny valley as effectively as Jake's ever could. With an outburst of grieving explanation, the surviving woman told of the attack, of how she'd killed one and Jake two others. Then she pointed toward the adjacent hilltop.

"They ran there. Two white men. Go kill them."

Big Elk needed no instruction, though. With a howling cry, he kicked his horse into motion and led the party over the hilltop in pursuit. In their absence, Jake gazed woefully at the surviving woman. Tears trailed through the dried buffalo blood on her face while she shook her head repeatedly, as if willing a different outcome.

"I am sorry," he said.

Jake began walking up the hill toward the rest of the hunting party with the dead woman in his arms. The bounty hunters were no longer his problem. He wasn't sure what Big Elk would do to them, but he hoped they'd suffer greatly before they died.

CHAPTER FIVE

Jake's hands still bore the stains of the murdered woman when the somber hunting party returned to the newly located village. In their half-day absence, three hundred lodges had risen in the flats between the Wind River and the foothills of the Rockies like a field of cream-colored haystacks. The smell of cook fires permeated the valley as residents awaited the bounty of the hunt. When Washakie informed the others of the young woman's killing, shock leached much of the excitement from those who waited, leaving grim expressions everywhere Jake turned his eyes.

Everyone recognized the danger of hunting buffalo and prepared for the death of a hunter beneath the feet or horns of the herd, or the gruesome injury of one thrown from a horse at a dead run. The killing of a young woman as she cleaned an animal after the danger had passed, however, came as a cruel afterclap. In their despair, some eyed Jake with judgment as he passed by, blaming him for the girl's death. They were not wrong. He could not have been more guilty if he'd slashed her with his own hand. Deep in the throes of remorse, Jake remained apart from the people, huddling with the mare beyond the village, staring into the distance. That was where Beah Nooki found him.

"Paynter."

Jake turned to find the elder stealing up as if fearful that his approach would send Jake into flight like some startled woodland creature. "Beah Nooki."

The old man motioned toward a flat rock. "Sit with me for a time. Let us speak of the hunt."

Jake turned the mare loose, knowing she'd not wander far, and joined his visitor on the rock. They faced the bustling village, only two hours beyond the tragic news. New buffalo hides had been stretched out on poles to dry, and the process of making jerky from buffalo meat was well underway. He could barely watch, knowing what his outlaw status had cost the Shoshone. The girl should be there among her friends and family, tanning hides and roasting meat. She should find a young man to woo her. She should raise children and grandchildren, become the wise old woman at the fireside, and die in her sleep at a ripe old age surrounded by loved ones. Instead, her cold body lay bundled and unmoving, all its future promise sent back to the Spirit at the hands of a man who'd wanted to kill Jake but had settled for an innocent. Jake was growing weary of innocents paying the price for his actions.

"You will leave now." Beah Nooki's words were more statement than question.

"If that's what the people wish."

He shook his head. "That's not what they wish. Not what I wish. But I see in your eyes that you are already gone from this place."

Jake heaved a deep sigh, realizing the elder was right. Sometime during the past hours, he'd decided to leave. He rubbed his hands together again, trying to remove the last of the bloodstains. "You see everything, Beah Nooki."

"Not everything. Just what is before me." He watched Jake's efforts to free his hands of guilt. "Her death is not your doing."

"It *was* my doing. Not directly, but still my fault. If not for me, she'd still be here." He leveled a determined gaze at Beah Nooki. "Others will come for me. Many more, I think. I have to leave now before more people die on my account. One is too many."

Beah Nooki nodded grimly and hummed empathy. "I understand. But stay the night. Feast with us one more time."

Though he was not hungry, Jake knew that to refuse the offer of food was a high form of disrespect, especially when refusing an elder. He swallowed the bile that had seemed to take up residence in the base of his throat. "I will stay. Thank you."

"That is good." Beah Nooki rose, peered at Jake for a moment with concerned eyes, and laid a hand on his shoulder. "You cannot forever run

45

from the ghosts that chase you. In time, you must face them all. Only in that way can you know peace. I know this from experience."

Jake nodded, wondering what ghosts Beah Nooki had faced. He knew the elder was right, though. He just didn't know how to stop running.

Jake had started a small cook fire in his isolated camp when Darwin Follows the Wind arrived on foot from the village. His face held a combination of regret and intrigue.

"Grandfather told me you are leaving."

"That's right."

"Where will you go?"

"To the Yellowstone country, I reckon."

"When?"

"Tomorrow morning."

Follows the Wind frowned. "Nothing will change your plans?"

"I don't think so."

The scout squatted and held his palms to the fire before rubbing them together. "Then you'll not want to know that outsiders have come to speak to you. You'll not want to know that they wait for you in the village with Beah Nooki."

Jake narrowed his eyes to slits. "Outsiders? More bounty hunters? Lawmen?"

"No."

"Who, then?"

"Come and see."

Follows the Wind stood and strode away, daring Jake to follow. He did but reloaded the Kerr as he walked. Twilight had deepened when they entered the village together and made their way toward Beah Nooki's home at the center. As they neared the lodge, Jake pulled the Kerr up in the holster, spun it sideways, and rested his fingers lightly against the grip. He didn't want to kill anyone else but would if forced. The thought of such an event pressed a lead weight into the pit of his stomach. Upon reaching their destination, Follows the Wind swept aside the flap and motioned for Jake to enter. He did so without losing contact with the revolver grip. As a result, it was only providence that he didn't shoot Stacy Blue when she tackled him.

"Paynter! You old dog!" She hugged him fiercely before letting him regain his feet. When Jake had been sent west as a federal prisoner to be hanged, Stacy, the half-Shoshone daughter of the wagon master, had befriended him immediately. Her ongoing loyalty continued to confound Jake, but he welcomed it nonetheless. Beah Nooki, who sat to one side with a blanket draped over his shoulders, smiled broadly, clearly amused by the chaotic reunion. Stacy's grandfather, Many Horses, had been his lifelong friend. He addressed her in the Shoshone language, his tone light with reprimand.

"Be calm, young colt. You will outrun your wisdom and fall into a pit."

She nodded deferentially and stepped back from Jake, allowing Gus Rivers to extend a hand. A flood of memories surged through Jake's brain at the sight of his oldest friend. Of the battles they'd fought together while with the Kansas First Colored Volunteers during the war. Of their time serving side by side in the all-black Tenth Cavalry of the Plains Army at Fort Bridger, a three-day ride to the south. Of those days on the Oregon Trail when they'd overcome impossible odds to defeat an unbeatable foe. Jake shook the offered hand and couldn't help but smile. It felt good to do anything other than frown, and he was happy to see his most trusted companions again..

"Gus. Stacy. Why the heck are you here? No offense intended."

"None taken," Gus said with a laugh. He stroked his smooth chin while pointing at Jake's. "The beard is new. Never seen you with one before."

"Never grown one before."

"I think it looks right fine," said Stacy. "Makes you look older. Like you might be important or somethin'."

"I ain't important. You know that better than anyone."

"There's lots a' folks who'd disagree with that."

"There's lots of foolish people, then." He

swung his attention back to Gus. "So, again, why are you here? I doubt you came to admire my beard."

"As much as I do admire it," said Gus, "we need to talk."

Beah Nooki waved a hand in disagreement. "Talk must wait. First, we share the bounty of the hunt and thank the Spirit for plenty."

Jake appreciated the elder's plan. Although he wanted to know what had brought Gus and Stacy on the two days' ride from South Pass City, he knew a meal and a moment to breathe would help prepare him for what they had to say.

CHAPTER SIX

While he finished a cut of fire-roasted buffalo flank, Gus studied Paynter like a man assessing a priceless vase after it had been shattered and reassembled. Had it come back together in a new configuration? Were any important pieces missing? His old regiment mate stayed mostly quiet, ceding the floor to Stacy and Beah Nooki as they conversed in a blend of English and Shoshone. Stacy's white father had done nothing to bury her mother's tribal heritage, and she appeared to revel in reacquainting with the amused elder. Paynter smiled here and there, but each attempt seemed strained. Forced. The peace Gus had hoped to find in his old friend was markedly absent. And he suspected why.

"Paynter."

Gus uttered the name with gravity, with a we-should-talk-now tone. Paynter's attention and the abrupt silence of the other two told him he'd hit the mark.

"Gus."

He wiped the grease from his hands onto the shins of his pants and settled back. "I know you been here, what, nine months now. But you don't seem like a man intent on stayin' much longer. Am I wrong?"

Paynter's mouth lifted in a half smile. "You know me better'n anyone."

"We all have our crosses to bear. So what's your plan?"

"And don't tell no stories," added Stacy. "We need the truth."

"Paynter always tells the truth," said Gus. "To others, anyway. He lies to himself from time to time until I tell him different."

Paynter shook his head. "You're like the mama I never had. Still tryin' to decide if that's a credit or a debit."

"A credit. I'm a good mama. And I'll box yer ears if you don't start explainin' what comes next."

"Right." Paynter folded his fingers together and stared at his hands. "A couple of weeks ago, two Texas Rangers came lookin' for me."

"You killed them?" said Stacy. Her tone carried surprised accusation.

"No, little sister, I did not kill them. They went away peaceably and with no permanent injuries. But they told me that every desperado in the territory is out for my head on a pike."

Gus sighed with relief. Paynter knew. At least he was spared having to share that bit of bad news. "So you know about the bounty and whose behind half of it?"

Paynter's eyes clouded. "I do."

"And you know you can't stay here, right? Your whereabouts are now public knowledge. I've seen at least three crews in South Pass City askin' questions about you."

"I gathered as much. Five bounty hunters came for me this morning. Them I did kill. With a lot of help, of course. But they had it comin'."

"Sounds like I might want a story after all," said Stacy. She sat cross-legged, propped elbows on knees, and set her chin in her hands. "Do tell."

Gus and Stacy listened intently as Paynter described in detail his encounter with the Rangers, the move of the village, the buffalo hunt, and the deadly episode with the bounty hunters. When he began speaking of the murdered girl, his voice left him for a time as he stared at the ground and traced a circle in the dirt. Then he cleared his throat.

"Anyhow, that's why I have to go. Beah Nooki understands."

The old man nodded, though he didn't seem very pleased by the prospect.

"At first light tomorrow," Paynter continued, "I'll ride over the pass and into the Yellowstone country. Beah Nooki will tell me the way."

Gus grunted. "It's a lonely place, so I've heard."

"I'm countin' on it."

Gus looked at Stacy. She returned his

glance with a nod and patted his hand with encouragement. "We have to tell him."

"Tell me what?" Paynter's somber expression melted into one of concern.

Gus spread his hands. "About what's happening in South Pass City these past two months. Immigrant gold miners are turning up dead. Three so far, all torn to shreds. Gutted and with entrails spread over the brush."

Paynter's eyes narrowed with bewilderment and affront. "A wild animal?"

"Some say it's a wolf," said Stacy. "Maybe a werewolf."

Gus waved a hand at her. "Don't be grasping at fairy tales. There ain't no such thing as werewolves."

"You don't know that. You don't know what's out there. It's a big world and we ain't seen the half of it." She turned to Beah Nooki. "Tell him."

Beah Nooki just smiled. "Not my argument."

"Regardless," said Gus before she could press her line of reasoning, "people are dyin' and everyone's afraid they'll be next. The associate justice seems concerned enough, but he's new there and the town marshal refuses to investigate. Says animal attacks aren't his jurisdiction."

"Spraggs." Stacy spit on the floor. "He's a coward and up to his neck in Lucien Ashley's pocket. O' course he won't investigate."

"And Judge Kingman is only in the area eight

days a month. Not much he can do with such a big circuit."

Paynter peered at Gus in thought, working his jaw back and forth. "What's your opinion, then? If it ain't wolves, regular or the fairy-tale kind, then what's this about?"

"I think the murders are about freein' up gold-mining claims so they can be resold to the highest bidder. And guess who's the highest bidder so far?"

"Ketchum," blurted Stacy.

Paynter's brow creased in disbelief. "Ketchum? The man who tried to kill us for gold on the trail last year?"

Stacy nodded, pleased with his surprise. "Yep. The jackass works for Lucien Ashley now."

"Which is why," said Gus in an attempt to reclaim the narrative, "I'm pretty sure Ketchum's a false front for Ashley."

Paynter's face grew the puzzled look Gus had expected. "Lucien Ashley? Why would he involve himself with gold claims six hundred miles from Boise? He'd have to ride for most of a month just to manage it."

Stacy leaned forward and lowered her voice. "You haven't heard, then."

"Heard what?"

"That the Ashleys didn't go on to Boise. They stayed in the Wyoming Territory."

Paynter's mouth hung open from the slackness

of his jaw, but his eyes became hawklike with startled interest. "Rosa . . . Lucien is still in the area?"

"They are," she said. "Bought a big spread of land east of the pass along the southern reach of the Wind River Mountains and three hundred head of cattle. They been building like mad beavers since they could scrape away the snow in March. House, barn, corrals. The whole nine yards."

Gus watched Paynter sink into himself for half a minute, the man's mysterious thoughts cartwheeling through his mind. When he raised his eyes again, they were no less haunted than before.

"I'm guessin' you've come for my help."

"Not just us," Gus said, "but all your friends. The Emshoffs. The Robersons. The Dunbars. They've all been whisperin' to the locals that you're the one to help them. That you fight for the little man. That you always find a way to win."

Paynter shook his head and frowned. "I ain't that man, Gus."

"I disagree, my friend. You've always been that man in my eyes, regardless of what you think you are."

Stacy tapped Paynter's kneecap. "We seen the bounty poster. It's not a good likeness, and they got the hat all wrong. An English bowler, of all things."

Paynter lightly touched the hat that he'd set to the side—a weathered slouch hat featuring the numeral 1 of First Kansas Colored on the crown. The hat he'd worn since '62 when he was the young white sergeant of Gus's all-black regiment, looking wet behind the ears if not for the desolation of his eyes.

"And they got you clean-shaven," Gus added. "The beard changes your looks. I doubt anyone but your friends would recognize you from it."

"Lucien and Ketchum would."

"There's that."

When Paynter fell silent, remorse struck Gus. What right did he have to ask a friend to endanger his neck to help people he didn't know in an affair that didn't involve him? Paynter had escaped the noose once. What he and Stacy proposed would return him to the firing line. "I apologize, Paynter. We shouldn't have asked. It's not our place to lay such a burden on you. You should head out for the Yellowstone first thing in the morning, like you planned."

When Paynter locked gazes with Gus, his eyes reflected an array of emotions shifting second by second. Gratitude. Concern. Guilt. "I suppose."

A glance at Stacy found disappointment crowning her usually amiable features. When her eyes narrowed, he guessed what was coming. She leaned back and folded her arms.

"There's one more thing you oughta know."

"What's that?"

"Over the past nine months, I've run into Rosalyn Ashley in town a half-dozen times. And every time, she asks about you. Have I heard from you? Are you well? What are your plans? And every time, I have to tell her that I don't know a blessed thing, not even if you're alive." Stacy let that sink in for a moment. "She pines for you, Paynter. And what's happened to you is slowly eatin' her alive."

Paynter seemed surprised but shook his head. "She should think of me no more. Find another man more her class, one that ain't on the run."

"You don't know much about the mind of a woman, do ya?"

"No."

"Thought so."

The conversation petered out with the dying fire, and soon everyone curled into a blanket for sleep. However, Gus woke several times during the night to find Paynter sitting in the glow of failing embers with his forehead against his knees.

CHAPTER SEVEN

Rosalyn had yet to grow accustomed to the spectacular sensory shift of the West. Twenty years of city living in St. Louis and Washington had trained her mind for a certain set of expectations. The murmur of people and steam engines all hours of the day and night. Light that never faded, gas lamps standing in for the sun when it set. And the smells, pleasant and otherwise. The offerings of bakeries and restaurants invading the air. The distinct odors of horses and oil and machines. Life in the cities provided a continuous feast for the senses, inescapable even when one wished to push away from the table. Her new home was literally a breath of fresh air.

After a restless night, she awoke in darkness to dead silence. Or nearly. A whisper at the edge of her hearing spoke of men snoring in the bunkhouse across the paddock from the house. Of the creek nearby, never ceasing in its labors. Of horses shifting their weight from side to side in the newly built stable. Only her cotton shift and the ever-present sage offered scent. She arose in darkness, changed into her sturdy dress, jacket, and knee-high boots, and donned the slouch hat that Lucien so despised. It reminded him of the one worn by Paynter, so he said, which was why he forbade her from wearing it. She disobeyed out of spite . . . and for deeper reasons she refused to admit to herself.

She tiptoed past Lucien's silent bedroom and took her shotgun from the wall. It was the best money could buy, a fourteen-gauge double-barrel fowling piece built by Samuel and Charles Smith of London. She'd balked when Lucien had bought it for her before the journey west but now cherished the security it offered when she carried it. By the light of a small candle, she loaded both barrels with paper cartridges and set the percussion caps. She didn't expect trouble but remained acutely aware of the rattlesnakes pervading the area—both the slithering kind and those that walked on two legs and eyed her possessively.

After slipping through the door of the sprawling log house, she began walking away from the rising sun. When she'd crossed the creek and covered a hundred yards, Rosalyn turned to survey what she and Lucien had built since they'd settled nine months earlier. The predawn glow revealed emerging shapes, some man-made, some formed by forces beyond reckoning. Twenty miles over the pass from South Pass City, the burgeoning ranch lay nestled in a green valley between fire-red canyon walls and hillocks that gave way to a long, smooth uplift of grass and sage favored by cattle. The hulking shadow of the Wind River Mountains rose to unseen clouds in the background, still hoarding snow on the high peaks despite the coming of proper summertime.

Rosalyn had seen many places in her short life. The gray Atlantic pressing the rocky shores of New England. The shattered beauty of the tree-encrusted Appalachians. The grandeur of the mighty Mississippi as it divided a continent. But she had never laid eyes on a more beautiful place than Red Canyon and Flaming Rocks Ranch. The long, single-story log house with four bedrooms and two parlors squatted beneath the canyon walls, separated by twenty feet from a kitchen sufficient to feed a ranch. The bunkhouse that slept thirty hands. The stables large enough for a dozen horses. The skeleton of a barn that would be finished by month's end. The large, fenced paddock for training horses. It had taken an army of men to raise the place from nothing in four months, but Lucien's gold had become a singular motivator of effort.

Satisfied, she climbed the uplift of grass, dodging cattle along the way, to greet the rising sun. When its first rays poked over the horizon, she checked for snakes and settled into the grass to watch the grand entry. Pink and gold runners fled along the sky from side to side, bleeding color into a landscape that defied simple explanation. This had become her favorite moment of each day. Of sitting in the stillness before the world awoke. Of assessing her list of necessary chores for the day. Of recalling a certain condemned man now disappeared into the Wyoming wilds.

Bathed by the warmth of the rising sun, Rosalyn lingered longer than usual. It was to her surprise, then, when she spied a single horse approaching from the east over the canyon rim and along the cut that drained the creek into the valley. She knew it wasn't *him,* but curiosity seized her. Retrieving her shotgun, she descended the slope much faster than she'd climbed it.

"Mornin', Miss Ashley."

A pair of ranch hands, still warming up for the day, greeted her as she crossed the creek and approached the compound.

She dipped her chin. "Gentlemen." She used the term loosely. None were anything like the gentlemen she'd known her entire life—well spoken, finely dressed, and guarded of emotion. The hands, however, possessed a code of honor that would surely put those "finer" gentlemen to shame. They worked hard. They protected one another. They tempered their rough speech in her presence and treated her like someone of importance. Sure, there were one or two she'd prefer not to be alone with, but she knew that the threat of retribution from the others acted as a deterrent. Upon entering the house, her eyes fell on the visitor as he conversed with her brother in the parlor. Both men stood when she entered.

"Rosalyn," said Lucien. "Allow me to introduce Mr. Venables, come from Chicago on the train to Laramie and by horse from there."

Venables, slim and slight, wore a well-tailored suit and spun an impeccable bowler in his hands. He bowed slightly. "A pleasure, Miss Ashley."

His proper English accent caught her by surprise. Most Britons out west hailed from the meaner streets of crowded cities or backwaters of the countryside, and their rough accents reflected it. She dropped a brief curtsy without thinking. "Mr. Venables."

A flash of insight struck Rosalyn as she deposited the shotgun beside the door—and within reach. Had her brother summoned this man to court her? The type of "gentleman" of which she'd just been reminiscing? Lucien motioned for her to sit and then put her fears to rest.

"Mr. Venables is a detective with the Pinkerton Detective Agency. He's come to South Pass City in search of Mr. Paynter."

Rosalyn tried to suppress the flare of alarm. Pinkertons carried a reputation of professionalism and effectiveness. His presence couldn't bode well for Paynter. "Is that so?"

"Yes. Indeed," said Lucien dryly. He knew her feelings well on the matter.

"You were telling me," said Venables, "about your half of the bounty."

Rosalyn's narrowed gaze locked with Lucien's until he looked away with apparent discomfort. "Your half of the bounty, Lucien? What does Mr. Venables mean by that?"

Venables raised his eyebrows. "My apologies. I did not know the lady was unaware of the details."

Lucien waved a dismissive hand and set his jaw. "She would've learned soon enough." He looked at Rosalyn. "I matched the government bounty of five hundred dollars."

She crossed her arms and glared ice that might survive the July sun. "Why?"

"You know very well why, but let's not discuss personal matters in the presence of a guest."

She did know why. Lucien had noticed her affection toward Paynter and took affront at his sister caring for a man whom he considered less than the mud clinging to the soles of his boots. Making sure Paynter hanged, even after he had saved their lives twice, seemed to Lucien an appropriate course of action. If anything had ever tempted Rosalyn to hate her brother, it was this.

"And while we are on the subject," said Lucien, "you may as well know the rest."

"There's more?"

"I've recruited a gang from Philadelphia to track him down. They specialize in such things. Hunting men."

The detective's flushed expression surely matched hers. He fidgeted with his hat. "Which gang, might I ask?"

"They call themselves the Flayers."

Venables pulled at his collar. "You've invited men of the Flayers? Here?"

"Yes." Lucien's reply reflected a new uncertainty. "You know of them?"

"I do. They are murderous cutthroats with a long history of violence and misdeeds. Even now, the Philadelphia police are working to stamp out their existence, no matter the cost."

Lucien nodded. "I see. Then I am fortunate to have employed them. When it comes to confronting Paynter, only violent, murderous men need apply."

Venables stood abruptly, clearly dismayed. "My apologies for intruding. I thank you for the information and will leave you in peace. But a word of advice before I go, Mr. Ashley."

"Yes?"

"Do not, under any circumstances, allow those men within a mile of your sister. Good day, sir, madam."

Rosalyn suppressed her seething anger until they'd seen the detective out the door and on toward South Pass City. When he'd ridden from earshot, Rosalyn wheeled on her brother.

"What have you done, Lucien? You've invited a band of devils into our house and offered them cash. In bringing the wrath of hell down on Mr. Paynter, you've endangered us all."

Lucien arched his spine and flexed his jaw. "I will handle them, Sister. Do not worry for me. As for you, now that the railroad is finished, you may return to St. Louis on any day of your choosing. I will not stop you this time."

She spun away and opened the door. "I might just do that."

Even as she reentered the house, though, she knew her threat to be hollow. She liked it here, despite Lucien's schemes. And if she returned east, she'd remove all hope of ever seeing Paynter again. Even now, though, her hopes were slim. Surely, he was far away and as unreachable as the moon.

CHAPTER EIGHT

Running away from trouble was like injecting morphine. Sometimes, it was necessary to prevent violent pain that might otherwise overwhelm a man. But every dose rendered it more the first reaction to pain rather than a path of last resort. Jake had already fled his problems too many times to stop himself from saddling the mare before the sun rose over the valley of the Wind River. He slipped away from the Shoshone village in the silence of predawn, drawing only half-hearted interest from a spotted dog and a couple of curious horses. The mare walked slowly, picking her way with care through the night-bathed sage. Jake didn't push her. His early start would put him beyond reach of persuasion before anyone woke to note his absence.

They doggedly climbed the stair step of hills beyond the river, rising higher with each ascension toward a pass the Mountain Crow people called Togwotee, meaning "from here you can go anywhere." When the sun finally breached the horizon, Jake urged the mare to an overlook that presented the vista of the Wind River wash far below. He dismounted, found a comfortable rock to sit on, and waited. The emergent sun revealed a land moored between mountain and hills, broken and reshaped over time by the endless flow of wind and water. The red, orange, and yellow of exposed rock embroidered the rippling cloth of grass and sage, green but trending gold in early summer.

In short order, smoke from early-morning campfires in the distant village began rising with the sun. Though the miles obscured echoes of animals and people, individual forms remained clearly discernable in the crisp morning air. Women huddling over fires. Men leading horses for water. Children chasing among the lodges. Still, he watched, his focus on the center of the camp, until Gus and Stacy emerged from Beah Nooki's lodge and trailed through the village toward the horse herd with saddles shouldered. He continued his lonely vigil as they saddled and mounted their horses, Gus on his buckskin and Stacy on her calico, and rode slowly in the opposite direction toward distant South Pass City. Toward people he cared for, and some he didn't. Toward a certain woman who saw him as a decent man instead of the corrupted soul he was.

Jake stood from the rock, brushed the dust from his pants, and mounted the mare. She cast a judging eye back at him, perhaps daring him to continue his knee-jerk flight toward oblivion. Instead, he did nothing but sit astride the saddle while pondering the trail ahead. Any moment, he expected to kick the mare's flanks to send her onward toward the Tetons and far Yellowstone. A minute passed, and then another until she began to complain about his indecision.

"Well, hell," he breathed.

Without a second thought, he pulled the mare around to return the way they'd come. In her excitement, she tried running ahead of his direction, ignoring his calls for restraint. They crossed the Wind River at a wide shallow spot along the base of the foothills, forging an intersecting path that would take them west of the village and make up at least a couple of miles on Gus and Stacy. He did his best to manage the mare, letting her gallop for short distances before returning her to a trot or canter. Given her head, she seemed prepared to race the entire distance. The mind of a horse was a thing of inscrutable beauty—perplexing, dangerous, and possessing an equine wisdom passed down by forebears who had spent a thousand lifetimes on the run. Perhaps he should listen more closely to her instincts. They had yet to fail him.

Jake continued onward through the long day and well past the setting of the sun, having fixed an eye on Gus and Stacy's position in the distance before darkness fell. A flaring pinpoint of light identified their campfire, drawing him on a line toward his well-meaning friends. He finally dropped from the mare and led her the final two hundred yards through crunching sage.

"Hello, the camp." His warning silenced the murmured voices of Gus and Stacy.

"Paynter?" Stacy's incredulous call greeted him as he led the mare into the firelight.

"In the flesh."

Gus laughed and pointed at Stacy as they both rose to their feet. "You owe me five dollars."

"I ain't got five dollars."

"You owe me later, then."

A grin found Jake's lips. "You bet on whether I'd change my mind?"

Stacy folded her arms and glared at Jake. "If you'd waited another couple a' days, I'd only owe him one dollar."

"Don't worry, little sister." He staked the mare in a patch of tall grass so she could restore her belly. "I'll pitch in half since your misfortune is my doin'."

"I don't need your charity."

"It ain't charity. It's justice. Gus knows me better than I know myself sometimes. He sharped you like a charlatan. Least I can do is ease the burden some."

Stacy turned her glare on Gus. "You knew."

He shrugged and sat back down. "I warned ya. It was you who insisted that we put money on it. And I'm always happy to take money from those desperate to part with it."

Her glare faded and she shook a finger at him. "I'll get you back, Gus Rivers. Wait and see."

"Of that, I have no doubt."

When Stacy sat, Jake joined them at the fire. A spit over the flames held a dripping hunk of buffalo meat. "Got enough for three?"

"And then some," she said.

"Good. I'm hungry. Been a long ride today."

They lapsed into silence, watching one another and the roasting meat for a half minute. Finally, Gus removed his hat and scratched the top of his head.

"Why'd you change your mind? You coulda been halfway up the pass by now."

Jake rubbed his chin in a maelstrom of thought. It was a good question—one he'd been asking himself the entire day since ending his latest run. The answer seemed at once simple and yet complex beyond comprehension. Turning around meant riding into the clutches of those who wanted to harvest him for money. It meant lunging directly into the teeth of impending disaster by his own choosing. But he had found himself unable to dismiss the needs of those who cared for him. He had found it impossible to deny his concern for them as well.

For the first time in his life, he was beginning to understand what it must be like to have family— and it was damned inconvenient. *Family.* Not just those related by blood but whose most meaningful attentions were wrapped in cruelty, but *real* family. People who offered safety, solace, and acceptance without conditions. People he would fight for. People he would die for, as fair recompense for those precious moments of belonging that he had sought from the worst of men before finding them with a better class of human being. People like Gus, and Stacy, and Rosalyn, and the families of the wagon train who'd welcomed a condemned killer and called him their own. These and other thoughts swirled through his brain after Gus asked him why he'd changed his mind, a storm of chaotic reasoning blowing through his head. He opened his mouth to explain as best he could.

"I don't know."

They rose early the following morning, intent on covering the final thirty miles to South Pass City before the day bled away completely. Discussion remained light, other than Gus and Stacy picking at each other as they volunteered details about the town, the families Jake knew, and the puzzling murders of immigrant miners. If Jake didn't know better, he'd have said his riding mates were engaged in an odd courtship ritual or a desperate power struggle—one of the two. But what did he know of such things?

"Come, now, Gus," said Stacy with dramatic affront. "You keep throwin' cold water on the notion of werewolves. Haven't you talked to the Emshoffs? They got stories from Bavaria that'll ice yer blood and pin one eye open at night."

" 'Course I heard from the Emshoffs. But even they call the stories fairy tales."

"Not the missus. She believes. Her mother saw one of 'em in the mist of the mountains when she was a youngster."

"Mrs. Emshoff is just workin' you, Stacy. Like she does her kids when she wants them to behave."

Talk of the Emshoffs resurrected pleasant memories for Jake. How they'd treated him as a hero instead of a condemned prisoner. How they'd fed him and welcomed him by their fire. How little Lisbet had fought diligently to break through his isolation even while she recovered from a gunshot wound. They were good people. He trusted their opinions and looked forward to breaking bread with them again.

"We're comin' up on it."

Gus's declaration interrupted Jake's reminiscing. He looked aside at his old company mate and blinked. "Comin' up on what?"

"The Ashley spread. We'll spot it from just ahead."

The information swept away Jake's recollections and deposited him squarely in the immediacy of the moment. He craned his neck in the direction Gus had pointed. Within minutes, they topped a ridge that gave them an astonishing view of a red-rimmed canyon, lush with green grass along an adjacent upsweep of hillside.

"Flaming Rocks Ranch, they call it." Stacy motioned to the distant huddle of buildings as she spoke. "All built in the last four months. Mighty impressive, even if the owner is a viper."

Jake peered intently into the canyon below as they passed it by. The buildings and corrals huddled between dramatic red walls and a line of hillocks that gave way to a rise of grassland dotted with cattle. In the fold of the canyon, he saw horses and a double handful of men wrangling them, building fences, or raising a barn. But no skirts. No feminine shape that might indicate the presence of Rosalyn Ashley. Gus seemed to guess his thoughts.

"She's there for sure. And Lucien too. So for your own safety, you should stay clear of that place."

The thought that Rosalyn was only a mile away brought Jake a fleeting feeling of peace that he hadn't realized he'd lacked until just then. It also brought him concern. He knew instinctually that he couldn't obey Gus's prudent advice and wondered what his future actions would surely cost him—and Rosalyn.

CHAPTER NINE

"We'll need to skirt the town," said Stacy. "We can't have anyone seeing you with us just yet. Some busybody might add up the numbers and figure who you are."

Gus nodded agreement. "Good thinkin', Miss Blue."

Stacy was pleased with her strategic reasoning and proud she'd been the one to suggest a plan. And Gus's compliment felt warmer than it should have. To make up for it, she tossed her head at him. " 'Course it was. You act like a woman can't muster up a good idea."

"Oh, no. I don't think that. My mama knew twice as much as everybody else and weren't the least bit shy about speakin' her mind." He shook his head slowly. "Nope. Don't think that at all."

His disarming response riled Stacy further, but she bit her lip. Mostly. "Don't forget that, now. I ain't got the time nor inclination to keep reminding you."

Paynter rolled his eyes at her and shook his head. "Can we at least get a look at the town?"

"I suppose. It can't hurt. Follow me."

They rode on for another three miles, trekking high ground that would avoid South Pass City while allowing an overlook view. When the town sprawled into view below, Stacy pulled up her horse just before they'd begin descending toward it. "Feast your eyes, Paynter."

He peered into the town for a while, twisting his jaw left and right. "It's grown since last I saw it. Maybe double."

"At least that," said Gus. "People been streaming in since the spring lookin' for a handful of gold nuggets or a pan full a' sparkly dust. Since the railroad finished, they been comin' from both coasts, just like Ashley said they would. Got a new bank, if that tells you anything."

"It means there's money flowing in."

Gus motioned to the large mining operation that dominated the high ground on the other side of the city as if to validate the point. "That's my thinking. I been supplyin' horses and mules for that big mine against the hill yonder."

"You're a horse trader?"

"Yep. I gotta eat somehow. It's honest work, and those buyin' care more about the strength of the horse than the color of the trader."

Paynter looked at Stacy. "And what about you?"

She puffed out her chest. "I work for Stillman Stables, caring for horses and whatnot. Pays three dollars a week, which is three dollars more than Pa ever gave me."

"Uh-huh." He eyed the town again. "Where exactly is the marshal's office?"

Stacy leveled a finger toward a new building across from the hotel. "Just there, with the brick walls. And the courthouse is next door. Not much to look at, but Judge Kingman holds court there when he comes through."

"Kingman." Paynter scratched his jaw. "You said he's inclined to help the miners?"

"Yep. Haven't met him, but he seems a decent sort. Spraggs won't have it, though."

"The town marshal?"

"Yes, him. And his no-account deputy, Duff. Word is, Ashley has 'em bought and paid for like painted women. They do what Lucien wants and wish hellfire on the rest."

"A pity, that."

"It's worse than a pity," said Gus. "Anyone who complains or stirs the pot too vigorously gets a sudden visit and a made-up fine. Them that resists are treated to the end of the deputy's boot."

Stacy watched as Paynter's eyes clouded. Even after all the time they'd spent on the Oregon Trail together, she didn't *really* know the man. But she'd come to recognize one truth of his mysterious nature. Nothing fired his anger like a bully. And right now, the flames behind his eyes lit his face.

"We'll see about that," he said before spurring his horse onward.

Gus took the lead as they followed a gradual

descent away from town and circled through a brush-covered draw. The arc took them behind a spine of hills and away from the creek along which most of the miners clustered their efforts. The arc bent more deeply upon itself into a stub of canyon perforated by a rectangular hole. Stacy punched Paynter's shoulder and motioned to the opening.

"Say hello to your new domicile."

Paynter cocked his head dangerously to the right. "A mine shaft?"

"Not just a mine shaft. An abandoned one."

"Abandoned for now," added Gus. "The owner died three months back, and the mine's in probate until some relative from back east shows up to dispose of the claim. He ain't due for another two months."

Paynter grunted. "Died. One of the victims of Stacy's imaginary werewolf?"

"No." Gus seemed to chuckle at Stacy's flash of indignation. "He died from beer."

"He drank himself to death?"

"Not exactly. He drank another man's beer and paid for it with a bottle upside his head. Turns out, the bottle was harder than his head. But, by God, he shoulda known better than to drink another man's beer."

"And the fella who wielded the bottle?"

Stacy jumped in, still annoyed by the whole affair. "One of the marshal's friends. Spraggs slapped his wrist and told him to get scarce. Hardly justice for murdering a man over beer."

A scowl crossed Paynter's face. "You already know how I feel about justice."

"How?"

"Ask Gus. I don't need him lecturin' me again."

"Wasn't lecturin'," said Gus. "It was pulpit-banging preaching that you needed to hear. The only way to guarantee lack of justice is to stop fightin' for it. If I ever stop fighting for it, then bury me where I fall 'cause I'll surely be dead."

The scowl fled Paynter's face, replaced by a wry but seemingly appreciative smile. "Another fine sermon, Reverend Rivers."

"Amen, Brother Paynter. Amen."

Before Gus could launch into a rendition of "Amazing Grace," they arrived at the mine entrance and dismounted. Stacy pulled an unlit torch from just inside the shaft. "Hand me a lucifer, Gus. I know you keep 'em handy."

Gus grinned, retrieved a match from his pocket, and passed it to her. "As Her High-and-Mightiness wishes."

She glowered at him while lighting the torch. "Let's go, gents, unless you're afraid of the dark."

She led the way inside, careful not to brush the flame against the ceiling and snuff it like she did the last time. Gus had only just stopped teasing her about that little blunder. The mine stretched back into darkness for maybe thirty feet, more or less straight as an arrow, until doglegging left, then right. From the double jig, it continued another fifty steps. At the end of the tunnel, the mine flared out as if the miner had planned to drive two shafts before the unfortunate beer incident. Paynter liberated the torch from her and swept it around the cramped space.

"I'm not so sure," he said. "Seems like a good place to die. Too much like a raccoon trap."

Despite his expression of uncertainty, he began retracing his steps slowly, watching the flame of the torch. After a dozen steps, he stopped abruptly and backed up, forcing Stacy to retreat from his back side. As she cocked her head in puzzlement, he moved back and forth over the same spot twice more, never taking his eyes from the flame. Then he handed Stacy the torch.

"This'll do."

Gus laughed. "This'll do? After grumbling about it not a minute ago?"

"That's what I said."

Stacy and Gus followed him back out of the mine to find dusk falling proper. She snuffed the torch in the dirt and set it back inside the entrance. When she turned, Paynter was already mounted.

"Didn't you just say this place would do just fine?"

"Tomorrow it will. For tonight, I'll set a cold

camp out in the brush. Got a little work to do before I take up residence."

"What're you talkin' about?"

Her question produced a laugh from Gus. "He's a soldier, Miss Blue. During the war, first thing we did at any new place was figure out how to defend it. We dug trenches, set pickets, posted scouts. Only then could we settle in without wakin' up dead. Me and Paynter musta dug three miles of trench between us."

"More like five. We spent more time grippin' our spades than our rifles. All the long guns were right jealous."

Stacy chuckled at the joke and marveled at this rare side of Paynter. She could count on one hand the times she'd seen him relax enough to take amusement. And as usual, a moment seemed more than enough for him.

"Give me your matches."

After Gus handed over the box, Paynter touched the brim of his hat. "Evenin', Gus. Stacy."

"Night, Paynter," said Gus. "We'll come for you this time tomorrow. Keep your head down in the meantime and don't do nothin' foolish."

"Since when have I ever done anything foolish?"

"Don't get me started, or we'll still be talkin' when the sun comes up."

Paynter waved a hand as he rode into the dusk. After Gus and Stacy had started back toward town, she fixed him with her gaze.

"Think he'll stay? Not run?"

"I'm sure of it." He cast a sly smile her way. "Care to put money on it?"

"Oh, Hades, no."

"No? Why not?"

"Because I saw his eyes when we talked about Spraggs and his deputy. There's a wrong here, and he's determined to right it even if he has to wrestle the devil himself."

Gus clapped his hands three times in mock applause. "Well done."

"Whadda ya mean?"

"I just mean that you're startin' to figure him out, and that ain't no easy task. Took me years to do the same."

"Maybe I'm just a quicker study than you, Augustus Rivers."

"No argument there, Anastasia Blue."

They fussed and argued all the way back to town, and Stacy felt happier than she had in years.

CHAPTER TEN

The best of fortresses can quickly become the worst of prisons for the complacent. Keenly aware of that fact, Jake decided not to allow his new hideout to become his final resting place. When he arrived back at the mine shaft with the mare in tow, the brilliant light of day was still but a promise. Only then did he realize the first flaw in his burgeoning plan. He stared at the mare for a solid ten seconds.

"I can live in a hole for a while. But you sure can't."

She tossed her head in agreement, her shaggy mane rippling in the predawn breeze. He scanned the darkness in every direction before craning his neck to take in the lump of hillside above the mine. "Up we go, then."

He circled out of the stub of canyon to what passed for a creek and let the mare drink her fill. When she belched and stepped away from the water, he mounted the hillside, pulling her along by the reins. She protested by keeping the length of leather taut as he all but dragged her zigzagging up the slope. When they reached the top of the rise, Jake's breaths came in ragged heaves and sweat soaked his forehead.

"Thanks for all the help," he groused. He took a knee to catch his breath and passed his hand over the ground. Grass. Mostly. He stood again, found a well-anchored sage half his height, and roped her to it. Rainwater had pooled in the hollow of a rocky outcrop within the rope's reach, and an adjacent jut of granite would provide her shade if the sun proved too intense. Fingers of light in the east marking the coming day gave him a view of the heights rising above surrounding valleys of shadow. He waited until the rays began reaching the bottoms, studying the cardinal directions.

From his vantage point, he saw nothing but sage, save one lonely miner's tent perhaps a mile out. Maybe the mare wouldn't draw too much attention. Regardless, she couldn't stay with him at the mine, and she couldn't stay on the hilltop for long. Eventually, someone would find her—a poor outcome for both of them. With her situated, Jake wandered the back side of the hill in the growing light until he found what he was looking for. A smile tugged his lips as he breathed a sigh of relief. He returned to the mare, checked her tether once more, and rubbed her neck. "Now, stay put. Don't cause unnecessary trouble while I'm gone. Only the necessary kind."

After picking his way down the hillside to the small box of a canyon, he returned to the mine entrance, lit the torch, and retrieved the abandoned pick and shovel he'd spotted the night before. He supposed the dead miner wouldn't much care if he borrowed them for a while. After all, they did have one thing in common. They'd both be below dirt for a while. He paced to the shaft's left-right dogleg, planted the torch, and began attacking the soft floor with pick and shovel until he'd accumulated a monumental pile. Rather than dumping it at the entrance, he dragged the loose gravel on a sledge to the larger room at the rear of the shaft. The less evidence of his residence, the better.

Jake repeated the process—digging and dragging—until the lip of the pit reached his chest. He climbed out and mopped his brow. The hole was four feet across and stretched from one side of the tunnel to the other. His old colonel would be proud that he hadn't lost his entrenching skills.

"That should do."

Jake snuffed the torch to conserve what might remain of it and returned to the entrance. He climbed the hill again to find the mare contently grazing around the rock, seemingly ignoring him in protest of having been abandoned. Satisfied, he returned to the vale and gathered limbs from the scraggly pines that clustered near the minimal creek. When he'd stacked a dozen inside the mine entrance, he sat, slid his blade from his boot, and began shaving the limbs into points sufficient to puncture man or beast.

A wan smile formed as he recalled the brief

history of his knife. How he'd borrowed it from a dead man to cauterize a wound that might've otherwise killed him. How Lucien Ashley had taken it from him when he was clapped in shackles after the mother of all wagon box fights. How little Lisbet Emshoff had returned it to him for the purpose of carving his name and hers on a rock along the Oregon Trail. He had no notion of how she'd managed to liberate the knife from his adversary, but the thought of it elicited a sad chuckle. He missed that little kid. She had made him feel like he was worth something.

On finishing the spears, Jake felt his way into the mine and edged forward to locate the lip of his pit with a probing boot. He climbed inside and, by feel, planted the sticks pointy end up before climbing out. Filling the pit with small tufts of sage consumed another hour, but by the end of that exercise, he had gotten his paces down. Forty-three steps from entrance to pit at a walk. Still working in darkness, he leaped back and forth across the armed trap a dozen times, learning the feel of jumping and landing without sight. Then, starting from the lip of the pit, he ran full bore down the tunnel to the entrance, counting. He repeated the action four more times until he had a number—twenty-one running strides between the entrance and the edge of the trap. When the time came, he'd more likely be running than walking.

With the mantrap finished, he started on the alarm system. This proved far simpler than the creation of the pit. He stood two rusted lengths of iron rail against either side of the tunnel about ten feet inside the entrance—just past where sunlight might easily reach. He tied a length of rope between them perhaps a foot off the ground, just high enough for a stray foot to catch it squarely.

When he tested his work by tugging the rope and jumping away, the rails fell forward with a clanging cry. Pleased with the effect, he reset the alarm, relit the torch, and moved to the rear of the tunnel. As he had the night before, he waved the flame slowly along the ceiling until locating the air shaft. He'd learned from a company mate that miners cut an air shaft upward to keep the mine's still air from suffocating them. Discovering one in this mine had convinced him to stay because air shafts served a secondary role—emergency escape route.

His hubris over finding the shaft faded when he tried to climb it. Though it angled upward toward the back side of the hill, gravity still conspired to yank him back into darkness. Poorly maintained handholds crumbled beneath his fingers and toes. Narrow spots convinced him the dead miner had possessed the shoulders of an adolescent boy.

With a heaving sigh, he pulled his knife and began firming up handholds and widening the narrow spots. Time passed as he strove for the pinpoint of light above, the exit he'd found on the hilltop that morning. He recalled what his pa had claimed so long ago—that you could see the stars in broad daylight from the bottom of a well. He stopped to rest and stared hard at the sky beyond the hole, hoping for stars. Nothing. Just blue. He shook his head.

"So much for promises."

The false claim came as no surprise. The only commitments his father had kept involved the promise of a beating. In the throes of dismal memory, the walls of the narrow shaft began to press in on him. He dug faster, clawing with knife and fingers as he raced for the blue above, stars or no. When he breached the surface of the hill and coughed dust from his lungs, the mare raised her head from the grass to stare at him. If he didn't know better, he'd swear she rolled her brown eyes before resuming her industrious foraging. He dragged his body through the hole, fell to his back, and stared at the sky while drawing heaving breaths until his heartbeat slowed to a maintainable rate. The sun had fallen nearly to the horizon, surprising him. He'd been at his labors for upward of fifteen hours, and he was weary.

Jake rolled to his feet and beat the dust from his clothes, pleased he'd left his hat with the mare. He unwound her tether from the sturdy sage. "Let's go. Company should be comin' soon.

And I imagine we could both use a deeper drink."

He gave the exit of the air shaft one last gander. If worst came to worst, that tiny hole could be his salvation. Or the opening to his grave. He just wasn't sure which.

CHAPTER ELEVEN

Jake heard Gus approaching before he saw him. The clop of hooves on rock echoed into the box canyon for half a minute before the familiar buckskin and rider appeared. Jake lowered his Henry and stepped from the mouth of the mine. Gus smirked.

"Still suspicious, are you?"

"Skepticism is the breath of life, Gus. And I'm still breathin', ain't I?"

Gus laughed softly as he pulled his horse to a stop. "Don't get me wrong. You should stay the skeptic. Anything less is foolish, given the army of miscreants who'd see you laid out on a table."

"Glad we see eye to eye on that." Jake pushed the rifle into its scabbard on the mare's flank and saddled up. "Where we headed, anyway?"

"Hush and see."

Jake fell in behind Gus as they exited the draw, crawled over a hilltop, and dropped into another vale. The presence of a sizable campfire and a number of people immediately unnerved him. The outlines of large tents and a pair of wagons dominated the space behind the fire. Before he could take Gus to task, Stacy called out.

" 'Bout time. Did you all stop off for a game of three-card monte?"

"Yep, and horseshoes," said Gus.

The lightness of their tone informed Jake of the safety of the place. He didn't understand why until a little blond person came bounding toward his horse.

"Mr. Paynter! It's me!"

He dropped from his saddle and crouched to meet Lisbet as she crashed into him. He hugged her fiercely, not quite understanding the visceral nature of his response. "Your leg seems all healed."

"It is," she said. "I can run real fast now."

She pushed away, grabbed his hand, and dragged him toward the others waiting beside the campfire.

"I'll tend to your horse," said Gus with a grin. "There's folks wantin' to reunite with you."

Jake nodded but his focus remained on the knot of bodies around the fire. They circled him when he stepped into its light. Lisbet's father was the first to shake his hand.

"Pleased to see you, Paynter. *Sehr gut!*"

"And you, Emshoff."

A mountain of a man gathered his hand next. "You're lookin' good, what with your fine beard and all."

Jake grinned a little at the Scotsman's mild taunt. "Don't go all jealous, Dunbar. You might

92

grow a whisker or two someday. How're Maddie and Lily?"

"Ask them yourself." He stepped aside as his wife, Maddie, embraced Jake with one arm while lugging Lily with the other. The toddler eyed Jake suspiciously before touching his beard.

"Tickles." She giggled.

And so it went as he became reacquainted with Mrs. Emshoff, her other children, Otto and Dora, and the four Robersons. It was with some surprise that he didn't find himself pulling away from their touches. A year earlier, he'd rather have put acid in his eyes than allow a mob of people to lay hands on him and gush over his presence. The long road from Missouri had changed all that. Fighting alongside others for mutual preservation had created a sacred bond that crumbled even the staunchest of barriers. The defeat of Sally's unbeatable army by a band of farmers and blacksmiths had created a circle of camaraderie among them that could never be replicated outside of shared sacrifice. He found the realization bewildering nonetheless.

"Come sit with us," said Mr. Roberson. He motioned to his son, now sixteen and taller than his father. "Fetch Paynter some grub. I imagine he's powerful hungry by now."

Jake sat and accepted a bowl of stew. He tucked in without shame. He was hungry, and he'd not tasted Mrs. Emshoff's Bavarian red stew in nigh on a year. He answered curious questions between bites, effectively describing how he'd overcome Blackburn and dodged the posse after escaping from Fort Bridger. He spoke of the long winter with the Shoshone in the land they called "Valley of the Warm Winds" and how he'd settled in over the spring before people had begun coming for his head.

"I am sorry for your troubles." The empathy from Mr. Emshoff was nothing new. He'd been the first to extend a hand of friendship when Jake was a condemned prisoner attached to their wagon train west. Jake scraped the bottom of the bowl, set it aside, and wiped his mouth with the back of a sleeve.

"No need to be. My neck remains unstretched, so I consider myself fortunate."

Without invitation, Lisbet chose that moment to crawl up into his lap. Jake tried not to allow his discomfort to show. Given his past, he had no business shepherding children. His angst multiplied when the six-year-old reached up to rub his cheek.

"Why'd you hide your face, Mr. Paynter?"

He leaned his head away from her hand. "Got tired a' lookin' at it. Thought I'd try a beard for a while."

She wrinkled her nose. "I suppose it's all right."

Certain that everyone saw through his facade, he decided to change the subject. "So tell me about yourselves. Is the smithy turning a profit, Dunbar?"

"Indeed. I've cornered the market on busted shovels, dull pickaxes, and bent mining pans. And since there's no doctor in the entire area, Maddie's been making her own living setting bones, stitching wounds, and delivering babies. Some folks call her Dr. Maddie, despite her best efforts to remain anonymous."

Jake nodded. "Anyone who worked the battlefields of the big war has got to be better than a quack with a couple of letters in front of his name."

Even in the low light, he saw a blush creep into Maddie Dunbar's cheeks. He had seen her pull a bullet from Ketchum's leg, though, so his praise wasn't hollow. He swept a hand toward the Emshoffs and Robersons. "And what of y'all?"

"We've thrown in together on a claim," said Roberson. "Managed to pull enough dust and small nuggets from the creek and hillside to feed ourselves and get ahead."

"Yes," Emshoff added. "We hope to raise eighteen dollars apiece and then some for expenses."

Jake recognized the amount. Eighteen dollars under Lincoln's Homestead Act would grant each family a claim to 160 acres of land. If they farmed it for five years, they'd own it.

"That'd be a fine chunk of land," he said.

Emshoff nodded. "My farm in Bavaria was but ten acres, and the king stripped it at his pleasure. To own more than ten times that amount and no one to take it? Why that would be . . ." He paused to gather a choke while Mrs. Emshoff patted his leg. "That would be the reason we came to this country in the first place."

"This is boring," said Lisbet with a fake yawn. "When will we talk about the werewolf?"

Her comment produced good-natured laughter around the fire. Jake thumped her shoulder lightly. "You shouldn't be hearing about this."

"Oh, but I have." Her eyes shone with morbid fascination. "How he tore men into pieces."

Mrs. Emshoff grimaced. "Enough, *kleiner Kind*. Go to the tent with your brother and sister."

Lisbet huffed while crawling from Jake's lap but obeyed her mother without guff. German mamas were not to be crossed. When the children had left, Jake lowered his voice. "So tell me about the killings."

Stacy seemed happy to launch the narrative. "It's like this. Three times, miners have been waylaid on their claims in the dead of night. They been split open from throat to crotch, and their entrails spread around the site."

"Anybody seen this happen?"

"No," said Mrs. Roberson. "Most of the wives and children stay in town while the husbands keep night watch over the claim. In fact, twice it's been the wife who's come upon the remains."

Those last words trailed away, exposing her concern for her own husband. Jake rubbed his chin in thought. "Why do people think it's a wolf, then, if nobody's seen it?"

"From the tracks," said Emshoff. "Large wolf prints at the campsite. And one wolf claw left behind in Mr. Zhou's chest when it took him."

"I see. But how do people jump from a wolf nobody's seen to a werewolf?"

Stacy almost stood with excitement before settling back down. "Because it only comes out in the light of a full moon, and the tracks are too big, and no wolf would mangle a body like that. It ain't like a wolf to make a kill and leave all the meat."

Jake agreed. That didn't sound like an ordinary wolf, or even a wolf at all, though someone was going to a lot of trouble to make it look that way. "Well, I ain't got no silver bullets, but I'll see what I can do. I'll need to think on it some and make a plan."

With the morbid topic set aside, the group fell into more pleasant conversation. They laughed and told stories and reminisced about their shared adventure on the Oregon Trail. As the hour grew late, Jake stood to take his leave.

"I thank you for the victuals and visitin', but I'd best be headin' back to my hole." He turned to Gus. "Keep the mare for me. She can't stay around the mine without drawin' attention."

"I figured as much," he said. "Until tomorrow evening, then."

"Until then."

Jake left the circle of light to plunge again into darkness, returning with nothing but his rifle in hand. Thoughts of how the married couples had interacted with affection set him to wondering again about his mother. What had she been like? If she hadn't died so young, might she have tamed his raging father or tempered the vicious instincts of his older brothers? He'd never know. But mired in recollection, Jake's first memory of Ambrose Blackburn came to him and how the charismatic captain of a Confederate raider band had appeared to Jake to be the father he'd always lacked.

• • •

"Who do we have here?" Captain Blackburn drawled the question while eyeing a seventeen-year-old Jake.

"Jake Paynter. From the Texas coast, sir."

"Well, well, Mr. Paynter from the Texas coast. You come to join us?"

It was the sort of question Jake's father might pose before burning him down with a tirade and a fist. The kind of question that served only to prepare a path for humiliation. Jake hesitated in his uncertainty.

"Yes, sir. I come to join ya. If you'll have me."

"Can you ride?"

"Yes, sir."

"And shoot?"

"Yes, sir."

He winced when Blackburn rose, expecting the fist. Instead, the man threw an arm around his shoulder and squeezed. "Wonderful. A strappin' lad like you should fit into this garrison right nicely. We've grand work to do and need all the fine men we can get. And I must say, you seem like a fine man to me."

Jake swallowed his doubt. "I suppose."

Blackburn laughed—but not at him. "Don't ever just suppose, Paynter. Be confident, boy! You're with us now, so you're somethin' special. We'll take good care of you and ask the same in return."

Jake straightened to his full height and smiled broadly. "Yes, Captain. I will give you all I have."

"That's all I ask, son. That's all I ask."

• • •

Jake scowled as he recalled that first meeting. Blackburn had taken care of him all right. He'd re-formed Jake into his own image—a stone-cold killer. And Jake had given his all to Blackburn as promised—including his soul—before fleeing the raider band to fight for the Union. Then, in a cruel twist of fate, Blackburn had dodged justice after the war by accepting a sergeant's commission in the Plains Army—under Jake's command. His former captain's malevolent presence as ally and then enemy had become a daily reminder of what Jake had sacrificed on the grim altar of misplaced loyalties. As he trudged through the inky blackness toward the mine, he wondered for the thousandth time how he'd allowed it all to go so wrong.

CHAPTER TWELVE

Jake took another crack at his escape tunnel the following day. For hours, he chipped away at the rocky earth to widen the passage and firm up handholds. Twice, he stopped to cart away the residue that had collected at the bottom of the shaft. Mostly, though, he got lost in the wilderness of his head, wandering through a landscape of isolation and regret. From time to time, a shining image would appear to beckon him toward more comforting ground. Gus's infectious laugh. Stacy's persistent spunk. Lisbet's insistence on pretending he was a good man. And Rosalyn, her green dress billowing in the breeze as she watched him with something much more than indifference.

The images only held him for a time, though, before he slipped back into the wilderness. Perhaps it was just the darkness of the mine shaft pulling his spirits downward like inescapable gravity. Maybe it was the way the breeze moaned over the entrance of the shaft, infusing him with the mournful sound. Periodically, he stopped to peer up the chimney in search of stars. They never appeared.

By the time Stacy arrived, he was tired,

famished, and one with the dirt. Stacy noticed the latter with a wrinkle of her nose as she approached astride her calico with the mare in tow.

"You look like somethin' grave robbers left by the side of the road, Paynter. I seen cleaner coal bins."

Jake continued beating the dust from his shirt and pants. "Sorry I'm not up to your lofty standards. I didn't realize we were goin' out for cotillion."

"Nothin' like that. But gosh all Friday, I'm the one that has to smell ya."

"I'll be sure to stay downwind."

As he donned his hat, his only relatively clean article of clothing, he suppressed a smile. Twenty seconds with Stacy had started to lift him from the swampland of his destructive thoughts. For most of his life, loneliness had been his preferred condition, far superior to suffering the company of others with their selfish motives and thoughtless actions that ranged from callous to brutal. Sometime during the past year, though, that had begun to change. As a result, he found himself revived by the thought of a few moments of companionship. He sheathed the rifle, rubbed the mare's neck, and swung into his saddle.

"Lead on, little sister."

"Try to keep up."

He followed her through fading light from

the small canyon and down the draw. When he realized she was taking them on a direct line toward South Pass City, he pulled alongside her. "We goin' for a whiskey first?"

"Shut up, Paynter. The widow of one a' the murdered miners lives in a shack at the edge of town. If you want a whiskey afterward, that's your funeral."

"Speaking of funerals, did you finally kill Gus?" She hadn't spoken yet of the reason for his absence. The question provoked a laugh and the slap of her thigh.

"No. Not yet, anyway. He's out ridin' watch."

Jake glanced at the moonless sky. A full moon was still two weeks away. "Why now?"

"I don't know. Maybe he just wants to feel like he's doin' something to help."

"That I understand."

A few minutes later, Stacy dismounted and began walking her horse toward a shanty clinging to the side of a hill marking the edge of the seam-busting town. He mimicked the action but took a moment to pull his rifle from its sheath. Stacy eyed the weapon as they tied off the horses.

"What's that for? The widow don't bite."

"Peace of mind. She might be harmless, but I trust no one."

"Suit yourself. But at least don't wave it in her face. She's wounded enough as it is."

"I'll be on my best behavior."

He followed her to the flimsy door that leaked light through gaps in the planks. She rapped it twice before calling out, restrained, "Mrs. Stefka? It's Stacy Blue."

No answer came, but shuffling sounded from inside the small cabin. The door cracked open to reveal a single, wide blue eye. "Did you bring *him?*"

The distinct accent marked her as hailing from one of the small countries on the flank or belly of Eastern Europe. Stacy reached back to grab Jake's shirt and pulled him into the crease of lantern light emanating from the door. "In the flesh."

The door cracked open wider to reveal an older woman, perhaps midforties. Her haggard features indicated that she'd barely slept since her husband's murder. The cabin held little but a stove, a collapsing bed, and a rickety table with two crates for chairs. The open pantry was virtually bare, testimony to a deeply interrupted income. She hurried them inside.

"I apologize. I have no cakes." She wrung her hands. "May I offer coffee?"

Despite the lure of a hot cup of coffee, Jake shook his head. He didn't want to dip into her meager supplies. She was suffering enough. "Thank you, Mrs. Stefka, but I am as full as a tick."

She smiled with what seemed gratitude. Stacy settled gingerly on the edge of the bed. "I'll sit here. You two take the table."

Jake removed his hat and sat on a crate while Mrs. Stefka settled across from him. Her eyes remained wary but impaled him with that uncomfortable stare he'd come to dread—like he could do something to right the wrongs.

"Tell me what happened," he said. "If it's not too hard."

She wiped tears that welled in her eyes before transforming. The steel that had brought her across two continents and an ocean straightened her spine and stilled her trembling hands.

"My husband, Andrei. He goes out to the claim each night. 'Not to worry,' he tells me. I believe him. But then . . ." She paused as the steel wavered before stiffening again. "The *vukodlak*, it comes. It kills him. Takes his heart."

"*Vukodlak*?"

"How you say? Werewolf."

Jake grunted. "Did you see this creature?"

"No. But I know."

"How?"

"I saw tracks of the *vukodlak*." The expression on his face must have betrayed his disbelief because she frowned. "I know you think I crazy old woman. But in the old country, they come on two legs and kill. They take the heart. Everyone knows."

Jake nodded. Her staunch belief swayed him, but just a little. However, he had other theories. "How long ago was your husband killed?"

"Six weeks."

"And has anyone squatted on your claim since then?"

Her frown grew deeper. "No. But bank man says I must sell to high bidder."

"I see." He stroked his short beard. "Has a man named Ketchum come to see you?"

"You know him?"

"Yes. But we are not friends."

Her frown melted. "Good. He is *zmija*. A snake."

"On that we agree, Mrs. Stefka. What did he want?"

She leaned forward with palms on the table. "He wants my claim. He says I should go back to where I come from. But I can't. I have nothing there. Not even my children survive."

Jake wondered about the disastrous hardships she'd left behind, only to find death in a new world. "I'm sorry, ma'am. You are right to decline the offer. Promise me you won't sell to him until I have time to figure this out."

A glimmer of hope lit her eyes. "I promise, Mr. Paynter."

There it was again—the misplaced belief that he might offer some sort of salvation. He shouldered the burden, though, adding it to the weight of what he already carried. "Tell me where the claim lies."

As Mrs. Stefka gave him the particulars, he captured them on a rough map pencil-sketched on the back of a used envelope. When she'd finished, he stood from the table.

"Thank you. I'll see what I can do. But make me another promise."

"Anything, Mr. Paynter."

"Don't tell anybody you saw me."

He could tell by the angst of her expression that she'd struggle to keep such a promise. At least she had the decency to lie. "I promise."

He and Stacy bid her good night and left the small shack. As they rode back, deep in mutual thought, Stacy finally ended the stalemate. "So whadda ya think? Is it a werewolf?"

"In a way, yes."

"In what way?"

Jake heaved a sigh. "The thing people forget about werewolves is that they're half wolf, half human. It's the human half that makes them monsters, not the wolf half. These killings are the work of men, one way or another."

She fell quiet as they rode on. She halted her horse maybe a half mile short of the mine and pointed into the darkness nearby. "Just so you know, there's a pool of water there deep enough to wash yourself in. In case you wondered."

"Thank God."

When he slipped from his horse, she chuckled. "What're you doing?"

"Takin' a bath."

She snorted a laugh. "Pardon me if I don't stick around for the show."

"I'll be fine. Take the mare, will ya?"

"G'night, Paynter. Don't drown yerself."

"I'll try not to."

When the shadows of the horses moved away, Jake stripped and waded into the pool with his clothes in hand. The crispness of the water briefly stole his breath. He washed his clothes as best he could before splaying them across a rock beside the bank. Then he returned to the center of the pool and submerged himself before floating upward on his back. Patches of stars among a scatter of invisible clouds led him down halls of memory to another cold creek during another hot summer in the year of '63.

• • •

Jake led the way as the Kansas First Colored Volunteers sprinted toward Cabin Creek while projectiles hummed past. A scatter of friendly cavalry held the far bank, but barely. As Jake hit the water, he lost his breath so suddenly he feared an enemy bullet had found his chest. When breath came in a rush, he realized it was just the shock of cold in the withering heat of early July. As he slogged through the creek, his mind strayed from the barrage of lead flying past his exposed head. The creek was cool. Oh, how he'd love to lie back in its comforting waters and watch the sky for a while. Forget about everything for a time. Only when Gus Rivers knocked down the man trying to bayonet Jake did he wake from his reverie. Jake finished off the attacker with a bayonet of hisown.

"Wake up, Paynter!" Gus shouted. "We're dyin' out here!"

Jake whipped his head side to side to find men—his men—falling under the enemy onslaught. His killer nature flared to life. "Let's git, dammit!"

He charged the Confederate pickets like a madman, not caring if he survived the act and only vaguely aware that his men had become efficient killers in his wake. He pressed the fight against desperate defenders, showing no quarter, until there was no one left to fight. When he collapsed in the dirt, it was not from exhaustion or triumph but from sudden lack of purpose.

• • •

The vivid memory stirred Jake from the creek. As he dressed, he considered his new purpose. His new mission. Unlike those bloody days of the war, he was tasked with saving lives, not taking them. He knew, though, deep in his gut, that it was only a matter of time before his killer nature would resurface. The thought of it left him hollow as he picked his way through the night toward the darkness of his cave, a wounded dragon of war seemingly unable to find peace.

CHAPTER THIRTEEN

Nothing hunts a monster better than a more terrifying monster. As such, Jake felt he was the perfect man to track down a werewolf. After lying low in the mine shaft through the heat of the day, he emerged during late afternoon, a creature from his lair, ready to hunt. Experience had schooled him deeply on the need to confuse his movements for any adversary who might be watching. With crude map in hand, his instincts drove him north away from the mine, east after a few minutes, and then south toward the claim. The sounds of distant voices and the clang of metal on rock identified adjacent claims hidden by the ebb and flow of the rippling landscape. Twice, he spied people but managed to skirt their proximity and attention.

When he reached the Stefka mine, enough daylight remained for a quick study of the earth beneath his boots. The place of the killing became immediately apparent. Ten feet from the remains of a collapsing canvas tent, an area of soil among the sage was stained a deeper brown. The faint odor of entrails lingered there. He squatted to find exactly what Mrs. Stefka had claimed— enormous wolf tracks much too wide for even the largest of timber wolves. The tracks were everywhere around the campsite, particularly at the point of the kill.

When Jake bent to study several of the deeper impressions, though, his doubt flared. Predators bore claws. They left prints that varied slightly one from the next depending on the flex of the foot and extension of the talons. In the process of dragging a man from his tent and killing him, a creature should have left a dozen variations of print. These, however, were all the same—each one identical to the other. As if frozen into a single form.

Jake sorted through the mess of tracks until he found the path that marked both the approach and retreat of the beast. He picked his way around intermittent tufts of sage and grass, following the path. Perhaps a hundred yards on, the prints stopped abruptly behind a protrusion of rock as if the creature had winked into existence at the spot and disappeared just the same way. He knelt, stroking his bearded chin in consideration. The fading light pressed against him, demanding insight before details could give way to darkness. Careful not to touch the ground where the tracks appeared, he leaned low on hands and knees to sweep his gaze around the soil adjacent to the terminal tracks. Within moments, he saw what he'd been looking for. Smudges in the dirt, smooth pressings marred by a few imperfections that repeated among the pressings in two distinct forms. He pushed up to his knees.

"Moccasins," he murmured. Early East Coast settlers had borrowed the footwear style from eastern tribes, and the practice had traveled west with each burst of expansion. The footprints could belong to anyone, native or European alike. Regardless, two gut instincts flared. One, someone had swapped out moccasins for a contraption with a sole shaped like a large wolf print, probably made of wood or plaster, in the interest of hiding human participation in the matter. Second, if the local tribes intended to kill miners, they wouldn't bother to employ such an elaborate ruse. There was no honor in trickery.

He studied the tracks further, both the wolf and moccasin variety, until the light failed. By that time, he had become aware of the stranger watching him from a distance. While crouching as if assessing prints, he cocked his Kerr and set it in his holster with the grip out. Though his hiding place lay roughly northwest, he rose and moved east. Quick glances into the twilight found the man following. Another bounty hunter, most likely. Jake continued east for a few minutes at a pace that reeled in the follower. After topping the roll of a hill, Jake ducked and crab-crawled to his right before flattening his form in the sage.

Half a minute later, his stalker topped the rise and stopped. Jake remained deathly still as the man seemed to scan ahead for signs of his quarry. He carried what looked like a rifle in his hand. After a few seconds of pause, the man began moving down from the rise in the direction Jake would've gone. After he passed, Jake rose silently and slipped up behind his pursuer. After first touching his revolver, Jake found his knife instead. Lisbet's knife. The stranger choked a startled cry when Jake circled his waist with an arm while pressing the blade to his throat.

"Drop it or die."

When his pursuer released what he'd been carrying, Jake pushed him to the ground, pulled the Kerr, and pressed it to the back of the man's neck. The follower spread his arms aside, fingers splayed in surrender.

"Don't kill me, mister," he said mournfully in a familiar Tejano accent. "I got a family. I don't wanna die."

"Why're you following me, then, if you don't wanna die?"

"I—I don't know."

"Tell me a different story."

The man exhaled in defeat. "My mine butts against Old Man Stefka's claim. I saw you poking around. Thought maybe you had something to do with his killing."

Jake finally glanced at the man's discarded weapon. A shovel. Not a rifle. He shook his head. "So you followed me in the dark, thinking I might've carved open your neighbor from gullet to gut, armed with naught but a spade?"

"Uh. Yeah."

Jake pulled the revolver's barrel from the man's neck and stood. "You're a brave man, mister. Stupid, but also brave. They're sons of the same mother most days." He holstered the Kerr. "What's your name?"

"Francisco Aguilar."

"Well, Francisco Aguilar. I ain't gonna kill you. Not today, anyway."

The miner rolled to his back. The absence of light left his face in shadow and likely meant he couldn't see Jake clearly either. Then he lifted a finger to point at Jake.

"Are you *him?*"

"Don't know what you're talkin' about."

"Him," Aguilar repeated. "The man Gus Rivers and Stacy Blue been telling folks about. The man who might help us. The outlaw. Are you him?"

Jake grimaced in the darkness. "And what if I was?"

Aguilar exhaled again, this time with seeming relief. "I'd thank him for trying to keep us alive. For trying to get justice."

"And the price on his head? You sure you wouldn't break his skull with a spade and bring him in for the bounty?"

"No, sir." Indignation dripped from his reply. "I would never."

"And why not?"

Aguilar rose slowly, gathered his spade, and stepped back from Jake. "Folks are frightened. They're losing hope. If I turned in the man trying to help us, they'd hang me from a high branch." He took one step forward. "I got a wife and three *niños*. I don't want them to go without a husband and father. This place is a trial as it is. For those without a way to earn a living, it's a grave."

Jake considered Aguilar's logic and appreciated the simple nobility of it. It was a nobility possessed by most of the westerners he'd met—not one that lorded over the weak but one that bound neighbor to neighbor with courage, dignity, and sacrifice. He'd seen the same from his company mates during the war.

"All right, then. But a word of advice, Francisco Aguilar."

"Sir?"

"Understand who you're tanglin' with before you tangle with 'em. And bring more firepower than a spade."

"Yes, sir."

"And one more thing."

"Yes?"

"Don't tell anybody you saw me."

Like Mrs. Stefka, the man paused. And like Mrs. Stefka, he made a false promise. "I won't."

Jake sheathed the knife that had been dangling

from his other hand. "Get on back to your claim, now. Stay vigilant."

"I will, sir."

Jake watched Aguilar's shadow disappear into the night before turning toward his impromptu fortress, wondering how he'd come to have so many strangers relying on him—again.

CHAPTER FOURTEEN

Gus arrived at Paynter's hideout shortly after sundown. Unlike before, Paynter did not show himself. The hairs of Gus's arms stood on end as a knot formed in his gut. He pulled his carbine, dismounted in a single, smooth motion, and trained the business end of his weapon on the dark hole.

"Paynter?" he called with a sharp this-better-be-no-joke whisper. No reply. He glanced at the horses. Neither seemed more nervous than usual, which was a good sign. Still, he lifted the rifle to his shoulder and crept toward the black opening, his finger caressing the trigger like a lover. When a pebble thumped his back, he spun and waved the carbine wildly into the darkness, ready to kill.

"You finally gonna shoot me after all this time?"

Paynter's voice from the shadow emerging from the night pulled the carbine from Gus's shoulder. "Dadgummit, Paynter. Why you do such things? I coulda blown your head clean off."

"Probably." Paynter came closer. "On the bright side, you could've collected a thousand dollars for your troubles."

"Don't tempt me."

Paynter laughed, a rarity from him. "Sorry. Didn't mean to startle ya. I just walked back from the place where Stefka was murdered. I got some ideas."

"I'd like to hear 'em while we ride."

"Fair enough. Where we headed, exactly?"

"To talk to the family of another man killed by the . . . whatever it was."

"That's precisely what I want to converse about."

They mounted up, Gus on his buckskin and Paynter on his foul-tempered mare. As Gus led the way, Paynter told him what he'd seen at the Stefka mine. The spot of the kill. The off-putting tracks. The disappearance of further tracks. The evidence of someone wearing moccasins and false footprints to perpetrate a ruse.

"So," said Gus, "you're thinkin' someone's playacting as a werewolf and using soft shoes to hide the fact that it was a person instead?"

"I do, with one caveat."

"Caveat. Now, there's a five-dollar word. And what would that *caveat* be?"

"I think it's two men. I found two sets of soft prints by the rock outcrop, different sizes. A bigger man and a littler man. Maybe a woman. One does the killin' while the other stands by with a gun just in case everything goes south."

Gus bandied the theory about in his head a few times. "That don't make me feel any better.

A man alone might be chalked up to criminal madness. But two men? That sounds like a plan. When it comes to murder, planning is a sure sign of larger forces at work."

"My feelings exactly. Larger forces usually mean money's at stake. It always comes down to gold in some form or another."

Paynter's comment reminded Gus of an unfinished task. He rifled through his saddlebag to produce a leather pouch with a drawstring. "Speaking of which, this is for you."

Paynter caught the tossed bag and hefted it twice. "Coins? What for?"

"I sold the horses we took from Sally's men that night they tried to kill us outside Fort Laramie. That's your share."

Paynter cocked his head. "I thought Lucien had claimed them for his own."

"Oh, he claimed them all right. But they all 'escaped' unexpectedly. Seems somebody left the gate open. Such a tragedy."

"You're a scalawag," said Paynter wryly. "And I mean that as the highest compliment. Thanks for the coins."

"Ain't but nothin'."

"But one more thing."

"Yes?"

"Don't tell anyone about my ideas yet. I'll need to check another claim first."

"It's your circus, Paynter."

Gus led onward until they encountered a series of five tents in the brush some distance removed from the rest of the town—an island of habitation tucked into the embrace of two hills. He caught Paynter looking at him with question.

"Chinese folk," said Gus. "They keep to themselves, mainly because they ain't welcome in town. Mostly families who came up from south of here after the railroad work dried up."

A smallish shadow walked out from the cluster of tents to meet them. "I watch your horses. Yes?"

Gus smiled at the boy. "Most grateful."

Paynter opened his newly acquired bag and offered a coin to the lad. The boy waved a hand in front of his face. "No money. No money."

Paynter cocked an eyebrow before returning the coin to the bag. They left the horses with the youngster and walked toward the tents. People had begun emerging from the shelters to gather in the area between—maybe twenty-five in all, men, women, and children. The glow of a small fire revealed wide-eyed curiosity in most faces, skepticism in others. The assembly parted to reveal a woman sitting on a blanket in their midst beside an older boy, perhaps in his late teens. The resemblance marked them as likely mother and son. An old man with a long, gray braid motioned for Jake and Gus to sit on the adjacent blankets clearly set out for their comfort. When they sat, the young man pointed to his nose.

"I am Zhou Li. I will speak for my mother. Her English is not so good."

Gus tipped his hat to the woman. "Mrs. Zhou."

She dipped her forehead and smiled, despite her careworn appearance.

Gus tapped Paynter's arm. "They've told me what they know, but I'd like you to hear it from them directly."

Paynter dipped his chin and leaned toward Mrs. Zhou, his expression grave. "Mrs. Zhou. If you would, tell us what happened to your husband."

She appeared to understand the question and began speaking to Paynter as if he understood fluent Mandarin. For his part, Paynter nodded from time to time as if he did. Zhou Li began translating her story.

"We lived in Shandong Province for many generations. We had a farm there. Fifteen years ago, the Yellow River changed course and destroyed our land. It destroyed the lands of many. We escaped with our lives but nearly starved. Hungry farmers joined the Nian Rebellion, and war nearly killed us all. One day, my husband said, 'We go to America where there is land for us.' But we had no more money when we arrived in California, so my husband and Zhou Li took jobs with the Central Pacific."

With that, Jake held up his hand and peered at the boy. "Just how old were you when you began working on the railroad?"

Zhou Li's chest swelled. "Nine years old. I crawled into tight places to set explosives. When I got older, I learned how to make powder and fuses. These were invented in China, so I was proud to learn those skills."

Jake nodded with seeming appreciation before motioning to Mrs. Zhou. "Please, continue."

She began again, still in Mandarin, as her son translated.

"When the railroad finished, Central Pacific had no more use for Chinese workers. We heard about the gold rush and came here one year ago. We have saved some money, but now everyone is afraid to work the claims. They are afraid of the beast that killed Zhou."

Paynter swiveled his attention to Zhou Li. "Did anyone see this beast?"

"No. But it left tracks." He made a circle between his hands to show how large. "Big, with claws. Many believe it is Fuzanglong."

"Fuzanglong?"

"The treasure dragon. It guards all treasures of the earth. Even natural treasures."

"Such as gold."

"Yes."

Paynter nodded slowly. "And what do you believe? You think it's a dragon?"

Zhou Li shook his head. "Those are stories told by old people. I have never seen a dragon. I do not think such things exist."

"What do you believe it is, then?"

Zhou Li glanced at his mother and the others, perhaps wondering if he should speak his mind. Gus held an open palm to him. "Say what you think. You've earned it."

Zhou Li nodded, but his face retained the frown. "In China, I saw no magical monsters. But I saw men do monstrous things. I think men must be the same everywhere. Even here."

As the gathering murmured, Paynter looked down at his hands, opening and closing them several times. He spoke without looking up. "You are a wise young man, Zhou Li. You know more than I did at your age."

"Thank you, sir."

Paynter produced a worn envelope and a pencil from his jacket pocket and extended it toward Zhou Li. "Can you mark on this map the location of your claim? I want to see for myself."

As Zhou Li marked the map, Gus looked at Paynter. He seemed suddenly withdrawn, and Gus knew why. Paynter saw himself in Zhou Li's description of despicable men. He always had, as long as Gus had known him, and had tormented himself for years over his guilt for whatever terrible things he'd done in the past. It was this very trait—this recognition of and resistance to his own darkness—that drew so many to believe in him. But Paynter seemed unable to realize that fact, and it was slowly killing him.

CHAPTER FIFTEEN

"Tell me again why you're showing your face in town in broad daylight?"

Stacy asked the question with all the derision she felt as she and Paynter rode away from his hideout at midmorning. Paynter turning up in the middle of South Pass City on a Saturday seemed a fool's errand. And the packhorse she dragged along at his request didn't bode well. After all, it could be used for hauling a dead body.

"I got my reasons," he said.

"Care to share 'em with me? I'll try not to judge you too harshly."

He stared ahead in silence for a time before speaking again. "Nobody ever won a war without mounting an offensive. Otherwise, you end up dying in your own trenches. It's better to die while tryin' to take someone else's trench."

Stacy blinked with confusion. "All right. But how is it a good idea to stroll into town on a day when everyone'll be there? And bounty hunters roamin' the streets asking questions about you? Seems like a death wish, not strategy."

"I understand your concern. But I can't avoid a fight forever. I don't intend to start one, but I'm ready if one comes." He waved a hand toward her. "Besides, you said it yourself. Nobody has a good likeness of me."

"And yet some of them found you with the Shoshone, desperados and lawmen alike."

"True. But they knew I was hidin' there and must've figured that the only white man in the area was the one they were lookin' for. And rightly so. Nobody's expectin' me to show up at their doorstep with such a price on my head. People have a curious way of convincing themselves of the truth and then ignorin' what's right in their face. They won't see me—not the real me. You watch."

"What about Mrs. Stefka? She'll know you."

"She promised not to talk. To those that might want to string me up anyway."

Stacy half-heartedly agreed with his logic but didn't have to like it. "I suppose you might be right. But what if someone with a gun and a Wanted poster does recognize you? What then?"

"We'll see what happens," he said darkly. "But promise me one thing."

"What's that?"

"If all hell breaks loose, stay out of it. The kind of men lookin' for me will shoot down a woman, no questions asked. And if they think you're helpin' me, they might just hang you for it. So promise me you'll stand aside if anything happens."

"I promise." She lied through her teeth but

figured the good Lord would forgive her that minor indiscretion. "But meanwhile, I'm gonna be the eyes behind your back."

Paynter grinned. "That's why I asked you to bring me to town. You've always had my back, and I don't trust anyone more than you and Gus."

His unexpected praise flushed her cheeks with pride. Which annoyed her. "Okay, then. But if you get yourself killed, I'll probably spit in your lifeless eyes."

"Fair enough."

"At least wear my hat. Yours is too recognizable. Somebody's bound to notice."

He stared at her for several seconds. "You ain't gonna leave me alone until I do, right?"

"You know it."

When he held out his hand, she pressed her forage cap into it. He removed his slouch hat, stuffed it into his saddle bag, and donned her cap. "It doesn't fit."

"It don't have to fit. It just needs to make you look like somebody else. Stop belly-achin'."

"Just sayin'."

Paynter's role in their conversation bled away as they approached town. His eyes became predatory, in constant search of a threat. Stacy eventually heard his unspoken message and joined him in silence until they rode up along a side street. She expected someone to point at Paynter and begin shouting alarm. That wasn't what happened. Folks just continued with whatever task they were about, oblivious to the fact that a thousand dollars was blowing right past them.

"What now?" she said finally.

"General store."

Of course. The busiest place in town. "You sure?"

"No."

They crossed the main street with heads down and landed at the general store. After tying their horses to the hitching post, Stacy held a palm to him. "At least let me scout the place. Wouldn't wanna run into somebody you know."

"I'll give ya 'til the count of thirty."

Stacy stepped inside and craned her neck over the stacks of supplies. No Lucien. No Ketchum. No Mrs. Stefka. She opened the door again and gave a quick nod. When Paynter slipped past her, he said, "Keep an eye on the door."

She did as he asked, lingering between the door and the cash register while thumbing through merchandise to give the impression that she might buy something at any moment. She didn't want to draw overt attention from the shop owner, Mr. Ellison. He was a weasel of a man and far too observant for his own good. Meanwhile, Paynter circled the store twice while accumulating a pile of dry goods on the counter. Beans. Flour. Coffee. Oatmeal. She knew he didn't have much in the way of supplies stashed at the mine, but the growing pile seemed sufficient for a small army. When she shot him a quizzical glare, he just winked and plopped a basket of eggs on the countertop.

Mr. Ellison, whose smile had widened as the pile grew, rubbed his hands together when Paynter stepped to the cash register with a bag of coins in hand. "Will that do for you, sir?"

"It will."

Ellison began punching the keys of the register as he brushed a hand over each item. "New in town?"

Stacy's attention fell on Paynter. He seemed unflustered by the question. "Yep."

"Where do you hail from?"

"Texas."

"Never been to Texas. Came here by way of Iowa, myself." He glanced up at Paynter. "You don't seem like a miner, unless you already got your own tools."

"That's right."

Ellison seemed confused. "So you're a miner or not a miner?"

"I'm doin' some digging."

"Ah," said the shopkeeper. "Most folks are. Whereabouts is your claim?"

Stacy sensed the shift in Paynter's stance. His right foot slid wider, and he squared his hips. Like a rattler coiling to strike. She slipped up next to the counter. "Howdy, Mr. Ellison."

"Miss Blue."

"Just Stacy. I keep tellin' everyone." She grabbed Paynter's upper arm and tugged him toward her. "This here's my cousin. He's just passin' through on his way to, uh, Montana. He'll be gone before you know it."

Minor disappointment colored Ellison's eyes as he seemed to consider the loss of a repeat customer who purchased in bulk. "Ah, well. More's the pity. But then again, we have people flooding in here day by day. Coming by train from back east and even from California to Laramie, then by wagon, horseback, or foot to here. People of all sorts. Mostly miners, but other types as well. There's even a ramrod do-gooder woman called Mrs. Morris from New York stirring up trouble."

Paynter, who'd eased a bit, lifted his eyes. "What kind a' trouble?"

"She's trying to rally the miners together, especially those with funny accents."

Paynter cocked his head, seemingly unamused. "Isn't that a good thing? People helping neighbors so they don't end up split open?"

Ellison appeared to sense the dangerous tone because he leaned away from the counter. "I suppose when you put it that way, maybe it's not such a bad thing."

Stacy, who still clutched Paynter's arm, squeezed it to remind him of his plan to avoid attention. He cut his eyes at her and nodded.

"But who am I to say?" Paynter's tone had lightened considerably. "I imagine she means well."

"Maybe. But Mr. Ashley says we don't need help from strangers. From outsiders."

Paynter lifted an eyebrow. "So this Mr. Ashley is opposed to Mrs. Morris's actions?"

"Yes."

"He been here a long time, then?"

Ellison frowned. "A year, perhaps."

"Doesn't that make him an outsider too?"

The shopkeeper laughed. "In most places, yes. But in a boom town, a year is like a generation. That, and he pays his bills on time. But he's got his hands full right now, what with building his ranch and beating the bushes for that outlaw they call Paynter."

Stacy squeezed the arm hard until it flexed beneath her grip, and Paynter placed a comforting hand on hers. "My *cousin* here mentioned as much. What'd he do? This Paynter fella."

"Let's see," said Ellison as he rubbed his forehead. "Killed his captain and a bunch of his men. Raided settlements with bands of hostiles. Shot twenty peaceful men heading west, for no reason whatsoever."

Under other circumstances, Stacy might have burst out laughing. But she was too worried over how Paynter might react to learning of all his supposed misdeeds. He just smiled. "Sounds like a dangerous man."

Ellison leaned forward conspiratorially and lowered his voice to a whisper. "Oh, he is. And let me tell you. I've seen no less than a dozen bounty hunters and a pair of Texas Rangers asking around about him this past month. Even Dutch van Zandt has a crew beating the bushes."

"Dutch van Zandt?"

"The outlaw king of Wyoming. He's got a small army north of here taking what they want. Seems like he's interested in taking Paynter's hide. But that ain't the half of it."

"What's the other half?" said Paynter.

"Word has it that Ashley hired a Pinkerton detective out of Chicago called Venables. And a gang from Philadelphia. Got 'em all staying at the Idaho House hotel up the street."

"Gang?"

"Professional criminals. Eight of them. Go by the name of the Flayers. Dress like gentlemen but will cut a throat without batting an eye."

Paynter only nodded at the disconcerting news. "What about the town marshal? What's his position on so many gunslingin' folks crowding his jurisdiction?"

Ellison waved a hand. "Ah, he doesn't care, so long as Ashley's happy. Judge Kingman is less pleased, but he's rarely in the area." His eyes drew into a squint and he lifted an index finger toward Paynter. "Say, I bet you're one of them. One of the bounty hunters lookin' for justice."

The wicked smile that crawled across Paynter's face sent such a shudder through Stacy that she released his arm and began gathering the supplies. He straightened his spine. "That's right. Just lookin' for justice."

"You'll need this, then." Ellison produced from beneath the counter a Wanted poster featuring Paynter's poor likeness, complete with the wrong hat and no beard.

Paynter frowned with amusement. "Seems a little soft for a killer. But I thank you for the poster."

"My pleasure," said Ellison. "By the way, what'd you say your name was?"

"I didn't."

Stacy dumped fifty pounds of beans and flour into Paynter's arms. "Come along, Joe Smith. We shouldn't take up any more of Mr. Ellison's time."

"Indeed."

Ellison waved as Stacy and Paynter hauled out the supplies. "Nice to make your acquaintance, Mr. Smith. I hope you get your man."

"Don't worry," he said. "I will."

CHAPTER SIXTEEN

After leaving the general store, Jake rode up the main street with his head down and cap pulled low as he and Stacy passed the town marshal's office. When they'd covered another thirty yards, he turned into a blind alley that ended unceremoniously in rocky hillside. Stacy rode up beside him in the narrow space, drawing behind her the packhorse loaded with supplies.

"Why we stoppin'?"

Jake slid from the mare and peeked around the corner of the adjacent building—the assay office—to find the front of the town marshal's office to his right. The Idaho House where Lucien's trackers lodged was situated diagonally across the street. Jake pulled back to find Stacy invading his space, her arms folded and an expression of what-the-devil plastered on her face. He pushed her a few steps into the alleyway.

"Remember what I said earlier. I need to go on the offensive, startin' with reconnoitering my enemy." He stabbed a thumb over his shoulder. "From here, we can keep an eye on the comings and goings of both the marshal's office and the hotel."

She unfolded her arms with the dawn of

137

understanding. "How long do we wait? And how do we keep folks from wonderin' why we're lurking in an alleyway like a couple a' thieves?"

Good questions, both. He could always count on Stacy to get to the fine end of a point. "First of all, get comfortable. We may be here a while. Reconnaissance never holds to a schedule. It tends to show you what you want ten seconds after you've given up waitin'."

"Fine, then. And about the nosy folk passin' by?"

Jake stroked his chin but failed to come up with an answer. Stacy's wry smile raised his suspicion that she knew something he didn't. "Let's have it."

She punched his shoulder and then slapped the wall across from the assay office. "Know what this is?"

"No." He'd not been along this route before. "But you're dyin' to tell me, so spit it out."

She folded her arms again and grinned triumphantly. "A blacksmith shop. And there ain't but one smithy in town."

"Glen Dunbar's?"

"Yep."

"Right. Let's wait there instead."

After beating back an army of raiders together on the journey from Missouri to Wyoming, Jake trusted Glen and Maddie Dunbar implicitly. They'd help him lie low. He led the mare around the corner of the building behind Stacy to find just what she'd claimed—a smithy. Within seconds, Dunbar emerged from the back room, wiping his hands on his apron. The large man froze, his eyes wide with surprise, before motioning them inside. After they led the horses into the open space, Dunbar pulled the ties holding back the canvas front, allowing them to close. He faced Jake with concern.

"Have you a death wish?"

Stacy snorted. "That's what *I* said."

Jake began unloading the supplies from the packhorse. "I don't have a death wish. Not on purpose, anyhow. But I've never been one to wait for trouble. I'd rather meet it on the way."

After Jake finished explaining to Dunbar what he'd found at the Stefka claim and his planned surveillance, the big Scotsman retrieved a chair and set it beside the seam where the two stretches of canvas came together. He motioned to Jake. "An eagle's-eye view. I'll ask Maddie to put on tea and cakes."

Jake knew better than to say no. He pulled up the chair, nudged the canvas open six inches, and waited. Stacy peered over his shoulder for a time before choosing conversation with Maddie and Glen over surveillance. Jake didn't blame her. Numbing patience was an acquired skill. He'd learned it well while hiding in the fields from his father or brothers, from huddling in trenches with the enemy in earshot, while riding patrol a hundred days in a row with no action. It served him well over the next four hours. People came and went from the Idaho House and marshal's office, oblivious to his observation. During that time, he counted at least seven gunmen, given away by their swagger and the wide berth shown them by the locals. Bounty hunters, no doubt.

During the third hour of his watch, a sharp-eyed man wearing a high-quality suit and a crisp mustache exited the hotel. Jake sat up, his attention riveted. The way the man stopped just outside the door to survey the length and breadth of the street before moving on. The way his eyes moved from face to face in constant surveillance. Jake pulled the canvas halves together until a slit remained, wondering. A U.S. marshal? The Pinkerton detective? Regardless, the man knew what he was about. Jake memorized his face, suspecting he'd see him again soon. In the man's wake, Jake lost interest in everything except the hotel.

It was the fourth hour, though, that held the biggest surprises. The first came in the form of a pimply-faced teen nearly stumbling over Jake as he blundered through the canvas crease.

"Oh! Sorry, mister." He picked up the burlap sack he'd been holding, stuffing a pair of horseshoes back inside. Jake slid the chair away from the gap and leaned back as if he'd been napping. Even a sixteen-year-old might take notice of what he was doing.

"Ned." Dunbar's greeting indicated that he knew the gangly young man. "Are those the shoes your ma mentioned?"

"Yes, sir." He seemed unenthused about his errand.

"I'll have them spruced up before I close." He glanced at Jake. "You can return for them later."

"Can't I just wait here?"

Dunbar withheld a reply until Jake nodded. "All right. Just stay clear of the forge."

"Yes, sir."

When Ned walked to the canvas and threw it wide, Jake grimaced and pulled his hat lower. The wider view, however, gave him a panoramic picture of a knot of strangers pouring from the hotel. Four men, all wearing matching black suits and bowler hats, gathered on the porch. The leader of the group, a swaggering man with a dangerous grin, became obvious from the deference shown him by the others. One of his followers was truly a giant who made Dunbar look frail by comparison. His tailored suit barely constrained shoulders well in proportion with a frame that challenged seven feet. Their raucous laughter rang up the street, scattering locals in a hurry.

"Oh, my Lord," said Ned. "Them's some of the fellas from Philadelphia. The Flayers."

The reverence in the boy's tone drew Jake's forehead into a crease. "You know 'em?"

"Oh, no. But I'd like to. They come to kill that outlaw."

Jake kept his eyes pinned on the men as they lingered on the porch, giving catcalls to the few women who dared venture by. When one of the husbands took mild offense, the gang showed him an array of cudgels that sent him scurrying away. Jake's gut clenched. He knew such men— the kind that viewed human life as a commodity to be bartered and spent. He'd ridden with such men. He'd been such a man, before he broke. Meanwhile, Ned oohed and aahed over them, clearly taken with their air of invulnerability.

After perhaps ten minutes, some of the gunmen Jake had seen earlier returned to the hotel—five in all. The tallest, a man who seemed constructed of saddle leather and molten steel, spoke in a condescending voice loud enough for everyone on the street to hear.

"Well, looky, boys. If it ain't the prissiest parade a' dandies I ever saw."

The suited men, who'd been lounging against posts and walls, went tense in an instant. The leader stepped toward the approaching gunmen, never releasing his grin. "Begging your pardon, mister. But are you speaking to us?"

The tall man seemed to miss the menace of the question, or at least doubted its danger. "Seein' as how you're the only prissy dandies here, then damn right I'm speakin' to you."

The cudgels appeared again as if from nowhere. Meanwhile, the other gunmen closed ranks and dropped hands to their hips. Clubs against revolvers didn't usually work out so well for them with sticks. This could get ugly quick. Jake stood in anticipation.

"Well, I'm sorry to earn your disregard," said the gang's leader as he stepped near the gunmen and held out a hand. "But I'd like to introduce myself. I'm Mr. Sweeney."

The tall man frowned, but one of his comrades laughed openly.

Sweeney cut his eyes to him. "What, might I ask, do you find so amusing?"

The laughing man lifted a lip into a sneer. "We ride with Dutch van Zandt. We don't shake hands with horse leavings."

Sweeney's face went blank, and he motioned to the giant. "Mr. Bollinger."

"Sir?"

"Introduce yourself to this man."

"With pleasure."

Bollinger closed the distance between him and the amused man in two strides before crushing his windpipe with a lightning throw of a ham-sized fist. The gunman fell like a brick chimney and began flopping like a fish. The Flayers were on the remaining gunmen before they could draw

143

and shoot. Clubs rained down repeatedly on ribs and skulls until a man erupted from the marshal's office.

"Boys! Boys!"

The easterners halted their carnage, seemingly prepared to turn it on the newcomer. He backed away a step and his voice went quivery. "I'm Spraggs, the town marshal. Mr. Ashley wouldn't want you gentlemen to be killin' nobody just yet. Then he'd have to send you away without your pay, and nobody wants that."

He backed away farther when Sweeney strolled his way. "Town marshal, is it?"

"Uh . . . yes."

"It seems your intervention is too late for that man." Sweeney jerked a thumb over a shoulder toward the man Bollinger had punched in the throat. The gunman had stopped writhing. And breathing.

"I—I see."

The easterner eyed the marshal in silence for a dozen heartbeats before his grim demeanor reformed into the dangerous grin. "I suppose you're right, copper. Wouldn't want to get sent home over a little misunderstanding." He turned to his men. "Would we, lads?"

"Oh, no, sir," they said with the earnestness of church choirboys. "We'd not want that."

Spraggs rubbed his throat. "Well, then. Glad we have an understanding."

Sweeney's wide smile failed to waver as he stared again at the lawman. "Oh, yes. We've an understanding all right. Good day to you, town marshal."

The gang wandered the opposite direction toward a tavern, but not before delivering a few parting shots to the moaning gunmen. In their absence, no one came to help the fallen men, and Spraggs retreated to his office.

"Lordy, Lordy," whispered Ned. "Did you see that? They busted up them gunslingers like they was china plates. Killed that fella dead with one punch!"

The awe in the young man's voice was all too familiar to Jake. He'd felt that same way the first time he saw Blackburn and his band of raiders when he was about Ned's age. He'd wanted nothing more than to be one of them, and they'd obliged. He saw in Ned that same desire and knew what it would cost him.

"Men like that'll steal your soul, boy. You best stay well away from them."

Ned peered at him, blinking his lack of understanding. "But you saw 'em. They mean business. And I gotta help feed the family."

Jake pulled the bag of coins from his pocket, extracted a silver dollar, and tossed it to the kid. "This'll help your cause. Don't get mixed up with that bunch."

Ned pocketed the coin, but the shine of his eyes

failed to fade. Jake was certain he'd wasted his investment. He rose from his chair and began reloading the packhorse. Stacy came up beside him.

"We leavin'?"

"Yep. Nothin' more to see here."

She eyed the distracted boy and leaned near to whisper. "We headed back to you-know-where?"

"We are. But we gotta deliver this food first."

"To who?"

He cinched down the last bag of flour to the horse's back. "Mrs. Stefka and Mrs. Zhou."

Stacy's brow smoothed and she smiled. "You're not as bad as you think."

He shook his head as he scanned the street before leading the horses outside. Stacy was wrong about that. But the least he could do was humor her with his silence.

CHAPTER SEVENTEEN

Rosalyn knew Ketchum wasn't the devil. But she was pretty sure he hailed from the same neck of the woods. His corrosive presence pushed her from the driver's seat into the wagon bed before they'd traveled a quarter mile from the ranch. He leered over his shoulder as she settled next to Mrs. Guilfoyle.

"You cut me to the quick, Miss Ashley. I'm startin' to think you don't love me at all."

Rosalyn ignored him, but the redoubtable Mrs. Guilfoyle did not. "I can poison ya real slow, Mr. Ketchum. 'Til your insides become outsides. You'd never see it coming."

He sneered and faced forward to drive the two-horse team. Rosalyn mouthed a "thank you" to the new ranch cook, more pleased than ever that she'd hired the widow.

Mrs. Guilfoyle waved a dismissive hand. "It was nothing. And I wasn't joking."

"It seems I have much to learn from you, Mrs. Guilfoyle."

"In the handling of rough men, I've much to teach."

Over the next three hours, she made good on that promise. Every time Ketchum began to step over the line, Mrs. Guilfoyle managed to beat him back with a combination of deflection, threats, and ridicule. By the last hour of the journey to South Pass City, Ketchum had stopped talking altogether. This nearly soothed Rosalyn's disappointment with her brother for sending Ketchum along with them to purchase supplies for the ranch. He had meant well, professing the outlaw's ability to protect the women from unwanted attention. But why him? Why the man who, along with Sally, had tried to kill them on the Oregon Trail until Lucien managed to buy his loyalties for a handful of gold? She'd sooner trust a scorpion not to sting her.

They arrived at the general store in South Pass City not long after midday. She ignored Ketchum's offer of a hand down from the wagon, opting to crawl over the side in the most unladylike of fashions. When her feet touched earth, a low whistle caught her attention. A grimy man with a brown smile clapped his hands together three times.

"Thanks fer the show, missy. Care fer a drink and maybe some fun?"

His shocking advance froze her. Ketchum appeared from her peripheral vision and planted a fist in the stranger's face. He fell to his backside, clutching a broken nose.

"What in the Sam Hill?"

Ketchum leaned over the man with a long

knife that had appeared from his boot. "Speak a word to Miss Ashley again, and I'll cut out your tongue. Savvy?" The man nodded. Ketchum pointed the knife at the crowd of men who'd stop to watch. "Same goes for the rest of ya. Now, run along."

The crowd broke up immediately and the stranger stumbled away in defeat. A chill ran up Rosalyn's spine. Where the others may have taken the threat as hyperbole, Rosalyn understood it to be a poison promise. Ketchum had undoubtedly cut out a few tongues and worse while riding with Union raiders during the war. For now, though, he was in service to her, but that could change in the blink of an eye if he received a better offer. What had Lucien been thinking?

"Come, Mrs. Guilfoyle. Let's satisfy our list." She peered at Ketchum. "And you'll look after the horses, sir."

Ketchum lifted one side of his lip and stomped back into the driver's seat. As she walked with Mrs. Guilfoyle to the store entrance, the older woman leaned her way.

"Now, that's how it's done."

Rosalyn couldn't help but smile as she pulled open the door. The storekeeper, Mr. Ellison, looked up in response to the bell as they entered the shop. He flashed a toothy smile and smoothed his overly oiled hair. "Miss Ashley. What a pleasure."

He dashed around the end of the counter to meet her. Ellison had been making advances toward Rosalyn since the first day they'd met, much to her chagrin. But before he could say a word, Mrs. Guilfoyle stepped between him and Rosalyn with an extended hand. "I'm Mrs. Guilfoyle, hired by the Ashleys to cook for the ranch. And yes, I'd be most obliged if you'd help me collect my supplies."

Thwarted, Ellison frowned before finding a false smile. "Why yes. Of course."

Mrs. Guilfoyle grabbed his elbow and dragged him away, leaving Rosalyn to trail behind in blessed peace. The cook kept the storekeeper so busy carrying armload after armload of goods to the wagon, ringing the register as he went, that he couldn't spare but a few words for Rosalyn. This pleased her. It wasn't until the wagon was fully stocked and they were settling the bill that he was able to again vie for her attention.

"So, Miss Ashley. It seems like your brother has this outlaw business well in hand."

She told herself to simply nod, but the subject of Jake Paynter always drew her interest. "How so, Mr. Ellison?"

He straightened, full of importance. "Why, the men he's hired. I spoke to that English detective, Mr. Venables. He seems the kind of man who could catch the wind with a net. Sharp as a tack, that one."

"Yes. I met him."

"And those fellas from back east. They seem full of piss and vinegar. Pardon my Greek."

"Yes. I met them briefly as well." She failed to mention that the gang of men from Philadelphia, the so-called Flayers, frightened her beyond words. She'd heard what Lucien had said of them. That they were the ablest of a criminal gang so vicious that the Philadelphia police had gone to war against them. That these particular men specialized in finding those who hid, by whatever means necessary, and exacted their price. She hoped for Paynter's sake that he was far away. Ellison leaned forward on his elbows.

"My money's on your brother's men to find the outlaw. But they do have some competition. Why, I spoke to one of them earlier this morning who seemed a capable sort. Stacy Blue's cousin."

"Stacy Blue's cousin, you say?" Rosalyn tried not to betray her surprise. Stacy had never mentioned a cousin. A creeping insight began to wriggle its way into her jittering thoughts.

"Yes," said Ellison, snapping his fingers. "What was his name, now? Oh, yes. Joe Smith."

"A Shoshone, perhaps?"

"No, no. He was a white fella, young and wide in the shoulders. From her dad's side of the family, I suppose. I gave him a Wanted poster for the Paynter fella. Seems like he was gunning for him."

This time, she did nod and began thumbing

cash onto the counter to end the conversation. As they left the store, Mrs. Guilfoyle eyed her suspiciously. "You all right, Miss Ashley? You seem a little pale."

"I'm fine."

The words had only left her lips when a voice called out in the street. "Well, looky, boys. If it ain't the prissiest parade a' dandies I ever saw."

Rosalyn turned her attention toward a brewing conflict between the Flayers and a cluster of wiry gunmen. She watched in horror as Mr. Sweeney and his band of cutthroats made short work of the tough-looking men before cowing the town marshal into retreat. A shudder rippled through her as the easterners strolled her direction.

"Come, Mr. Ketchum. Mrs. Guilfoyle. We had best return home while we have the light."

She climbed quickly into the wagon, joining Ketchum on the seat. As the men neared, they noticed her and doffed their bowlers.

"Miss Ashley," said Sweeney with a reptilian smile. "What a pleasure to encounter you so far from the ranch on such a fine day."

She required every ounce of restraint to settle her voice. "Mr. Sweeney. Gentlemen."

Ketchum pushed back his hat to reveal his mop of red hair and an appreciative grin. "Nice work back there, fellas. Bastards had it comin'."

"Indeed, Mr. Ketchum. Join us for a drink?"

"A kind offer, but I'm tasked with returnin'

152

Miss Ashley to the ranch. But slosh one down for me, will ya?"

"And then some."

Rosalyn breathed a sigh when the men moved on toward the Red Hen saloon. Ketchum just kept grinning. "Nice boys. Coulda used a few of 'em in the war. Especially that Bollinger fella. A one-man army, he is."

She turned away to keep from disagreeing to Ketchum's face. And that was when she saw him. Three blocks away, Stacy Blue rode in the opposite direction on her familiar calico, back toward Rosalyn. And beside her rode a man whose form she recognized instinctively, even from a distance.

Jake Paynter.

She nearly rose from the seat to chase him down but stopped. Any such action would draw Ketchum's attention to what she saw, and he was shrewd enough to figure it out. She turned abruptly back toward Ketchum.

"Tell us, how'd you get so proficient driving a team of horses, Mr. Ketchum?"

He grinned at her, oblivious to Paynter's slow disappearance down the street. "Why, I grew up on a farm."

She kept him talking as they left town, though her mind reeled with chaos. Paynter's presence was an answer to unspoken prayers and a disaster waiting to unfold.

CHAPTER EIGHTEEN

Every good scout knew that the report after a reconnaissance mission was as important as the mission itself. In the absence of a superior officer, Jake had to settle for Stacy after they'd left food with a grateful Mrs. Zhou.

"So," she said as they made their way toward the Zhou mine. "What'd you learn from watchin' the street today?"

"Been thinkin' about that." He removed Stacy's ill-fitting cap and handed it back to her before retrieving his hat and settling it on his head.

"Well?" she said impatiently. "Start with them eastern boys."

"Brutal," he said. "Vicious, like tigers on the hunt. Men raised in alleyways, brothels, and opium dens. Men without morals or hesitation. Men who'll do most anything for money, or for recognition, or just for the hell of it."

"They got you spooked, then?"

He shook his head. "Not spooked. Thing is, I know my way around such men. I've spent my life since childhood around that sort, and I've learned two important lessons about 'em. One, if I avoid them long enough, they just might turn on each other."

155

"And the other lesson?"

"They can't be avoided forever. I'll have to fight 'em eventually, to the death."

Stacy swallowed hard and her expression went slack. "You think it'll come to that?"

He gave her a tight smile. "It always does with me. I think it's my destiny to fight 'em all until I ain't breathin' anymore."

"But don't you want better? Don't you want a country porch with a rockin' chair and a few other gray-hairs to recollect with?"

He grunted at the thought of such an ending. It would be nice. "I won't live that long, Stacy. What we *want* usually gets trampled underfoot by what we *get*."

She frowned at him, perhaps hoping he was joking. He wasn't. She exhaled heavily. "All right, then. So what about the Pinkerton fella?"

Jake nodded thoughtfully. "Now, he's the one that worries me. Those Flayer boys will shout their coming from a mile off. But the detective, now he's different. He seems all precision and stealth. He'd be the one behind me when I turned around, the one above my bed when I opened my eyes. That concerns me far more than a frontal assault. You can't shoot a shadow. You can't wrestle a ghost."

"Sounds like you're afraid of that dapper little man." She said it with a mocking tone, probably expecting a denial. He hated to disappoint her.

"Of course I'm afraid of him. Only the stupid and the dead are unafraid. That same fear, though, will keep me alive like it has a hundred times before. But that's not the worst of it."

"What could be worse?"

"If Venables and the Flayers join forces. My chances of survival would diminish greatly with his brains directin' their violence."

Stacy frowned with concern. "You think they'll do that?"

"I hope not. But in the meantime, I wonder if you and Gus would see fit to keep a close watch on the whole lot of 'em until we solve this puzzle."

She leaned from her saddle to punch his shoulder. "As if you'd even have to ask."

A few minutes later, they arrived at the Zhou mine. The sun was fading into a line of clouds that hugged the horizon, so the investigation needed to happen at a pace. As he slipped from the mare, Stacy fell in behind him.

"See there," he said. "The darker ground where Mr. Zhou was relieved of his innards. And look there."

She squatted to peer at the oversized tracks. "Looks like a wolf. A big one. Maybe even a werewolf."

"It's not a werewolf."

"You don't know."

"Sure. But tell me. What's wrong with the tracks?"

She blinked at him before looking again. She put a finger down to trace the outline of three different tracks before looking up with sharp eyes. "They're all the same. Like a carving, almost."

"Exactly my thoughts." He pointed toward the brush. "Now, follow them."

He stood aside as Stacy trailed the tracks through the jumble of sage and rock until they ended behind a juniper bush. She squinted at him. "Where'd they go?"

"Take another gander. Not just at the wolf tracks. Look at everything."

She dropped down again and studied the earth for the better part of two minutes before popping to her feet. "There's other tracks. Hard to see, though. Smooth. Like . . . like . . ."

"Like someone wearing moccasins?"

Her face lit with epiphany. "Yeah! Just like that."

He shared with her what he'd told Gus the day before about his suspicions of two men working together to take down lone miners. Her unease mirrored Gus's. "So people are behind this after all."

"That's right, and they're laying down just enough of a ruse to fool anyone who doesn't care to take a closer look. Like the town marshal, for instance. And since the dead are all immigrants, nobody else seems willing to dig any deeper."

She smiled and shook her head. "Except you."

"There's that."

She rubbed her forehead. "Why? Why are they doin' this?"

"That's the right question. I don't know, but I'm nursing some suspicions."

"So whadda we do now? Do you want us to take this to the marshal? Or maybe the judge?"

"Been thinkin' about that too." Jake scratched his jaw. "And no. But what time do you rise in the mornings?"

Her brow furrowed. "Just before the sun, like any decent person. Why do you ask?"

"Because I'd like you to bring me the mare as quick as you can in the morning."

"The morning? Why?"

He turned away from Stacy, expecting judgment. "Because I need to ride out to Lucien's ranch and scout it some. See what else I'm up against."

The judgment came, but only after she'd stepped in front of him with a solid glare. "Don't tell me you're gonna risk yer neck to see Rosalyn."

It stung. Too close to the truth. "Nope. I plan to keep her out of it. But if I happen to spy her from a distance, well, that can't be helped, can it?"

She folded her arms and shook her head. "I'll bring yer horse, but I don't like this one bit. And tomorrow's Sunday, anyway. You should rest, like the Good Book says."

Jake's favorite proverb found his lips. " 'No rest for the wicked,' so the Good Book also says."

"The wicked? You mean Lucien? Or the Philly boys?"

"Yep. Them too."

CHAPTER NINETEEN

For a boy who'd grown to manhood under the benevolent oppression of the salt marshes, mosquitoes, and humidity of the Texas coast, Jake reckoned Wyoming on a summer's morn was akin to the sweet breath of God. As he rode the downslope of South Pass toward Red Canyon, the Wind River range sat on his left shoulder as a gentle reminder of his insignificance in the grand scheme of the world. To make up for it, the rising sun warmed his face while scattered meadowlarks and magpies gave voice to the music of the morning. The gentlest ghost of a breeze played with the mare's mane as she trotted east with her usual diffidence. Yep. If he could have chosen anywhere on earth to be right then, he wouldn't have changed a thing.

He continued riding, touching peace for a small window of time, until he neared the place Rosalyn now called home. He recalled the view when he'd passed by a year earlier in irons on his way to Fort Bridger to hang. Even then, he remembered marveling over the majestic beauty of the lonely spot. When the mare topped a roll of ground, he caught his first sight of the startling red rocks in the distance. A sweep of crimson canyon stretched toward the foothills of the Wind Rivers, as if the world had opened a vein to nourish the ground. A grand sweep of grassy slope rose opposite the rocks, green as polished glass. Another thirty strides brought the ranch into view at the base of the canyon walls. Aware of his exposed position, he prodded the mare toward the back side of a ridge that would allow him to draw much closer without notice. He followed the uplift of rock for another mile or so before dropping from his mount and rubbing her neck.

"Stay put, girl." He swept his hand around. "There's some fine-lookin' grass just beggin' to be eaten by a fine but disagreeable horse such as yourself."

She tossed her head and set to work filling her belly. Rifle in hand, Jake ambled to the top of the ridge until he possessed an eagle's-eye view of the canyon below. When he settled behind a boulder to assess the situation, he couldn't help but be impressed by what he found. A large log house, twice as long as it was wide, seemed to be the sun around which the rest of the ranch revolved. To one side lay a small building billowing smoke—the kitchen, no doubt—and a long bunkhouse. To the other side were a corral with another under construction, a stable, and a barn. And all around the structures were men. A few were feeding horses, but most idled, given that it was Sunday after all. Several pitched horseshoes. Some reclined against the bunkhouse wall with a front-row view of the cattle strung across the hillside opposite them. Jake counted the men, as was his nature. Twelve in plain view. Probably others in the kitchen, bunkhouse, and barn. Call it sixteen or eighteen. That seemed a lot of men to manage a few hundred head of cattle and horses. His gut told him that not all were cowhands or vaqueros. Some were likely hired guns. He already knew that the bounty hunters in Lucien's employ were staying at the hotel in town. These men had another purpose, of that he was certain. But what?

He watched and waited, hoping to find some sign of Lucien. When a skirt appeared from the kitchen, he almost rose from his post. The wearer, however, had light-colored hair, not mahogany brown. His vigil continued for another ten minutes before he decided that Lucien was probably still in bed. Crouching low, Jake clambered back over the ridge and found the mare mowing the hillside. He swung up into the saddle.

"Let's head back. Stacy'll have a bucket of oats for you, so long as you behave."

As he pulled the mare around toward the west, the faint nickering of another horse rose from behind. When he kept spinning the mare back toward the east, she complained with a whinny.

With any hopes for stealth dashed, he should have hightailed it toward South Pass City. On a hunch, though, he prodded the mare toward the sound of the other horse with his hand resting atop the Kerr's grip. His heart jumped when the strange horse came into view on the back side of the ridge, headed toward the ranch. Riding atop the chestnut was a familiar woman wearing a wide-brimmed riding hat and a memorable green skirt. She hadn't seen him yet. He began to turn the mare away but hesitated.

In his moment of indecision, her eyes cut his way and she yanked her horse to a stop. Ten seconds passed as they sized up each other across the rock-strewn hillside. Then she raised a gloved hand. The gesture drew him, like gravity. She nudged her mount into motion, and they met halfway, circling slightly at the joining with twenty feet of soil between them. Her eyes were bright, uncertain, relieved, and more—all at once. Jake didn't judge. He likely looked the same. He touched the brim of his hat and nodded.

"Miss Ashley."

"Mr. Paynter."

"It's good to see you."

"And you." She glanced skittishly toward the unseen ranch. "I was afraid you might be . . ."

"Unhappy to see you?"

She shook her head. "No. Not that. I've feared you might no longer be among the living, that's all. Until I perhaps saw you in town yesterday with Stacy Blue."

He grimaced, suddenly questioning his risky trip the day before. If she'd seen him, others might've as well. "I was there."

Nothing but the breeze interrupted the stretching pause between them. She looked again toward the ridge that blocked the view of the ranch. Then she moved her horse a few steps nearer until he could see the scatter of freckles across her cheeks, like a constellation of stars.

"Where have you been all this time?" Her question was not accusatory. Just supremely curious and more than a little relieved.

"I wintered with the Shoshone up range. Stacy's mother's people. Chief Washakie let me stay so long as I pulled my weight." He drew a deep breath. "I might still be there if folks hadn't started showin' up to kill me or recruit me."

Her eyes narrowed with concern. "Kill you?"

He told her about the Texas Rangers, the bounty hunters, and the coming of Gus and Stacy. He relayed their explanation of the killings in South Pass City and his intent to get to the bottom of it. She nodded understanding as he told the tale.

"You should know something, then." She drew her horse nearer still until he could almost extend a hand to touch her. "Lucien has all manner of men looking for you. He's hired a Pinkerton detective from Chicago. And a gang of cutthroats from Philadelphia with a reputation for hunting down even the most elusive of prey."

"I saw them yesterday."

"Then you know you cannot stay around South Pass City, right? You know they will catch you eventually. A thousand dollars is too tempting a prize."

He knew she was right. He should just head west until he ran up against the Pacific Ocean and then try to carve out a new life. But he couldn't. That meant abandoning people who cared about him and who were counting on him to deliver them from evil. It also meant abandoning the woman facing him, even though he could never have her.

"I am grateful for your concern, Miss Ashley. But I promised to help. I won't go back on my word."

"I expected as much."

When she glanced at the ridge for a third time, he was reminded why he'd come so far afield. He motioned toward her. "About the killings. You wouldn't have heard anything from your brother on that subject?"

She leveled an unwavering gaze at him for the space of several breaths. "You think Lucien is involved somehow?"

"Yes." His eyes found the ground between their horses. "When I heard he'd decided to carve out his empire here, I thought of him first. I apologize for that."

She sighed heavily, drawing his eyes again. "No need to apologize. You are right to consider him suspect. My brother is a corrupt soul in certain ways, particularly when money is involved."

"But . . ."

"But he possesses some admirable qualities. He is afraid of nothing. He is determined. And he takes care of his own."

"Like you?"

"Especially me. Which is why he wants you dead." She laughed softly. "He thinks you have designs on me. And I wonder . . . Is he right?"

Her face fell when he shook his head. "You're too far above me for that, Miss Ashley. I'm just a bit of country nothin' compared to you."

Her eyes flashed at his words. "There you go again, demeaning yourself as less than you are. But I know the truth. You are a much better man than you believe, Jake Paynter. And I am . . ." She hesitated. "I am less than you know."

"I doubt that." When she gathered more chastisement, he raised a palm to beg restraint. She held the words, waiting. He lowered his hand. "But if I was a better man. If I was a gentleman and not what I am, I'd put on my best suit and buy you flowers and perfume and come to the ranch to court you proper. That's what I'd do."

She ducked her face as color climbed her cheeks. "You mean that?"

"I do. But since I'm not a better man, I'll have to settle for the offering of a compliment. You look well, Rosalyn. Like the end of a long night and the coming of the sun."

She lifted her face, her eyes shining with the promise of tears. "And you also look well. Your beard makes you look older. It suits you."

"Appreciate it."

She turned her eyes toward the ridge a final time. "I'd better be going before Lucien sends out a search party. That wouldn't end well for either of us."

He nodded agreement. "Will you keep my presence in the area a secret, then?"

"You didn't even have to ask."

"Right." He touched the brim of his hat again. "Good day, Miss Ashley."

"Until we meet again, Mr. Paynter."

As Jake rode away from her, an ache opened inside him that no balm could soothe.

CHAPTER TWENTY

After leaving Rosalyn behind, Jake violated the first rule of the cautious fugitive—never travel a well-worn path. Perhaps it was the distraction of speaking to her for the first time in nearly a year. Maybe it was just the grinding nature of living life under the gun finally wearing him down. Whatever the reason, he followed the main trail back toward town rather than skirting the fringes like he had on the way out. What happened next, then, was surely his own damn fault.

Along a curving sweep of trail that disappeared behind distant junipers, he looked up from his hands to find a crowd riding toward him some few hundred yards out. The uncooperative breeze had hidden evidence of their approach. And they had spotted him for certain, given the gestures in his direction. Nothing would arouse suspicion like a sudden dash into the wilds, so he pulled his hat low and pressed ahead. Within seconds, he began regretting that decision. Eight men wearing identical black suits and bowler hats bore down on him with the slow confidence that only comes from violent experience and appropriate firepower, headed for Lucien's ranch, no doubt.

"Steady," he whispered to the mare. She seemed

as tautly strung as he was. If he played his hand right, they'd pass by without connecting him to the poorly rendered Wanted poster. He'd be past them in no time. His alternatives had evaporated quickly. Five shots from the Kerr might keep him alive for ten seconds, but he'd be dead before he retrieved his rifle to handle those left standing. As the gap narrowed, the murmured chatter among the men bled away to silence. Eight pairs of predatory eyes pinned Jake as they rode single file toward him. Sweeney led the line. He wore a demeanor of boyish mischief, a slight smile on his face as if he were just about to tell a crude joke. His eyes, however, told a different story. Jake was beast enough to recognize an equal hunter when he encountered one. When not more than four strides of the horses separated them, Sweeney lifted his chin toward Jake.

"That's a fine hat, mister."

And it was a fine hat, the last vestige of his days riding with the First Kansas Colored and unique in all the territory. Jake's basest instincts reacted on his behalf, recognizing how near Death stood with scythe in hand. Even as Sweeney grabbed for his pocket pistol, Jake careened the mare toward his horse and shoved the man from his saddle. He spurred the mare through the erupting chaos of spinning horses, slashing with the knife he hadn't known he'd grabbed from his boot. The mare had been involved in enough of his fiascos to know what to do. She buried her head toward the earth and grew wings. Three shots rang out behind him, all errant, though one whizzed near enough to sizzle the air next to his ear. He ventured a glance behind to find the Flayers struggling to turn their horses in the right direction. Apparently, the streets of Philadelphia offered little in the way of equestrian experience. With each subsequent glance, they fell farther behind.

That was when he noticed the mare's pronounced limp. He twisted in his saddle side to side until he found the reason. A stream of blood flowed from her left rear flank, already beginning to coat the leg beneath it. One of the bullets had not been so errant after all. Over the next mile, the laboring mare slowed noticeably. Sweeney and his gang had stopped receding in the distance and were making up ground. And flowing blood like she was, the mare would never outpace them long enough to lose the pursuit. The hunter within him was of no help at all when hunted. He shoved aside the rising red haze in an effort to clear his thoughts of primal instinct. If they laid hands on him, he'd be a dead man when his Kerr emptied. But his pursuers weren't confident horsemen. He needed to use that fact to his advantage. Within moments, he knew what he must do. He leaned low and rubbed the mare's neck.

"Sorry for this, but I need another mile from ya."

She responded by increasing her pace, limping

171

dramatically with each long stride. After a few hundred yards, he guided her off the main trail toward a rise of land strewn with boulders that culminated in a rocky spine stretching away into the distance. He'd spotted it on the way to the ranch, never thinking he'd need it so soon. By the time they reached the spine, Sweeney's men had drawn near enough to take potshots, hoping to get lucky. He rode along the ridge of rock before finding what he sought. They moved over the ridge before he dismounted and yanked the mare along behind him.

"You're gonna need to trust me on this."

She showed him the whites of her eyes and jerked her head twice, but her legs kept moving in the right direction. They reached a point where the rock seemed to fall away into nothing, a death step if ever there was one. However, a seam of rock angling downward provided just enough purchase for man and horse. She'd already shown a willingness to climb rocks, so why not the other direction? When he began edging down the cut, a thirty-foot drop-off just inches to his right, the mare balked.

"Come on, girl." His voice exuded the calm of death. "It's this or the end of us."

She began to follow, placing hooves carefully before her, reining in her mounting momentum with each pair of footfalls. They were halfway down when voices rang out above.

"Where'd they go, for Joseph's sake?"

"Can't have just disappeared."

"You three, go there. We'll take a gander over the edge. Maybe they fell."

Ten feet from the ground, Jake leaped and pulled the mare with him, covering the rest of the descent in two bounding steps. He swung into the saddle before she could stop, and they flew away from the cliffs like Pegasus and Apollo, gods destined to fall in time. Lead whistled past but spared them both until they'd outrun the range of whatever peashooters the easterners considered guns. A dodge into a gulch took them from the Flayers' sight. Jake slid from the mare to inspect her wound. When he mashed a hand against it to stop the bleeding, she whipped her head around with the clear intent of biting a hole in the back of his neck. Fortunately, he ducked.

"You act like you never been shot before. It ain't so bad."

Regardless, she was done running. He dragged her along, angling for the creek he'd seen on the outbound journey. After two minutes, he found it, a trickling flow of water called Beaver Creek barely worthy of its name. He gathered up a double handful of mud the consistency of clay and packed it into the bullet wound. Meanwhile, the mare tried to trample him into a pulp in gratitude for his concern. He would've preferred gauze, and the clay couldn't stay or it would surely infect the wound. In the meantime, though, it might keep her from bleeding to death.

After they'd come to a peaceful accord, Jake led the mare along a circuitous route back toward town while waiting for sunset, along the way skirting the large mining camp the locals called Atlantic City. The occasional voice of a Flayer drifted on the wind, evidence that they were beating the bushes for him. And surely, they'd already sent a couple of their number back to town to watch for his arrival. Under other circumstances, he'd return to his fortress shaft and wait. But his horse was shot. He couldn't let her die.

The light of day had burned away to a whisper when Jake led the mare into South Pass City. They slipped over the natural berm that stopped the alleyway running alongside the Dunbars' smithy, aiming for the back door. Light leaked from the partially ajar door when he pulled the mare up to it. She balked when he opened it and tried to pull her through.

"We've no time for arguments," he said, hoping he sounded soothing rather than agitated. "You need help."

She dipped her head and darted into the smithy. Jake turned to find Glen and Maddie staring, dumbfounded. He tipped his hat as if dropping by for a Sunday visit.

"Sorry to bother, Mrs. Dunbar. But do you still

have those bullet forceps you used on the trail?"

She blinked at her husband and then at Jake. "I do. Three varieties."

"You ever remove a bullet from a horse before?"

Understanding dawned in her eyes. "In fact, I have. The battlefields of Pennsylvania and Virginia weren't kind to horses. They make for large targets."

He motioned to the mare's flank. "It seems the battlefields of Wyoming are no kinder."

Maddie stepped forward to study the wound. Without looking away, she said, "Glen, make sure Lily's still abed and fetch my bag. Paynter, bring her into the light and lay her down."

Jake scratched his jaw with concern. He'd taught his military horses to lie down on command, but the process had taken time. The mare was just as likely to bite off his nose as she was to do what he wanted. "I'll try. But I'll need Glen."

He led the mare to the large open area alongside the forge and stripped her saddle. With the intake of a here-goes-nothin' breath, he grabbed the ankle of her right foreleg and forced her to bend the knee. He rubbed her neck when she resisted. "Easy. Easy."

When Glen loomed over his shoulder, Jake made eye contact. "I'm gonna make her back up now. You reach across her back and pull her toward ya. Hopefully, she'll get the message."

With the mare's foreleg still bent, Jake drove a shoulder into her chest while Glen pulled her spine to the right. She took a pair of backward steps before bending her hind legs to settle and then rolled to her right side. Jake was more than surprised that she'd cooperated. She must've really been hurting. He soothed the mare while Maddie settled over the hindquarters, well away from powerful legs that might shatter her skull. She dug away the mudpack until the wound became visible.

"She's not going to like this. You'll need to pin her down as best you can."

Jake laid his body across the mare's neck while Glen put his weight against her ribs. He nodded at Maddie. "Work fast."

When she poured alcohol over the wound, the horse spasmed. But when Maddie plunged the forceps into the wound, all hell broke loose. The mare began complaining mightily while trying to kick a hole in the world. Her white-soaked eye stared at Jake as if he'd just betrayed her to the minions of the underworld. He and Glen just held on. Somehow, Maddie managed to ride the thrashing and emerge with a slug of lead. She jumped back from the haunch and held the bullet high. The mare immediately stilled, free of the puzzling pain for the first time in hours. She nickered contentment and lay still.

"She'll need at least a week of rest. No riding."

"Understood, Doctor Maddie."

"I'm not a doctor."

"You are in my book."

She blushed and proceeded to clean the wound. Glen stood, brushed his big hands free of horsehair, and looked at Jake with morbid curiosity. "Kindly explain what happened."

Jake told them about his visit to the ranch, his disastrous encounter with the Flayers, and the escape. He also told them what he'd discovered at the Zhou mine—identical to what he'd found at the Stefka claim.

"I've heard tell of a third murder," he said. "You wouldn't happen to know where the dead miner's claim lies?"

"I do," said Glen.

Jake produced the now-grimy envelope with his crude map drawn on the back. "Can you show me?"

Glen stabbed a finger onto the paper. "Just there."

Jake and Glen cocked their heads in unison, noticing the same pattern at the same time. Glen was first to comment. "The three claims lie on three sides of a box. A claim-sized box."

Jake nodded agreement. "We need to find out who owns that box."

"The assay office is just next door. It will open tomorrow by eight o'clock in the morning."

"Then that's where I need to be, eight in the morning."

"I'd be happy to investigate on your behalf," said Glen.

"Thanks, but no. This I need to do myself." He couldn't stand another day of just waiting in a hole for someone else to do his work. He looked long at the mare, who seemed to be resting comfortably. "Do you mind if I sleep on the floor tonight?"

"Nonsense," said Maddie as she continued to monitor the mare's wound. "We've a spare cot. Glen will move it next to your horse."

"Thank you. I appreciate all you've done."

Sometimes, Jake offered thanks because he knew it was the proper thing to do. This time, though, he meant it deeply.

CHAPTER TWENTY-ONE

Gus knew that he and Stacy were oil and water in the early mornings. His optimism springing from the promise of a new day seemed to set her nerves on edge. And she appeared to require an hour and a cup of coffee to erase the tragedy of having to abandon sleep. Despite that, he was pleased she'd agreed to meet him at the Dunbar place for their weekly visit. As they approached the smithy on foot, they found the canvas front securely drawn.

"Strange," he said. "Glen's usually airin' out the place by now." He pried the canvas open and motioned to Stacy. "After you, Miss Blue."

She shot him a warning glance and ducked inside. He stepped in behind her, nearly colliding with her frozen form. His eyes soon found the reason for the abrupt stop.

"What the . . ."

Paynter's mare stood in the middle of the smithy, pestering a man on a cot. Paynter. He tried waving away her invasive nose before noticing the visitors. He rose quickly and raked a hand through his hair.

"Gus. Stacy. What brings you?"

As if in response, Maddie and Glen emerged from the portion of the building that was their

179

home with Lily toddling after. Maddie held a pot in one hand and a plate in the other. "The coffee's hot and the shortbread's sweet."

Seemingly bewildered, Paynter accepted coffee and food when Maddie shoved it into his hands. He sipped his cup and eyed Gus. "This a regular event?"

"Every Monday morning since we got here last year. Makes for good neighborin'."

"Sound reasonable."

Gus watched Paynter continue to drink his coffee as if the presence of him and his horse inside the smithy was unremarkable. Stacy lost patience before he did.

"By Josh and Joan, Paynter! What're you doin' in the middle of town again and with your horse? I stayed up half the night waitin' for you to bring her back."

A sheepish expression crossed his face. "Sorry about that. Wasn't thinkin'."

"Well, why would you start now?" She crossed her arms. "At least tell us what happened. You owe me that much."

"Fair enough."

Paynter explained the disconcerting events of the previous day before showing them the hand-drawn map. "I'll be headed next door shortly to find out who owns this claim."

Gus's skin crawled. The move was risky in broad daylight. "You should let us do that."

"Can't."

"Why?"

"This could be a hornet's nest. My neck's already in a noose. I won't let anyone else risk theirs."

"Too late for that." Gus sighed. "At least let us run scout for ya."

"I suppose."

"And leave your hat here," said Stacy. Her obvious annoyance had abated with a spiritual indwelling of coffee.

"Good idea."

Fifteen minutes later, Gus and Stacy were on the main street, surveying. The assay office had opened a few minutes early and no one had visited yet. The marshal's office, on the other hand, remained closed. Spraggs had apparently adopted banker's hours. Meanwhile, the hotel seemed quiet. Most lodgers were likely still in bed or breaking their fast in the dining room. Stacy gave Gus a nod, and he signaled to the smithy. Paynter moved with earnestness from the shop to enter the assay office. Gus and Stacy converged behind him to step inside.

"I'll watch the door," said Gus. "You watch Paynter. Keep him from knockin' the place down, will ya?"

Stacy smiled and followed Paynter to the clerk's counter. A smallish man with a wispy mustache and hair parted down the middle greeted him. "What can I do for you, sir?"

"I'd like to inquire about the ownership of a particular claim."

The clerk pulled a map from a cubby and unrolled it across the counter. "Which one?"

Paynter slapped the envelope on top of the map and pointed to the space that bordered the claims of the murdered miners. "That one."

Gus watched as the clerk's eyes went wide with discomfort, perhaps even fear. "I, uh . . . well, that one. Now that I recall, I don't believe I'm allowed to provide such information without the owner's permission."

When he tried to roll up the map, Paynter slapped a palm over it. His smile was ice. "I think you can. I think you'd just rather not. Which disappoints me considerably."

Stacy leaned toward the clerk. "What my friend here is tryin' to say is that you need to tell us who owns that claim. Whoever you're afraid of ain't near as dangerous as we are."

To his credit, the little man stiffened his spine. "I am an agent of the federal government. I'll not be bullied into the dereliction of my duty."

At that moment, a tall, silver-haired woman wearing dark gray entered through the front door, catching Gus a little by surprise. Upon recognizing her, he stepped aside to let her pass. As if oblivious to the woman's presence, Stacy and the clerk argued back and forth for half a minute until Paynter seemed to have his fill. He reached across the counter to grab the clerk by the collar and pulled him close.

"Let's have a chat about your *duty,* shall we?" His voice was deadly calm.

"Uh, okay?"

"Isn't it the highest duty of any federal agent to establish justice and insure domestic tranquility? Like the Constitution says?"

"I—I reckon."

"And doesn't that include supporting any attempt by well-meaning citizens to prevent the murderin' of their neighbors?"

"Yes, sir?"

"Then I'll need to know who owns that claim."

Before the stuttering man could spit out a coherent reply, the tall woman stepped to the counter. "Good morning, Mr. Bohannan."

Still in Paynter's grip, the clerk forced a smile. "Mrs. Morris."

"Do you require my assistance?"

"Yes, ma'am. Your assistance would not go unappreciated."

She turned toward Paynter, her eyes nearly level with his. "Sir, would you be so kind as to unhand Mr. Bohannan? In a neighborly fashion, as it were?"

Paynter slowly released his grip while peering at Mrs. Morris.

She faced the clerk. "There we are. Assistance rendered. Now, I require a favor in return."

"Anything, Mrs. Morris."

She tilted her head toward Paynter. "Answer this man's question."

"Ah . . . well . . . yes. Give me a moment." He disappeared into the back room.

The woman held out a hand to Paynter. "Esther Morris."

He shook her hand. "Joe Smith. And this is Stacy Blue, and that's Gus Rivers by the door."

She dipped her head toward them. "I've encountered Miss Blue. Haven't had the pleasure of meeting Mr. Rivers." The smile abandoned her eyes and she was abruptly all business. She tapped the map on the counter. "If you're looking into the killings, then you and I are here for the same purpose."

Gus had suspected as much. He knew of Esther Morris by reputation. She and her second husband owned a mine, and her son, Archie, was bootstrapping a local newspaper. The powers that be didn't much like her because she shined too much light on misdeeds and injustices. However, Judge Kingman called her friend, so she remained untouchable. Meanwhile, Paynter just studied her, likely assessing whether she was friend or foe. Stacy tried to help him out. She nudged the back of his shoulder.

"She's good people, Pay . . . Joe."

Paynter cut his eyes at Stacy and nodded before

smiling at Mrs. Morris. "Nice to know you, then."

Seconds later, the nervous clerk returned with a document in hand. He held it near his chest before reluctantly setting it atop the map. Paynter leaned forward to study the paper. He froze for ten seconds, and a shudder seemed to pass through his body before he became as still as a morning lake. A single name escaped his throat in the form of a growl.

"Ketchum."

Again, Gus was not surprised. A year earlier, Ketchum had been willing to murder peaceful travelers for gold. Miners would be no different.

"Ketchum," said Mrs. Morris. "You know this man?"

Paynter scowled. "Too well. He's a dog, no offense to dogs. And these days, he's Lucien Ashley's right-hand man."

"Are you suggesting that Mr. Ashley is the true power behind this scheme?"

"I am."

She stood taller, if such was possible, and cast an appraising eye at Paynter. "I like an honest man."

"I'm not a good man, Mrs. Morris."

"I said 'honest.' Good or bad is subjective. But the truth never is." She tapped the document with a forefinger. "As it happens, I am organizing the independent miners into a mutual self-defense pact. I'd like us to join forces. I need all the honest men I can find, good or otherwise."

Paynter's jaw flexed. "A kind offer, ma'am. But I work alone. I wish you well."

He tipped his hat and brushed past Gus as he left the assay office. Gus groaned. The look in his friend's eyes was one he'd seen a hundred times over the years. Jake Paynter was going to war—and on his terms.

CHAPTER TWENTY-TWO

Great change normally happens over time, like the erosion of a riverbed from the repetitive passage of water and debris. Sometimes, though, change is like a boulder breaking free of its perch on a steep hillside—one moment at rest, the next hurtling forward with unstoppable force. When the clerk had confirmed Ketchum's likely involvement in the murders, Jake had experienced the latter, all in a compressed instant. The red haze had risen in a raging rush, but he had contained its spread with the force of iron will. When he ducked back into Dunbar's smithy, the world had shifted on its axis. The haze remained pervasive, but he held it tightly in his grip. In that odd reality, his thoughts never seemed crisper, his vision never clearer. Gus apparently noticed the change.

"You all right, Paynter?"

"Maybe." He waited for Stacy to duck beneath the canvas curtain. "Take care of the mare for me. I'll proceed on foot for a while until she loses her limp."

Jake retrieved his rifle and slung it over a shoulder, infantry style. He picked up his hat and studied the emblem on the crown. If he were more careful, he'd just buy a new hat. Brown, nondescript, unmemorable. But he couldn't. When the commanding colonel of the First Kansas Colored Volunteers had promoted him to lieutenant, he'd placed the hat in Jake's hands. "You've earned this by putting your men first," he'd said. "Go and earn it again, every day." It was the highest praise and toughest mission Jake had ever been given. When the company tailor had stitched the red numeral 1 on the crown, the hat had become a living entity. To replace it was to abandon any progress he'd made since then.

"Right," he whispered. But his new clarity urged him to be smart. Rather than placing the hat on his head, he mashed the crown and front brim together in his left hand and strode outside bareheaded. As was her nature, Stacy tagged along.

"Good idea to hold your hat 'til yer outside a' town."

"I reckon."

"You headed back to . . . you-know-where?"

"I am."

The words had only left his mouth when Ned, the young man so taken with the Flayers, stepped from a corner to block his path. He leveled a rusting revolver at Jake's face, two feet away. Enough to shatter Jake's skull.

"Hold there, mister," said Ned. "I've been thinkin' on it. I know who you are."

The young man's voice quivered as he spoke. Jake had to admire his courage, though. To take on a killer, face-to-face in broad daylight. He assessed the weapon for the space of two heartbeats before snatching it from Ned's grip and turning it toward its former owner. The would-be assassin stared at his empty hand in disbelief before alarm overtook him. He stumbled back a step and raised his hands. Jake closed the gap until the barrel held steady six inches from Ned's forehead.

"If you're gonna pull on someone," Jake said, "you should at least make sure your weapon's ready to fire."

Ned blinked when Jake pulled back the hammer of the revolver to cock it. The young man's eyes glazed as he faced the reality of his mistake, the one that would kill him. Instead of pulling the trigger, though, Jake lowered the hammer and flipped the gun to catch it by the barrel and held the butt toward Ned. "And you need to make sure you kill him *and* his friends before they return the favor. Now, whatcha gonna do, kid?"

Ned cut his eyes toward Stacy, who stood to the side with a scatter gun pointed at his gut. He swallowed hard and reached gingerly to accept his weapon from Jake. Then, without a word, he turned and fled. In his absence, Stacy glared at Jake.

"That was a mistake. He'll tell everybody."

"That's what I'm countin' on. Everybody's gonna know soon enough anyway. Including him."

Stacy's eyes followed the motion of Jake's head to find a man approaching from the direction of the hotel. The Pinkerton detective. Jake pinched his hat together tighter. The man walked with care, hand hovering near his weapon while giving the impression of ease. His sharp brown eyes appraised Jake and Stacy as he closed the distance. He stopped ten feet away to raise a hand.

"A fine maneuver, sir. I rather expected that one or both of you would lie dead after your encounter."

Jake frowned. The man's stiff-collar English accent seemed out of place in the rambunctious West. "He's just a stupid kid."

"As if there is any other kind."

Jake grunted with amusement. "I suppose you're right. I was as ignorant as a fence post at his age."

The detective tipped his hat. "Venables. From Chicago in the employ of Mr. Lucien Ashley. And you?"

"Joe Smith. This here's my cousin, Stacy Blue."

Venables tipped his hat a second time. "Miss Blue."

"Just Stacy. What do you want, mister?"

He held up his hands. "Oh, nothing, other than to commend your actions. Any avoidance of

190

bloodshed is certainly commendable, don't you agree?"

"I do."

"Very good. I happen to be searching for a certain fugitive, and I hope to avoid a killing—him or me. Perhaps you've heard of him. Jake Paynter."

A year earlier, this would've been the point where Jake drew on Venables and hoped he was faster. But he had begun to harness his rage, doling it out as time and opportunity required. "Yes, sir. I've heard of him. He's the one who brought me here as well."

The best lies are those that are mostly true. Such lies can be spoken with confidence and no shame. Jake Paynter *had* brought him to South Pass City. He knew without a doubt that his statement sounded sincere. The detective nodded, seeming to have swallowed the line.

"I see. It seems we are in competition, then."

"Maybe."

The detective's glance fell to Jake's hip. "And might I add how much I admire your weapon. The side-mounted hammer is distinctive, indeed. Nobody built a better revolver than the London Armoury Company, and they produced no finer device than the single-action Kerr." His eyes rose to lock with Jake's. "You don't see those much out west. I'm a Smith & Wesson man myself, but the Kerr is nevertheless a truly fine piece."

In that moment, Jake knew the truth. Venables had identified him. But he was smart enough not to challenge two guns to his one. The detective seemed to sense the mutual recognition and flashed a casual smile.

"As we are pursuing the same man, perhaps we might compare notes."

Jake sensed a trap. He should've just walked away. However, he saw in Venables a more dangerous foe than even the brutal Flayers. This was an opportunity to probe with a bayonet to determine the man's mettle. "Sure. One question each."

Stacy's hand gripped his sleeve. "Joe. We should be goin'."

He cut his eyes toward her. She was terrified. "Don't worry. I don't mind sharing information." He looked at the detective. "You first."

Venables stroked his chin in thought. "This is my question. Why would Mr. Paynter risk coming to South Pass City when he could lose himself inside ten million acres of wilderness?"

Jake had expected something more specific. He pursed his lips in consideration. "Who's to know? But maybe he cares about certain folks more than he does his own life."

"Which folks?"

"You had your question. Now, here's mine. If you were to encounter Paynter alone, man on man, would you shoot him?"

"It depends."

"Depends on what?"

Venables smiled. "Which one of us got the drop on the other."

Jake returned the smile with an upward tic of his lip. "Makes sense. Let's hope it doesn't come to that."

"Indeed," said the detective. He tipped his hat a final time. "Well, I've kept you long enough. I'll bid you farewell and hope our next meeting is just as pleasant."

"The same."

When Venables walked away, Stacy peered at Jake, mildly bewildered. "He seems a decent fella."

"Don't believe it. I know a killer when I see one. Mr. Venables is a force to be reckoned with. And for that reason, we should part ways now. I'm gonna need to take the long way back to the mine."

"I'll see you tomorrow, then?"

"Maybe. Make doubly sure nobody follows you. They'll figure out soon enough that you might be the key to my whereabouts. I'm sure Venables already knows."

"Will do. Take care."

As he promised, Jake left town in the opposite direction of the path to the mine. For the next two hours, he continued south to make sure no one followed. Then he turned west to begin a tortuous course back to his hiding place. The sun was low in the sky when he finally arrived at the mine, thirsty, hungry, and weary of walking. He trudged through the dark entrance and was soon swallowed by the welcome abyss, a momentary refuge from his foes before the war began in earnest.

CHAPTER TWENTY-THREE

"Paynter. You in there?"

Gus's call into the dark shaft met with nothing but a dying echo. Stacy had told him about their encounter with the Pinkerton man earlier in the day. Had the detective tracked down Paynter? A jolt of suspicion drove Gus's hand to his Colt. He crouched at the entrance with weapon pointed into the darkness, waiting.

"Lower your piece, Gus. I'm comin' out."

Gus stood as Paynter emerged from deep shadows into lesser ones. His friend scanned the area before facing him. "What brings you here so late?" He sounded dog-tired.

Gus clamped a hand on his shoulder. "The Emshoffs want to feed you supper. They got a cook fire set up on their claim."

Paynter hung in the entrance for several seconds, seeming as if he'd just melt back into darkness and stay there. When he finally began moving into the tunnel, Gus nearly grabbed his arm until he heard the explanation.

"Just let me fetch my hat." He pointed to the pool of darkness near his feet. "Don't step inside or you'll trigger the trap."

Paynter was gone long enough that Gus

wondered if he'd decided to stay after all. He reappeared, though, stepping over an invisible trip line. "Let's go."

Paynter rode double with Gus on his buckskin, given that his horse was enjoying a medical holiday in town. They wound around the perimeters of two adjacent hills before the Emshoff campfire came into view. The aroma of Mrs. Emshoff's Bavarian stew saturated the glade as they rode into it. Paynter seemed to appreciate the effect. He inhaled deeply.

"Lord Almighty, that smells good."

Lisbet was the first to greet them again, running perilously up to the moving horse but somehow avoiding its startled hooves. In an instant, she was hanging from Paynter's pant leg.

"Mr. Paynter! You came. We're having stew and bread. And beer!"

They dismounted, Paynter first. Much to Gus's surprise, Paynter swept the little girl into his arms and carried her to the campfire. Mr. and Mrs. Emshoff met him along with the older children, Otto and Dora, and a nervous Stacy. Gus motioned for Stacy to relax, and she exhaled audibly.

"Herr Paynter," said Mr. Emshoff. "So pleased you could join us."

"The pleasure's all mine."

He set Lisbet on her feet and pulled up a rock while Dora fetched him a bowl and spoon. Otto followed with a mug. Paynter dove into the bowl without a word and was halfway through before he took a breath. He glanced up sheepishly.

"Apologies. Dry provisions and jerky get downright monotonous after a week. This tastes like a bowl of heaven, Mrs. Emshoff."

She lifted her spine and smiled. "You flatter too much."

"No, not nearly enough."

When Dora took his bowl to refill, Paynter leveled a suspicious gaze at Mr. Emshoff, Stacy, and Gus. Dammit, he knew. "What's really going on here?"

Gus scratched his neck, wondering how Paynter could so easily spot a ruse. "How'd you know?"

"Just a feeling. Am I right?"

Mr. Emshoff spread his hands. "You are. And regardless, you are welcome at our table anytime it suits you. It is the least we might offer after what you did for us. So my apologies for bringing you here under false pretenses."

"All is forgiven," said Paynter. "That said, what are the particulars of the pretense?"

Stacy laid a hand on Paynter's sleeve. "Promise not to leave immediately."

"I make no such promise."

"Fine, then." She whistled into the darkness. "Come on in."

Paynter groaned when Esther Morris stepped into the firelight, towering. He glared at Stacy. "This your idea?"

She glared back, just as hotly. "What of it?"

He swung on Gus. "And you allowed it?"

Gus held up a hand. "You should know by now that Stacy does as she pleases. In this case, I decided to swim with the current instead of against it. Just hear Mrs. Morris out."

Mrs. Morris strode toward Paynter until she loomed over him. "Mr. Paynter. Given enough time, I can wear down a small mountain. Why put us both through such an effort? If you'd allow me five minutes of your time, I'll not pester you again."

He peered up at her from his rock. "I don't believe you'll stop pestering me regardless."

"You're a wise man. Now, about those five minutes."

Paynter spat in the dirt and folded his arms. "Let's hear it, then."

Mrs. Morris settled on the log that Mr. Emshoff had vacated for her. She and Paynter stared at each other across the flames as if about to battle to the death with hands and teeth. She stripped off her black bonnet to reveal curly hair of hard-earned silver.

"I hear from those who know you," she said, "that you're a man who won't abide a bully. A man who keeps his promises. A man who fights for others when they are overmatched. Have I heard correctly?"

He ground his jaw back and forth as his hands dangled between his knees. "I suppose."

"Good. Then we are cut from the same cloth, you and I. And right now, the common people of this town face a slew of bullies, and they are overmatched, and I have promised to help them. As have you, or so I've heard."

Paynter picked up a stick and stirred the fire. "I work alone."

Mrs. Morris's hard gaze failed to waver as she sat in dead silence. Gus almost laughed but caught himself. She was a tough biscuit. She'd have made an excellent field commander during the war. Paynter must have felt something similar because he finally looked up from the fire. She waited another five seconds before speaking.

"Mr. Paynter. Only the dead work alone. And you are not yet dead." She paused again and her eyes softened. "What I propose is a complementary partnership. A left hand and a right hand. A set of parallel rails, as it were."

Paynter watched her for a moment, squinting with one eye. "Go on, then."

The hard line of her lips tilted up ever so slightly. "Mr. Morris is my second husband. My first husband died after only two years of marriage, leaving behind considerable properties. However, the State of New York prohibits women from owning land. I dug into the lawbooks as best I could and railed my cause at the top of my lungs, but the state would not relent. So I shook the dust of New York off my feet and went west to Illinois a changed woman. I decided then and there that I'd not be bullied ever again. By any man, any woman, or any unjust law. That pledge, Mr. Paynter, has compelled me to fight for my new neighbors. Most of them are uneducated in matters of the law, but I have learned much over the years. I can help them."

Paynter listened without blinking. "And concerning this complementary partnership?"

"I'm helping to organize the workers into a unit dedicated to patrolling and self-defense while exploring means to grant them legal protection from more powerful men." She lifted her index finger toward Paynter. "You are already undertaking the mission, sir. I ask that you allow me to feed you information, and in turn, you help our cause as necessary."

Paynter lifted his left eyebrow. "And?"

Gus didn't realize there was more to be said, but Mrs. Morris smirked before lowering her brow to peer at Paynter. "If circumstances warrant the need, you put that revolver of yours to good use."

Gus grimaced. He knew how those Paynter had killed haunted him. He held his breath, waiting for him to leave without a word. The stalemate stretched for a dozen heartbeats before Paynter surprised him.

"All right, then."

Mrs. Morris smiled, truly, for the first time since she'd arrived. "I was hoping we might reach an accord, for I have more to offer."

"I'm listening."

"You are a fugitive from the law because of noble actions, or so I'm told. Perhaps we might carve for you a less onerous path."

"How?"

"I have made many powerful friends."

Paynter frowned and expelled a breath. "Pardon my skepticism."

"I understand," she said. "So in the first act of this partnership, may I ask what your next maneuver is?"

Paynter stared at the firelight, his eyes blank. "I need to prove Ashley's involvement in this blood parade. Which means I'll be returnin' to his ranch."

Gus cocked his head at Paynter, but it was Stacy who voiced the objection. "Didn't you nearly die the last time you went there?"

Paynter nodded slowly without dragging his eyes from the fire. "No man can live forever. The way I figure, you're either tryin' or you're dyin'. For now, I choose to try."

CHAPTER TWENTY-FOUR

The coyotes had quit their singing when Jake stepped from the mine in the depths of night to relieve himself. Two bowls of rich stew still lay heavily in his stomach, picking apart his sleep with the precision of a three-armed surgeon. Clouds had crept in, obliterating the stars. He finished his chore and, with nothing interesting to observe, turned back toward the hole. A distinctive click brought his hand to a holster-free hip and froze him on the spot.

"Raise 'em," said a gruff voice. One Jake recognized from recently. He lifted his arms slowly, cursing himself. He hadn't even brought his knife.

"Turn about," said the stranger. Jake complied and found five shadows facing him, armed with revolvers and long guns. The speaker struck a match and held it toward Jake. "That him?"

"Yes, sir. Just like I said."

Jake groaned softly. Ned. Dang, stupid kid. "You made a poor decision."

Ned's shadow shifted. "I did what I had to."

"How'd you find me?"

"Followed you from that German camp," said

the leader. "The one with the pretty little blond girls."

Jake's rage flared, but he tamped it down. "You touch a hair on their heads, and I'll send you straight to hell."

"Shut your lip. Step this way, hands up. One sideways move and you're full a' holes."

As Jake stepped forward with slow deliberation, he studied the shadows. All wearing hats but none of them bowlers. "Ned. I thought you were aimin' to throw in with those eastern boys. This ain't them."

Ned coughed a nervous laugh. "I tried. They spat in my face and knocked out two of my teeth. Mr. Royster here was more inclined to listen."

"Royster. You that same fella who got his head handed to him by them Flayer folks? What would your boss, van Zandt, say about that?"

"I said shut it. Keep comin' this way."

"My apologies," said Jake. "But I just think it's a shame Ned had to join up with your lot. Those boys from Philly beat you stupid in front of God and everybody. But then again, maybe you were already stupid."

This earned a crack of a rifle butt against Jake's jaw, and he stumbled to the dirt.

"Get up, jackass."

Jake remained on his knees, hunched over and working his jaw back and forth. Nobody saw him pick up the stone. He stayed in that position until someone kicked him over to his back.

"We should just shoot 'im now," said one of the others. "He's still worth a thousand dollars dead."

"I'll do it," growled a third.

Jake decided he'd better spring the first trap before someone made good on that idea. "You'll never find it, then."

Royster held up a hand to stop the advancing gunman. "Find what?"

"All the money I stole." It was, of course, a lie. But he'd learned to lie like a politician—boldly and without remorse. "You probably heard."

"He took down a pay wagon out of Fort Leavenworth." Ned's misinformed claim was breathless and without doubt.

"And there was the bank he robbed in St. Louis," said another. After thirty seconds and three more claims, Jake had become the most accomplished thief since Robin Hood. The lure of tens of thousands in money, gold, and jewels proved too much for Royster. He shoved a rifle barrel into Jake's chest.

"Tell us where, and maybe we'll forget about the bounty."

Jake spread his hands and jerked a thumb toward the mine. "Fair trade. It's buried inside that hole behind a closed-up shaft. But it's well hid. You could dig for a year without sniffin' it out."

The barrel pressed more resolutely into his chest until Royster decided. He swung his weapon toward Ned and the muzzle flashed. The young man cried out as he sprawled backward to the night-soaked ground. As Jake lurched toward his feet, another hammering rifle butt returned him to his knees. He glared at the shadowy outlines, his gritted teeth matching the clench of his body. "Why'd you shoot him?"

"Less to share, and he talked too damn much. Now, show us your stash. You got a torch?"

Darkness welled up inside Jake, whispering violence in oddly specific detail. "No. But if you strike up a lucifer and light a piece a' sage, that should do well enough."

"Ernie. Light one up."

Jake rose to his feet to watch but didn't extend his hands. No use showing off the stone just yet. In half a minute, Ernie had a lit sage held at arm's length. It threw more smoke than light, but everybody knew it would. Which was why Jake had suggested it. Royster pressed his rifle barrel into Jake's midriff.

"Lead on, Paynter."

Jake did as he was instructed and entered the mine, burying his rage beneath a layer of false compliance. Where he high-stepped, though, Royster dragged his foot through the trip line. The metal rails crashed together behind him and in front of the next man. In the shock of sound,

Jake whirled to belt Royster's skull with the rock so hard it crumpled. He stripped away the rifle as the man fell and turned to run, counting. Taking into account that he'd been three strides deep before starting, he ticked off eighteen steps and leaped. Expecting a spike up his groin, he instead crashed to the soft earth beyond the pit. Shouts of pursuit rang out from the others, as did a number of wild shots into darkness. Just as he slipped past the dogleg and squatted, the first of his followers found the pit. Or rather, it found them. The anguished cries of two men gave him the number. He stepped from cover and opened up into the darkness, emptying the rifle of bullets without so much as a single shot of returned fire.

In the aftermath of unspeakable acts, regret tended to visit Jake eventually. This time, it showed up in five seconds. He'd just killed four men. Not because he'd wanted to. Not because he had to. But because he was remarkably good at it. For some reason, the world kept sending men with guns and malice in his direction. And he was growing weary of it.

"It hurts."

The muffled cry pierced the quiet like a peal of thunder. Jake set aside the empty rifle and moved carefully toward the voice in the flickering light of the smoldering sage. He leapt the pit, now occupied by two unmoving bodies, and passed two more still forms along the way until arriving at the source of the cry. He knelt over Ned, guided by the sound of feeble breaths bubbling blood.

"Don't move, son."

"Mr. Paynter?"

He inhaled a sharp breath. "I told you they'd steal your soul, boy."

"Shoulda listened."

"Uh-huh."

Ned stirred then, frantically. "Oh, my mama. My sisters."

Jake put a hand to the side of Ned's face, now wet with blood. "Nothin' you can do now."

"Don't tell 'em . . ."

"I won't say a word."

Ned's head drifted downward and became still. Jake rolled to his haunches and put his hands to his face.

"Dammit," he said, then quieter. "Dammit all."

He sat that way for maybe an hour, remembering everything while trying to remember nothing. Every killing he could recall paraded through his mind. Some faces were mere shadows, unknown men whose grave mistake was wearing the wrong uniform or following the wrong man. Others were vivid, like oil paintings hanging on the walls of some great house. Ned's smooth-cheeked face had joined the latter. He was what Jake would've been with a little less luck. Just another young man who'd heeded a deadly piper's call and paid for it with his life. But for reasons he could not fathom, death kept engaging Jake in a twisted game of tag that left him still standing after the shooting had finished, only to make him play again.

Approaching dawn stirred him. He couldn't just let the bodies lie. He rose in the darkness and went searching for the bounty hunters' horses. He found them a few hundred yards out tied to a stand of junipers, roped them into a train, and led them back to the mine. One by one, he dragged the dead men from the places where they'd expired, hoisted them each onto a horse's back, and tied them to the saddle with the respective horse's bridle. By the time he finished, the midmorning sun stood judge and jury over what he'd done. Despite the risk of exposure, he led the horses eastward until he found Francisco Aguilar working his claim. When the man spotted him, his eyes went wide.

"Mr. Paynter! What happened?"

"Bounty hunters. Tried to kill me this mornin'. I need you to bury all but one of them, quiet-like."

The courage that had led Aguilar to pursue Jake into darkness held him steady now. He looked from Jake to the bodies and back before nodding. "All right. What about the other?"

Jake stepped to the side of the lead horse and touched Ned's back. "Some young colt called Ned. You know him?"

Aguilar frowned with sadness. "Yeah."

"He joined the wrong cause, and they made him pay for it."

"Seems like."

Jake handed a bag of coins to Aguilar, what he'd collected from the dead men and most of what he had left of his own. "Take Ned to his family. Give 'em the money. Tell them he died trying to save someone from outlaws."

"That true?"

"Not exactly. But it will be after you tell it that way."

Aguilar nodded again. "Understood. And the horses?"

"Yours to sell or give away. Gus Rivers and Stacy Blue can help you with that, if you like. Split the profit with them."

"I'll take care of it." He watched Jake for a few seconds. "Will you leave the area now?"

Jake turned to head back toward his hole. "Nope. I still have promises to keep."

CHAPTER TWENTY-FIVE

Rosalyn was thinking of Paynter when his eight assassins arrived on horseback wearing matching bowler hats. They formed two complete sets of the Four Horsemen of the Apocalypse, though with less empathy. She spied them descending from the ridge above the canyon while she trotted her horse around the corral. She jerked the reins, beelined straight for the stables, and shut her mount in a stall without removing the saddle.

"I'll be back."

She flew toward the house, her nerves jangling. Although the Flayers worked for her brother, she didn't trust them as far as she could spit after having met them in town upon their arrival from the East. And she was not a proficient expectorator. They were just another version of Ketchum—all swagger, big talk, and violence—but who could be bought by a higher offer. Or tempted by easier prey. She burst through the door, breathing hard.

"Lucien?"

Her call must have carried every ounce of the angst she felt, because Lucien jumped from his office into the main room, his eyes lit with concern. "What's wrong?"

She drew a couple of breaths and pointed generally toward the ridge. "Eight riders are coming. Your Philadelphia mashers."

Rather than sharing her alarm, Lucien chuckled. Relief swept away his disquiet. "About time, then. They're late."

She stormed over to him. "You invited those animals here? To my house? Without warning me?"

"Easy, Rosalyn. You'll overstress yourself."

"Having eight killers in my home is more than sufficient reason for overstress! I watched them murder a man in the street!"

He just shook his head. "And here I thought you'd become partial to killers. To animals. Haven't you?"

His jab at her interest in Paynter stung, because it was true. But she didn't care for Paynter because of his capacity for violence. She was drawn to him for his restraint. She'd seen him offer up himself—his very life—for others when violence was his better option. He'd killed men; that much was certain. But he wasn't a killer. The Flayers, on the other hand, delighted in the prospect of taking lives.

"Just send them away, Lucien."

He spread his hands and raised his eyebrows. "That wouldn't be neighborly, particularly since I told them to come. Now, put on some coffee."

"You put it on, Lucien. I'll not serve them."

Red gathered in his cheeks and he was making a pair of fists when a knock sounded at the door. He glared at her for three seconds. "I'll get it."

He shouldered her aside and opened the door. The eight men stood waiting, hats in hands and wearing self-congratulatory smiles. Senator's son that he was, Lucien immediately buried his discord and flashed an enormous grin. "Gentlemen! Come in! Come in!"

"Don't mind if we do," said Sweeney.

They filed in one by one and proceeded to take over the chairs and corners of the big room. Too big for either, Bollinger lounged against the wall, his head nearly scraping the ceiling. Ketchum followed them in, seemingly enthused by their malicious presence. "Those are some fine suits you're wearin'. You'll put all the other pallbearers to shame."

The intruders laughed at the implications of their assignment. Sweeney slapped Ketchum's shoulder. "Only the finest tailors in Philadelphia will do for us. We'll be happy to take your measurements and send you something once we get home."

Ketchum clutched his heart in a false display of alarm. "Measurements? For a casket or a suit?"

They all laughed again. "The latter, my yokel friend. The latter."

All the while, Rosalyn edged nearer the door, trying to disguise her distress and disgust. Lucien just kept grinning, as if not noticing her reaction. Or perhaps he did and was exacting what revenge he could for her audacity to disagree with him. Sweeney, however, did appear to notice. His eyes found her—all of her—and his grin slipped into a smile less warming, more speculative. He gave a half bow.

"Miss Ashley. You're looking a wonder today."

She shifted her gaze to Lucien to find a shadow passing over his features as he watched Sweeney watching her.

"Rosalyn," he said calmly. "Perhaps you should leave us while the men conduct private business."

Under other circumstances, she would never allow her brother to dismiss her from a conversation in such a manner. However, she knew he was doing her a favor. She dropped a brief curtsy. "I'll see to my horse."

Rosalyn left without a word. Instead of moving toward the stables, she crouched and crept urgently to the side window that she'd left open to allow a breeze to pass through the house and leach away heat. Lucien was already talking when she arrived.

"So, gentlemen. I expected you on Sunday. That was two days ago. Did you work out a truce with van Zandt after declaring war on him? The last thing I need is a war with an outlaw army. I've already survived one and do not care for another."

"We did strike the deal that you proposed.

Van Zandt is nothing if not a greedy man. And deepest apologies for our late arrival. Truth be told, we had intended to join you on Sunday and were in fact en route when we were, shall I say, distracted by a rabbit."

"A rabbit?" Lucien paused. "What kind?"

"We were headed this way and not but five miles up the pass from here when we saw a man approaching. From this direction, I might add."

Rosalyn bit her knuckle. She knew which man and where he'd been. The clop of Sweeney's boots sounded on the floor as he paced and continued to explain.

"He was riding a smallish brown horse and was unmemorable in most respects. But as we drew near, I noticed his hat. A unique hat it was."

"Unique in what way?" said Lucien. She could tell he was beginning to fume.

"It was an army type, tassels plain as day with it pulled low over his eyes. But it was the emblem on the crown that drew my attention." Sweeney paused, likely for dramatic effect. "A numeral 1, some shade of red. I seemed to recall you mentioning such a hat."

Though she'd guessed they were speaking of Paynter, confirmation doubled her distress. Had they captured him? Killed him? Lucien seemed to be of the same mind.

"Then what?" he growled. "Please tell me you have his body."

"Sadly, we do not."

Rosalyn slapped a hand over her mouth to stifle a cry of relief. Lucien was not nearly as pleased. His response sounded somewhere between the spitting of nails and the gnashing of teeth. "Why? Why do you not have him?"

"Easy, Boss. Easy. We thought to bring him in alive. We figured you had words to say to him. Unfortunately, he slipped through us, but not before we winged his horse. We gave chase, and just as we were about to catch him, he and the animal leaped from a cliff."

Rosalyn's chest thudded again, while Lucien seemed to find a ray of hope. "So you don't have his body because it lies broken on the rocks at the base of the cliff?"

An hour ticked by, or perhaps just a few seconds, before Sweeney replied.

"Ah, no."

"But you said he jumped from a cliff."

"Indeed, he did. Thirty feet at least. But he raced away, unharmed. We had to circle around to continue the chase, but he'd eluded us by then. We searched until dark, to no avail."

Rosalyn shrank against the wall as Lucien stepped to the window. She heard him inhale what to others might sound like a calming breath. She knew better. He was just stoking his inner fire with more air. He spun away to face the visitors.

"Did I not warn you? The man is a ghost. A phantom. He eludes death like a thistle blown before the storm. I've seen it with my own eyes. A dozen guns turn his way, but no bullet finds him. Imprisoned the day before his hanging, and then he is gone. You should have shot him on sight and continued shooting until he stopped breathing. He will never be taken alive, of that I am certain."

The room had gone silent, short of bated breaths. Lucien exhaled his rage.

"I've paid you handsomely to travel across the entire country to do one job and will triple that when the deed is done. And why did I hire you? Why? Because my contacts back east assured me that you were the men for the job. That you were known far and wide for making sure men died very suddenly and violently. That's why I hired *you,* in particular. I have nothing to say to Paynter. I don't wish to see the look in his eyes as he dies. I just want him dead. Understand?"

As Lucien explained, Rosalyn's hands balled into fists of rage. She'd known how her brother despised Paynter. She hadn't realized the extent of his vitriol, though. She hadn't understood the depths of his dark malice.

"We understand very well, Mr. Ashley." Sweeney's sober reply filled the silence. "We know the sort of man of which you speak. A killer with principles. A beast with a mission.

217

And we know only one way to deal with such a man. Bollinger?"

"Yes, sir," boomed the giant.

"How do we deal with such a man?"

"We beat his skull until his brains flow out. And then we beat him further until he has no face. And then some more until no head remains at all."

"Aye," said Sweeney. "And that's just what we'll do, just after we shoot him a dozen times."

Lucien grunted. "Very well, then. We are in agreement. And now that we know where he is, let me tell you how to find him."

"We're all ears, Boss."

"He's got friends in town. Some immigrant families, a buffalo soldier, and a half-breed girl. You watch them. You follow them. They'll lead you right to your man. They can't help themselves. They like him for reasons I don't understand, more than they liked me for sure, even though I'm the one who provided them the opportunity to come west. It makes no sense."

Rosalyn disagreed. It made perfect sense. Though Paynter sought isolation, he always had people's backs. Though he shunned leadership, he always led the fight. Though he was strong, he poured himself out for the weak and defenseless. No wonder he drew everyone to him. That Lucien couldn't understand his appeal was a family tragedy.

"So," said Sweeney, "tell us about these friends of his, starting with where to find them."

"Of course."

Rosalyn crept away rather than listen to the further betrayal of Paynter into the clutches of demons. She wandered numbly toward the stables. They were going to kill Paynter and anyone who got in their way. Unless she did something about it. Resolve began rising within her. She'd need to concoct an excuse to go to town and then slip away from the eyes of Ketchum to warn someone. Perhaps it was time to mail a letter to her father in Washington, explaining what was happening. Not that he'd care. In fact, he'd likely approve of Lucien's initiative. Regardless, it would provide reason enough for a trip into South Pass City.

CHAPTER TWENTY-SIX

Time alone in reflection can be the best of medicines or the worst of poisons. It is all a matter of mental trajectory. After obliterating four men without breaking a sweat and watching another kid die in his arms, Jake felt he was headed for a lower road. In the past, he'd simply given himself over to the downward spiral. This time, though, he fought against the enticing pull. Fought for meaning. Fought for purpose. Fought for whatever remained of his shredded soul. As a result, when Gus arrived after nightfall, he'd mostly sorted out what had happened and perhaps how to carry on.

"Paynter." Gus's whisper into the mine's entrance proved moot, because Jake was waiting for him in the shadows outside.

"Here."

Gus jumped and cursed. "Don't go doin' that. Scared three years off my life."

"Sorry. But I've been waitin' for you since sundown."

The shadow of Gus's head tilted on his shoulders. "You got somethin' to tell me?"

"I do. Make yourself comfortable." He motioned to a jumble of small boulders piled outside the mine entrance. He sat on one of them and Gus joined him.

"So tell me what happened. What'd you do?"

Jake grunted a laugh. "I swear you live in my head sometimes."

"Let me out, then. That place ain't fit for a friendly visit."

"No, it ain't." Jake looked at his limp hands draped over his knees. "They found me today."

"Who?"

"Bounty hunters. And that kid . . . Ned. But it doesn't much matter who. The point is, somebody traced my whereabouts and came to kill me."

Gus was quiet for a moment. "I'm sorry. Francisco Aguilar told me some of it. But I'd like to hear the details, if you're willin'."

Jake inhaled a breath and told the tale. Of the bounty hunters' catching him flat-footed and without a weapon. How they'd shot Ned after Jake had told his lie about buried riches. How he'd lured them into the mine. How he'd killed all four with rock, spike, and bullet. He even recounted his last words with a dying Ned. When his voice trailed into silence, they just sat together for a time watching clouds wash past stars and a waxing moon.

"The death of this kid, Ned," said Gus finally. "It's eatin' at you pretty hard. Like the other kid you never talk about."

Gus was right, as usual. If Jake could figure a

222

way to make the man his conscience, he'd do it. It'd save him a lot of trouble. He leaned his head back against the rocky hillside, resigned. It was time Gus knew who he really was.

"I killed a boy, no older than six, before I showed up in Kansas to join the regiment. Back when I rode with Blackburn and his raiders."

Gus hummed acknowledgment. "That don't seem like you. Can you recount the particulars?"

To his surprise, Jake told him the unvarnished truth. How he'd torched a shed knowing that there might be fugitives from slavery inside and how they'd cried in anguish as the flames tore through their bodies. How the kid had run from the inferno into his arms, his skin burning away. How he'd reached for Jake, wondering if he were his pa instead of the man who'd just murdered him. He sighed long and hard.

"That kid could've been mine. That kid could've been me, under different circumstances."

When Gus listened in silence, Jake went on. He talked about the raids and how he'd gunned down the enemies in his path, driven by Blackburn's violent fervor that bordered on religion. He talked about the things he'd done and hadn't done to please his captain and earn his place. He talked about how he'd surrendered his soul for glory and respect and had come away with neither.

"So you see," he said, "that's the man I was the day I showed up at the recruiting office in Kansas. I was runnin' away from what I'd become and figured any job would do. When they offered me rank with First Kansas Colored, I agreed without a second thought. And I was okay with dyin'. Hopin' for it, maybe. But somehow, I lived through the entire mess and maybe did some good in the process."

Gus dropped a hand onto Jake's shoulder. "You were a prime jackass when you showed up to join us. Half the men wanted to shoot you after the first week. The other half just wanted to stick a knife in your chest. But you ended up doin' some good regardless. You ain't that man anymore, Paynter, the one from before. And Ned died because of what *he* decided, not because of anything you said or did. Don't ever doubt that."

Jake chuckled sadly. He could always count on Gus for the truth, no matter how painful. He barely recognized the kid he'd been then. He rubbed the sides of his face. "Anyways, those dead men trailed you here, so you can't come back to this place until it's over, one way or another. In the meantime, I'll manage on my own. I got a plan."

"You always got a plan. What do you have in mind?"

"I need to catch 'em in the act and get them to confess to Lucien's involvement no matter what it takes. The only way I can do that is to patrol at night on foot. There are four more claims that butt up against Ketchum's, so I'll limit my surveillance to those areas. Sleep during the day. Become one with the night. Like a bat or a coyote."

"Makes sense," Gus said slowly. "But you can't shoulder this burden yourself."

"I must. Any association with others puts us all at risk."

Gus harrumphed in disagreement. "That's always been your problem, Paynter. You send away help when you need it most. As it turns out, I've already been keepin' a watchful eye on the area. There's a full moon comin' in about a week. So I'm gonna stay at it. Maybe we'll cross paths in the night."

Jake nodded in the darkness. "Maybe we will."

"Just don't take me for a werewolf and shoot me. I'd not appreciate that one iota."

Jake turned to Gus and nudged his shoulder. "How long we known each other?"

"Seven years, I suppose."

"That's about right." He cleared his throat. "I could never shoot you, Gus Rivers. I may have had a father and two older brothers, but you're just about the only kin I've truly ever had."

Gus expelled a breath that sounded something between a laugh and a snort. "Well, never thought I'd say this about a skinny white boy, but you're just about the only kin I have left."

An awkward silence settled between them

before Jake found his feet. "You better leave, now, before we start holdin' hands."

Gus laughed as he stood. "You wish, Paynter. You wish. But I'm saving myself for someone else."

"Someone who rides a calico and infuriates you most days?"

"I don't know what you're talkin' about." Gus stepped to his horse and mounted. "But remember not to shoot me. If you learn anything, you know where to find me."

Jake watched him ride away. And despite Gus's absence, he felt a little less forsaken than before.

CHAPTER TWENTY-SEVEN

Jake hiked out of his stub canyon with the Kerr holstered, Henry loaded, and canteen filled. The pouch on his left hip held jerky, dried fruit, and extra ammo for the weapons. The claims in question lay a couple of miles distant, scattered around a pair of uplifts that lent amorphous contour to the map. He figured the trip would cover six or seven miles of broken earth in darkness illuminated only by an occluded half-moon. Even with a careful pace and stops to surveil each of the four plots of ground, he should return to the mine well before sunrise. He placed his left shoulder to the Big Bear and headed more or less east. The night birds kept him company as he walked, calling to one another about concepts and notions too lofty for the likes of men. Eventually, the coyotes began lifting their songs in competition.

After maybe an hour of following memorized folds of terrain, Jake arrived at the first target. He waited on a rise until the scudding clouds allowed passage of enough moonlight to illuminate the area. A square canvas tent across from a hole in the adjacent hill marked the claim. The tent flap hung limply open, and no dying coals glowed in the firepit. After minutes of no movement, Jake unshouldered his rifle and skittered down the incline to reach the tent. He halted to listen intently. No sounds at all.

He pushed aside the flap further with the rifle barrel to find the tent empty but well maintained. Blankets were neatly folded across a wooden crate, and a pair of shirts hung from hooks in identical formation. He stepped to the firepit, squatted, and waved a hand over the ashes. The memory of warmth leaked through. In all likelihood, the owner had headed for safer territory before sundown, unwilling to spend the night at his mine. With nothing more to learn, Jake moved on.

The second mine proved the opposite of the first. A larger tent supported by a wooden frame and an assortment of clothing strung on a line indicated that the miner's family lived on the claim. Undulating moonlight revealed two forms sleeping on the ground next to the tent, probably guarding the entrance. Once again, he slipped near, silent as a cold breath. Two men, he assumed, based on size and build. At least one cradled a long gun. And both seemed fast asleep.

Jake shook his head at the gaffe. What sense was it to post two slumbering sentries? A more sensible pair would've taken turns sleeping so that one set of eyes was always alert for danger. For an instant, he considered prodding the men awake to educate them on the finer points of not getting killed in their sleep. He hesitated, though. Waking a man who clutched a rifle was a sure way to get someone shot in the face. Instead, he retreated from the camp, settled in against a rock, and waited.

After an hour passed with no movement from inside the camp or without, Jake went on his way. What he found at the next claim was more to his liking. Two people slept outside a lean-to, one of them perhaps a woman. A third sat in a chair with a rifle balanced across his lap and head held steady. After a minute, the man's head moved to scan the area. Jake crouched in the brush on the far side of the stream separating him from the watcher, trying to avoid notice. After fifteen minutes, the man stood and nudged the woman.

"Your watch, Eleanor."

"All right," she mumbled. "Stop kickin' me."

She rose and accepted the long gun before taking the man's place in the chair. The former sentry crawled under a blanket and began to snore almost immediately. After a few minutes, Jake was satisfied that she remained attentive. As he began to backtrack, the heel of his boot found a wayward sage, which complained mildly at the indignity. The woman surged to her feet and pointed the gun in Jake's general direction. He froze and stilled his breathing. After a couple of tense minutes, she resumed her chair. He waited a while longer to allow her suspicions to dull before finishing his retreat. He passed through the now-abandoned claim of the dead Mr. Zhou to reach the fourth and final plot that abutted Ketchum's claim.

As with the first target, this one featured a seemingly empty tent and dead firepit. After listening for a bit, Jake moved toward the tent to verify. As he reached for the flap, a rustle of brush to his right caused him to drop and roll behind the tent structure. He lay prone with the Henry trained into the darkness while his breaths assumed a slow and silent cadence. Not so for the other. Rapid huffs of shallow breathing emanated from twenty yards away. Jake waited and his patience bore fruit.

"Who goes there?" The question from the unseen man was tremulous and treading the edge of panic. "I'll shoot, by God."

Jake believed him. Panic and loaded weapons made for an indiscriminately deadly combination. He inhaled through his nose and pictured perfect peace—the memory of Rosalyn in her billowing green skirt atop Independence Rock a lifetime ago. He needed to sound utterly benign, something he inherently wasn't.

"Easy, friend. I mean no harm."

Brush crumpled as the man reacted to his voice, as if he'd fallen over. More crunching of brush ensued, followed by silence. Jake decided to offer a second olive branch.

"I'm here to help. To watch."

Silence, and then, "How can I be sure?"

"If I was whatever you were expectin', you'd already be dead."

"Oh." A pause. "Oh!"

"Let off your trigger and I'll do the same."

After a few seconds, the man rose from the brush and began moving slowly toward Jake, a long gun dangling from his hand. "Are you *him?*"

Jake waited by the tent. "Depends on who 'him' is."

"*Him.* The outlaw the Emshoffs speak of. The man Gus Rivers knows who fights for them what needs help. The one Stacy Blue says can bring down an army with his handgun and a box a' bullets. The one come here to kill the monster and preserve us all."

The awe of the stranger's tone drove a shudder of discomfort up Jake's spine. It made him sound like a gallant knight of yore, come to seek a holy grail or to slay a few dragons. High expectations always made for bruising falls, and he wanted no part of it.

"Whatever they said of me, divide it in half and then half again, and maybe I can answer to that."

"It is *you.*" The man cackled. "Hot jiminy. You're here. You're watchin'. Hot dang."

Jake stepped back with his rifle across his chest

to keep the man from embracing him. "Yes, just watching. You by yourself?"

"Yes, sir."

"You been up all night?"

"Most of it."

"Crawl into your tent. Get some shut-eye. I'll keep watch 'til near dawn."

The man stripped off his hat and held it over his chest. "Thank you, sir. I will."

After he slipped into his tent, Jake leaned in. "What's your name?"

"Manasseh Johnson. And no need introducing yourself. I already know who you are."

Jake put a finger to his lips. "Don't tell a soul about this."

"I won't." Johnson sounded disappointed. "But wait a moment."

Jake heard him rummaging through his supplies until he stood and shoved a glass jar into Jake's hand. "Take this."

He ran his fingers over the contours of it. One of those fancy mason jars with the screwed-on lids. "What's in it?"

"Peaches. Carried it all the way from Mississippi."

Jake extended it back to him. "I can't take this."

Johnson held up his palms. "It's a gift. For what you're doin'. I insist."

Jake nodded and retracted his arm. "All right. Thank you. Good night, then."

"G'night, Mr. Paynter."

Jake grimaced at the sound of his name on a stranger's lips. Still, he'd made a promise and had been paid in jarred peaches. He traipsed into the brush where Johnson had been and found a clear swath of soft dirt. He settled in, popped open the jar, and retrieved a slice of peach. It went down smooth and tasted like a home he'd never had. He slurped the syrup from his sticky fingers and closed the lid, remembering for a brief, shining moment what it felt like to have a higher purpose.

CHAPTER TWENTY-EIGHT

Stacy knew the best remedy for fretting was a heavy dose of hard labor. She'd been mucking stable stalls for an hour in an attempt to bury concern over what Gus had just told her about Paynter's run-in with bounty hunters. They'd found him; who might locate him next? And could he keep fending off mobs of desperate men intent on killing him? She was starting to regret dragging him away from his refuge with the Shoshone. She'd always known things could go badly sideways, but that had seemed a distant prospect—until now. Her scattered thoughts kept her from noticing the visitor until she spoke.

"Stacy."

She jumped to find Rosalyn outside the stall, her expression grave. Stacy instantly suspected that she'd come with a report of Paynter's death. She carefully leaned the shovel against an empty corner and steeled herself for the bad news.

"Miss Ashley. What brings you?"

Rosalyn lifted an eyebrow as if recognizing Stacy's mounting distress. "Hopefully not what you suspect."

Stacy stepped from the stall and surveyed the

length of the stables. A woman unknown to her stood in the doorway watching the street. Stacy motioned toward the stranger. "Do you know her?"

"Mrs. Guilfoyle. The ranch cook and my trusted confidante. She'll warn us if anyone comes."

"Where's your shadow, then?"

"You mean Ketchum?"

"Yes, that bandit bastard."

Rosalyn offered a wry smirk of agreement. "I gave him two dollars and sent him to the Red Hen saloon. It'll be an hour before he comes looking for me, and his senses will be sufficiently dulled by then to not pay much attention."

Stacy nodded with mild relief but was still thrown by Rosalyn's secretive visit. "What's goin' on?"

Rosalyn grabbed Stacy by the hand and pulled her farther from the door. "Those Philadelphia, uh, gentlemen paid us a visit yesterday at the ranch. Lucien sent me outside so he could speak to them in private. I eavesdropped, of course."

"Naturally. What'd they say? Do they know where Paynter is?"

Rosalyn shook her head. "They do not . . . for now. That's why I've come—to warn you all."

"About what?"

"Those men intend to watch you, Gus, and anyone else who knows Paynter. They assume that one of you will eventually lead them to his hiding place, wherever that might be. You do know where he's hiding, right?"

"I do. Just me and Gus and nobody else. Until yesterday, that is."

This time it was Rosalyn's turn to show alarm. Her eyes went hot. "What happened?"

Stacy told Rosalyn what she'd learned as relayed from Paynter through Gus. "So Paynter's already told us to stay away for our safety and his. He's a man alone now, watching through the night and waitin' for the next attack. And the full moon is only a few days off. We ought to be hearin' from the killers soon."

"Killers? There's more than one?"

"Paynter thinks so, as do I." She told Rosalyn about what they'd found at the Zhou claim and how it had matched the tracks at the Stefka mine.

"So," said Rosalyn, "if he catches whoever's doing this, he'll be at a disadvantage."

Stacy laughed. "You know as well as I do that it takes more than two men to put Jake Paynter at a disadvantage. I'm happy to be on his side of any battle, and not across from him."

Rosalyn lowered her eyes and nodded. "I suppose you're right. But we should do what we can without getting in his way or placing him in danger."

"You have something particular in mind?"

"Yes." She looked up again. "If I learn anything that might help him, I'll pass it along to you. In the meantime, I must behave as if I never knew you or Gus or anyone else who traveled with us from Missouri. Lucien's men could be watching any of you at any time. Further visits from me might alert Lucien to the fact that I'm working against him."

Stacy cocked her head, intrigued by Rosalyn's admission. "That must be hard, goin' up against your blood. Against your own brother."

Rosalyn shook her head slowly. "Not as hard as you think."

"Is that so?" Stacy frowned. "Why?"

Rosalyn turned away to speak to the wall, and her words came methodically. "Lucien's not actually my blood. After he was born, the doctors told my mother she'd have no more children, but she was desperate for a daughter. So my father bought me from a poor farmer and his wife who couldn't support a child. I wasn't but six months old. Shortly afterward, they had second thoughts and tried to get me back. So my father—Lucien's father—ruined them. Bought the note on their land and foreclosed. Forced them to leave Missouri under the threat of further recrimination. I don't know what became of them." When she turned back to face Stacy, her eyes were wet. "Lucien doesn't know, so you must never tell him . . . or anyone else for that matter."

"I won't. Swear to God."

"Thank you." Rosalyn heaved a sigh. "I only learned of my origins by happenstance a few months ago through an unexpected letter from the woman who'd made the arrangements. I confronted my father by correspondence, and he admitted the truth but communicated no remorse for what he'd done. So though I'm grateful for the life I was given, and though I owe my father for what he has taught me, I never again wish to see his face."

Stacy didn't handle the emotions of others very well. Which was why she liked Gus so much. He was as steady as cast iron and nearly as predictable. However, she knew what it was to lose a parent, and Rosalyn had lost four. To her great astonishment, Stacy leaned forward to embrace Rosalyn and whisper in her ear, "You got family now."

Rosalyn produced a single grateful sob before pulling away and wiping her eyes. "It seems I do."

"Still, though, you're puttin' your neck on the chopping block for Paynter. Riskin' the wrath of your brother and maybe your life. I have to ask. Why? What are your intentions with him?"

Rosalyn's spine straightened and she lifted her chin defiantly. "He believes in me. Not for what everyone else thinks I am but for what I can become. For that, he has my deepest gratitude. In return, I will do everything in my power to help him survive until he must leave again."

"Anything else?"

"There can be nothing else. Not for now." She arched one scrutinizing eyebrow. "But what of you and Gus?"

Stacy stifled a nervous laugh. She told the necessary lie that kept her feelings in check. "He has no designs on me."

"I wouldn't be so sure of that."

Stacy tangled her fingers together to contain the sudden fidget. "It's just that . . ."

"That what?"

"That I don't know how to be a proper woman. Not like other women. Not like you. Pa raised me on the trail, so he raised me like a boy. To be strong and frank and as rough as I need to be. I can't imagine any man takin' interest in such as that."

Rosalyn dropped a hand on Stacy's wrist. "Isn't that the way of the West, though? That to survive, we should all be strong and frank and as rough as we need to be? That I should become more like you and not vice versa? That Gus might appreciate you *because* of who you are and not in spite of it?"

The way she said it nearly made Stacy believe that such a thing was possible. Nearly.

"I suppose so."

"Good, then. Do not doubt." Rosalyn glanced at the door, which was still guarded by a diligent Mrs. Guilfoyle. "But look, I really should be going. We've taken an undue risk as it is. So until we cross paths again, I wish you the best. With everything."

"Same to you."

After Rosalyn left with Mrs. Guilfoyle, Stacy watched the empty doorframe for a time, deep in thought. Then she retrieved the shovel and continued scooping manure, though a little higher above it than she was before.

CHAPTER TWENTY-NINE

To avoid emerging from his hiding place into another trap, Jake made three strategic changes. One, he dug a latrine in a corner of the mine to minimize his excursions. Two, upon each return after a night patrol, he waited and watched from a distance for daylight to reveal anyone lying in wait. Three, he began entering and exiting the mine solely through the ventilation shaft. He'd strengthened the handholds, so leaving in darkness was relatively straightforward aside from negotiating his rifle up the narrow chimney. Returning into a one-hundred-foot pit without sight proved more daunting. How ironic it would seem for him to survive dozens of bloody battles only to die falling into a pit of his own design. Still, the strategy offered better odds than inviting ambush every time he decided to make an appearance.

His second night patrol went much as the first did. An empty first camp. Sleepers and sentries at the next two. And a brief conversation with a weary Manasseh Johnson before allowing him some sleep. After that, word apparently spread to those involved. When Jake climbed the shaft for his third patrol, he pushed aside the wad of sage he'd pulled into the entrance hole atop the back side of the hill. Persistent clouds had quit the area, leaving a wash of stars challenged only by the burgeoning moon. He replaced the sage before scanning his surroundings for movement that might betray human watchers. Nothing stirred in the stillness of the night. Securing his rifle, he set off on his now-familiar rounds. The moonlight made for easier traveling through stretches of rock and brush that otherwise might conspire to break an ankle.

Before he knew it, Jake walked up on the first of the claims. He nearly blundered into the camp before instinct drove him into a frozen crouch. The formerly dead firepit still glowed with embers, and someone huddled beside it. The person straightened and shifted a long gun in his hands.

"Mr. Paynter?" The sound of his name from someone he didn't know once again put him ill at ease. After a few seconds, the man stood. However, the gun remained cradled in his elbows—not exactly a picture of hostility. Jake lowered his Kerr and took a chance.

"That's right."

"Thank God." The man's voice went soggy with relief. "Johnson told me you've been lookin' out for my claim. I figured I'd stop hiding and help out, especially with the full moon approaching. Before my wife thinks I'm no man at all."

Jake rose from his position. "You need a break for a while?"

"I could use a few winks."

"Crawl in, then. I'll wake you in a couple of hours."

"Thank you, sir."

The man entered his tent and was soon snoring softly. Jake kept watch as he'd promised, accompanied only by the natural creatures of the night. After the stars had marched ahead long enough, he stepped to the tent and prodded the man awake with the barrel of his Henry.

"I best be movin' on now. It's yours until daybreak. And do me a favor."

"Name it."

"Don't tell a soul I was here."

"Done and done. Thanks again."

Jake left before the sleepy man could strike up a conversation. He wasn't there to make friends. His second stop, which had featured sleeping sentries before, was alive when he arrived. Both men were awake and talking in low tones beside a still-burning fire. His gut told him to walk away without notice, to leave well enough alone. His conscience, though, warned him what would happen if the killers caught both men sleeping as they had been the night before.

"Oh, Jerusalem crickets," he whispered to himself with disapproval. Then louder, "Hello, the camp."

The men jumped up, rifles at the ready. "Name yourself!"

"A friend."

One lowered his weapon. "Mr. Paynter?"

"The same."

The second man's rifle drifted away to dangle from his hands. "Step in, then. Warm yourself by the fire."

Despite another warning from his good sense, he did as they asked. They sat in silence for a while, just watching one another across the fire. Finally, one of them seemed to overcome his surprise.

"You seen anything, then? While you've been out patrolling'?"

"Not yet."

"You expect to see anything?"

"I do. The killin' ain't over."

The two men exchanged disappointed glances, clearly rattled. One of them motioned to Jake. "My compadre thinks it's a beast. I think it's a man. What's your reckoning?"

"Not quite either. I'm thinkin' two men at least, tryin' like the devil to make it look like a beast." Jake told them what he'd noticed at the sites of the Zhou and Stefka murders. The men digested the information, each an individual crucible of discomfort. After a minute, Jake resumed his feet.

"You seem to have it covered, but a word of advice."

"Sir?"

"Every time I've been here, you both been sleepin' or both been awake. The night's long and you need your rest. Post one sentry while the other sleeps, then trade off. Two hours at a time. Four hours is a long time to stay alert without company. And tell no one you saw me, lest you invite trouble to your doorstep."

"Will do, friend."

Jake moved on yet again, concerned. Clearly, Manasseh Johnson had spread the word. Jake only hoped that he'd limited his audience judiciously. Everyone who wished Jake dead knew by now that he was in the area. He didn't want them to also know where to find him during the night. His unease mounted when he found the next site in a similar state—a fire going and two watchers. He sighed heavily. This again.

"Hello, the camp."

The next minute proceeded as before. Surprise, the calling of his name, and an invitation. And as before, he joined them—a Mr. and Mrs. Beckett. The third watcher, her brother, remained sleeping in the tent. As Jake sat, he surveyed the area around the claim. High ground surrounded three sides. In other words, a death trap for anyone in the camp should adversaries arrive with malicious intent. He motioned in a circle around them.

"You've done well rotating sentries. But you're sittin' ducks in this pit."

Mrs. Beckett nodded as if she'd already worried about what he claimed. "What can we do?"

"How good's your marksmanship?"

She nudged her husband and grinned. "At least as good as his, most days. I'm an Arkansan. And my brother can shoot the eyelash off a gnat at a hundred yards."

"Good. Then here's my advice." He pointed to the highest rise, a looming shadow in the moonlight. "Dig yourself a bunker up there with cover from behind and a clear view of the campsite. Put your watcher in it. That way, if someone comes to pin you down, you'll have a clear shot from a fortified position."

Mr. Beckett nodded with enthusiasm. "We'll do just that. It seems you've done this before."

"Too many times. Been lookin' over my shoulder for eight years, so I view every place as a potential battleground."

"I'm sorry for that," said Mrs. Beckett. She twisted her hands together and chewed her lip. "Is it true what they say about you?"

The question was not unexpected. He'd heard variants of it for years, and lately more often. "Depends."

Mr. Beckett put a hand on his wife's arm. "Eleanor. It ain't neighborly to pry."

"I don't mind," said Jake. "What've you heard?"

"They say you were a cavalry officer who killed his captain."

"That's true."

"That you attacked your own men."

"Not true."

Mr. Beckett leaned forward. "I heard you killed twenty men on the Oregon Trail."

"True. Maybe more'n that. But they were bandit raiders tryin' to murder a bunch of farmers travelin' west. I did my best to make sure they failed."

"I heard that as well."

Mrs. Beckett peered into Jake's eyes from across the fire. "I heard one other thing."

"Yes?"

"You're not getting anything of value for helping us."

Jake chuckled softly. "Not exactly true. I'm hopin' to get my soul back, if even just a little."

The Becketts exchanged a long wordless look before he nodded once. She left briefly and returned with a small cloth-wrapped packet in one hand and held it to Jake. "It's not much."

He frowned but accepted the gift and folded back the cloth to reveal a small loaf of sourdough. His frown softened. His journey from the pit of a personal hell had begun with a gift of bread from the Emshoffs. This new offering seemed only fitting.

"I thank you. Haven't eaten sourdough in a coon's age." He stuffed the packet inside his shirt, collected his rifle, and stood. "I'll leave you folks in peace. But I'd appreciate you not mentioning that I was here. Don't want anyone to come lookin'."

"We'll stay quiet," said Mr. Beckett. "Godspeed."

He walked away to find Manasseh Johnson. The man clearly needed further instruction on what it meant to hold his tongue.

As the moon waxed fuller, the next two nights proceeded in a similar fashion. At least one person at each claim met Jake's arrival, tried to engage in conversation, and offered him food or drink. He disentangled as best he could, but not before he'd collected several items for his growing pantry. Just as a modicum of predictability had settled in, though, Esther Morris threw a spanner in the works. When he arrived at Manasseh Johnson's claim the second night, she was waiting there for him. She looked unrested and sober, as if her vigil had lasted all night. He suppressed a grimace and joined her anyway.

"Mrs. Morris."

"Mr. Paynter. We need a word."

Given the tone of her statement, Jake half expected her to box his ears. However, she was all business from the get-go. "I've organized a meeting of the mining families to be held north of town a few miles, at Beaver Creek alongside the

Red Canyon trail. The event will masquerade as a communal picnic to avoid suspicion."

Jake knew the place of which she spoke. It lay no more than a mile from the rocky spine where he'd escaped the Flayers. "What's your plan if you get 'em to show up?"

"We will organize a legal defense union and sign a compact. Each family will pledge to aid their neighbors through physical and legal defenses, so that their combined strength might stand against powerful men who'd take what they wanted."

It seemed a reasonable idea—one she could handle without him. "Why tell me this? My concern is catching some killers, not preserving civilization from a fall."

Her grim expression nearly cracked to reveal a smile. "Right to the point, then. You see, Mr. Paynter, some are hesitant. They don't trust anyone but their own family. But most of them seem to trust you."

Jake narrowed his brow in surprise. "How's that possible? Most of them have never met me, and the exceptions don't truly know me."

Then, she did smile. "You're wrong, sir. They all know you, or at least the myth of you. And I can assure you that the force of myth nearly always overcomes the resistance of reality. You have become their lord protector, their rogue knight—the one willing to vanquish the monsters they cannot defeat."

Jake had suspected as much but hearing it from Mrs. Morris only pressed the burden more firmly onto his weary shoulders. He'd rather not carry such a load. "What if they plan to crack my skull and turn me in for bounty? A thousand dollars split a hundred ways can still feed a family for a month."

Mrs. Morris shook her head adamantly. "They will not. You cannot buy a savior for a thousand dollars."

"I ain't their savior."

"That's not how they see it. Will you come, then?"

He looked away into the night, wondering how this whole affair would end. Wondering when strangers would quit looking to him for leadership he didn't want. Wondering if he'd ever find peace at last.

"I'll think on it."

"That's all I ask."

He bid her good evening and took to the high ground on a return path to his hiding place. It was from that vantage, then, that he saw them. A pair of riders on stationary horses occupied an adjacent ridge, studying the vale below. Jake kneeled to watch them. After a quarter hour, the men wheeled around their mounts and disappeared from view. His instincts weren't always right, but they were sending him a loud message that something wicked had just ridden away.

CHAPTER THIRTY

As Gus rode up on Beaver Creek, the Sunday meeting of miners seemed more spectacle than secret. He shook his head at Stacy, who rode alongside him.

"It seems the best way to spread a secret is to swear people to silence. It'll eat 'em up until they tell a friend and demand they keep it to themselves."

"Seems like half the town is here, and folks from Atlantic City too," she said with a grin. "Mrs. Morris probably planned it that way. She's a shrewd one."

Gus thought the same but didn't dare temper her opinion. One counter word about Mrs. Morris would likely earn a sock to his jaw from Stacy. They dismounted at the creek as knots of miners with their families peeled off the trail to gather. Some had driven wagons and carts while others had ridden. The vast majority, however, had walked the five miles, even the children. He didn't wonder why, though. Most of them had hoofed it a thousand miles to get here in the first place. A ten-mile round-trip walk to a picnic seemed a simple family outing by comparison. He waved as the Emshoffs and Robersons sauntered in his direction. Little Lisbet had probably walked twice as far as the rest, the way she circled the group in relentless motion. Mr. Emshoff waved back.

"Gus. Stacy. I wondered if you'd be here. You've no mining interests, after all."

Stacy folded her arms with good-natured affront. "We have neighborly interests, though. We'd be mighty poor friends if we stayed away."

He laughed. "You're anything but that."

They greeted everyone with handshakes or hugs. Otto, growing tall now at just shy of ten years old, tugged Gus's shirt. "Papa says I'm nearly old enough for a horse. You trade horses, right?"

"That I do."

"Will you keep your eye out for one? Not too big. Brown or black."

Gus tapped the side of his nose. "I'm on it. You'll be the first to know."

Otto grinned and skipped away to join Dora and Lisbet in chasing the other kids around the grass. Gus stepped up on a tumble of rock to watch the growing crowd. He tried to get a number but lost count after a hundred due to the incessantly milling bodies. Maybe twice that, he figured. Within a few minutes, though, folks began spreading blankets on the wild grass that dominated both sides of the creek. Meanwhile, Stacy had laid out a blanket and was unpacking meat, cheese, and bread. Gus wandered over.

"Mighty fine picnic you packed."

She looked up at him and slid aside to open a spot on the blanket. "I packed for two."

"You expectin' someone?"

"Shut up and sit, Gus. Before I find better company."

He sat, took the cloth she offered, and waited while she piled it high with food. He had just begun to enjoy a hunk of ham when Esther Morris strode up. Stacy popped to her feet and brushed off her denim britches.

"Ma'am." Yep. Stacy was impressed. Gus didn't blame her, though. Mrs. Morris cut a physical presence equal to any man's but with twice the brains as most.

"Miss Blue," she said. "And Mr. Rivers."

Gus stood as well. "Seems like a good crowd. Those Philadelphia boys could hardly miss it with all the excitement."

The hard line of Mrs. Morris's mouth curled into a wicked smile. "Ah, yes. It seems those particular gentlemen are all hungover at the hotel. My husband is a prodigious drinker and proceeded to drink them all under the table last night with brandy donated by me. His humble contribution to this affair. We'll not see hide or hair of them out here today."

Her smile faded as she glanced around the area. Gus shook his head. "He's not here."

"Do you think he'll come?"

"Don't know. Public gatherings aren't exactly his cup of tea. Not to mention the risk he'd be taking by showin' up here."

"Ah, well. I had to try. We'll just need to make do with a loud and opinionated woman who often doesn't know when she's outside her depth."

"No," said Stacy. "Don't talk that way about yourself. People listen to you."

Mrs. Morris laughed. "I'm loud. They have no choice."

With that, she strode to Gus's rock outcrop and stepped up. Two hundred sets of eyes turned toward her and conversations fell to a murmur. She lifted both hands.

"Good people of South Pass City and surrounds, thank you for joining our fair outing today. I could bore you with a politician's speech or a minstrel's tale, but I'd rather arrive directly at the point. We are here today for the purpose of one another's mutual interest."

With that, she began explaining the details of a compact that would help them preserve what they'd already acquired and seek greater opportunities in the future. Stacy watched with a slack jaw while Gus watched her. When she caught him looking, she frowned.

"What're you starin' at, Augustus Rivers?"

"Oh, nothin'. You seem enthralled."

Her frown melted. "It's just I never seen a

woman talk like that before. Like she owned the place. Like she was in charge and afraid of nothin'." She looked again toward Mrs. Morris. "I wish I was like that."

Gus reached to take her hand. She cut startled eyes at him and lifted a quizzing eyebrow. He smiled softly. "You already are, Anastasia Blue."

She ducked her eyes as a blush climbed her cheeks, but she kept hold of his hand. He was pleased about that. He focused his attention once more on the speaker.

"We are not in this alone," said Mrs. Morris. "Judge Kingman presses the town marshal to investigate the killings. He should arrive this afternoon to stay awhile. However, we must take the initiative to protect ourselves and not wait for a miracle. I hope that each of you will consider signing the compact."

Gus peeked over a shoulder to gauge the towns-folk. Some seemed skeptical. Most, though, wore their fear just below the surface. As he scanned expressions in search of optimism, he spied a despicably familiar face.

"Wait here, Stacy."

Gus hopped up and strode toward the figure lingering at the back of the crowd. He lifted a finger as he drew near to the man. "Ketchum. You're not invited. You best be leaving."

Ketchum just sneered at him. "You gonna make me?"

"If it comes to that."

Ketchum's disdain melted into a self-satisfied grin. "You know what happens if you attack a white man, don't ya? They'll have you up a tree in a gnat's breath."

Gus stepped closer, nose to nose. "Whadda ya say we find out about that. Nothin' between us but air and opportunity."

A lifetime of injustice settled into the ends of Gus's fists, a pent-up torrent waiting to be unleashed. He knew if Ketchum took a swing, Gus would send him to hell. What happened afterward didn't much matter. Ketchum's nostrils flared as his anger mounted. It was only a matter of time.

"Do it, Ketchum," said a voice from beside them. They both turned to find Paynter standing six feet away. "I've seen Gus bury men twice his size. You, he'll just break in half. We'll have to dig two graves. One for the pieces and another for your poor judgment."

Ketchum's bravado wavered. He clearly hadn't expected the most wanted man in the Wyoming Territory to show up in his face. He glanced at Paynter's hand resting atop the butt of his revolver and then the rifle slung over his shoulder. The sneer reappeared when he looked again at Gus and stepped back. "I was just headin' to the ranch anyway." He nodded at Paynter. "Wouldn't want to keep Miss Ashley waitin'."

Gus prepared for Paynter to finally shoot Ketchum as the man so richly deserved. Instead, he just watched with a stony brow as the former raider moved along toward his horse. Finally, Gus grabbed Paynter's sleeve. "Come on. We'll finish that job eventually."

"I'll flip you for it."

As they walked toward the blanket Gus had shared with Stacy, Mrs. Morris called out, "Mr. Paynter."

Paynter winced visibly. "Ma'am."

"Now that you're here, might you address these fine folks?"

He blew out a deep breath, one eye squinting. "I suppose."

Mrs. Morris relinquished the rock dais and Paynter stepped up. He dragged his gaze over the collected faces, all of them watching him with wide stares.

"You already know who I am," he said. "Half of what you've heard of me is true. Good and bad. I've killed a lot of men. I've done unspeakable things. And it all began by trusting the wrong person." He looked back and forth across the still-silent crowd. "I'm here to tell you something. Don't trust anybody who makes promises too good to be true. Don't trust anyone eager to own you, no matter the honey they pour in your ear. Trust only those who look out for you. Trust only your neighbors and stand for them in turn."

In the drifting silence that followed, one miner stood. "How can we trust you, then?"

Paynter nodded at the question. "Because I make no promises and ask for nothin'. But I will give you a truth. The only way to defeat the concentrated power of the few is with the combined power of the many. A single stick is easily snapped, but a bundle of sticks is unbreakable. You have numbers if you choose to pull together. But do what you want. The choice is yours."

Without another word, Paynter stepped down, walked past Mrs. Morris, and strode away into the hills. It didn't come as much of a surprise to Gus that most folks stepped up to sign the document in his absence.

CHAPTER THIRTY-ONE

During the war, Jake had charged across a dozen battlefields into the teeth of enemy fire bent on plowing burning holes through his exposed body. He vastly preferred that to retreating. A bullet to the back seemed the most futile of deaths—to fall after having given up the fight. Futility dogged the small space between his shoulder blades as he walked away from the Beaver Creek meeting toward a jumbled granite mound. He knew Ketchum had a rifle trained on him while debating whether he could make the kill at such a distance. Hopefully, the raider was still better with a revolver than with a long gun. The naked vulnerability only began fading as he rounded the base of the mound. Most folks would've surrendered to alarm and begun running. Jake was not most folks. The first rule of any effective retreat was to give hell while quitting the field.

After rounding the mound, Jake ventured a glance back the way he'd come to find it absent of followers. He clambered up the mound to a pair of junipers that clung to a pocket of soil tucked among a chaos of loose boulders. Within half a minute, he had stacked a few rocks into a makeshift barricade and settled behind it with his Henry covering the path he'd just taken. His wait proved short. A horse and rider emerged from around the mound, the latter scanning the distance for signs of his quarry. Ketchum slowed his horse as confusion took hold of his features. Jake waited until Ketchum's eyes went wide before announcing his presence.

"I'm gonna need to borrow your horse and rifle."

Ketchum yanked his frantic gaze toward the sound of Jake's voice before narrowing it on the end of the Henry's barrel. For a pent moment, it seemed to Jake as if the man would spur his horse away in a desperate attempt to escape.

"Don't do it, Ketchum. I could put twelve holes in your body before you covered fifty yards. You know I can."

Ketchum did know. He'd seen Jake pin down twenty men all night with a rifle and a bag of cartridges. Resignation crowned his features. He removed his hat, ran a frustrated hand through his crop of red hair, and replaced the hat with indignation.

"All right. Steady yer trigger finger." Ketchum dismounted with deliberate slowness and stepped away from his mount. "Now what? This where we dance a polka?"

"I'm gonna need your revolver too. Drop your belt."

"C'mon . . ."

"I'm thinkin' about where to put that first bullet."

Ketchum sucked in a deep breath, unbuckled his holster, and lowered it to his feet. "I'm forever losing revolvers to you, Paynter. You must have quite the collection by now."

"Now the boots."

"My boots? You gonna take my boots?"

"That's what I said."

"And if I don't give 'em up?"

"Twelve bullet holes. Nobody'll miss you except the vultures after they finish. You're a fully grown man, though. Your choice."

Ketchum pried off his boots one at a time while standing and dropped them next to the abandoned holster. "You got my boots. I suppose you'll be wantin' my trousers next?"

"Keep 'em. Now, start walkin'."

"Where?"

"Doesn't matter. Back to Missouri, for all I care."

"I'll kill you for this, Paynter."

"If the devil don't get me first. Now, walk. Don't look back."

Ketchum threw back his shoulders and began high-stepping in socked feet back toward the gathering at Beaver Creek, no doubt to beg a ride. After a dozen steps, he began singing. " 'When Johnny comes marchin' home again, hurrah, hurrah. When Johnny comes marchin' home again, hurrah, hurrah . . .' "

Jake maintained his aim until both Ketchum and his off-key serenade had disappeared from his senses. He descended the granite mound, secured the discarded boots and holster to the horse, and rode away in a sweeping arc that would bend toward town. After a few minutes, he retrieved the scrap of paper Mrs. Morris had slipped him as he'd departed the meeting. Unfolding it revealed a short message.

Mr. Paynter, Judge Kingman wishes a word with you alone. Walk away afterward. Stroke of midnight at the courthouse if you please. E. H. Morris.

His first instinct was to toss the note aside and stay well away from Kingman. On further reflection, though, his opinion began to shift. Mrs. Morris was nothing if not trustworthy. She spoke her mind and hid little. She held a lofty opinion of the judge. In the throes of deciding, Jake circled into the lonely hills away from town and waited out the day. Long after nightfall, he rode into South Pass City with nearly enough doubt to outweigh his curiosity. He led Ketchum's horse on foot down the mostly empty main street and tied it to a hitching post outside the marshal's office. A grin briefly stole across his face as he envisioned

Ketchum's disgusted reaction when he found it there.

Though the courthouse sat next door to the marshal's office, Jake circled behind. Levering open a poorly fitted window took only seconds and left him standing in the main court room. It was tiny by most standards, with room for maybe forty souls and a jury. He followed the soft glow of a lamp and muffled conversation toward the judge's chambers.

"Have faith." Mrs. Morris's voice leaked from the room. "I believe he will come. Another ten minutes."

A man chuckled. "Ten minutes, my eye. You'll have me here all night, I'm certain."

"If you insist, Judge."

Jake filled the doorframe in silence for five seconds before the man looked up with a start. He stood from a weathered desk littered with paper. "Mr. Paynter, I presume?"

"Judge Kingman?"

"Indeed." He motioned to a chair next to the one occupied by a grinning Mrs. Morris. "Won't you sit?"

"I'll stand here, if you don't mind." Jake folded his arms and lounged against the frame.

"Fair enough."

Mrs. Morris leaned toward Jake. "Thank you for accepting the invitation. I wasn't certain you'd come."

"That's not what you told me," said the judge with a wry smile. "With such ease of prevarication, you'd make a fine attorney."

"With all due respect, faith and fabrication are quite different. It's all in the intention."

Kingman waved a playfully dismissive hand at her before looking again at Jake. "Normally, I disallow weapons in my courtroom."

"Normally, court is not in session at midnight."

"Fair point. Now," said the judge, "let's chat."

Jake expected a line of questioning about his crime or outlaw status. Kingman surprised him. "Tell me about your investigation into the killings of the miners. Mrs. Morris informs me that you've made progress."

Jake cocked an eyebrow and nodded. "I have."

With an economy of words, he told the judge about his findings at the Stefka and Zhou claims, his certainty that it was the act of two or more people, and his suspicion of Ketchum as the instigator. Kingman listened carefully before rubbing his chin in thought.

"According to my understanding, this Mr. Ketchum is certainly capable of such brutality, given his checkered service record during the war. However, I wouldn't have thought him able to conceive of such a patient plan. Am I wrong?"

Jake grunted. The man possessed a keen eye for reality. "No, sir. I suspect his actions are under the direction of Lucien Ashley."

The judge whistled out a breath. "My, my. Mr. Ashley is a well-regarded citizen of the area. That's quite an accusation."

This was more of what Jake had expected. Dismissal. Power using power to preserve the powerful. However, Kingman surprised him again. "Can you prove this, Mr. Paynter?"

"I hope to."

"Carry on, then."

Jake mistook the unexpected statement for the end of the conversation and turned to leave. Mrs. Morris rose from her chair.

"Wait." She looked at the judge. "About the other matter."

"Of course." Kingman addressed Jake again. "Mrs. Morris tells me that the story of your conviction is both compelling and misunderstood. I'd like to hear your account, if you don't mind."

Jake felt his head cock to one side. This was interesting. "I don't suppose I mind."

He told his tale of that day above the Green River when he'd shot his captain to prevent a massacre of Arapaho women and children. He recounted the trial and the farcical mistreatment of favorable testimony. Finally, he described his escape, omitting all details about those who'd helped him.

"Now, every man west of the Mississippi with a gun and a fancy is lookin' for me. As you know."

Jake felt the judge sifting his soul with gray

eyes before the man nodded. "And yet you stepped into the fire to help your friends."

"I did."

Kingman rose slowly from his chair. "The law says you are guilty. As a regional associate justice appointed by the president of the United States, it is my duty to uphold the law regardless of my personal feelings with respect to the morality of the situation."

Jake leaned away from the doorframe and dropped his arms to his side. "So what will you do about it?"

The judge turned to his desk to begin bringing order to the scatter of documents. "I will pretend I never saw you. In the meantime, Mr. Paynter, keep digging."

Mrs. Morris gave Jake an I-told-you-so wink before she turned to face Kingman. Both of them studiously ignored Jake. "Now, Your Honor," she said. "About that shot of whiskey you promised."

Jake melted into the darkness, returned through the window, and hiked back to his fortress while trying to figure out just what the hell had happened.

CHAPTER THIRTY-TWO

Jake shouldn't have cared a lick what Judge Kingman thought. He was well accustomed to going his own way without concern for the opinions of others. But wink-and-nod support from the local arm of justice quieted his doubts and renewed his fervor for the mission. The next two nights, he resumed his lonely patrol of those camps most likely to fall victim to evil men impersonating werewolves. He continued to slip through the shadows along his route, observing without alerting the miners to his presence.

The nearly full moon challenged him, though, madly stripping away shadows with an ethereal wash of light. However, that same light gave him evidence of riders on the ridge above Manasseh Johnson's claim. Each night, he waited for them to leave before retreating to his tunnel refuge by sunrise. He chuckled at the irony. He'd become as much a creature of the night as any Brothers Grimm monster.

The blooming of the moon into its full glory on the third night drove Jake toward a different strategy. On a hunch, he traveled directly to Johnson's claim, mounted high ground opposite the ridge used by the watching riders, and waited prone with the Henry ready at his side. Down below, Johnson remained the lone guard over his claim. Jake wondered what decisions in the man's life had driven him to such solitude. Did he have no family? No friends? Was he so unlikable that no one shared his burden or came to his aid?

Regardless of the answers, Jake felt a bond with him. Those who walked the path of solitude were a breed apart, brothers of different mothers. He'd been on a lonely course since he was six years old and had constructed tall and dangerous walls to bar others from entry. Even though many people were working hard to breach the barrier, the walls still held.

Jake's drifting thoughts sharpened as the night progressed. His study of the opposite ridge intensified with each passing hour. During the smallest hours of the morning, his vigil bore poisonous fruit. Shadowed outlines appeared on the ridge, this time bereft of horses. They settled on the crest and lapsed into stillness, watching. Johnson, who had managed to pin his eyes open for hours, was already exercising the long maneuver of descending into sleep. He'd moved from his chair to the ground, and his slump had grown pronounced.

After perhaps half an hour, he completed his fall by drifting to one side while cradling his rifle. Another interval passed with no movement from the miner before the watchers rose. After they put heads together briefly, one began descending the ridge with the slow deliberation of a lion stalking a water hole. Save for a long knife that gleamed with reflected moonlight, he was unarmed. As he grew nearer, Jake saw that his face was covered—a bandanna perhaps. In response, Jake tugged his rifle into position beneath his chest, cocked it, and aimed for the intruder's chest.

He waited as the figure reached the bottom of the slope. He slowed his breathing as the shadow crossed the creek without a splash. He lifted his finger to the trigger as the man stepped up to the miner and began raising his knife for a killing stroke. Jake exhaled and blew a hole through the attacker's neck, sending a spray of liquid into the night. Johnson stumbled to his feet, his head on a swivel, as his would-be killer flopped backward into the dirt. Jake yanked his aim toward the opposite ridge just in time to find the other stalker's head disappearing from sight.

Jake leaped to his feet and began his pursuit, shouting as he went. "Hang on to that body and stay alert! I'll be back!"

The thought crossed his mind that the miner might shoot him in panic. But he'd probably miss. No lead plums crossed his shoulders, so apparently Johnson had understood Jake's identity and intention to help. He ran onward in the moonlight over rock and brush. The flow of the ridge carried him toward town and a stand of scraggly trees perfect for tying off horses maybe half a mile from the ridge—far enough to muffle the grunting of the animals. Jake surged toward that point, hopeful that he'd rightly guessed the strategy of the killers.

Twice he stumbled in the twilight before reminding himself toward caution and a slower pace. Nevertheless, his breath was heavy as he approached the rendezvous spot. He smiled on spying a pair of horses roped to the trees. The crushing of brush underfoot marked the flight of the second killer. The man managed to fling a wild gunshot before Jake belted him with the blunt end of his rifle. The stricken man sprawled to the earth just shy of the stamping hooves of the alarmed horses. Jake shouldered his weapon, dragged the man away from the animals, and yanked the bandanna down to his neck.

Spraggs! The man entrusted with keeping peace in the area. Jake began lashing the marshal's cheek none too gently.

"Wake up, you son of a mule. We need to chat."

The marshal moaned as he stirred back to his senses. The man's eyes fixed on the shadow that was Jake and blinked. "You killed Duff."

Jake grunted. The lone deputy had been the one to wield the carving knife. "Damn right I killed Duff. And you're next, Marshal."

Spraggs lifted his hands in defense. "No! Please!"

Jake knotted the shirt below the marshal's neck and drew his torso toward him. "Better yet, I won't kill you. I'll just shatter your shins and leave you here for the coyotes. Nobody will come to help, not after they learn what you did. You might survive tonight if you don't run outta blood. You might even survive tomorrow. Even an injured man can live a day without water. But the pack'll be here tomorrow night to start in on what's left of you. They'll eat just about anything, so long as it's meat. Even corrupted flesh."

The marshal's shadowed eyes remained wide in the darkness. "What do you want?"

"The truth would be nice. Starting with who you take orders from. You don't seem smart enough to think of this all by your lonesome."

When Spraggs hesitated, Jake pressed a knee into his groin. "Coyotes go for the genitals first."

"Ketchum!" He exhaled a ragged cry. "This is Ketchum's business."

"What's he got over you? Did he threaten you with death?"

"No. He . . . he paid us."

"How much?"

"Two hundred to split."

Jake hit Spraggs again.

The marshal spit out what seemed to be a tooth. "Why'd you do that?"

"That was for Stefka." Jake punched again. "And one for Zhou. Now, tell me about Ashley."

"What about Ashley?"

He pressed harder with his knee until the marshal screamed. Jake growled. "Ketchum gets his orders from Ashley, doesn't he?"

"I don't know, I don't know, I don't know!" The stream of denial arose as a rising screech and sounded believable to Jake. And tore at his loyalties. If Lucien was behind the orders, Jake would see him brought to justice. But Lucien's involvement might also mean that Rosalyn knew. His mind couldn't hold such a desolate scenario. He lessened his knee pressure.

"Hear me, Marshal. Are you listening?"

"Yes."

"I didn't hear you."

"Yes." The man's voice rose louder.

Jake lowered the marshal to the dirt. "You're gonna hang. Nothin' you can do about it now."

"But . . . I don't . . ."

"Shut your trap. You're gonna hang, and the only unanswered question is who hangs with you. Will you swing from that rope all by yourself, or will the men truly responsible join your parade?"

Spraggs lay motionless but for his rapid breathing. "If . . . if I help, will you put in a good word for me?"

Heck, no, thought Jake. "I'll think about it. Now, tell me something useful. Or maybe I'll just start cracking shins."

Spraggs lifted his hands again. "A book!"

"What?"

"Ketchum keeps a book in his desk at the Ashley place. He writes down everything, like when he paid us to, well, you know."

"Why does he keep the book?"

"I don't know." Spraggs lowered his hands. "Maybe to use against Ashley if necessary?"

Jake agreed. Ketchum could be bought and sold at will. Lucien had bought his temporary loyalty with a handful of gold. Ketchum's record book might come in handy to a higher bidder when the time came to switch allegiances. "Tell me exactly where to find his desk."

Spraggs must have sensed reprieve because he seemed happy to comply. He was wrong about that, but Jake didn't bother to correct him. After Spraggs told him where to find the book, Jake yanked him to his feet. "Grab the horses. March 'em back to where I shot Duff. One staggered step and I'll bury you two together."

Just beyond the barrel of the Henry, Spraggs led the horses back to the claim, silent as death and very careful with his steps. When they arrived, others had gathered. Manasseh Johnson rushed to meet him.

"The neighbors heard the shot and came lickety-split." Jake recognized the Becketts from the adjacent claim, and Mrs. Beckett held a torch. Johnson gaped when his eyes caught Spraggs. "You brought the marshal?"

"Nope. He's one of the killers. That's his deputy lyin' cold on the ground."

"Holy Hades."

Jake gripped the marshal's arm and dragged him away from the horses into the torchlight. "Tie this bastard up good. Make sure he doesn't go anywhere for the next few days. Dig a grave for the other one. And one more thing?"

"Yes?" said four voices.

"Don't tell a soul about this. Got it?"

They all nodded, but Jake knew a truth this big couldn't stay buried. They'd start talking, and before long, everybody would know. Any chance of him implicating Lucien hinged on quick and definitive action. He needed to lay his hands on Ketchum's book, and soon. Without so much as a "by your leave," he spun on his heels and strode into the darkness.

CHAPTER THIRTY-THREE

"Mrs. Guilfoyle."

The cook wiped her flour-covered hands on a well-worn apron. "Miss Ashley?"

"I'd like a private word with my brother, if you don't mind."

Mrs. Guilfoyle removed the apron and reached for her bonnet as she strolled from the dining table toward the door. "Seems a good time for a walk and some fresh air."

The door thumped closed behind her, leaving Rosalyn alone with Lucien for the first time in days. He looked up at her from his chair in the parlor while wearing the grim expression that had drawn her concern of late. She sat across from her brother, hoping he was in the mood for conversation. If he wasn't, she'd know in ten seconds.

"What's eating you, Lucien? You've been sour for days."

This was the point where he'd often tell her to mind her business before finding a sudden interest in some unfinished project. However, he blinked slowly several times, though still maintaining a champion glower.

"It's that Mrs. Morris and her do-gooding."

Rosalyn lowered her brow in confusion. "Do-gooding? Such as?"

"Organizing the miners into some sort of mutual protection pact."

"Isn't that a Christian effort? Looking out for your neighbors?"

He folded his arms. "It would be if they'd involved me. But I've not heard scat from Mrs. Morris or any of the miners about this business. They even held a well-attended meeting on Sunday. Not a word to me."

Rosalyn's confusion deepened. "Why *would* they involve you? They prospect for gold. You're a cattle rancher. It doesn't seem as if you qualify for attendance."

"It just so happens that I do."

She folded her arms to match his. "What are you not telling me, Lucien? And don't subject me to the disrespect of saying, 'Oh, nothing.' "

Lucien's reply came only after a lengthy pause. "I hold a vested interest in a few claims not far from town. A partnership, as it were."

Her brother was in the mining business? And hadn't bothered to inform her? "Why did you keep it from me? After the gold fiasco on the trail, I thought we were finished keeping secrets from one another."

He pinned her with a cool gaze. "I wonder. What secrets do you keep from me, dear sister?"

If Lucien knew of her continued involvement

with Paynter and his friends, he would fly into a fury. Rosalyn willed her trembling hands to stillness and strengthened her voice. "Don't change the subject. We are talking about the fact that you've decided not to tell me about a significant financial transaction. Why is that?"

"I didn't want to involve you. I need your attention focused on the day-to-day workings of the ranch. The mining business is just a distraction."

She showed him her steeliest frown. "I thought you were grooming Mr. Ketchum for that job. As a replacement for my services."

Lucien grunted a laugh. "Ketchum. Absolutely not. He can't be trusted. Why would I set aside the one person in the world who actually cares for me in favor of a man who would plunge a knife into my chest if he thought it would further his cause?"

Rosalyn shook her head at the enigma of her brother. His morals were as gray as day-old dishwater but he would probably lay down his life for her. Every day brought a new contradiction that either pulled her closer to him or sent her running.

"So," she said. "About the miners. What is your plan given their seeming dismissal of your participation?"

"Who says I have a plan?"

"You always have a plan, for better or for worse."

"You know me too well."

"About your plan . . ."

Lucien leaned back into the chair and drummed his fingers against his forearms. "I will have my say. That's all you need to know at this time."

Rosalyn stiffened her spine in a counter move against his relaxed posture. With all the grit she could muster, she called up the question she'd been harboring for days. "Are you somehow involved in the killing of those miners?"

Lucien's eyes flashed with mild affront. "How could you ask such a thing?"

"Because I know you. I've seen what happens when your ambition outruns your soul. It clouds you sometimes and pushes you into dark corners where you should not go."

His grim demeanor softened slightly. "And just what would you do if I was, as you say, somehow involved?"

Rosalyn didn't hesitate. She'd thought it through a dozen times already. "I would leave at first light. Pack what I can carry and ride away."

"Where would you go?"

"It doesn't matter, but I'd never lay eyes on you again in this life."

He watched her through hooded eyes, working his jaw back and forth. "I assure you, Rosalyn, I know nothing of the killings. Probably just a wolf or bear. And now, if you'll excuse me, I must see to the progress on the new corral."

With conversation terminated, Lucien stood, snatched his hat, and slammed the door on his way out. In the sudden silence, Rosalyn considered his claim of ignorance. She wanted to believe him, but doubt plagued her.

CHAPTER THIRTY-FOUR

Jake often wondered about the meaning of the phrase from the Twenty-Third Psalm: "the valley of the shadow of death." He had walked, run, or generally crawled through many places that seemed to fit the description. Dark roads littered with refugees and bodies. Lines of burning cabins in forests and on hillsides. A dozen killing fields where a carpet of dead obscured the mud on which they'd fallen. While peering down from the ridge into the night-washed canyon, he wondered if the idyllic place would join his list of horrors. The Ashley house was not his primary concern. The two dozen mostly sleeping gunmen scattered around the property, however, begged him to reconsider his plan. As usual, Jake failed to listen to his own prudent advice. He descended the back side of the ridge in an attempt to make amends with the mare just in case he died.

"Stay here 'til I get back," he told her. "Sorry to drag you into this quagmire again."

She failed to lift her head from the grass, choosing to ignore the apology. He couldn't complain, though. She had accepted him back in the saddle earlier that evening with minimal fuss and had betrayed no signs of a limp. Yes, she was just a horse. But her cantankerous presence lent him some comfort that if he died in the valley below, at least one creature would notice his passing. She might even miss him for a while. He patted her neck and hiked back up the ridge and over.

Rather than dropping straight into the canyon, he followed the flow of the high ground as it curled away from the sloping meadow opposite the canyon rim. His stealth would be for naught if lowing cattle cried warning of his approach. Instead, he slipped down the steep incline of the canyon wall, its brilliant red lost to the night. The effect was one of descending a two-hundred-foot ladder. The lone sentry never spared a glance in his direction, choosing instead to watch the more likely approaches.

When Jake reached level ground, he waited for the guard to saunter toward the barn on his languid rounds before stealing up to the rear of the sprawling house. He moved left to the last window, a horizontal slit near the eave sufficient to allow in light, block out cold, and remain above drifting snowbanks in winter. Jake pulled himself up to peer into blackness inside. No movement. If Spraggs had told the truth, this was the office used for ranch business—payroll, orders, and record keeping. If not, then he'd probably fall into a hornet's nest.

Jake levered his body through the window,

catching himself before falling awkwardly—and loudly. His groping foot found a flat surface. A desk, just where Spraggs had claimed one would be. Dodging the paperwork left on the desktop, Jake picked his way onto the floor with the speed of a slug on an uphill slope. He froze for a while, listening. Nothing.

"Easy, Jake," he whispered faintly.

With deliberate movements born from an abundance of caution, Jake swept his hands over the top of the desk but found no book. He then turned his attention to the three drawers on the left side of the desk and found them mostly empty. The first two on the right side produced the same lack of results.

"Lord have mercy," he mouthed in silent appeal.

The final drawer was locked. He tugged the handle a second time in hopes of a simple jam. No luck. He stood straight to consider his options. A locksmith could likely spring the lock with a set of pins. However, he was no locksmith and possessed no tools for the job. He couldn't even afford to light a match for fear that the distinct odor of sulfur spreading through the house would arouse a sleeper. Alternatively, he could lever open the drawer, grab the contents, and make a run for it. He shook his head in frustration. The action would create a ruckus, and two dozen men would be taking potshots at him before he got a hundred yards. Regardless of the plan's flaws, he'd nearly convinced himself to try the smash-and-run approach when a whisper sounded behind him.

"Ketchum?"

He spun toward the shadow of a person and stabbed their throat with his hand while flicking the Kerr from its holster. In the space of a heartbeat, the barrel rested against the person's temple as his finger touched the trigger. The scent of perfume stopped him short of mayhem. He loosened his hold on the soft throat.

"Miss Ashley?"

When she coughed softly, he yanked his hands away. She stumbled back to rest against the wall, rubbing her throat. The leak of moonlight through the narrow window left her face completely in shadow. He holstered the Kerr and stepped near her with hands lifted in appeal. She extended a palm to hold him at bay.

"Mr. Paynter." Her whisper was hoarse, a result of his actions. He discreetly closed the door at her side.

"I'm sorry. I didn't know it was you. I . . ." His whisper trailed away into unspoken remorse.

"I am fine. You just frightened me."

Truer words had never been spoken to Jake. He was a loaded spring who'd nearly killed the only woman who saw him as a worthy man. He calculated how long it would take for him to jump through the window and return to the mare. Rosalyn stopped him from the rash reaction.

"Why are you here?"

He answered without thinking. "I'm tryin' to stop the killing of miners. I know Ketchum gave the orders."

"Do you . . ." She paused. "Do you think my brother is involved?"

"I don't know. Maybe. But I need Ketchum's record book to find the truth."

He expected her to leave. To slide through the door and never speak to him again. Instead, she stepped around Jake, crouched next to the outer wall, and came away with her hand clenched. She stood and pressed a metal object into his palm. "I keep a key to the drawer in the seam between the lowest pair of logs. Ketchum doesn't know I have it. But this is *my* desk, after all."

Bewildered, Jake weighed the key in his hand before squatting before the drawer. The key turned the lock and the drawer slid open at his pull. When he fished inside, his hand came away with a book. He stood and lifted it for Rosalyn to see. "All the answers may be in here."

"I know."

"Will you stop me, then? One shout from you and your brother is safe."

She swayed in the moonlight. "No. I won't stop you. But make me one promise."

"Anything."

"Just don't kill him. Please."

"I won't," Jake said, "unless he leaves me no choice."

When she remained silent, he slid the book into his shirt, stepped up on the desktop, and faced the window. He looked back over a shoulder. "I am truly sorry, Miss Ashley. For hurting you. In every way."

Her hand found his and gave it a brief squeeze. "I know. Now, go. Do what must be done. I will survive."

Jake withdrew his hand and pressed his body through the window, already regretful. He waited for the absence of the sentry before returning the way he'd come, up the canyon wall and along the ridge. The mare was where he'd left her. He pressed his face into her mane.

"I'm a first-rate fool. But I suppose you already knew that about me."

She turned her head toward him as if to say, "Stop whining and climb aboard. I need my oats."

He followed her unspoken suggestion and mounted. She turned toward town without direction from him and set off at an energetic pace. In that way, the mare was superior to him. Her plans ended with oats and brushing. His plans tended to culminate in fire and fury.

CHAPTER THIRTY-FIVE

Stacy was up to her ankles in horse manure when Gus decided to show up. It was then that she knew God must have a wicked sense of humor.

"Miss Blue."

The scoop slipped from one hand as she turned with a start, splattering dung all over her boots. She threw the shovel down in disgust. "Don't you ever knock?"

Gus flashed that disarming smile that made everyone believe he could probably run for president. "Knocking's so impersonal."

She rolled her eyes and kicked the filth from her boots. "What do you want?"

He held up his hands with mock surprise. "Hold your fire. Our presence has been requested next door."

"At Dunbar's smithy?"

"Yep."

She frowned with curiosity but followed Gus from the stables. When she saw the canvas front of the smithy uncharacteristically shut tight, her suspicion mounted. One step inside confirmed her guess.

"Paynter!" she said much too loudly. Then softer, "Why are you here? And with your horse inside again. Did you get her shot the first day out? I told you to take care of her."

"Easy, little sister." He patted the mare's rump. "She's healthy as a, well, horse. And I'm pleased to see you too."

When Glen Dunbar laughed at her, she folded her arms. It was too late to prevent embarrassment, so she decided to spread it around. "Keep pounding iron, Scottish lunk. Meanwhile, Mr. Paynter better start explainin' before I poke him in the eye."

"She's in a mood," said Gus. "I suggest you not test her."

"Right." Paynter waved Stacy toward the table at the rear wall behind the forge. She and Gus followed him over while Glen resumed striking a shoe with his hammer. It seemed he already knew whatever she and Gus were about to learn. Paynter pulled a book from his shirt and laid it on the table. She tapped it with a forefinger.

"What's that?"

"In a moment. First, you need to know what's happened."

She folded her arms and smirked. "About you gunnin' down Duff and keepin' Spraggs locked away in a mine?"

Paynter cocked his head with alarmed affront. "You know about that?"

"Yes."

"Already?"

290

"Just said yes."

"It's only been a day! I swore those people to secrecy."

Gus chuckled. "Seems like they didn't listen. Mrs. Beckett found me the next day to tell me all about it. She told me to keep quiet but thought I should know since you and me are friends. We *are* still friends, right?"

"Who else knows?" said Paynter.

"I'll take that as a yes. I told Stacy and nobody else."

Stacy stretched taller. "I told not a soul. I ain't into church-lady gossip."

Paynter massaged his forehead with one hand. "That's good. But half the town'll know before long. Including them who'd like to put a bullet in my back."

Stacy wondered why it mattered if everyone knew. The end of the killings should be cause for celebration, not a shameful secret. Even if the culprit was the town marshal. "What's the harm if everybody knows? They'll be happy to pack a picnic and the kids to attend Spraggs's hangin'."

"It ain't just Spraggs."

Paynter's declaration brought silence to the conversation, punctuated only by the repetitive clang of Dunbar working iron. Paynter leaned toward them. "He was takin' orders and money from our old friend Ketchum."

Stacy hurled a gob of spit to the floor in disgust. "Ketchum. Evil bastard."

"What about Ashley?" asked Gus.

"That's where the book comes in." Paynter proceeded to tell them about his nighttime trip to Flaming Rocks Ranch. How he'd slipped in. How Miss Ashley had discovered him but had helped his cause rather than alerting her brother. That bit didn't surprise Stacy in the least. When the good Lord had handed out character to the Ashley family, Rosalyn had received nearly all of it. She eyed the book with the curiosity of a cat that should know better.

"So what's in the book?"

"Almost everything," said Paynter. He flipped it open to the middle. "It's a ledger of cash in and cash out for the ranch."

Gus squeezed in beside Stacy to run a finger down one of the columns. "Sales of cattle. Ranch supplies. Payroll. Doesn't seem that interestin'."

"Mostly, it's not. But look here." Paynter thumbed backward a few pages and tapped an entry. Stacy read it aloud.

" 'Forceful liberation of claims. Strong-arm services regarding claim rights. Mr. Spraggs and Mr. Duff. Two hundred dollars.' " She looked Paynter in the eye. "Is this what it looks like?"

"It is. Spraggs even mentioned the amount."

"I don't understand," said Gus as he scratched the stubble on his neck. "Why would Ketchum even write it down? If anybody found this, it would cost him his neck."

"I don't think he meant anyone to see it. He didn't know about the second key to the desk. Spraggs thinks Ketchum means to use the ledger to blackmail Ashley at some point. I think he's right. But look here. That's not all."

Paynter led Gus and Stacy through additional pages that he'd dog-eared. Each contained one or more entries that hinted at dubious dealings. Payments to the assay office clerk for the "accidental" misplacement of competitive bids for available claims. Reimbursements to the hotel for the "Philadelphia company." A pair of hundred-dollar sums to those same men for "surveillance." Payments to people she didn't know for the rigging of cattle prices, contesting of water rights, rebranding of strays, and the "goodwill" of the Union Pacific Railroad. The sum of those entries told a story of corruption, coercion, and grift that would make a New York politician blush. She had to commend Ketchum. He'd made thorough notes, and she hadn't even believed him literate. But the ledger contained no mention of Lucien Ashley whatsoever. Gus said it aloud before she could.

"I don't see Ashley's name anywhere. Maybe he don't know all the details."

" 'Course he knows," she said. "How can he not know? Every entry in this book is about

293

his money. It ain't Ketchum's gold on the line."

Gus nodded before shaking his head. "But I don't think Ashley'd allow his dirt to be written down like this for all to see. He hired the Flayers to catch Paynter, not to run a grift campaign. If he don't know about the ledger, then maybe Ketchum's running his own business on the side."

"But we both know Ashley well. He was willin' to let innocent farmers die to preserve his gold. Man like that's capable of just about any snake-infested scheme you can think of. Including killin' miners to make his pile of gold a little taller."

"Which is why," said Paynter, "I need more time. I've got to prove that Lucien's hand is the one pulling the trigger."

"Tell me," said Gus, "what's your brilliant plan?"

Paynter leaned with his palms on the tabletop and head down. "Ketchum will soon know the ledger's missing, if he doesn't already. He's gonna panic. If Lucien's involved, he'll get wound up right quick. Either way, the anthill's been kicked over, and it should be swarmin' soon enough."

Stacy nodded agreement. The dam was about to break with uncontrollable consequences. "What can we do to help?"

"Just watch and listen. And get word to Mrs.

Morris to meet me here today. We'll need her help for when we involve the judge in this mess."

Gus frowned, mirroring Stacy's concern. "Is that all you got? Just keep our eyes open?"

"No." Paynter leaned back from the table. "If anyone can dig up the truth, it'll be Miss Ashley. She shares a house with her brother. She's also smarter than he is, and he doesn't realize it. I gotta go see her again. Tell her what I found."

Stacy put a hand on his arm. "You sure about that? You've almost been killed once goin' out there. You keep returning and you'll end up shot before long."

"Probably so. But what else can I do? I can't just leave. I can't ride to the Yellowstone and pretend there wasn't more I coulda done. I couldn't live with that."

His confession put a smile on Stacy's lips. Despite his preference for solitude, she was certain he'd die for those he protected. And she'd likely do the same for him. She released his arm.

"You're not planning on strollin' out of this smithy in broad daylight, are ya?"

"No. I'll wait 'til after nightfall. After the drunks go home or pass out in the street. Glen or Maddie can bring the mare to the stable later. In the meantime, I expect you to send Mrs. Morris my way."

"You got my word. Until later."

"Later."

She dragged Gus toward the door. After they'd slipped outside through the canvas flap, she turned to him. "We gotta watch out for him."

Gus chuckled deep in his chest. "Watch out for him? Whadda ya think I been doin' for the past seven years? We've pulled each other outta more fires than you've ever seen lit. More'n once we literally stood back-to-back fending off the enemy. At this point, I could write a book about how to watch out for Jake Paynter. It'd be a good book too."

Stacy laughed, and it felt nice to stop frowning. "You're a good man, Gus Rivers. Paynter's lucky to have you as a friend."

"Tell *him* that."

"I will, next time I get the chance."

She hoped the opportunity would come soon but wasn't so certain.

CHAPTER THIRTY-SIX

Jake watched Glen Dunbar repair a plowshare, a saddle buckle, two door hinges, and five horseshoes while waiting for his next meeting. He was just shy of asking the blacksmith to let him take a turn with the hammer when Esther Morris showed up. After pressing her long frame through the still-drawn canvas flap, she strode directly to Glen at his forge.

"I'm to meet a certain mutual friend at this location. Do you know his whereabouts?"

Jake pushed back his hat and lifted a hand. "Over here, Mrs. Morris."

She looked over Glen's shoulder and her eyes lit. "Mr. Paynter. I failed to notice you in the darkness of the corner."

"By design." Glen chuckled. "I've just finished for the day. Let me fetch you a chair."

Jake rose to meet Mrs. Morris as she approached. "Thanks for comin', ma'am. We've a couple of important matters to discuss."

"As I'd hoped." She accepted the wooden dining chair Glen brought for her, settled into it, and folded her hands. She regarded Jake with her familiar stony expression. "I've heard a fantastical rumor. Perhaps you might begin with that."

"What sort of rumor?"

"About the foul deeds of a certain town marshal and his wayward deputy."

Jake restrained a groan. "Who told you?"

"Mr. Emshoff."

"And who told him?"

"Not sure."

"Wonderful." He rubbed his face with both hands. "Everybody knows by now, I reckon."

"Only the dead keep secrets, Mr. Paynter. But why don't you tell me directly. I may have heard incorrectly."

"I suppose." He stared at the ceiling. "It all started happening a couple a' nights ago under the full moon."

Jake relayed the tale of killing Duff and capturing Spraggs after they tried to gut the sleeping miner. He recounted the marshal's confession and the subsequent visit to Lucien's ranch to gather evidence, including Rosalyn's role in assisting him. Mrs. Morris listened intently, asking for details here and there. When he mentioned coming away with the book, she licked her lips.

"You have this ledger?"

He nodded and retrieved it from beneath his chair.

She eyed it with interest. "May I?"

"Certainly." He handed her the ledger. "I've dog-eared the pages of concern. Tell me what you think."

She shifted her chair to catch light from the forge and torches. He watched her expression as she studied the marked pages one by one. Curiosity. Surprise. Concern. Anger. She slammed the book closed after reading the last dog-eared page.

"Well," he said, "whadda ya think?"

"I think Mr. Ketchum has made a mockery of the law. And by implication, so has his employer."

"Is it enough to convince Judge Kingman of Lucien Ashley's involvement?"

She stared vacantly at the floor while running a thumb along the book's spine. "Most likely. But it won't convince a jury. Everybody's too fearful of retribution from Mr. Ashley. They'd need more certainty before venturing out on a limb against him."

"That's what I suspected. You're sure about the judge, though? Is he fearful of Ashley too? Or beholden to him somehow?"

She looked up from the floor, and a smile cracked her normally stoic demeanor. "I am certain. Judge Kingman is a rarity in these parts. A powerful man who is also truly decent. A man like you, Mr. Paynter."

He shifted uncomfortably in his chair. "I ain't truly decent and I've no power of any kind."

"Your friends tell me that you are nearly always right. But you are most definitely wrong about that. Indecent men don't stop to pull the injured from the ditch. They don't fight for those trod underfoot. They don't run into fires to save the perishing."

A vision of blazing cabins and a burning child knifed through his brain. He rubbed his forehead to will it away. "None of it seems to matter, though."

"Wrong again." She frowned as if she were a terrible schoolmistress preparing to take him to the woodshed for a switching. "I've talked to a score of people who claim otherwise. Because of you, folks have stopped cowering. They've stopped jumping at shadows. They've started taking a stand and, most importantly, standing for one another. All because of you and your valiant friends, Mr. Rivers and Miss Blue. They act as if the heavens parted and sent forth three angels of mercy."

A skeptical laugh escaped Jake's throat. "I been called many things over the years, few of them flattering. But I've never been called an angel."

Mrs. Morris's frown softened. "Then let me be the first."

He shook his head. Didn't the angel of death slaughter the firstborn of Egypt? Wasn't the devil a fallen angel? If Jake was an angel, then those two were more his ilk. He ran his palms over his thighs, wishing he were elsewhere. However, he remained impaled by her imposing gaze. Changing the subject was his only salvation.

"So tell me about the pact," he said.

"I thought you'd never ask." She relaxed into her chair. "Nearly sixty families have signed on. Every one of them promises to cling to their respective claims unless they receive a fair market price from a bidder. They've pledged to raise arms in defense of one another. And they've promised funds toward any legal defense, should litigation come before the courts."

Jake couldn't help but be impressed. This middle-aged woman recently arrived from back east had molded a collection of strangers into a community in their hour of darkness. Building community was a skill that continued to elude Jake. He wouldn't know where to start. But if a band of neighbors needed a monster to patrol their walls, he was the man for the job. "What's next for the pact, then?"

"Glad you asked. We'll gather again at Beaver Creek a week from Sunday to assess the union and formulate legal strategies for protection against Ketchum, Ashley, and anyone else who wishes us to grovel before the threat of a gun. I hope you'll come but understand if you cannot."

"We'll wait and see what happens."

The conversation lapsed into silence as she regarded him with the cock of her head. He experienced the distinct feeling that she was sifting his soul like one might stir the ashes of a dead campfire looking for glowing remnants. Finally, she pursed her lips. "And what of you? Will you hand over this book to the judge?"

His intentions hadn't changed. He still knew what he must do. "Not yet. I need more proof of Lucien's role. Enough to convince a jury to risk dispensing justice."

"How?"

"A journey into the belly of the beast. Which is where you come in."

Mrs. Morris leaned forward, her gray eyes sparkling with interest. "Oh?"

"Miss Ashley comes into town every Saturday for supplies. That's tomorrow. I need you to pass her this message for me, if you're willin'."

She accepted the slip of paper he extended toward her. "I am willing."

"Thank you."

"My pleasure."

She offered the ledger to Jake. He held up a palm. "Hold it for me. It'll be safer in your care."

With a nod, she rose from the chair, stuffed the message in her reticule, and turned to leave. Before taking a step, she looked back over a shoulder.

"There's one more thing, Mr. Paynter. I've debated telling you."

Jake's curiosity drove him slowly to his feet. "I'm listening."

"Judge Kingman requested your military records from the U.S. Army. They declined the request initially, but the judge is a stubborn man."

Jake's brow creased. "My military records? Why?"

"I don't know, hence my debate over telling you. But have a little faith. And good night, sir."

She departed the smithy, leaving Jake alone with the dying forge and a single word hanging in the evening air—*faith*. His past reliance on others had usually ended badly for him, them, or both. Reliance on himself, though, had kept him alive and moving forward through the darkest of hollows and deepest of mud. To trust his fate to the goodwill and competence of others was like asking him to climb the sky and retrieve the stars. He desperately wanted to perform such a miraculous deed but couldn't see past its improbability.

CHAPTER THIRTY-SEVEN

Rosalyn had been raised to do as she was told. First by her mother, then by her father, and now by Lucien, with a hundred authoritarians in between telling her what to wear, how to walk, how to talk, what to say and not to say, what to do and not to do. She was frankly weary of it, and Paynter's surprising note had stirred her audacity. In an act of rebellion, long after everyone had retired to bed, she donned Lucien's trousers, coat, and hat, grabbed her shotgun, and stepped outside. Every ladylike convention would suffer her wrath this night.

She waited near the door on the expansive porch, watching for the sentry. He needed to see her, but not too clearly. After a while, a cowhand called Paddy trooped by the house with rifle in hand, headed for the corrals. Rosalyn pulled the hat low and lifted a hand. Paddy waved back.

"Mr. Ashley."

The sentry ambled away without further conversation, having dismissed the coat and hat creeping from the porch as nothing of concern. Rosalyn turned in the opposite direction and began running to lose herself in the night. The Wyoming skies conspired to assist her, blanketing the still-bright moon with a patchwork of scudding clouds. She followed the ranch road that angled up the eastern rim but turned straight uphill long before it merged with the main trail. A deeper darkness loomed above her—the ridge guarding the eastern flank of the valley. Her detour from the road grew steeper and more beset by obstacles of rock and brush.

She shifted the shotgun to the crook of one arm and used her right hand to help propel her body over hurdles, thankful she'd worn Lucien's deer-hide gloves. Twice she stumbled to a knee, each time acutely careful not to lose the grip on her weapon. The cantankerous piece had a propensity for discharging when dropped. Rising howls in the distance reminded her why she'd brought it along. That, and caution over the two-legged beasts with hats and unhealthy appetites that might haunt the high roads at night. On the brighter side, rattlers would be securely tucked beneath rocks at this hour.

Her lungs were heaving and fire burned her thighs before the incline became more forgiving. The furnace in her legs paled in comparison to the cryptic message burning through her pocket. It drove her forward. She wondered why Paynter would risk meeting her so near the ranch. A heavy sense of foreboding settled in her chest as she climbed through the night, head down. After a brief eternity, she became aware that she had topped the ridge. Three points of light scattered in the far distance marked a claim, a cabin, or a campfire in the direction of South Pass City or the Atlantic City mining camp. She couldn't tell for sure. After watching the points for a few seconds, she cursed herself.

"Stupid girl."

Standing atop a ridge in the dead of night was a sure way to show anyone below where you were. Paynter had taught her that on the long walk from Missouri, along with another piece of advice. Those watching the high ground in the dark of the night usually weren't up to any good. She scrambled down the backside of the ridge, nearly turning her ankle as she went. When a new light flared ahead in the darkness, she froze. Grabbing the shotgun with both hands, she lifted it halfway.

"Paynter?"

"Present and accounted for." The light fizzed out as she started toward it. His shadow emerged from the gloom, trailed by a much larger figure.

"You rode."

"I thought about walkin', but the mare wouldn't hear of it. She thinks I'll find trouble unless she's around to keep me straight."

Rosalyn chuckled. "Is she correct?"

"Absolutely."

The mare grunted and stamped a hoof, letting it be known she would not be the subject of idle gossip. Rosalyn stepped to her neck opposite

Paynter and rubbed it. "That's right. We ladies have to keep Mr. Paynter from suffering the consequences of his poor decisions."

He laughed softly. "Too late."

She circled the mare's nose to stand before him. "Speaking of poor choices, why did you come all this way to meet in the dead of night?"

He tipped his face skyward, silent for a time. "Do you still watch the stars, Miss Ashley?"

She followed his gaze to find a window of deeper sky sliding past, revealing a scatter of stars bathed in moonglow. "Every night."

"Me too."

She recalled vividly the first conversation they'd shared on the trail. He was still a prisoner then, watching the skies. He'd responded to her gift of corn bread with a short but revealing story of the man beneath the rough exterior. "Because of what you told me that evening on the trail? Of how your grandmother taught you the constellations?"

"Yeah," he said. "That, and now another reason."

She rubbed a hand along the bridge of the mare's muzzle, wondering. "Care to share the other reason?"

"Nope."

She understood Paynter well enough by now to know when further probing would meet with futility. "Then tell me about the note."

"I can do that." He leaned against the mare and faced into the unseeable distance. "I found the werewolves. Marshal Spraggs and his deputy. They're no longer a threat to the miners."

His declaration took her by surprise. He'd stopped the killers, and they were lawmen. "Did you . . . Did you have to . . ."

"One of 'em. The deputy, Duff." He sounded weary, defeated. She knew how the burden of such violence bowed his shoulders and crushed his spirit. How much he wished to be left alone to live in peace. But death appeared to follow him, throwing opportunities into his path unasked.

"What about the marshal?"

"Held prisoner by a few of the miners until . . ."

After a long silence, she prodded him. "Until when?"

"Until I can prove who paid for the killings."

A cold wind knifed through her soul. She wanted to walk away without hearing the rest but knew she must. "Was it my brother?"

"Probably."

He told her what he'd found in Ketchum's ledger. Each new piece of information came as a shock and sank her spirits deeper into the muck. She knew Ketchum was capable of the underhanded dealings Paynter described. But Lucien was just as capable. She couldn't imagine that Ketchum would transact such evil business beneath Lucien's nose without him knowing about it. She also knew that Paynter didn't come all this way without a deeper reason.

"You need my help," she said.

"Yes. I know it's too much to ask. To turn against your own flesh and blood. If you'd rather not, I won't blame you a penny's worth. I'd understand."

She leaned her face against the mare's muzzle, seeking an answer. It came to her despite her objections. "I will help. No matter the outcome."

Paynter leaned away from the mare and turned his shadowed face toward her. "I am grateful. Truly."

"Thank you." She ran her fingers through the lock of mane drifting down between the mare's eyes. "I might know a way to learn the truth."

"Oh?"

"Mrs. Guilfoyle."

"Who?"

"The ranch cook . . . a widow. I trust her like a sister. And I think Ketchum is sweet on her, even though she harangues him continuously when he's around."

"And?"

"Ketchum also likes his whiskey, and guess who holds the key to the liquor cabinet?"

Paynter chucked. "Mrs. Guilfoyle?"

"Yes. Perhaps she might water him down sufficiently to get him talking."

"Good idea. Ketchum loves nothing better'n

talkin' about himself. A few shots of whiskey ought to loosen up his defenses."

"My thoughts exactly. In the meantime, I'll continue to listen in on Lucien's meetings."

"Why, Miss Ashley," he said, "I didn't think you were one to eavesdrop."

"I am a senator's daughter, sir. Eavesdropping is a highly prized skill in my family. Lately, I've become rather good at it."

His chuckle died away. "Just be careful. Most people don't care to be spied on when they're plottin' foul doings. Even when the spy is blood kin. Sometimes, especially when it's blood kin."

She agreed, even though Lucien didn't know the truth of her parentage. Every time she'd overheard one of Lucien's meetings, she feared what would happen if he caught her. On the one hand, she knew he'd protect her with his life. But nothing shattered loyalty more completely than betrayal. And in this scenario, she was definitely Judas. "I will take care."

Silence overtook them as the matter seemed settled. However, Paynter appeared unready to leave. She waited and her patience paid dividends.

"One more question," he said.

"Ask it."

"What'll you do if he's guilty? If the full fury of the law falls on him?"

She'd been asking herself that same question

for days—ever since her previous encounter with Paynter. "At first, I thought I'd just return to Missouri and to the life I knew. But I'm thinking differently now."

"How so?"

"My life in Missouri was hollow. I had nothing to do but entertain the gentlefolk of high society. That is no longer enough for me." She exhaled a deep breath. "I'd probably stay and try to make a go of the ranch."

"You'd stay?" Surprise colored his voice even though his expression remained in shadow.

"Yes. Particularly if I had other reasons to remain here."

She hadn't meant to confess so much, and he wasted no time correctly guessing her meaning. "You can't stay around for me, Miss Ashley. I'm a fugitive from the law. And no matter what I do, it always seems to end with me puttin' a bullet in somebody. That's no life for you."

"But . . ."

"But nothin'. You're as far above me as those stars up there. Nothin' you can do to change that." He swung into his saddle with a suddenness that startled her. "G'night, Miss Ashley. I'll keep watch 'til you make it down the ridge."

With the meeting abruptly adjourned, she returned over the ridge, never looking back. She knew he was there, though, and that would have to be enough.

CHAPTER THIRTY-EIGHT

"Everything in moderation."

That was what Jake's grandmother had often told him when he was a small boy. He'd always known what she meant by it—that too much of anything, no matter how good, will eventually kill you. Too much food. Too much drink. Too much sun. Too much thinking. It was the last of those that sealed his fate. He should've listened more carefully to his wise old grammy.

After leaving Rosalyn, he'd ridden through the night back toward town. Instead of remaining alert to danger as was his nature, his thoughts had been filled with Rosalyn and the chasm between them. In his fog, he had ridden on the road straight into South Pass City, certain that darkness would cover him from prying eyes. In his distraction, he'd returned the mare to her stall and set out on a direct line to the hidden fortress. If not for his preoccupation, he would've taken the mare to the Emshoffs or Francisco Aguilar to return on his behalf. He'd gone and gotten stupid. And stupid gets men killed.

The ghostly echo of hoof falls behind him first alerted Jake to his mistake. He'd already reached the mouth of the stubby canyon, so the mine proved his only path to cover. As he slipped inside the tunnel, the thump of hooves was joined by voices, urgent and jubilant. Counting strides, he avoided the trip line and pit of spikes that had claimed the bounty hunters earlier. He turned into the dogleg and waited for his pursuers to follow him inside. The clatter of several horses outside indicated a troop of men.

"Mr. Paynter." Sweeney's voice echoed into the mine shaft. "We've come to make a social call. Me and the boys."

Laughter from the other Flayers indicated their appreciation for the joke. Jake remained silent, hoping they'd either enter the shaft or leave. They did neither.

"Come now," said Sweeney. He seemingly hadn't moved from the entrance. "I know you're a bit surprised, but you did lead us here after all. We've had men watching the stables every night for a week now. When we saw that little horse a' yours missing, we figured whoever brought her back might lead us to you. But no! 'Twas the great Jake Paynter himself who did the deed. The rest was child's play. Just follow you away from town to where your capture might not raise such a fuss. For some reason, the good people of South Pass City seem to hold you in some regard. We didn't want any heroes complicating our task."

"Come out, come out, little pig," said the

booming bass of the giant, Bollinger. "We'll huff and we'll puff!"

"What would Miss Ashley think?" said another. "Her beau hiding in a hole like a sewer rat."

Without giving it much thought, Jake leaned around the kink in the tunnel and flung lead toward the glow of the entrance. Shadows dove away, one of them cursing loudly. "Sons of Joseph, he got me!"

"Where?"

"My bloody arm."

"Bind it up," said Sweeney. "I've given you worse myself."

A bullet sailing past Jake's ear sent him back around the dogleg. He pressed the Henry to his chest. "I'm waitin' if you're man enough to come my way."

Sweeney laughed. "My, my, Mr. Paynter. That *is* a sweet invitation. But no, thank you. We're not a band of yokel bounty hunters who'll fall into your traps like that bunch who left to kill you and never returned. No, indeed. Every one of us cut our teeth building snares to keep rivals away from our domiciles. We'd shame our poor sainted mothers if we got caught up in such a web at the hands of a drifter."

Jake inhaled deeply, finally thinking like prey. Fear of traps would keep them out, but for how long? Daylight would expose at least one. They could stand to wait. He couldn't. Thoughts of the air shaft began circling his brain. Those were cut short by gunshots and a hail of bullets pinging against the shaft wall three feet away. He ducked and covered his head against the spray of rock chips flying at his face. The barrage continued for some time as the attackers apparently took turns rearming and shooting. Three or four times, Jake reached around the dogleg to return fire, shooting blindly. Then, as suddenly as it had begun, the shooting stopped.

"Oh, Mr. Paynter," Sweeney called. "Still breathing, my friend?"

Jake cleared the acrid smell of gunpowder from his throat. "Why don't you come and see?"

Seconds passed as the Flayers exchanged mumbled conversation. Silence fell for a time.

"They say you were a rich boy." Sweeney's voice echoed down the tunnel again. "That your daddy owned a sugar plantation and three hundred slaves. That true?"

"Maybe."

"Not like us, then. My parents were food for worms before I turned five. I ate what others threw into the street. I slept in a coal bin to keep from freezing to death. I learned to catch rats and gut them with a piece of glass. I begged, borrowed, and stole enough to reach the age of seven without surrendering to the Reaper. Then the Flayers took me in, those benevolent souls. By my fifteenth birthday, I captained my own crew. My own boys.

And we took care of one another with the flat of our fists and the bend of our clubs. The poor of our streets had nothing to fear from us so long as they shared what we asked. But rich boys like you? We hunted them for sport."

Jake knew better than to engage, but Sweeney's painful dig raised his ire. "My father was wealthy, sure. But money ate him alive from the inside out. It turned him cruel. He beat his sons until we bled and beat the others 'til they died. I left as soon as I could and took only what I carried. As for his money? I didn't take a single cursed penny. Been livin' meal to meal ever since, and not sorry about it."

"Then you know what it's like." Sweeney sounded almost amiable in his commiseration. "To have your belly press your backbone until both ache. To shake so violently from cold and starvation that you fear your teeth will fall out. To throw fists with a man knowing that to lose is to die."

"I do."

The conversation burned low before Sweeney added another log. "I heard you killed thirty men who were trying to murder regular folk—farmers and such. And the Ashleys. Is that true?"

"It was twenty at most. My friends and the Arapaho took care of the rest."

"Ah," said Sweeney. "He's humble too. Maybe you and I are not so different. We do what we must to survive. We take down those who would stand in our way, of necessity. Doesn't that make us kin of sorts?"

Good question. Were he and Sweeney cut from the same cloth? Men shaped by cruelty to cut down those who stood against them? He wanted to disagree, but the line between him and the Flayer remained blurry.

"Why not come out?" Sweeney's question was disarming. Brotherly. "Out of respect, we'll not kill you. You have my word as a gentleman."

A laugh nearly escaped Jake's throat. There was nothing gentle about Sweeney or his methods. He wore a tailored suit but was as corrupt as Jake beneath the finery. They were both bound for hellfire. But he wanted nothing of the man's brotherhood. "You'll have to come fetch me."

"I thought as much."

Minutes passed with nothing but the mumbling of voices and echoes of vague activity that culminated in recognizable sounds. The stacking of brush.

"Last chance," Sweeney called.

"Go to Jericho across lots."

"It seems we'll need to burn you out, then. Mr. Bollinger?"

"Sir?"

"A match, if you please."

Shortly, the smell of burning sage and juniper began drifting into the shaft. Unseen smoke

318

pricked Jake's eyes, forcing a retreat to the nether regions of the mine. The Flayers must have redoubled their efforts, because the air soon grew thick with smoke, sending Jake into a coughing fit. He ran his hand along the roof of the tunnel until he found the air vent. If he waited much longer, he'd die unconscious. Now or never. After slinging his rifle, Jake pulled himself into the escape tunnel and began feeling his way upward. Acrid smoke followed him, gathering as he climbed.

He tilted his chin upward in the pitch-blackness of the shaft, striving for stars and counting steps. And hoping that a mob from Philadelphia didn't know enough about mining to consider the concept of air vents. When the count reached seventy, he waved his hand overhead to contact the tuft of sage he'd pulled into the exit hole. He shoved it aside as he continued to climb and crawled out into blessedly clear air and the soft wash of moonlight. He might have gloried in the moment if not for the rifle barrel pressed into the back of his skull.

"Mr. Paynter. Good to see you again."

Jake briefly wondered if he could draw his Kerr before the rifle opened a channel though his brain. He spread his hands instead. "Detective Venables. You're late for tea. What brings you out this time of night?"

"I'm hunting wolves. And look here. It seems I just caught a fine specimen."

CHAPTER THIRTY-NINE

"Keep your hands wide and exit the shaft. Remain prone."

Jake did as Venables told him, continuing to crawl until he'd left the hole. Just when he was ready to roll quickly and yank the rifle barrel, the detective stepped away. He must've known that particular trick. Jake exhaled. "Now what?"

"With all the care of a man standing barefoot on razor blades, reach to your belt and remove your Kerr. Two fingers only. A third finger will force me to shoot you immediately."

Jake obeyed. He believed Venables could make good on such a threat, unlike those who boasted of great plans but wilted in the oppressive heat of reality. He used his thumb and forefinger to toss the Kerr out of his reach.

"Now your rifle. A Henry, is it?"

"Yeah."

"Another fine piece. Unsling it and set it aside, half speed."

He followed the instructions and pushed the rifle away.

Venables pulled it out of Jake's reach with a foot. "Now, the knife in your boot."

"What makes you think I have a knife in my boot?"

"You're an intelligent man, Mr. Paynter. Every intelligent man keeps a knife in his boot."

Jake reached carefully to pull the sheathed blade from his boot and tossed it aside with the Kerr. In the distance, he heard the Flayers begin calling to him with taunts and laughter, certain he was choking to death in the mine. He nearly smiled, but metal clanking to the dirt beside his head restored his attention to the enemy at hand.

"Put them on, Mr. Paynter. I believe you know your way around wrist irons."

Jake did. He'd worn them for half the journey from Missouri to Fort Bridger. He hated the infernal things. These, however, were smaller than the deadweights he'd worn before. They locked without a key when he closed each ring around a wrist.

"What are these?"

"They're called handcuffs. Designed by Mr. W. V. Adams, an American gent. Quite an improvement over the older style. Now, stand tall."

Jake stood to face his adversary and cut his eyes toward the Kerr in the grass. Venables must've noticed. "I'm a crack shot, Mr. Paynter, I assure you. I've had ample opportunity to practice over the years."

"During the war?"

"Yes, but not the war you might think."

The man was English, so Jake guessed. "Crimea?"

The detective chuckled with seeming surprise. "Seventeenth Lancers, as a matter of fact."

"Them from 'The Charge of the Light Brigade'?"

Though the moonlight barely illuminated Venables's face, Jake could practically hear his eyebrows rise. "You've read Tennyson's poem?"

"Once or twice."

"Fascinating. However, the real event wasn't nearly as glorious as the poet made it seem. But then again, you know how inglorious war is."

"I do."

Venables cautiously retrieved the knife, Kerr, and Henry, never letting his gaze or rifle barrel leave the center of Jake's chest. Then he motioned with his weapon toward the back side of the hill away from the mine entrance. "Start walking. I've two horses waiting for us in the vale."

Jake moved, with the detective trailing him by about six feet. Far enough that if Jake turned on him, he'd die before reaching the man's gun. Close enough that Venables would blow a hole through him if he darted away. As they walked, the carried voices of the Flayers dissolved into the night. He decided to keep Venables talking, hoping for a lapse in attention. The strategy had worked against Blackburn, so why not against the detective?

"How'd you find me, anyway?"

"Mathematical triangulation, if you must know."

"Triangu . . . What the heck is that?"

Venables chuckled. "Triangulation. I learned it from artillery men and have found other uses for it. In brief, it is a method of determining location by considering multiple trajectories."

"Speak American."

"Fine, then." The detective waited until they'd both clambered down a shelf of rock. "I guessed that your friends, Mr. Rivers and Miss Blue, knew where you were. I watched them as they came and went from town. Which direction they took. How long they were gone. I also collected rumors about places you'd supposedly been seen. I then plotted the information on a map of the region—points, lines, and arcs. The result showed a possible intersection in this general area. Lo and behold, a visit to the assay office revealed an abandoned mine nearby. I watched the entrance for two days before realizing you might be using the ventilation shaft for access. And there you were."

Jake shook his head. He'd figured Venables was his most dangerous adversary. The explanation proved his suspicion right. "You know about mine construction, then?"

"My mother's Welsh. I'd be a poor son if I didn't know about mine construction."

The hill began to flatten as it reached low

ground. Jake continued to keep the detective talking. "How long did you watch me?"

"Nearly a week. I watched you leave every night and return before daybreak."

"Why'd you wait?"

"I think you know."

"Tell me, anyway."

Venables prodded him with the barrel. "Turn to your left and follow the bottom. As for why I waited, you are a supremely dangerous man, Mr. Paynter. Between the war, the cavalry, and your trip west, a horde of men have tried to kill you. They all failed, and a great many of them died in the attempt. I knew that confronting you alone was a coin flip at best. I decided to bide my time and hope for an opportune moment."

"Such as the Flayers tryin' to burn me out?"

"Exactly."

A pair of horse-shaped shadows in front of Jake resolved into flesh-and-blood animals. They stamped their hooves to acknowledge the approaching men.

"Mount up," said the detective. "The one to your right. And don't forget, as former cavalry, I am a proficient shot from horseback."

Jake lifted his foot into a stirrup and swung onto the horse. "Where exactly are we going on this little jaunt?"

He suspected the answer. Venables didn't disappoint. "Mr. Ashley's ranch."

"Not to the town marshal?"

The detective let loose a hearty laugh. "I'm afraid not. It seems that the town marshal has gone missing, along with his ridiculous deputy. But it's likely just as well. I suspect that Spraggs was behind the killings of the miners, given all reasonable evidence. Perhaps a concerned citizen took matters into his own hands. You wouldn't happen to know about such, would you?"

Holy Mary. Did this man know everything? "I couldn't say."

Venables laughed again. "Well, if I ever find that citizen, I will surely shake his hand. I cannot abide a lawman who uses his authority to line his pockets. Whatever befell Marshal Spraggs was surely justified."

Jake took the detective's words as a hopeful sign. Perhaps he could reason with the man's sense of justice. "Lucien might just kill me, you know. Claim that I tried to run, or grabbed a gun, or choked in my sleep."

"I doubt that."

"And then there's the Flayers. If you turn me in for bounty, they'll be mighty disappointed at missing out on their share. I imagine you might meet with a tragic accident before you can board a train east."

"That, I do not doubt."

"But you're willing to take the risk?"

"I am."

"Then why'd you come all the way here from Chicago, if only to die?"

The detective fell silent for a bit as the horses moved away from the hill in the general direction of Red Canyon, carefully picking their way over unseen obstacles that could snap a foreleg. Words finally found Venables as they reached unbroken ground. "I first read about the American West while huddling in a frozen trench near Sevastopol, from a pamphlet courtesy of a dead man. The words lifted me from the muck and the blood into realms of imagination. Grass as far as the eye can see. Mountains that scrape the sky. Native peoples who live by the horse. Unending herds of buffalo. Hardy souls crossing a vast and untamed continent for the promise of land. Desperate men willing to live and die by the gun." He paused again. "Since that day, I'd always intended to witness the place described by the pamphlet before it disappeared. When I heard that the younger brother of Anthony and Edwin Paynter had become a wanted man, I found my excuse to make the journey west."

Jake twisted in his saddle with surprise that bordered on shock. "You know my brothers?"

"Yes, unfortunately. They tried to break into a bank in Chicago. I killed one, sorry to say."

Jake looked ahead again. "Which one?"

"Anthony."

"He had it comin', I'm sure."

"Perhaps. I'd have preferred him to surrender."

"What became of Edwin?"

"He escaped, but not before shooting down my partner." Venables paused. "I thought you might know where he is."

Jake emitted a grunt that was half disgust, half intrigue. "Haven't seen 'em since the day I left home in '61. Don't care to run across either one of them again. Thanks to you, I've one less to worry about."

Venables didn't respond and the stillness of night gathered them in. After maybe half an hour, the detective pulled alongside Jake, his rifle still trained on his prisoner. "This is far enough."

Jake reined his horse to a stop. "You gonna shoot me now? Was that your deal with Lucien?"

Venables shook his head slowly. "No, Mr. Paynter. I'd rather not continue risking the horses by traveling through the wilderness in darkness. We'll stop here until first light. And know this. A Pinkerton never sleeps on duty."

"I don't imagine you do."

CHAPTER FORTY

Dawn caught Jake and Venables engaged in a stalemate of epic proportions. After stopping, they'd settled atop a flat rock, facing each other about eight feet apart. Venables had positioned his cocked rifle across his lap but pointing toward Jake, and his fingers never strayed more than three inches from the trigger. They'd spoken from time to time through the night but had mostly watched each other like a pair of polecats ready to spar. Jake's hope that Venables would drift into sleep had faded as the stars marched across the sky. The coming sun revealed the detective's eyes still trained on him.

"I suppose that's enough," said Venables. He stood and stretched his back. "Are you as tired as I am?"

"Most likely." Jake found his feet and rubbed his wrists beneath the cuffs. When he moved toward his horse, Venables held a palm to him.

"Not yet. I brought breakfast."

Jake grunted with amusement. "You were so optimistic about apprehending me last night that you planned for breakfast?"

"Not really. I always plan for success. I've packed breakfast for a week, just in case."

Venables continued to cover Jake with his rifle while instructing him where to find the food. The meal consisted of biscuits, jerky, and cold coffee. During the war, Jake had grown accustomed to going without food for days at a time. For that reason, breakfast was a simple pleasure that he'd never take for granted, even one with cold coffee. Afterward, he returned the remnants to the saddlebag where he'd found them.

"All right, then," said the detective. "Off we go, but let us avoid the road."

They mounted and continued as they had during the night with Venables trailing Jake. The detective seemed content to let him lead the way as they snaked through hills, brush, and rocks in the general direction of Ashley's ranch. Jake waited for Venables to make a mistake. To drift too far back so he could bolt. To draw too near so he could jump him. But the man was like a machine, maintaining a perfect trailing distance, his rifle unwavering. Jake turned his thoughts toward what would happen when he arrived at the Ashley ranch. Maybe he'd find an opening then. However, the Flayers upended his plans a mile from their destination. Jake reined his horse to a halt when he spied them.

"Hold up, Venables."

Eight horses stretched across the saddle of earth below the ridge overlooking the ranch. The riders wore dark suits and bowler hats. One raised a hand to wave, the universal sign for "I see you."

"Make for the ridge, frank speed." The detective's command was as taut as a strung bow. When Jake spurred his horse toward the high ground, the Flayers burst into motion. A more practiced band of riders might have intercepted Jake and Venables, or at least drawn near enough for a decent shot. However, the men's struggles with their mounts allowed their would-be prey to thread the needle and occupy the high ground. As one, Jake and Venables leaped from their horses. The option of continuing toward the ranch had evaporated. A perilous and cautious descent through the boulder field would allow the Flayers to cut them off.

"Give me my Henry," said Jake as they crouched low to watch the men assembling below them.

Venables twisted his mustache to the left as he appeared to consider the strategy. "I don't know you well enough. I must decline your request. Now, extend your hands where I can see them and don't move. Not so much as a twitch."

Jake said nothing and focused his attention below. The Philly boys assembled, grouping like cattle. They were killers, but clearly, they'd never fought on a battlefield. A shooter could fire with his eyes closed and bring down two or three of them. The same notion must have occurred to Venables.

"Foolish," he hissed. "Fish in a barrel."

As if in reply, Sweeney pointed at Jake. "That's our prisoner, Pinkerton. He belongs to us."

"And yet I'm the one who captured him," shouted Venables. "How odd."

Sweeney turned his head aside, his smile visible even at distance. "Did ya hear that, Bollinger? He thinks he's a funny man. Telling jokes. Do you find him amusing?"

Bollinger, whose bulk threatened to overwhelm his poor horse, shook his head and slashed a finger across his throat. "Not a bit."

Sweeney again looked up the hill. "We'll just take him, then. There's one of you and eight of us. I'd make book on those odds."

"I'll take those odds," said Venables. "I've a Sharp's carbine. Bloody accurate it is, and I can squeeze off ten shots per minute. And Mr. Paynter has asked for the return of his Henry. I'm strongly considering his request."

The smile faded from Sweeney's face. Without it, he looked hardened and capable of slitting his mother's throat. "Let me explain your situation, then. To collect the bounty, you'll need to turn over Paynter to Mr. Ashley or the army. Either way, we'll be nearby when you collect your reward. And we will take it from you eventually and leave what's left of your body for scavengers."

Jake frowned deeply. The threat was valid. Despite the detective's cunning, he was a man alone. The Flayers likely knew a hundred ways to isolate and destroy an individual. He glanced aside at Venables but found him grinning.

"You won't do that," he shouted to the men below.

"Oh? Why's that?"

"Because I know every detail of your operation in Philadelphia. Your gambling dens. Your protection rackets. Your political influencing. Where you keep your money. Where your families live. I left the records in Chicago, care of an associate. If I fail to return by winter, my associate will send the information to the Philadelphia police." He paused while Sweeney's expression went blank. He'd struck a nerve. "On the other hand, if we can reach an amicable agreement concerning the bounty, perhaps I might 'lose' the information upon my return east. What say you?"

After a few seconds of silence, Sweeney broke into laughter. "My, my, Pinkerton. You look the part of a worthless dandy but you think like a criminal. I'll give you twenty percent."

"I'll give *you* twenty percent, as I currently hold the upper hand."

Jake watched as the two men negotiated across the distance. He might've found it amusing if not for the fact that they were splitting hairs over the share of his death. Within a minute, they'd agreed to a forty-percent cut for Venables.

"Nice doing business with you," Sweeney called. "Send Paynter down."

The detective shook his head. "Go on to the ranch. We'll follow at a safe distance."

"How do we know you won't run off?"

"You have my word."

Sweeney laughed again and said something unheard to his men. No doubt mocking the detective's promise. Nevertheless, they turned their mounts toward the ranch. Venables whispered aside to Jake. "I was prepared to take twenty-five percent. Ah, blessed serendipity!"

Jake peered at Venables with narrowed eyes. "Do you really have detailed records on the Flayers?"

"Of course not. But I'm a confidant liar."

"You seem like a decent fella, Venables. Any chance you'd cut me loose right now?"

"No." He motioned to the horses. "Shall we?"

They descended the ridge in single file, with Jake leading. The Flayers reached the ranch minutes ahead of them, stirring the place into a buzz of activity. Jake scanned from building to building until he saw her on the porch of the great house. Rosalyn raised her eyes in his direction. She hiked her skirt and began running toward him, calling his name. Ketchum sprinted from the house and knocked her into the dirt. Jake's rage flared and he spurred his horse into a gallop.

"Easy!" shouted Venables. "You'll only end up dead."

He slowed his horse and gritted his teeth as Ketchum flung a flailing Rosalyn over his shoulder and returned her to the house. Lucien appeared seconds later through the same door. He and the Flayers met Jake on the way. The Philadelphia men enclosed Jake and Venables in a deadly circle and dismounted. Lucien nodded to the detective.

"Who made the capture?"

"We worked together," said Sweeney.

"That we did," said Venables.

"What's the split of the bounty?"

"Sixty for us," said Sweeney, "with forty to the Englishman."

"Glad you came to an arrangement. After all, your cause was common." Seemingly dismissing the other men, Lucien leveled a triumphant gaze at Jake. "I knew I'd find you eventually. You can't seem to stay away from my sister. That's your Achilles' heel, Paynter. Your particular brand of poison."

"What did you do to Miss Ashley?" His question was more growl than speech.

"Don't worry over her. I take care of my own, especially when they choose a destructive path. My sister will forget you soon enough."

"Tell Ketchum I'm gonna kill him."

Lucien's eyes went wide with mock surprise. "Oh, I'll tell him. Meanwhile, we have some

335

excellent accommodations. Newly built, just for you. I think you'll be impressed." He turned to Sweeney. "Show our guest to his room."

Sweeney nodded to Bollinger. The giant dragged Jake from his horse and threw him over a mile-wide shoulder like a sack of flour. Jake suffered the indignity in silence but added Bollinger to his list alongside Ketchum. After a short walk, the man dumped him to the earthen floor of a hut constructed of log posts and plank walls. As Venables removed the handcuffs, he made eye contact with Jake.

"Sorry about this. It's just business."

Jake looked away while Sweeney and Bollinger stretched his arms to either side and tied them in twin loops of rope at shoulder level, each attached to the wall by a multistranded rope about six inches long. When they stood, Sweeney laughed. "You look rightly crucified, Mr. Paynter."

Jake was left alone with Lucien when the others departed the hut.

"What's next, Ashley? A hangin' tree?"

Lucien shook his head, grinning slyly. "You know as well as I do that there's no tree out here tall enough to hang you from. But I do recall a fine set of gallows at Fort Bridger built with you in mind."

He left without another word. Jake spent maybe twelve seconds feeling sorry for himself before turning his thoughts toward a plan for escaping.

CHAPTER FORTY-ONE

Gus's grandmama had always figured him for one with second sight. Seeing what others didn't see, knowing things he shouldn't know. He considered her opinion mostly horsefeathers. What she ascribed as supernatural was just Gus keeping his eyes wide open, clinging to even the smallest of details, and sorting through it all during quiet moments. It was this trait that brought him bolt upright in his bed on Tuesday morning with one thought shouting in his head—Paynter was in trouble.

He was fully dressed and pulling on his boots before he understood why he thought so. Two days had passed without a meaningful reference to his friend. His name was still on people's lips, but nobody had reported laying eyes on him. Meanwhile, the Philadelphia toughs and Pinkerton detective, both of whom had been omnipresent for a week, had seemingly crawled under a rock. Individually, those facts were worrisome. Partnered together, they spoke dread.

Gus slipped from his rented room near Main Street to fetch his buckskin from the stables. When he took the reins from the boy working the stalls, he produced a nickel and pressed it into the kid's palm.

"Tell Miss Blue I'm lookin' for her. Can you do that?"

"Yes, sir."

"Good boy."

He swung his mount onto the street and began beating a more or less straight line toward Paynter's hiding hole. He hadn't returned to the mine since realizing his visits could lead dangerous men directly to his friend. Going there in growing daylight was a risk, but the day was young. Most folks were still abed and likely thinking he was in the same condition. Over the course of the two miles, Gus envisioned one of two outcomes—Paynter mocking him for his concern or Paynter in a shallow grave. What he found at the mine struck a squarely middle road.

He dismounted in the stub canyon to study signs of activity. A dense array of boot prints marked the passage of many men since the last rain shower five days earlier. A splash of blood spoke of an injury—a stab wound or a gunshot. But whose blood? When he poked his head into the shaft, his gut lurched. A mound of ash marked the conflagration of sage and juniper, enough to blacken the walls and ceiling. Someone had tried to suffocate the occupant. He cupped his hands to his mouth.

"Paynter? You there? It's Gus."

No answer. He led his horse up the hill to the ventilation shaft Paynter had told him about. After five minutes of searching, he found it. Loose earth around the mouth still showed imprints of hands and knees. Likely Jake had escaped as planned. The two sets of tracks leading from the hole puzzled him, though. Emshoff? A miner? He could only guess. At a dead end, Gus mounted and rode back to town with burning urgency. South Pass City was stirring to life when he pulled up at the hotel and entered. The desk clerk, a slack-jawed man of maybe twenty, gave him a death stare.

"You ain't allowed in here."

"No?" Gus reached over the bar, grabbed a fistful of the man's shirt, and hauled him bodily onto the countertop. He buried his forehead in the clerk's temple. "You the one gonna throw me out?"

"Ah, ah, no."

"Didn't think so. Now, answer me a question."

"Ah, what?"

"Those easterners from Philadelphia. They still here?"

The clerk balked. "I—I can't tell you . . ."

Gus rolled him to his back and backhanded each cheek with sufficient gumption to draw blood from the man's nose. "I'd hate to make your face any uglier than it already is, but I'm willin' to try. Now, answer the question."

"Uh . . . they still have rooms."

"Didn't ask if they had rooms. Have you actually seen 'em?"

He seemed to finally have the clerk's undivided attention. The man's eyes rolled up to the ceiling in panicked recollection. "Not since Sunday supper."

"You sure?"

"I think so."

Gus straightened the clerk's collar but kept him pinned to the countertop. "What about the Pinkerton detective?"

"He's here." The man had become downright enthusiastic in his cooperation. "Came in yesterday noon and asked not to be disturbed."

The information gave Gus pause. Venables had been a dynamo since he'd arrived. Retiring to his room for an entire day meant he had either given up or had finished the job. Gus gently slid the clerk back over the bar to his feet.

"There. That wasn't so hard, was it?"

"No, sir."

He turned to leave but cast a finger back at the cowed clerk. "We'll talk again later."

Stacy was waiting for him when he stepped outside, armed with a frown. "I heard you were lookin' for me."

"I am. Let's ride together."

She settled her calico alongside his buckskin as they left town, and he recounted the events of the morning. She listened carefully, nodding agreement with his intuitions.

"Interestin'," she said. "So you think he's at the Ashley ranch?"

"Yep. That's the only place I can think they'd hold him. Especially with Spraggs out of the story."

"What's yer plan? Storm the valley?"

"Nope. Reconnaissance first. Then we'll see."

So much for Gus's plan. A mile short of Red Canyon, Ketchum and two men in black suits met them on the road. Gus pulled his carbine from its sling and laid it across his lap. A wide-eyed Stacy mirrored his action with her shotgun. He whispered aside to her. "Stay calm. But if it comes to shootin', take Ketchum's head off and then fly like the wind back the way we came. Understand?"

She nodded as her eyes went wider still. Gus raised a hand to Ketchum. The raider lobbed a wad of spit onto the road and waved a revolver at Gus.

"Get on back, Rivers. You ain't wanted here."

"People keep tellin' me that today. Startin' to feel unwelcome."

Gus pressed his horse forward, closing the gap between him and those who barred his way. Ketchum watched him with hooded eyes, unflinching. He knew as well as Gus did that an exchange of gunfire would probably leave them all bleeding. Gus pulled his horse to a halt ten feet from Ketchum's. The pair of Flayers eyed him with cautious contempt. But they were young. He addressed the one with the haughtier demeanor.

"You got lots a' Flayer friends in Philly, do ya?"

The man lifted one side of his lip. "Yeah. So what?"

"How many?"

"Forty or more."

"How far's it to Pennsylvania from here? Two thousand miles?"

"Maybe."

Gus nudged his horse nearer until he could see the sweat glistening on the man's upper lip. "I got friends too. Eighty-nine, to be exact, all mounted and armed to the teeth courtesy of the United States Army. They could be here in three days." The threat was not hollow. His and Paynter's former comrades were still stationed at Fort Bridger—an all-black Tenth Cavalry troop filled with hardy men who the local tribes had begun calling "buffalo soldiers" as a show of respect. Gus swung his gaze back to Ketchum. "If it's a war you're lookin' for, I can bring an actual army and right quick."

When Ketchum blinked, Gus knew he'd gained the advantage. Ketchum flared his nostrils. "What do you want?"

"A word with your boss, and then we'll be on our way. Promise."

After a brief battle of unblinking glares, Ketchum turned his horse. "Sheath your guns and stick close."

Gus holstered the rifle but rested a hand on his revolver, just in case. He glanced aside at Stacy. She was terrified, but it was a terror he recognized. He'd seen it on a thousand faces during the war in those gasping moments before battle. It was the look of one who saw death beyond the door but pushed through anyway. He was no less fearful—just more accustomed to dwelling with it. He flashed her a reassuring grin and hoped it was enough to temper the fear for both of them.

Ten minutes later, Lucien Ashley stood on his porch glowering at Gus, Stacy, and Ketchum in turn. He started with the last.

"Ketchum. Did I not insist that no one approach the ranch?"

"You did." The raider didn't seem overly concerned about Lucien's umbrage. "But he'll get to ya, one way or another. Might as well get all the talkin' done now."

Lucien turned his glare on Gus. "Speak your piece."

"Where's Jake Paynter?"

A thin smile captured Lucien's lips. "Haven't the foggiest notion. And here I thought *you* knew.

Or maybe that excuse of a woman next to you knew."

Gus commended Stacy for remaining silent and not drawing on the man. If she did, though, he wouldn't hold her back. He pinned Lucien with a silent gaze and clenched his jaw. "Sure you don't want to amend your answer?"

"I am. And who knows? Maybe Paynter died in an unfortunate accident. Or perhaps he lit out, abandoned you again. He seems to have a knack for leaving you behind."

It was all Gus could do to keep from leaping from his horse to wring Lucien's neck like he would a barnyard hen. "Maybe we should ask Miss Ashley that question."

"I'm afraid not. She's gone away for a while. Now, clear out before I call Sweeney over here. He and his boys are bored as Hades and itching to fight."

Gus touched the brim of his hat. "Whatever you say."

He held a downward palm to Stacy as they rode away, a call for silence. When they'd climbed from the canyon, he finally looked her way. Instead of finding distress, he was met with the very picture of angry determination.

"Pit snake," she spat. "He was lyin' through his teeth. He's got Paynter."

"My thoughts exactly."

"Whadda we do about it?"

Gus had been thinking about just that question since they'd ridden away from the ranch house. "They'll be holding him in the barn or one of those smaller outbuildings. For now, we keep watch. I'll take first stand. You go back to town, gather some supplies, and relieve me tomorrow. I'll set up shop on the ridge."

She nodded slowly and began to pull ahead. "Take care, Gus."

"I always do. Except when I don't."

CHAPTER FORTY-TWO

Jake's empty stomach had been gnawing at him for two days. He wouldn't begin starving for another couple of weeks. In the meantime, he inhabited that dismal space between— where resistance fought a slow but losing battle against hunger. Twice a day, one of the Flayers had entered the hut to pour water down Jake's parched throat and release one of his hands long enough for Jake to relieve himself. Otherwise, he was left alone in a constant struggle to keep his suspended arms from growing numb and useless. With little room to move, he shifted from one hip to the other on the hard-packed dirt floor to keep creeping agony at bay. Lucien seemed intent on breaking him before whatever happened next. To Jake, the punishment seemed spiteful and petty, the desperate act of a small man.

Light prying through the cracks between wall planks began to fade, announcing the coming of his third night in confinement, when heavy steps thudded up to his prison. The door swung open and a body blotted out the light that attempted to wedge through the doorframe. Jake squinted to make out the visitor when a rumbling timbre filled the space.

"You don't look like much of nothin'. From all the stories, I expected a little brother of Hercules."

Jake's pupils constricted to identify Bollinger's dismissive lip curl. The giant ducked his head to enter. He held in one hand the familiar crock containing Jake's water ration. Bollinger squatted in front of Jake, an expression of mild contempt spreading across the expanse of his face. After a few seconds, he nodded.

"Yep. I've used better men than you as battering rams to kill other men."

Jake returned the man's gaze unblinking. "You know I'll be the one to kill *you*."

Bollinger threw back his head and laughed. "You're a funny man. Tell me another, sewer rat."

When Jake fell silent, the Flayer hocked up a massive ball of loose phlegm from his throat and spat it into the crock. He held the pitcher to Jake's lips with challenge. "Drink up, mate."

Jake began swallowing down the contents without hesitation or losing eye contact with his tormentor. Halfway through, Bollinger let the crock fall to the ground between Jake's knees. It shattered into three pieces, sending the remaining water sloshing across his crotch. The big man grunted with amusement.

"Looks like you won't need a latrine. Seems you soiled your britches."

"That's what your mama thought when she birthed you."

Bollinger's grin faded. His mammoth hands closed around Jake's skull, and he began pressing his thumbs with ever-increasing pressure into Jake's eyes. In the space of a heartbeat, Jake's rage overflowed the banks. He hammered Bollinger so violently in the crotch with the point of his boot that the vibration shuddered his entire body. When the giant stumbled back with a yelp, Jake planted the second boot squarely in the middle of his face. Blood sprayed between Bollinger's fingers as he clutched his mashed nose. He rose like a fallen god of thunder over Jake, his eyes going cold with impending murder. He lifted a ham-sized fist for a killing blow.

"Do that and I'll blow a hole through your spleen."

Bollinger halted in midstrike and turned to face Lucien. His eyes fell to the shotgun aimed at his gut. Rosalyn's shotgun.

"He dies by my hand," said Lucien, "or at the end of a rope. If you kill him, you'll not receive a penny."

A taut moment passed between the two men before Bollinger growled and pushed past his employer. Jake inhaled a pair of deep breaths to quell his violence as he watched the big man stalk away. Lucien stepped inside, now training his weapon on Jake.

"I could've just let him kill you."

"You should've," he replied. "What do you want?"

"What? No gratitude?"

"Go to hell."

Lucien smiled coldly. "Sooner or later, but you first." He leaned against the doorframe, not repeating Bollinger's mistake of standing within Jake's striking distance. "Your friends came poking around yesterday. Rivers and Blue. What a ridiculous pair."

The revelation caught Jake off guard. He hadn't expected anyone to notice his absence so quickly but was grateful to Gus. A lifetime of moments flashed through his recollection—of all the many times Gus had saved him, lifted him up, and otherwise watched his back. For a second, he was sorry for not having appreciated it more.

"Do they know I'm here?"

"No. I don't think they're that astute. Regardless, I warned them away under the threat of a dozen guns. If they show up again, they'll both be dead. As you can see, I don't have much control over those Philadelphia boys. No telling what they'd do to a black man and a half-breed woman. I shudder to think."

The sarcasm was as thick as the empathy was thin. Jake flexed his jaw. "Not if I kill the Flayers first."

Lucien shook his head in bemused wonder. "Don't you ever know when you're beaten?"

"Never. I'm colossally stupid that way."

"That's not what Venables said."

Jake's thoughts turned toward the enigmatic detective. He'd still be free if not for the Englishman. "Is he here too?"

"No," said Lucien. "He's gone back to town to wait."

"Wait for what?"

"I had him issue a telegraph to Fort Bridger announcing your capture. They'll be sending an escort to South Pass City along with the government's portion of the bounty and should arrive by Sunday. Venables will guide them here. Bounties will be paid, and you will return to Fort Bridger to hang."

The finality of Lucien's declaration fell on Jake like a mantle of darkness. After inhabiting the dismal space for a moment, he clawed his way through to daylight. He wasn't ready to die just yet. Words remained unspoken and deeds undone.

"What have you done with Miss Ashley?"

Lucien's eyes rolled upward as irritation flooded his face. "She's not your concern, Paynter. She's my problem. You'll not lay eyes on her again."

"If you harm her . . ."

"I know. I know. You'll escape, fight your way through two dozen armed men, and kill me."

"That's right."

351

"Not if I just kill you now."

Jake sharpened his glare and leaned as far forward as his bound wrists would allow. "Like you killed those miners?"

Lucien's eyes narrowed and his mouth went slack. "I don't know anything about that."

"Ketchum does. He ordered the killings. He takes his direction from you."

Lucien shook his head in clear denial. "I just tell Ketchum what I want. How he goes about delivering is his business."

"Your sister won't see it that way."

"She won't ever know."

Jake stretched his neck and flashed a fierce smile. "She *already* knows."

Lucien's face contorted. He strode forward and hammered the side of Jake's skull with the butt of his rifle. "Damn you, Paynter! You should've died a long time ago."

He stormed out and locked the door behind him. Jake squeezed his eyes shut to will away the pain while contemplating Lucien's parting words. The man was right. He should've died long ago. But here he was, still breathing.

CHAPTER FORTY-THREE

Caging a human is a coin-flip proposition. It will either break the person or render them unbreakable. During the four days following Jake's capture, Rosalyn trended magnificently toward the latter. She paced the house in a seething rage, challenging the men guarding the door and harassing Lucien until he locked her in a bedroom for hours at a time. Twice, her wardens nabbed her as she was halfway through a window. Another time, she made it thirty feet from the house before Bollinger knocked her to the dirt.

Only the continuous presence of Mrs. Guilfoyle kept Rosalyn from tearing through a wall. During quieter moments, she fantasized about finding where Lucien had hidden her shotgun and blasting a path to the blockhouse confining Paynter. It was during one such quiet interlude that she overhead her brother in whispered conversation with Ketchum and Sweeney. Like a tigress, she padded swiftly toward the hushed voices, stopped outside the office, and eavesdropped with the skill of a royal chambermaid.

"You sure they'll gather?" The question came from Sweeney.

"Yes," said Lucien. "Mrs. Morris's obstinacy is

her greatest weakness. It makes her predictable."

"Any suggestions on how to break the union?" said Ketchum.

"Not particularly. I trust that between you, Sweeney, and van Zandt's people, you'll think of something suitable and severe. Are you sure the truce with van Zandt will hold?"

Sweeney laughed. "I think so. There's too much money in it for him. And not to worry, Mr. Ashley. Me and the boys have shattered more than a few unions. We know how it's done."

"Very well. They meet again in two days. You should head back to town this afternoon to prepare."

"I'll ready the horses," said Ketchum.

Rosalyn barely had time to duck inside the adjacent room before Ketchum's boots went clicking down the hallway toward the front door, followed by another pair. She flattened herself behind a bed when footsteps approached her hiding place. Lucien's boots appeared in the doorway. "Rosalyn?"

She held her breath, praying he'd not enter the room or squat to look beneath the bed. The boots hovered for a few seconds before moving to the other bedrooms. She sprang up and hurried toward the front door, willing her steps into silence. She flung the door open to make good her escape, only to find Sweeney waiting. He snatched both her wrists.

"You shouldn't eavesdrop on the conversations of men, Miss Ashley. They might soil your delicate sensibilities."

"Unhand my sister." Lucien stalked through the door and pushed Sweeney back. The lead Flayer glared blue ice at Lucien but released Rosalyn's wrists. He raised a finger.

"Control her, then, so I don't have to." He eyed Rosalyn with a wicked smile. "I'd tame you soon enough. I'd show you how to please a man, unless you're already a harlot."

Without thinking, she laced his cheek with her palm. Sweeney went red with rage. Lucien dragged Rosalyn back and stepped between her and the advancing Flayer until the two men touched chest to chest, nose to nose. They held steady like two raging bulls, ready to lock horns. Sweeney broke first. His boyishly charming smile returned, and he retreated a step while straightening his jacket.

"Easy there, Boss. Wouldn't want anyone to get hurt, now, would we?"

"Just earn your pay."

"Righto, sir." Sweeney saluted too enthusiastically and turned on his heel. He began shouting with a dangerous edge to his voice. "Rally up, my boys! We've a night on the town ahead of us!"

As Rosalyn watched him go, her eyes drew up to find a trio of riders approaching the house, dragging a packhorse. Lucien saw them too. He pulled his revolver, grabbed Rosalyn by the wrist, and dragged her along to meet the intruders. A pair of Lucien's cowhands circled the strangers from the sides, rifles trained on them. The three riders made for an unusual sight. Two sported silver hair beneath their wide-brimmed hats and looked as if they'd been baked into marble over the course of decades. The third man, maybe twentysomething, flashed an infectious grin. He was also chained at the wrists. Thirty yards from the house, Lucien halted. The strangers reined back their horses and peered down at him. The smaller of the leather-faced men doffed his hat.

"Good day to ya, mister. I'm Chancellor." He swept a hand to the left. "This is my associate, Hyde. And this knucklehead is Frank Nimbles."

Nimbles bowed with a flourish, only to catch his hat before it fell. "The one and only Frank dubbelya Nimbles, at your service."

"Shut up, Frank," said Chancellor.

"What can we do for you?" Lucien's question featured all the charm of a cornered wolverine. It sounded more like, "Go to Jericho."

Chancellor replaced his hat. "I understand your lack of hospitality, mister, and forgive you for it. Me and Hyde are Texas Rangers from down Austin way. We rode up to fetch Frank here off the Powder River for some nastiness back home."

"The ol' judge had it comin'," said Frank. "He hanged my pappy and my brother, so I hanged

356

him. He was pretty dang surprised when I strung him up. You shoulda seen the look on his face."

"Shut up, Frank," said Hyde. He looked to Lucien. "We been ridin' away from Montana for a week solid with death stalking us most of the way. We're a mite weary and wonderin' if we could hole up here for the night before movin' south again. A night's sleep without worryin' what's slippin' up on us in the dark is all we ask."

Lucien alternated his scrutiny between the older men. "How do I know you're Rangers? Aren't you a bit far from home?"

Hyde retrieved a paper from his saddlebag and offered it to Lucien. When her brother didn't move, Rosalyn stepped forward to retrieve the document. Her eyes swept over the paper. "It's a warrant for the arrest of Frank Nimbles, granted to Chancellor and Hyde of the Texas Rangers." She returned it to the man. "Seems legitimate, Lucien."

Her brother expelled a frustrated breath. "Fine. You may set a camp by the second corral. But don't go poking your noses into anything. All structures are off-limits."

Chancellor tipped his hat again. "Much obliged, Mister . . ."

"Ashley." He recaptured Rosalyn's wrist. "Come on, little sister."

He dragged her away from the newcomers and shoved her toward the house. She resisted enough to make clear her point. When they reached the porch, Lucien shouted to a cowhand.

"Jim Jackson! Come over here."

The young man in question came loping onto the porch. "Mr. Ashley?"

"Don't let my sister leave the house until I get back."

"Yessir."

Lucien pushed her through the door. "Stay put. I need to run cattle check on the high pasture."

She planted her feet in the open doorway with arms crossed.

Lucien rolled his eyes. "Suit yourself."

After he walked away, she and the cowhand fell into a steely-eyed stalemate. He seemed nervous, and she was determined to make him suffer for his assignment. After a few minutes, the clink of spurs drew her attention. Chancellor and Hyde walked up to the porch, the latter standing a head taller than the former, but otherwise both lean as posts.

"Miss Ashley," said Hyde.

She looked toward the corral. "What about your prisoner?"

Hyde laughed. "Lashed him to a split rail. We need the reprieve. The man talks a blue streak."

"We're sorry to impose on you," said Chancellor, "but we wondered if you might offer us a drink of somethin' other than canteen swill. Coffee. Tea. Anything will do."

"And one for the young man here," said Hyde as he slapped the cowhand's shoulder.

Something about the gleam of the men's eyes spoke of conspiracy. Rosalyn turned away. "I'll speak to Mrs. Guilfoyle."

While she and the cook fetched tea for the men, she heard them on the porch introducing themselves to the cowhand, Jim, and talking up a storm. When she returned with three glasses, the Rangers each took one and pushed the third at Jim. He drank with them, a grin plastered on his starry-eyed face as Chancellor launched into a story about tracking down a gang of cattle thieves in '47. By the time he finished, Jim seemed half in love. Chancellor punched his shoulder again lightly.

"Say, there, Jim. Would ya mind helpin' Hyde put the horses up for the night? I just need to rest my old bones for a bit." When the boy balked, he added, "I'll make sure the lady don't leave. Ranger's honor."

Jim nodded and walked away with Hyde to tend the horses. Chancellor maintained his grin until the men disappeared around the corner of the house. The smile fled his face instantly, and he met Rosalyn's eyes with a granite gaze.

"Where they keepin' Paynter?"

The question nearly flattened her. She recovered quickly. "How did you know he was here?"

"An English fella let it slip when we asked after him in town. Or maybe he told us on purpose. Couldn't rightly tell."

"Are you here to take him in, then?"

Chancellor removed his hat. "No, ma'am. We are not. Is he in one of the little blockhouses near the barn?"

She didn't know the man, but his forthright earnestness begged her trust. "Yes. The one nearer the creek."

"Can you spring him?"

"I—I don't know for sure."

"Are you willin' to try?"

She lifted her chin. "I've been trying for days now. I will continue to do so."

"Good, good," he murmured. "Me and Hyde will wait about a mile beyond the back side of the high ridge for three days. After that, we gotta head on. If you bust Paynter loose, send him our way."

"Why? What will you do with him?"

Chancellor smiled warmly, transforming his face into a geological map of hard-earned lines. "We'll give him a fightin' chance. We owe him that much after he spared our lives."

Rosalyn blinked. They knew Paynter and owed him their lives. They really were trying to help. Before she could pester him for details, the Ranger leaned his head toward her and lowered his voice.

"By the way. Who's the lady up in the brush watchin' the place?"

"Lady? What does she look like?"

"Long black braid, forage cap, wears britches. Carries a shotgun, maybe."

A grin crept across Rosalyn's face. "She's a good friend. Stacy Blue. Don't hurt her."

"Wouldn't think of it. We don't shoot women lest they shoot us first. Then the rules are off." He cocked his head to the right. "This friend. Would she try to shoot us?"

"If she thought you were hurting Paynter, probably."

"Duly noted." He wedged his hat back onto his head. "We'll see about a truce, then."

Rosalyn's skepticism warned her that the Ranger's pledge of support might be nothing more than an attempt to squirrel away Jake to claim the bounty. However, she oddly trusted the man. He reminded her of an older Jake Paynter— as principled as he was dangerous.

CHAPTER FORTY-FOUR

Stacy spent a restless night wandering the halls of speculation over the three riders who spent the night at Lucien's ranch. Were they bounty hunters? Some of Dutch van Zandt's outlaw crew? Lawmen come for Paynter? The fact that one of them appeared to have his hands bound led her toward the last of those conjectures. However, the visitors never approached the guarded outbuilding that likely held Paynter. When they rode away over the southern rim shortly after sunup, she dismissed them from her thoughts and spent the next three hours instead focused on the ranch.

That proved to be a mistake.

"Set down your scattergun, missy."

Stacy flinched hard and almost spun to unload on the voice at her back. Almost. The cool and certain tone of the request stilled her hand. One of Lucien's men, no doubt. She set aside the shotgun and raised her hands, wondering if she could reach her knife when he came for her.

"Call me 'missy' again and I'll cut out your tongue," she said with more composure than she felt. "So what's your beef, mister?"

The man chuckled. "You Stacy Blue?"

"In the flesh. You got a point?"

"Maybe. But you should keep a better eye on your blind side."

"Good advice," said another voice from farther away. Gus! "Drop your piece easy-like."

The stranger swore beneath his breath. When Stacy heard the clunk of iron in the dirt, she leaped for her Lefaucheaux and brought it to bear on the stranger. He was an older man, smallish though seemingly constructed of leather stretched taut over a wire frame. A bushy mustache all but obscured thin lips. Funny thing, though. He didn't seem overly concerned about the turning of the tables. She stepped toward him with her shotgun leveled at his chest as Gus closed the gap at the man's back.

"You one a' Lucien's men?"

"No, ma'am."

"So, it's 'ma'am' now?"

"Yes, ma'am. You're the one holdin' the firepower."

"Why'd you steal up on me with a gun?"

Gus reached the stranger and pressed his rifle barrel into the man's kidney, none too gently. "I'd like to know the same. I been watchin' you slippin' up on her for half an hour."

Stacy frowned at Gus. "And you let him?"

"Easy, Anastasia. I didn't know his intent."

She lifted one lip at him. "Well, you do now. Thanks for nothin'."

"You're welcome as always. Now . . ." He prodded the stranger again. "Answer Miss Blue's question before she decides she don't want to hear it."

"Settle down, kids," said the man. "I'm old enough to know that walkin' up on someone keeping vigil is a recipe for taking a bullet. I meant no ill. Just didn't count on reinforcements. But I shoulda known better. Every time I go after Paynter, it ends up this way."

Stacy caressed one of the triggers. "You're after Paynter, then?"

"Not like you think. I'm here to help. Me and my partner, Hyde."

Stacy eased her finger from the trigger. She knew who the man was. Paynter had told them. "Are you those Texas Rangers who came for Paynter in the Wind River country?"

"Yes, ma'am. Name's Chancellor."

"Start talkin', then."

"Can I drop my hands?"

"No."

"Fine." Chancellor sighed. "I spoke to your friend Miss Ashley. It seems Paynter is held prisoner in that blockhouse out past the barn there. She's plannin' to break him loose and send him our way over the back side of the big ridge."

Stacy narrowed her eyes. "How's she gonna break him loose?"

"She didn't say."

"How long will you wait?"

"Three more nights. Can I put my hands down now?"

"No." While Stacy mulled the information, her eyes found Gus's gaze. The set of his jaw, the flare of his nostrils, the intensity of his eyes spoke what he hadn't said yet. She lifted her chin toward him. "What's going on, Gus?"

He didn't appear surprised by the question. "There's a storm brewin' back in town. The Flayers rode in last night with Ketchum, and I counted at least six of van Zandt's bunch wanderin' around."

His point was clear to Stacy. They were needed back in South Pass City, and pronto. She pinned her eyes on the Ranger, wondering if she could trust him. After all, he'd tried to capture Paynter once before, so why not again? "Tell me," she said to him. "Why I should take you at your word."

A familiar expression rippled across Chancellor's features. Affront. He stretched his spare frame bolt straight and returned her gaze, steel for steel. " 'Cause if I don't keep my word, then I'm no better than the desperados I bring to justice. If that were true, then you'd best shoot me now and with my thanks."

She lowered her shotgun, infused with belief. "Put your hands down, mister."

When he did, Gus stepped around him to pull

366

Stacy aside. He leaned into her ear, his voice low. "Can we trust him? A thousand dollars is a fortune to a lawman."

"Paynter seemed to."

"Paynter's got a history of givin' his trust to the wrong people."

"He trusts you, though. Right?"

"That's different."

She huffed in his face. "How?"

"He got lucky one time."

"So I don't count? Is that your meaning?"

A smile spread across his face and he shook his head. "You win, Stacy."

She punched his shoulder hard enough to bruise a knuckle. "I always do, and don't you forget it."

"Can't. You won't ever let me."

Stacy strode up to Chancellor. "All right. We'll leave the vigil to you and your partner. If we don't see Paynter in three days, we'll be back and loaded for bear."

"Fair enough," said the Ranger. "Send someone back with his horse, stacked with provisions. Enough to carry him far from here."

"And weapons?"

"Miss Ashley will see to that. If not, we've got spares."

"Very well." She stabbed an index finger into Chancellor's chest. "Don't disappoint me. I'll ride all the way to Texas to hunt you down."

The Ranger laughed and removed his hat to

wipe his forehead. He replaced the hat on his head. "Heard and understood, Stacy Blue. Mr. Paynter is lucky to have friends like you all. It's a gift. I should know."

Stacy agreed. True friends—those willing to walk through fire for others—were a rare breed. She counted as precious two of those and was bound and determined not to lose either one of them.

CHAPTER FORTY-FIVE

Jake had just grown comfortable with the onset of starvation when the cavalry arrived in the form of a woman he'd never met. The guard, a young cowhand called Jim, had just finished giving Jake his final water ration of the day and the opportunity to relieve himself. Jake had only just settled down when a feminine voice greeted the guard.

"Howdy, Jim. They keep assigning you guard duty, it seems."

"You don't hafta remind me."

"I'm sorry. But look on the bright side. It shows Mr. Ashley's trust in you."

"I reckon."

"All pleasantries aside, I'm here with food for the prisoner."

Jake bolted upright from his slump with that announcement. Food? After five days? Was it a last meal, or had his military escort arrived early? Either way, the change didn't bode well. Starving seemed the more hopeful option.

"Ma'am, I can't let you do that," said the guard. "Mr. Ashley ordered water only."

"Jim Jackson, I am sorely disappointed in you." Her tone was one of gentle rebuke. "What would your mother think about your role in starving a man to death?"

"Well, I don't . . ."

"She'd be sorely disappointed as well. I mean, this man is confined and no threat to anyone. He'll be gone from here tomorrow to hang. Why not show him a bit of charity with a couple of buttermilk biscuits?"

"I don't know . . ."

"It'll be our secret. Nobody will know but you, me, and the prisoner. And I don't think Mr. Paynter will be inclined to tell anyone. How about it? Two biscuits. Buttered and spread with gooseberry jam, but two biscuits and no more."

A relenting sigh sounded through the closed door. "Oh, all right. For my mama. But hurry inside before someone figures out what you're doin'."

The door creaked open to reveal a woman of perhaps forty with dimpled cheeks and carrying a basket looped over one arm. She brushed past young Jim and stepped into the small space, her eyes on Jake.

"We'll keep him bound to be safe," she said over a shoulder. "I'll feed him the biscuits myself. And you better close that door a bit." Jim narrowed the gap but continued watching Jake through a slit, clearly nervous. Jake, meanwhile, eyed the woman, still suspicious over the change of routine. She kneeled, set the basket down, and clasped her hands together.

"I am Mrs. Guilfoyle. I cook for this mob and serve alongside Miss Ashley as an island of femininity in this sea of gravel-throated men."

"Folks call me Paynter."

She flipped a wrist at him. "I know all about you, Mr. Paynter. But enough chatting. I imagine you're right ravenous."

Jake's mouth burst with saliva when Mrs. Guilfoyle peeled back a thick napkin to reveal a mound of biscuits, still hot as evidenced by the steam rising from them. She stuffed the napkin beside the pile, broke one biscuit in half, and plopped a portion into his mouth. He gobbled it down, barely tasting it. The second piece he savored. His eyes closed as he inhabited the miraculous combination of bread, berry jam, and heavy butter. While he was having a spiritual moment with the biscuit, Mrs. Guilfoyle began chatting with the guard.

"Where are you from, Jim?"

"Kentucky. Little place called Maysville."

"Kentucky? Why, I'm from across the river in Ohio. We're practically cousins. What brought you to the territory?"

"Pa died and my mama needed my help. I came for gold but couldn't afford a claim. Mr. Ashley offered me work on account a' my experience with horses. Got me doin' guard duty lately, though."

Mrs. Guilfoyle did not answer immediately. Jake opened his eyes to find her leveling an intense gaze at him, her back to the guard. She lifted another half biscuit toward his mouth.

"Let me assure you that Miss Ashley is grateful for everyone on this ranch and glad you're here."

"That's kind of her," said Jim. Jake accepted the next hunk of biscuit, his attention fully on Mrs. Guilfoyle as he realized her words were likely for him.

"Indeed. Miss Ashley is especially grateful because she knows any one of you could move on at any time. In fact, someone could leave this very night. They could head east over that big ridge and never look back, toward whatever destiny awaited them there."

Jake swallowed the bite. She was definitely talking to him, not to the young guard. He nodded slowly to communicate his understanding. She blinked both eyes deliberately and offered him the last piece of the second biscuit.

"And if anyone did leave this night," she said, "Miss Ashley would miss him greatly. But she would understand. In fact, she would extend him her best wishes for a good and peaceful life. Every time she lifted her eyes to the stars, she'd think about the friends that had to go away."

Jake looked aside from Mrs. Guilfoyle as he swallowed the last bite. He didn't want her to see him falter. When he looked back, she was studying his left wrist.

"Why, Mr. Paynter. Your wrist is bleeding. Let me clean that for you."

His wrist was chafed but not bleeding. "Thank you."

She retrieved the napkin from the basket and leaned toward his wrist, blocking it from Jim's view. Instead of wiping it down, she shoved something long and cold down his sleeve, leaving one end protruding into his palm. When he circled his fingers around the exposed end, she moved away.

"There. All better." She whirled to her feet, drawing Jim's attention. "I brought a few biscuits for you as well."

The guard's eyes went wide with interest as Mrs. Guilfoyle piled four biscuits into his outstretched hands. "Much obliged, ma'am."

"There's more where that came from," she said while pushing him through the door and closing it behind her. "Next time you're up to the house, I'll make sure you don't go away hungry."

After her voice trailed away, Jake waited in the dark for the guard to come inside to inspect him. He didn't. After a few minutes, Jake uncurled two of his fingers to reveal the hilt of a long knife. His knife. The one he'd taken from a dead man for an episode of self-surgery that had saved his life. The one he and little Lisbet had used to carve their names into Independence Rock. No matter how many times he lost it, the blade kept returning to him. He wasn't one to believe in signs, but this seemed as close to one as he'd ever experienced.

With great care to avoid dropping the knife, he wriggled the blade from his sleeve until it came free. He stretched the binding away from the wall until it grew taut, cocked his wrist uncomfortably, and began sawing with short, limited motions. After several hundred strokes, a single strand parted. He sighed before determination settled in. It would take a while to cut the first bond. The others would go quickly. Regardless, he needed to finish before daybreak, or all the underhanded efforts of Rosalyn and Mrs. Guilfoyle would be for naught.

CHAPTER FORTY-SIX

The wind began moaning with a vengeance during the lonely hours of the night, a warm and raucous funeral dirge swelling from the south. *Perhaps Texas is sending me its last respects,* thought Jake as he continued to saw his bonds. He welcomed it, though. The relentless creaking of wind-blasted planks obliterated the sounds of his attempted escape. As night wore on, the bond grew thinner strand by strand. The fatigue of his wrist forced him to rest it for minutes at a time before resuming the task. Twice, he nearly dropped the knife before catching it with two fingers. He had no reasonable means to reach it again if it fell. Otherwise, the night passed in the numb monotony of ten thousand repetitive motions. So numb, in fact, that the snapping of the final strand caught him by such surprise that he did drop the knife. He peered at the spot in the darkness occupied by his newly freed hand.

"Son of a gun."

Jake retrieved the fallen blade and attacked the bond restraining his right wrist, making short work of it. When he tried to stand, his knees buckled. His thighs and buttocks had gone perfectly numb and his head was light from hunger. He braced a hand against the wall and tried again. With paranoid stealth, he marched his legs in place and pumped his arms until they felt somewhat restored—and ready for what came next. He stepped to the door, knife in hand, and pushed against it slowly. It moved half an inch before stopping.

As silent as death, he slipped the blade through the seam and slid it upward until finding the latch. The latch rotated upward as he pressed carefully with the blade until the door began to open. He caught the door with three fingers and froze it in place. When he pressed an eye to the crease, he spied Jim hunched on the ground nearby but facing away. What little moonlight remained revealed no further detail. Jake inhaled deeply through his nose and burst into fluid motion. He was on Jim before the boy could move. His blade found Jim's throat and bit into it.

"The next sound you make will be your last. Hear me?"

A mousy cry escaped Jim's throat, but he nodded as much as the blade against his neck would allow. Jake lifted him to his feet, stripped away his rifle, and dragged him backward through the door before pulling it shut. He shoved the young guard against the same wall where he'd been restrained for five days. The encompassing night left Jim a shadowy figure, but the boy's rapid breathing audible over the vociferous wind spoke of his terror. An earlier version of Jake Paynter would've slit Jim's throat as the price of survival. The newer rendition cried out for another path.

"You seem like a nice kid," he said. "I bet they got a lot a' nice kids in Maysville, Kentucky."

"Yes, sir." Jim's voice trembled even with those two words.

Jake circled him. "It seems we have a few options here. I could just kill you, but I'm not inclined to. You could fight back, but *you* don't seem inclined to. Either way, you'd be dead. Do you want to die right now?"

"No, sir."

"All right. Then let's keep tickin' through options. I could just leave you as you are. But I imagine Ashley'd blame you for my escape and let his band of animals deal with you accordingly. I could stick my knife in a place that won't kill you or belt you unconscious so you can claim you put up a fight. That might save your life but not your job."

The loss of life or livelihood must've overcome the boy. He fell to his knees and dropped his head. "Better to just kill me, then."

Jake stepped forward to yank him up by his collar. He slapped Jim across the face. "Don't ever surrender like that, boy. You keep fightin' until there ain't no other option. Understand?"

Jim rubbed his cheek. "Yes, sir. But what can I do?"

"Leave," said Jake. "You got a horse?"

"In the corral."

"Good. Go fetch it and leave this rotten place. Ride to town and find Esther Morris. Tell her I recommended you. She'd find you a job, no questions asked."

"Aren't you afraid I'll raise an alarm after you go?"

"That possibility does concern me. But you know what Ashley's like. Would he give you the same chance I'm offering?"

A pause. "Not likely."

"So what would your mama back in Kentucky tell you?"

"She'd tell me that evil company corrupts good morals, like the Bible says. She'd tell me to fetch my horse and leave quietly."

Jake touched the brim of his hat. "Then I'll leave you to your conscience. Do what you must. But I'll be taking your rifle, just in case."

He spun and pushed his way out of the blockhouse into the steady wind. The half-expected shout of alarm never happened as he forged a path toward the ridge overlooking the canyon. He stopped halfway up to rest his burning thighs and cast his first backward glance. The ranch remained perfectly still aside from a lone figure leading a horse away from one of the corrals.

"Good choice, boy."

Turning again uphill, Jake resumed picking a path through the boulder field until he surmounted the ridge. There he halted, recalling Mrs. Guilfoyle's cryptic message. "East over the big ridge . . . to whatever destiny awaited." Swiftly scudding clouds brushed past the moon, leaving the landscape momentarily alight before plunging it again into darkness. He waited for the Big Bear to reveal herself, put her on his left shoulder, and continued east. He stumbled for a while through the darkness until spying a knot of swaying shapes ahead. He redoubled his grip on the captured rifle, dropped to a crouch, and pressed ahead.

"Paynter? That you?"

Jake froze at the calling of an oddly familiar drawl. Could it be? Against his better judgment, he stood and walked toward the knot, which soon revealed itself to be three men and five horses. He stopped short of them.

"Chancellor?"

"The very same."

"Why are you here? Last I saw, you were headed to the Montanas in search of a fugitive."

Hyde laughed. "That's right. We found our man already."

"Frank dubbelya Nimbles, the one and only outta Bandera, Texas," said a third voice. "May all the world quake before me."

"Shut up, Frank," said Hyde.

Jake stepped nearer. Clearly Rosalyn had meant for him to meet up with the Rangers. She wouldn't have sent him this way only to again become a prisoner. He lowered the rifle. "How'd you find me?"

"You don't know by now?" said Chancellor. "It's what we do. Find things that don't want ta' be found."

"More importantly, *why'd* you find me?"

"Good question. Hyde? You wanna answer that?"

"Don't mind if I do." He leaned forward in his saddle. "In the execution of fetching this fugitive off the Powder River, we engaged in a rather tense parley with a band a' Cheyenne who were none too keen on our presence. I figured we'd seen our last sunset. But then, for reasons I can't explain, I mentioned you."

"Me?"

"Yep," said Chancellor. "The second he mentioned we were friends of Jake Paynter, the Cheyenne lowered their weapons. We enjoyed a much more civil discourse after that."

Jake struggled to wrap his brain around what they claimed. "Because you mentioned my name?"

"Surprised us too."

"And me most of all," said Frank. "I about fell off my horse, and I never fall off my horse."

"Shut up, Frank," said Chancellor.

"Anyway," said Hyde, "they told us what you

done for their allies down on the Green River. Not that we thought you a liar when you told us the same, but their corroboration laid to rest our justified skepticism."

Chancellor grunted agreement. "After some spirited discussion, me and Hyde decided to come back your direction to offer apology for tryin' to string you up or otherwise kill you."

Jake swung his baffled scrutiny between the two shadowy figures. "So that's it? You just wanted to apologize?"

"Yes," said Hyde. "But we also told the judge over at South Pass City what we heard. And we came to an agreement with your friends who've been watchin' the ranch since you were taken."

"My friends?"

"Mr. Rivers and Miss Blue. They gave us somethin' for ya."

Chancellor rode forward with one of the unmounted horses in tow. He dropped the reins when the horse pushed toward Jake and nearly bowled him over. Jake grabbed the horse's neck. "My mare?"

Chancellor chuckled. "Seems she missed you. She's loaded with provisions, compliments of your friends. Including your Henry rifle and this."

He tossed a holster into Jake's free hand. His probing fingers caressed the Kerr. "How'd you get this from the ranch?"

"Your girlfriend took care of it. I hope it don't put her sideways with her brother when he finds the weapons missin'."

Jake set down the borrowed rifle and buckled the Kerr onto his hip while adding another entry to his growing book of things for which he owed Rosalyn. He mounted the mare, who took a swipe at his leg while he did so. It warmed him that she hadn't lost an ounce of her fury.

"Anyhow," said Chancellor, "your friends wish you well and suggest you light out for the Yellowstone country or head west 'til nobody knows your name. But now we must be off to Texas. Best a' luck, Paynter. And if you're ever down Austin way, look us up."

"Thank you. I will."

The Rangers stuttered into motion, heading south. Frank turned back to wave his manacled hands at Jake. "And if you're ever down Bandera way, look me up. I'll tell ya how I killed these Rangers."

"Shut up, Frank," said Chancellor and Hyde in unison.

Jake watched them recede into darkness. Suddenly adrift, he struck out north toward the Wind River country with a muddled plan in his head and a steady wind belting him from one side. He would let Mrs. Morris handle it from here, including showing the ledger to the judge. Maybe that would be enough to bring Lucien to justice, though he doubted it. Instead, he'd drop in on the Shoshone and beg for more provisions. Then he'd plow a path to the Yellowstone. Make a dugout so he could survive the winter. Bring down some game and salt the meat. Then, then . . .

The plan circled the drain of his head for five miles before he halted the mare and dismounted. He plopped down on a rock, grabbed a small stone, and began rolling it around his fingers while watching runners of dawn rise in the east. His thoughts turned toward the dark forces he was fleeing. A hundred men who wanted him dead. A thousand people who knew his name but not his black soul. A nation that had chewed him up, spit him out, and sentenced him to die.

Gradually, though, pinpoints of light invaded the darkness of his recollections, filling it with an amber glow. Each wore a face. Gus, Stacy, and Rosalyn, who'd risked everything for him. The Dunbars, Emshoffs, and Robersons who'd made him a neighbor. Esther Morris and Francisco Aguilar who believed in him more than he believed in himself. What would become of them now? Lucien Ashley still employed a band of dangerous men, and every bounty seeker west of the Mississippi was still looking for him. As long as Jake remained free, these men would harass his friends for news of his whereabouts. Those he cared for would never experience a moment's peace. He clenched the stone and hurled it away.

"Double dammit."

Jake rose to his feet, mounted the mare, and turned back toward South Pass City. The dawn beckoned but made no promises.

CHAPTER FORTY-SEVEN

Jake rubbed dust from his eyes to better view the gathering at Beaver Creek as he returned toward town. Though at least a mile distant, the relentless flapping of skirts and spectacle of runaway hats was on full display. It seemed most folks had walked again, given the small number of carts and wagons scattered across the field. His best guess put the crowd size at a hundred, give or take a dozen. The imposing gray-clad figure of Esther Morris stood out as she apparently addressed the gathering. The vicious wind, however, whipped away any semblance of sound from his ears.

He briefly considered joining the congregation before shaking away the foolish notion. Showing his face to the public wouldn't help anyone. He needed more time to implicate Lucien in the killing of the miners. After that? He could save his friends a load of trouble by turning himself in to the judge. Could he surrender his freedom when the time came? Or would he just run again with no destination, no plan, no future? The last time he'd given himself up for the sake of others, unexpected freedom had offered him a second chance. Maybe he could hope for one more miracle. Or maybe he should finally put aside such delusions. Regardless, he rode onward.

Not two minutes later, a cluster of riderless horses in the distance drew his attention. Maybe two dozen were lined up, side by side, tethered to an unseen rope stretching between two trees. Alarm bells clanged in his head. He wheeled the mare about to put the steady wind at his back and cupped his hands over his eyes to peer into the space between the horses and the gathering of miners. His stomach fell. A parade of men upwind from the meeting was spreading out, clearly armed with torches. In an instant, he knew what would happen next. His prophecy transformed into reality within seconds as the men began setting grass alight. Digging his heels into the mare's flanks, he let loose a cry.

"Git on!"

His bursting angle toward the miners brought him within two hundred yards of the men and newly billowing smoke. Ketchum, black-suited men wearing bowlers, and a dozen he couldn't identify had abandoned the torches in favor of long guns. When Ketchum raised a rifle, Jake fell prone across the mare and swerved her away from the advancing flames. Two shots rang out, but neither struck him. Man and horse barreled toward the miner meeting with the intent of shouting alarm. That proved unnecessary. The bawling wind drove a cloud of smoke at those gathered, scattering them. Gus and Stacy rushed among the chaos, shouting commands. Jake glanced north to find the spine of rock that had saved his life once before, perhaps a mile and a half distant, and he knew what to do. He pulled his kerchief over his nose and flashed onto the meeting grounds with shouts of instruction and exaggerated gestures.

"Cover your faces! Ford the creek! Run for the rocks!"

As he repeated the commands, others took them up. Gus and Stacy raced to head off those who'd bolted toward the fire to turn them north instead. In groups of five and ten, the adults gathered up children and crossed Beaver Creek. A man attempting to flee in his cart succeeded only in miring the vehicle in the stream.

"Abandon the wagons!" Jake shouted. "Cut loose the horses and run!"

He leaped from the mare to help the miners and their families cross the creek. Mrs. Morris was already on the far side, directing everyone toward the distant rock spine. Jake waited for Gus, Stacy, and the stragglers before pushing past the creek. He looked back to study the advancing flames. The fires were darting forward in two lines separated by maybe a hundred yards, with a smoke-obscured mob of men advancing between them. The first fire line jumped the creek to his left even as he watched. A bullet striking dirt at his feet prompted him to move. He led the mare at a trot until catching the rear guard of the fleeing miners.

"Mrs. Morris!" She stopped and he leaned into her ear. "Take my horse. Mount up the children and elderly and lead them over the rock spine. The back side is steep and barren. We can shelter there while the fire burns past."

He stripped away his rifle and ran ahead to Gus to repeat the instructions. His old friend seemed simultaneously pleased to see Jake and horrified by the mounting catastrophe. "Already on it."

Jake understood Gus's dismay. A hundred men, women, and children fled on foot ahead of advancing flames while the relentless wind billowed choking smoke at them, and maybe ten horses among them. He ventured another backward glance to find that the second fire line had leaped the creek. Twenty armed men marched in the gap, their mouths and noses wrapped with cloth. If not for the men, the gap could provide an avenue of escape between the twin walls of flame and smoke. Jake knelt and lifted his rifle, knowing he didn't have enough bullets to take them all. The smoke, though, conspired against even his tempered expectations. His eyes watered as he knocked down two men.

The ensuing hail of shots from the attackers sent Jake into full retreat, cursing. It couldn't be done. The flames would join into a single line before he took down half the men or before he died—whichever came first. He caught up with the stragglers, urging them forward as the flames closed. The remains of the gap hosted a menagerie of progressing men who disappeared and reappeared as smoke swirled. Dismal realization set in. Half the party wouldn't reach the rocks ahead of the flames. With angry impatience, he picked up an older woman who'd fallen and threw her across his shoulder.

"Run or die!" he shouted to the others.

Spurred by panic, the slowest kept running with morbid determination. But not fast enough. After a few hundred strides, Jake halted long enough to cough up a lung and scan the approach of certain death. The flaming walls had closed the distance to the runners by half. The gap between the walls had narrowed until the advancing party clustered in what remained, blocking retreat, firing potshots toward the miners. He set the woman down.

"Run and don't stop!"

She tore away from him, crying. Jake knelt again and readied his Henry. At least he could take a few with him. He chambered a cartridge before freezing as a rumble of thunder reached his ears. A glance skyward revealed nothing indicating a storm. He returned his attention to the advancing men in time to see one fall. Then another. Then two more. The rest scattered, risking flames, even as others fell to the reports of gunshots. Jake blinked with confusion before spying a blue wave rushing his way, a determined tide plunging through the narrowing gap.

Distinctive bugle notes met his ears. He bolted to his feet. The oncoming tide resolved into a column of horses sprinting full tilt, driven hard by buffalo soldiers with rifles cracking.

The Tenth!

Jake waved his arms to draw the column. He grabbed the extended hand of the lead rider and swung into the saddle behind him. The eyes of Sergeant Stubbs, his former K-Troop subordinate, cut back at him above a face obscured by a yellow bandanna.

"Round up the stragglers!" he told Stubbs. "Carry them to that rock ridge ahead!"

The sergeant saluted as Jake slid off the horse. When Venables flashed past to help, Jake was not surprised. The detective and the fifty or so troopers scooped up the runners, one by one, as Jake ran along to boost bodies onto horsebacks. After tossing a limping man onto a horse, Jake found himself abruptly alone and watching the receding haunches of four dozen horses. He continued running with lungs heaving. Burning sage arced over his head, carried by gusts, to light the field before him. He pinned back his ears and dodged among sprouting wildfires as an impenetrable cloud of smoke encompassed him. Robbed of sight, he could only keep running and hope his line was true.

A shadow burst from the haze to congeal into the form of a familiar horse and rider. He seized

Gus's outstretched hand to swing up behind him. When the buckskin surged free of the worst smoke, Jake found K-Troop hauling the last of the civilians up a cut through the spiny ridge. He and Gus were the last to climb the crease and descend into the shelter of rock. He scrambled down from Gus's horse, ready to bark orders.

Before he could begin shouting, though, he found everything well in hand. Mrs. Morris and Stacy had pressed the families against the rock wall, making sure each person's face was swaddled in cloth. Venables was helping cover the children. Sergeant Stubbs and the man who'd taken Jake's place, Lieutenant Stallings, were directing the troopers in the stripping of saddles and the use of blankets to wrap the heads of their horses. When Jake spotted his mare among the cavalcade, he relieved her from a surprised soldier.

"I got this one, Corporal."

Instead of removing the mare's saddle, Jake jumped astride and nudged her along the spine, intent on flanking the fire. Gus chased after him.

"Paynter?"

"Keep everybody down, Gus. Keep 'em alive."

"Where you goin'?"

Jake lowered his brow and growled. "Hunting."

He turned away from Gus and dug his heels into the mare's flanks. She buried her head toward the earth and barreled ahead, seemingly as furious as he was.

CHAPTER FORTY-EIGHT

Jake drove the mare along the spine of rock for a half mile before finding a navigable gap. The horse burst through the wall into unburned ground as smoke billowed off her left flank. Circumventing scorched earth, they raced to Beaver Creek and over, bound for the place where Jake had spotted the mass of horses earlier. He found them in his sights, some mounted, others draped with bodies of those cut down by shots from him and the Tenth. With the mare in full flight, he pulled his Henry, took aim, and added one to the death tally from two hundred yards out. The riders burst into motion, splitting immediately into twin parties flying away from each other. The strangers turned northeast, hauling their dead along behind them. The Flayers didn't bother. The five survivors abandoned their cold brothers and fled behind Ketchum toward distant Red Canyon and the safety of Lucien's ranch. Jake grinned viciously. He would run them down long before then. Ignoring the strangers, he fell onto the trail laid by Ketchum and the men in black suits.

While the Flayers struggled to remain in their saddles at a gallop, the mare chewed up the gap like so much prairie grass. Five times Jake straightened to squeeze off a shot. He missed twice. He barely spared a glance for the dying and the dead as the mare bounded over them. Ketchum had long since disappeared around a jumble of rock, with Sweeney and the giant falling behind. Jake drew a bead on Bollinger's wide back and pulled the trigger.

Click.

He sheathed the empty rifle and drew his Kerr, but not before Bollinger had cut around the rocks. The mare slowed, exhausted and cautious on a rock-littered rise. Jake trained his eyes on the dirt, following the hoofprints left just seconds before. His preoccupation with tracking left his defenses wide open for attack. A flash of movement in his peripheral vision drew his attention to find Bollinger bolting from behind a boulder.

The man struck the mare squarely in the neck as he gripped her halter. She twisted violently to the right while Jake kept going. The bone-jarring impact against the ground ejected the Kerr from his grip and left an ocean of stars swimming across his vision. As he spun on his knees in search of his revolver, iron hands grabbed his biceps and lifted him skyward. His eyes found the flushed and maniacal glare of Bollinger.

"Greetings, sewer rat!"

Bollinger tossed him like a bale of hay. Jake tumbled backward through space before landing roughly on the back of his shoulders and somersaulting ass over teakettle to land on his knees. The Flayer charged and swung a mighty kick that would've separated Jake's skull from his neck had he not sprung aside. Instead, Bollinger's boot caught Jake's shoulder with a glancing blow still sufficient to spin him full circle. Jake let the new momentum carry him away from his attacker and to his feet. He turned toward the bull with fists raised. A hungry smile grew across Bollinger's wide face, and he stripped off his coat with a ripple of massive shoulders. He ignored the weapon at his hip and instead lifted balled fists.

"Let's dance, Paynter."

Though his head still spun from the double falls, Jake had no choice but to fully invest in the conflict. One well-placed swing of the Flayer's fist would end him. Bollinger waded into Jake with hammer strokes. He dodged one, then two, then three. The fourth caught the left side of his chest. He left his feet briefly before crashing to the dirt yet again and rolling up against a rock pile that abruptly stopped his progress. Bollinger roared with delight.

"Not so mighty without your shooter! Get up, rat!"

Jake stumbled to his feet and lunged at the giant. His fists met flesh with seemingly no effect. Bollinger laughed again and wrapped his arms around Jake in a killer clench. Jake pressed both hands against the man's lantern jaw to no avail. The mounting pressure of Bollinger's clasped fists against the base of Jake's spine ripped a cry of anguish from his throat and raised the looming specter of death. But the grinding pain also opened his eyes. The red haze returned to settle around him, gathering him into its loving embrace. In the blood warmth of the malevolent cloud, Jake became one with his darkest demons. He went briefly limp before plunging two fingers into Bollinger's left eye and ripping it free of its moorings. A second later, he was on his knees where the Flayer had dropped him.

Bollinger stumbled back and pressed a hand against his empty eye socket. He emitted an ear-shattering scream of wounded rage, a torrent of sound that echoed across the landscape. As Jake stood, Bollinger's remaining eye fell on him, and the man's features became those of a beast. The clutching hand fell from his face to join its mate as twin claws intent on murder. With another bellow, he charged. Still firmly entrenched in the violence, Jake threw his body toward the giant in a hurtling crouch. As they collided, Jake caught an arm and a leg to catapult Bollinger onto his shoulders. He flowed with the momentum of the impact to ram all three hundred pounds of the Flayer into the rock pile, headfirst. Jake disentangled from the resulting jumble and crab-walked backward. Blood sprayed from Bollinger's scalp as he shook his head and stood. He watched Jake rise and hurled another threat.

"I'm gonna rip your heart out!"

The promise would have sent most any man into flight. But Jake was not most men. He smelled the hint of doubt in Bollinger's threat. A hint was all he needed. He strode in toward Bollinger, ducking a wild swing and lashing upward with a fist to crack the Flayer's jaw. He fell back a single step, dodged another panicked swing, and crushed Bollinger's nose. When the big man stumbled backward, Jake launched himself at Bollinger's leg and staved in his left knee with the heel of his boot. The giant swayed and fell across his ruined leg. Jake caught him in midfall and carried the bulky body earthward. His legs circled the Flayer's waist from behind as he wrapped the man's throat in the crook of his elbow.

Bollinger rolled until Jake was beneath him, perhaps hoping to use his bulk to suffocate the smaller man. Jake grabbed the fist of his encircling arm with the other hand, arched his back, and pulled like he was dragging the world uphill on a chain. Bollinger tried to pry the arm away and clawed at Jake's head, but Jake had become burnished bronze, immovable. The Flayer thrashed his four limbs wildly to rid himself of the man who would kill him. He failed.

Jake continued to squeeze Bollinger's neck long after the dead man had stopped moving. As the red haze dissipated, Jake let his arms fall limp to his sides. He lay pinned beneath the body with eyes half-closed, drawing ragged breaths while summoning the strength to push Bollinger off him.

"Pretty damn impressive."

The sound of Ketchum's voice drew Jake back to alertness. The raider stood ten feet in front of him with a revolver leveled at Jake's forehead. Jake's revolver. The Kerr. Ketchum seemed amused by the sight.

"Never thought I'd see anyone take down Bollinger. Then again, never thought you'd be unarmed when I finally killed you."

Jake's limp arm inched toward the holster strapped to Bollinger's hip. "Just answer me one question before you kill me."

The barrel of the Kerr drifted imperceptibly downward. "What question?"

Jake's fingers found Bollinger's revolver and cocked it. He twisted the end of the holster upward and squeezed the trigger, hoping the chamber held a cartridge rather than empty air. A red ring blossomed from the center of Ketchum's chest. The raider fired the Kerr before he fell to his back, but the shot found Bollinger's unmoving chest. Jake heaved the dead man away, crawled to Ketchum, and stripped the Kerr from unresistant fingers. Ketchum looked down at his chest to find a spreading stain.

"Well, hell. That ain't no good." His eyes turned to Jake. "What was the question?"

"Do you wanna die with your boots on?"

Ketchum grinned before his head fell back and his eyes went blank. Jake wiped blood from his nose with the back of a sleeve and plopped into the dust next to Ketchum's corpse. He flipped open the chamber of his Kerr, reloaded the empty slots with supplies from his ammo bag, and shut it. Only when he returned his attention to Ketchum's stationary form did realization strike. Ketchum was dead, and along with him any chance to implicate Lucien. The only consolation was the defeat of the Flayers, Sweeney excepted. He was probably halfway to Philadelphia if he had any sense. Regardless, Jake was still a fugitive with a heavy price on his head, and everyone he cared about was suffering as a result of his continued presence.

He jumped as a shadow fell over him. The mare peered down with well-practiced annoyance. Her judging eyes seemed to say, "What next, jackass?" Jake chuckled in spite of the darkness of his reality. Every bone in his body ached. Blood seeped from a dozen wounds. His head felt like someone was carving it into a jack-o'-lantern. His gaze fell to the dead man at his side.

"So, Ketchum, what would you do if you were

me?" He paused. "What's that? You'd grab what you could and quit the territory?"

Knowing what Ketchum would do in his place made up Jake's mind. He rose to wobbly feet, found his hat, and dusted if off. The mare followed him impatiently. He rubbed her nose with reassurance.

"It's been a good run for us, girl. We got one more ride to make and then you'll be free of me."

With a clean but heavy heart, he eased into the saddle and directed the mare toward South Pass City.

CHAPTER FORTY-NINE

If not for the fact that she'd nearly died, Stacy might've felt like the grand marshal of a parade. She glanced past Gus at her side to the eye-popping cavalcade behind. Fifty blue-clad cavalry troopers rode in two-by-two formation, led by Venables and Mrs. Morris, the latter of which rode double with the detective. Mrs. Morris's rangy frame behind the compact and trim Venables nearly drew a laugh from Stacy. The troopers sobered her, though. If not for their arrival, maybe fifty men, women, and children would've been consumed by the fire as it raged past. She faced forward again. Her peripheral vision caught Gus gazing at her.

"You did good, Miss Blue," he said. "I'm proud of you."

The unexpected compliment brought heat to her cheeks. Which never failed to annoy her. "I'm gonna chat with the detective. Don't get us lost, Augustus."

He laughed as she fell back to ride alongside Venables and Mrs. Morris. Mrs. Morris seemed entirely uncomfortable with the situation, with the thin line of her mouth seemingly carved in stone. The detective tipped his hat to Stacy.

"Miss Blue."

"Just Stacy. Now, tell me again what happened."

Venables motioned to the column of the Tenth behind him. "They arrived just after nightfall but camped outside town. Lieutenant Stallings and Sergeant Stubbs found me shortly after breakfast, and I led them out, bound for the Ashley ranch. When we saw smoke from the road, we diverted to investigate. Stubbs was the first to recognize what was happening." He glanced back at the sergeant. "His family got burned out during the war by folks who didn't care for the notion of black neighbors, so he'd seen it before. Anyway, you know the rest. The lieutenant ordered a mounted charge. K-Troop took it from there."

"That they did," said Stacy. "It was like a miracle."

Mrs. Morris snorted. "I find that most miracles happen only after a healthy dose of diligent work and preparation. The Tenth's arrival was good fortune but also the result of years of training and three days of hard riding."

"When you put it that way . . ."

They continued to converse as the parade wound its way into South Pass City. Folks out for Sunday walks stopped to stare, some with hand-covered mouths. She didn't blame them—not too much, anyway. Most of them probably hadn't seen so many buffalo soldiers in one place before.

Stacy lifted her chin as if to say, "They're with me." She caught up with Gus and led the line down muddy Main Street to the courthouse—a modest white slab of a building. Judge Kingman must've heard their approach because he stepped onto the porch to meet them. He cocked his head at Mrs. Morris.

"This seems like a fascinating tale, particularly given the smoke on the horizon. Come tell me about it."

They dismounted and followed him inside—Mrs. Morris, Venables, Stacy, Gus, Lieutenant Stallings, and Sergeant Stubbs. Before he stepped through the door, the sergeant leveled a finger at one of the troopers. "Corporal Jefferson. The command is yours. Don't make me come out and fight ya."

Jefferson fired a crisp salute offset by a wry grin. "Yes, sir."

Kingman leaned against the witness stand with folded arms while the rest of them fanned out in the first two rows of benches. He nodded toward the assembly. "The honorable Mrs. Morris has the floor."

With a direct but dramatic approach that impressed Stacy, Mrs. Morris recounted what had happened. The judge grew alarmed when she talked of the Flayers and the band of strangers lighting the malicious fires.

"Who were the strangers?"

"Nobody knows for sure, but probably van Zandt's people. They rode northeast afterward."

"Go on, then."

When she'd finished the recounting of events, Kingman heaved a deep sigh. "It seems we owe a great debt to the Tenth Cavalry K-Troop. And to Mr. Paynter, wherever he may be. But who would order the attempted murder of a hundred civilians?"

"I can answer that."

Stacy whipped her head around to find Paynter standing at the door. She bolted from her seat and tried to push him back outside. "Why are you here? You should run."

He gently pulled her hands away. "If I run, you'll never know another moment's peace. There will forever be someone tryin' to leverage you to get to me."

"But, Paynter . . ."

"There is no 'but.' This has to end. I'm tired. I've had my fill."

Only then did she really look at him. He stood stiffly, favoring one leg. His haggard face and neck were a mass of budding bruises with claw marks descending one cheek. Dried blood ran in a diagonal smear across his forehead, and his knuckles looked as if he'd gone three rounds with a brick wall. She dropped her hands and stood aside, dejected. He gave a tight smile as he stepped past her to approach the judge.

Kingman watched him with hooded eyes. "Miss Blue asks a good question, Mr. Paynter. Why are you here?"

"To turn myself in for killin' the deputy and orderin' the marshal held prisoner."

The judge seemed unsurprised. "And why'd you do that?"

"To keep Duff from gutting the miner beneath his knife. And to keep Spraggs from escaping justice."

Kingman nodded and paced the floor with chin in hand. "I see. Mrs. Morris has hinted that you've gathered evidence to back your suspicions of Ketchum and Ashley."

"Yes and no," he said. "Ketchum for sure, but not Ashley. And Ketchum's dead."

"Dead?"

"I shot him an hour ago. He needs a burial before the coyotes get him."

"And the Philadelphia men?"

"Dead too, but for one. You're gonna need lots of shovels."

Relief burst inside Stacy. She pointed at Gus. "I told you he'd hunt down them bastards and send 'em to hell! Didn't I?"

"Miss Blue," said Kingman.

"Judge?"

"Mind your language in the courtroom."

She dipped her chin but failed to wipe the smile from her face. "Yes, sir."

"And about the fires?"

"Ketchum too," said Paynter. "No doubt under orders from Ashley, but again, no longer provable given the lead ball in Ketchum's chest."

The judge approached Mrs. Morris, his mind seemingly awhirl. "Can you show me that ledger?"

"Yes, Your Honor."

Gus, who'd remained silent, shifted sharply in his seat. "What about Paynter?"

"My question exactly," said Lieutenant Stallings. "We were sent here to collect him for a hanging, but me and the men would be just as pleased to ride away empty-handed."

Judge Kingman leaned against the witness stand again and peered at the floor for nearly a minute. Paynter just stood in place with his distinctive hat clutched in both hands, staring out the cloudy window at who knew what. Finally, Kingman looked at the lieutenant.

"I took an oath to uphold the law and dispense justice, first and foremost. The law requires me to hand Mr. Paynter over to you for transport to Fort Bridger. But justice also requires that I keep him here until the matter of the killings and the fire can be settled. So if you don't mind waiting, I'd like a few days."

The lieutenant stood. "Don't mind at all. Sergeant Stubbs."

"Sir."

"Let's reestablish camp southwest of town and settle in for a few days. Relay those orders to the men."

Stubbs grinned conspiratorially as he replaced his hat on his head. "Yes, sir. That's a fine plan."

The soldiers marched out, leaving the civilians alone. In their absence, the judge approached Gus and placed a hand on his shoulder. "Mr. Rivers. I understand you're a military man with years of leadership experience and handy with a carbine."

"True on all accounts."

"Then please stand and raise your right hand."

Gus's eyes narrowed, clearly communicating Stacy's similar bewilderment. He stood and raised his right hand.

"Gus Rivers," said Kingman, "I hereby deputize you as an officer of the court and authorize you to take Mr. Paynter into custody. Do you accept the position?"

Gus's hand faltered as he looked at Paynter. His old friend met his eyes and nodded. Gus's features sagged briefly before he addressed the judge. "I do."

"Then please show this man to a cell in the adjacent marshal's office. And get him some medical treatment, for God's sake."

Stacy followed Gus as he marched Paynter out of the courthouse and into the marshal's office. She watched, horrified, as Paynter helped himself to one of the two cells. Gus gathered the key but froze before the cell door, a monument to unwilling betrayal. Paynter reached through the bars to guide Gus's hand to the lock.

"It's what I want, my friend. No hard feelings."

Gus turned the lock. "No hard feelings."

"No hard feelings?" Stacy shouted. "Maybe for you! But I'll never forgive you for not runnin' when you had the chance!"

He just smiled at her softly and nodded. "I know, little sister. That's why I like you so much."

Stacy ran from the marshal's office, angry and devastated. God help any fool who dared step across her path.

CHAPTER FIFTY

As Gus sat vigil over Paynter in the marshal's office, he couldn't help but recall his grandpappy's funeral, two weeks after the cannon shots at Fort Sumter had ignited the war between North and South. The old man had outlived his wife and all his children by blood and by marriage, including Gus's parents. Despite counting only Gus as his remaining family, Polidore Rivers was a spiritual father to an entire county. The mourners had begun arriving just before nightfall from a dozen adjacent plantations, with or without permission. The tightly packed crowd of two hundred men, women, and children had sung in the nightfall and thumped drums in defiance of those who would prohibit such acts.

As young and old alike had given testimony of Polidore's influence, the night had gathered closer, barely beaten back by the feeble glow of a few torches. In the sacred hollow of light carved into the darkness, Gus had felt the spirits of his ancestors on two continents gathering at the margins to welcome home his grandpappy. Near midnight, Gus had leaned over Polidore for a final farewell. The man's skin had gone pallid, trending slowly toward the color of death—white.

Gus had driven the nails to shut the body inside and helped lower the box into the moist Alabama earth. As each dollop of dirt from his shovel had struck the casket lid, it had sounded to Gus like a whispered word.

"Free. Free. Free."

The next day, Gus had slipped away from the eyes of the overseer, dodged dogs and trackers for a week, and never looked back. Now, watching the imprisoned Paynter from the corner of his eye, Gus felt the experience repeating. A farewell to family, a burial, and an unknown journey into the future. Paynter sat placidly for hours on the bunk in his cell, staring at the ceiling, the bars, the window, only to repeat. Gus honored the impromptu wake by remaining silent. The dead have no need to talk. Spraggs lay on the bunk in the adjacent cell, drifting in and out of consciousness. The miners had beaten him to the borderlands of death before turning him over to the judge. The only sounds he emitted were a wheezing rattle through his broken nose and a periodic groan. Evening was fast approaching when the hallowed moment collapsed into chaos.

"Send him out!"

Gus jerked up from his chair and strode to the door. Perhaps fifteen armed men stood outside on the street, facing the marshal's office and fronted by Lucien Ashley.

"Send him out or we come in after him!" shouted Lucien.

Gus glanced over a shoulder at Paynter to find him still staring at the ceiling. Paynter waved a hand. "Better see what he wants."

If not for the gravity of the situation, Gus might've laughed. He donned his holster, pulled his Spencer carbine from the gun rack, and stepped onto the porch. He recognized a couple of the men from watching the Ashley ranch. The rest were unknown to him.

"Whadda ya want, Ashley?"

Lucien lifted half a lip. "We want Paynter."

"Why?"

"To hang him. It has become abundantly clear that his friends from the Tenth are not up to the task."

Gus glared without response, choosing instead to train his carbine somewhere in the vicinity of Lucien's crotch. A barrel pointed at the head would make a man angry and desperate. A barrel pointed at his manhood would make him uncomfortable. Gus wanted Lucien to wallow in discomfort.

"Stow those weapons!" All eyes turned to find Judge Kingman striding from the courthouse, red in the face. "What in God's name is going on here?"

"Mr. Ashley wishes to hang Paynter," said Gus. "But I disagree."

When Kingman waded into the space between him and Lucien, Gus drifted the carbine's barrel aside—but only just. The judge turned his calibrated wrath on Lucien.

"If you lynch the prisoner, you will violate multiple statutes of federal and territorial law. I would think a man of your public standing would be unwilling to risk everything to hang a man who is already condemned to die."

Much to Lucien's credit, he didn't bend. He eyed the judge coolly. "Paynter has been under sentence for nigh on two years now. And yet he still breathes, just inside that door. Pardon me if I don't trust the army to properly finish the job."

Kingman waved a hand at the other men. "You understand that Mr. Ashley is attempting to violate the law, do you not? He is dragging you into a federal crime."

One of the men, a deeply tanned brute with curly mutton chops, spat on the street and grinned. "We ride with Dutch van Zandt. He don't give a damn about the law, and neither do we."

Lucien rocked forward as the men crowded behind him, intent on overrunning the marshal's office. When Lucien shoved Kingman aside, Gus raised his weapon, expecting to die. But Lucien froze just before mounting the steps to the porch. Gus blinked to find Venables pressing a Smith and Wesson to Lucien's temple.

"Mr. Ashley," Venables said crisply. "This is not justice, and you owe me money. I would like to see both rather than a bloodbath."

Van Zandt's men apparently cared little for either, because they continued shuffling forward as Gus pressed his back to the door. He aimed his weapon at the mutton-chopped man who'd spoken. "You're first."

The leader stopped with his shotgun leveled at Gus's face. It seemed only a matter of seconds before one of them would squeeze the trigger and mayhem would ensue.

"Stop or drop!"

The outlaws jerked their collective heads around to find Francisco Aguilar and a dozen miners swarming from behind the hotel, pointing long guns at the mob. A woman stepped from the hotel balcony to level a musket at them. Shopkeepers wearing aprons emerged from storefronts with an assortment of rifles and revolvers trained on the lynch mob. Glen Dunbar marched from his smithy, hammer in hand and destruction in his eyes.

Lucien appeared to assess the unraveling situation and made an executive decision. "Fall back. Lower your weapons."

Mutton Chops glared at Lucien. "Afraid of a fight, are ya?"

"Never. But you should be." He jerked a thumb toward the far end of the street where fifteen mounted buffalo soldiers were setting up a fire line. Sergeant Stubbs motioned the horses forward in a slow but ominous advance.

"You gotta go through us," shouted Stubbs. "And if one of us takes so much as a single bullet, the U.S. Army will hunt you to the edge of the continent."

The man growled and spat in the street a second time. He shoved Lucien's shoulder. "Another time, then. C'mon, boys."

The townspeople gave the outlaws a wide berth as they filtered by and disappeared down a side street. Venables holstered his revolver. "A prudent choice, Mr. Ashley."

Lucien glared at the judge. "How long, then, must I wait?"

"I need to conduct a hearing over your man, Ketchum, and his book. Paynter is the principal witness."

Gus grinned as Lucien's face went ashen. "When?"

"A few days. Perhaps a week."

Lucien swallowed before clenching his jaw. "Right, then. One week, and I'll be back. You tend to Paynter or I will."

Gus watched Lucien and his five remaining men traipse down the street past the still oncoming troopers, collect their horses, and ride out. Sergeant Stubbs dismounted when he reached the marshal's office. "Havin' some trouble?"

"A little," said Gus. "Nothin' I can't handle."

"I figured." He motioned to the door. "Mind if I check up on the lieutenant?"

"Not at all."

Gus led him inside to find Paynter still contemplating the ceiling. "Brought you a visitor."

Paynter cut his eyes at them and chuckled. "Stubbs." He kicked his feet off the bunk to sit and pointed at Stubbs's shoulder. "I see by your stripes you made first sergeant."

The soldier lifted his chin with pride. "Yes, sir. The position came open three weeks ago, and the new colonel made the terrible mistake of promotin' me."

Paynter's brief grin flickered before fading into a frown. "What happened to Blackburn, then?"

Gus understood his friend's concern. The former first sergeant had robbed Paynter of his soul during the war and had haunted him like a specter ever since.

Stubbs circled the cell bars gently with gloved fingers. "He mustered out. Said he was gonna collect the bounty on ya. Two birds with one stone and all that." He sighed. "Watch yer back, Lieutenant. He's in the wind and still hell spawn."

Paynter nodded. "Thank you, First Sergeant. I owe you double."

"My pleasure, sir."

Stubbs strolled out with his head hanging low. The closing of the door plunged the office again into silence. Gus stepped to the marshal's desk, opened a drawer, and retrieved Paynter's Kerr. He extended it between the bars. "Just in case."

Paynter studied the revolver before gingerly accepting it. "Thank you, Gus."

He slipped the weapon beneath his pillow, swung his feet onto the bunk, and returned his gaze to the ceiling. Gus settled into his chair to continue the vigil and gather more wool from days forever gone.

CHAPTER FIFTY-ONE

Rosalyn had never understood how a single straw could make the difference between a functional camel and a defective one. Surely, the camel would raise a righteous defense before accepting such an injustice. She maintained this opinion until the moment Lucien broke her back with not one but two straws.

"Paynter has turned himself in to Judge Kingman," he had told her. "I'm taking some men to hang him."

Despite her protests, Lucien had mounted up and ridden away. Before he left her sight, what should have lasted eternally instead failed spectacularly. As she lamented what her brother had become, the bond that had joined them since childhood snapped. He died during those moments—as far as she was concerned. Without a word, she returned to the house and packed a canvas bag. Mrs. Guilfoyle appeared at the door of Rosalyn's room as she buckled the bag tight.

"It's finally happened," said the cook.

Rosalyn met her sad gaze. "What?"

"You've endured enough complicity with your brother's actions. You've decided to go."

Rosalyn lifted the bag to her thighs and hauled

417

it through the door as Mrs. Guilfoyle stepped aside. "I have. Don't try to stop me."

Mrs. Guilfoyle laughed. "Wouldn't dream of holding you here. If I didn't need the job, I'd leave with you now. Mr. Ashley's vigilante mob is a reach beyond the pale."

Relief swept Rosalyn. She wasn't irrational after all. "Thank you for understanding."

"Think nothing of it. I'll pack some victuals and meet you at the stables."

Rosalyn grabbed her shotgun from the wall and lugged her bag through the door toward the stables. A cowhand repairing the corral stopped to watch. Undoubtedly, Lucien had told him to keep an eye on her. She decided to seize the proverbial bull by the conceptual horns.

"You, there. Come help me."

The man pointed to his chest with eyebrows raised. She placed hands on hips.

"Do you see anyone else behind you?"

"No, ma'am."

"Then come fetch my bag."

He dropped the mallet from his hand and slipped through the rails. He wore a look of bewilderment. "What for?"

"I'm riding into town for an extended stay."

"I don't think Mr. Ashley would take kindly to . . ."

She stepped into him and stabbed a finger into his chest. "Mr. Ashley is not here. And he would be most displeased with anyone crossing swords with his beloved sister. Therefore, you may assist me with this bag or get the hell out of my way."

The man's eyebrows lifted further, and Rosalyn surprised even herself. She'd never before uttered a curse word. The cowhand proved himself a prudent man by hoisting the bag onto one shoulder, hauling it to the stables, and strapping it to a packhorse. Meanwhile, she saddled her mount. The cowhand watched her with obvious discomfort, stirring her empathy.

"If my brother asks, I threatened you with my shotgun."

He straightened his shoulders. "If it's all the same to you, ma'am, I'll do no such thing. Mr. Ashley had no right to confine you the way he did. Take care."

As the cowhand departed the stables, Mrs. Guilfoyle entered with a bundle. "It's not much, but it'll tide you over a few days. Do you have money?"

"I opened an account at the bank the week we arrived and have been secreting money there ever since. I have plenty for the winter. Besides, I've already spoken to one of the councilmen about the appalling lack of a schoolhouse. I intend to rectify that."

"And where will you stay, dear?"

"Esther Morris offered me a room should I ever choose to leave. With luck, the offer still stands.

If not, perhaps the Dunbars might spare a spot of floor for me. I don't need much."

Mrs. Guilfoyle wiped away a tear and smiled. "I'll miss you here. Take care on the road. Don't let your brother see you."

Rosalyn embraced Mrs. Guilfoyle. "I won't. Take care as well. If I find you a job, I'll send word."

What she failed to disclose was her intention to stop Lucien before he stormed the jail.

Rosalyn's plan unraveled thread by thread on the ride out. First, it was the packhorse refusing to cooperate during the climb out of the canyon. Instead, her horse practically dragged its counterpart up the slope to the high road. After resting both animals, she started along the trail toward South Pass City. Two hours on, she spied a group of riders approaching from the direction of town. She hid, even though it became clear they'd seen her. However, when they turned aside toward the Atlantic City mining camp, she realized that none of them were Lucien or his men.

Annoyed by the delay, she pressed the horses toward town. The packhorse again took exception and fought her urgency every step of the way. When she was little more than a mile from her destination, she again spotted a band of riders on the trail. Thanks to a fortunate bend of the road, they appeared not to notice her before she pulled the recalcitrant packhorse off the trail and into a hollow. As the riders neared, their voices carried on the breeze. One was Lucien—no doubt about it. Warring emotions captured her. Fear that her brother would see her from the road and drag her back to the ranch. Dismay that his return likely marked the demise of Jake Paynter. She huddled in the low land, waiting for Lucien and the emotional avalanche to pass. When she finally led the packhorse onto the trail, it was with a new measure of grim resolve. She couldn't turn back. She couldn't avoid the truth. Her only available recourse was to stick to the original plan, regardless of its cost.

The first thing she noticed when riding into South Pass City was the lack of a publicly displayed dead body. That fact gave her little solace, though. Surely, Paynter's friends would've cut him down as soon as Lucien left. For a moment, she regretted not having fired both shotgun barrels at her brother as he'd passed by. When the grim vision passed, she found a better one—a band of blue-clad soldiers at the grocer's loading supplies. One she recognized from Fort Bridger a year earlier. She spurred her horse ahead, yanking the packhorse in her wake.

"Sergeant Stubbs!"

The soldier gave her a suspicious sidelong glance before recognition lit his features. "Miss Ashley, is it?"

"Yes. You're a friend of Mr. Paynter, right?"

"I served under him." A smile crawled across his face. "I suppose we was friends too."

Rosalyn swallowed hard and wavered in her saddle. "Was?"

Stubbs blinked before seeming to recognize her alarm. "Oh, no, ma'am. He's not dead. We sent those boys packin' in a right hurry."

She had spent all day preparing herself for the worst. As a result, relief nearly finished the job of knocking her from the saddle. "Where is he?"

"Jailhouse, up that way." He jerked a thumb over his shoulder. "Sergeant Rivers is watchin' over him, along with the rest a' the town. Ain't nothin' gonna hurt him until the judge holds his hearing."

Rosalyn dipped her chin. "Thank you, Sergeant. I'm much obliged."

"Don't mention it."

She left the troopers behind and pushed her horses doggedly up the street to the marshal's office. After securing them to the hitching post, she bulled into the office without knocking. Gus was on his feet with revolver drawn before she cleared the doorway. Only then did she realize the folly of bursting in on an armed man who expected nothing but enemies through the door. When she froze, he sheepishly returned his gun to its holster.

"Apologies, Miss Ashley."

"The fault was mine, Mr. Rivers."

She cut her eyes toward the pair of cells to find the marshal in one and Paynter in the other, each at the edge of their bunks. The sudden fight faded from Paynter's eyes as he stared at her. Then, slowly, he lay back down on his bunk and curled toward the wall. Memories flooded back to Rosalyn from those days on the Oregon Trail—of how he'd tried to push his friends away when his death seemed a foregone conclusion. She drifted to his cell and placed one hand on the bars. He stayed put. She lifted her chin, intent on coaxing him from isolation once more.

"It seems as if I'm forever looking at you through bars or in chains." She kept her voice light. "I might suspect that you prefer the condition."

Paynter didn't respond, but Spraggs slapped his knee. "Come over here and talk to me, then, sweetheart. I know how to get on with a woman."

Paynter's head lifted and he glared war at Spraggs. The marshal went quiet, and Paynter laid his head again on the bunk. Rosalyn redoubled her grip on the bars and gathered patience.

"As I was a prisoner at the ranch the last time you saw me, you might wonder about my presence here." She paused, but he remained motionless. "Lucien suspected I was helping you. He accused me of orchestrating your escape, which I denied. I've never lied to my brother before, so it wasn't easy. And then, when he departed this morning intent on hanging you, I packed my bags and left. I'm sorry I wasn't here in time to warn you."

Paynter's head lifted a few inches from the bunk but didn't turn. "You left Lucien?"

"Yes—for good. Mrs. Morris has a room for me. I plan to open a school and teach the youngsters."

After a few seconds of silence, Paynter rolled to face her. "Good. You'll make a fine teacher."

"Thank you."

Spraggs expelled a laugh. "What? Is that all it takes to earn your regard, Miss Ashley? One pitiful compliment? Why, a beerhouse painted lady would need more than that."

In a flash of motion, Paynter leaped toward the adjacent cell, grabbed Spraggs by the collar, and pulled his skull into the bars with a clang. The marshal fell to the floor clutching his head.

"Damn you, Paynter! I hope you suffocate when they hang you."

"Maybe I will, Marshal. But I take consolation in the fact that you'll hang first."

The specter of Paynter's death flooded Rosalyn abruptly. Her knees nearly buckled and her eyes went bleary with tears. Before she could wipe them away, Paynter was standing before her, his fingers wrapped around hers. He reached through the bars to smudge tears from her cheeks. His mouth hung open, but he seemed unable to speak. In the yawning silence, grief over unrealized what-ifs settled into the nooks and niches of Rosalyn's soul. She sniffled and pulled away from the cell.

"I shouldn't have come."

Gus held the door as she walked through. In her wake, Paynter finally found his voice.

"Thanks for always treatin' me better than I deserve."

She halted on the porch, swaying, before descending the steps of the marshal's office. The sound of the door closing threatened to unmoor her.

CHAPTER FIFTY-TWO

For five days, Jake became a jackrabbit—all ears and without voice. The parade of visitors would invariably arrive expecting conversation but leave disappointed. Most of them endured his silent head nods and grunts for thirty minutes, but none lasted an hour. Not the Robersons, the Dunbars, Francisco Aguilar, Lieutenant Stallings, Mrs. Stefka, Esther Morris, or the kid, Jim Jackson. Little Lisbet Emshoff almost cracked him, though.

"Why is he not answering my questions?" she implored her mother. She faced Jake with a huff. "Why are you not answering my questions?"

A reply nearly found his lips before he doused it with a vague grunt. The little girl glared at him until he dropped his eyes. She spun about and headed for the door.

"I'm gonna go talk to a rock. It's better than talking to Mr. Paynter right now."

When she slammed the door, Jake glanced at the remaining Emshoffs. Mr. Emshoff slapped his thighs and stood. "Well. I suppose it's time we left you in peace." He motioned to his family. "*Meine Liebe*, Dora, Otto . . . shall we?"

Mrs. Emshoff shoved a bundle of bread

through the bars and refused to move until Jake accepted the gift. She rounded up her other two children with a disappointed frown. *"Kommt, Kinder."*

Their departure left Jake feeling guilty. Just a little, though. Gus, who was leaning back in his chair with boots on the desk, shook his head. "You're a jackass sometimes."

"Only sometimes?"

"Good. You can still talk. I figured you swallowed your tongue."

"Don't you start on me, Gus."

"Got to," he said. "Don't want your final acts on this earth to be shunning your friends and disappointing little girls."

"I'm still talkin' to Stacy."

"She ain't a little girl."

"Glad you noticed." Jake nearly grinned. "But she won't talk about anything except how to spring me. Gettin' a mite predictable."

Gus chuckled. "Say that to her face."

"I'm a jackass. I ain't stupid."

"In that case, I'm gonna tell another story."

Spraggs stirred from his bunk. "I like your stories."

"I don't," said Jake.

Gus smiled. "Don't matter. I still have the keys to your cell. And I do love me a captive audience."

Jake lay on his bunk, hands behind his head,

and gazed at the ceiling. "Fine, Gus. Do your worst."

He did.

"Wake up, Paynter."

Jake's eyes flitted open to find Stacy standing at his cell door. He rubbed his face and sat up. "You breakin' me out, now?"

The ash that fell across her face told Jake she wasn't in the mood. She kicked a set of wrist irons through the bars. "Gus sent me. Put those on."

He complied while studying her face. "Where we goin', little sister?"

"Your hearing with Judge Kingman."

He snapped his jaw shut. He'd expected more warning. When Jake stood, Stacy unlocked his cell and let him out before repeating the routine with Spraggs. The marshal eyed her speculatively while snapping shut his irons. "Can't believe the judge sent a little girl to fetch prisoners."

Jake impaled Spraggs with his deadliest glare. "She'll drop you like rotten timber, Marshal. And if she don't, I will."

Spraggs held his tongue while Stacy trailed them from the jail to the courthouse next door. She handed the prisoners over to Gus, who seated them to one side facing the empty judge's chair. Jake cut his eyes at the small gathering to find Lieutenant Stallings, Esther Morris, and Lucien Ashley. The last eyed him with thinly veiled contempt. Jake returned the death stare until Lucien looked away. But he faltered when Rosalyn entered the room. She slid onto the back bench behind her oblivious brother and stared straight ahead. Jake adjusted his position and turned his eyes toward the judge, wishing Rosalyn wasn't present. She'd seen him die too many times already.

"All rise." Gus's baritone filled the small room. Everyone stood as Judge Kingman walked five steps from his chambers to his chair. He flicked a palm to those gathered.

"Sit, folks."

Jake resumed his seat and watched the judge shuffle through Ketchum's infamous ledger for at least a minute. Without looking up, he lifted a finger toward Jake. "Mr. Paynter. Please tell the court how you obtained this document."

Jake described his infiltration of the Ashley ranch in great detail. After recounting finding the locked desk drawer, Lucien jumped to his feet.

"This man broke into my house and stole from a locked desk! Surely, this would invalidate whatever he found. For all I know, he manufactured the ledger and attributed it to a man who cannot counter his claim because Paynter killed him."

Jake gritted his jaw and cut his eyes at Rosalyn. He met a determined gaze. When she nodded twice, he cleared his throat.

"I did enter the house, but I broke nothing. Miss Ashley was kind enough to provide the key to the drawer of *her* desk and hand over the ledger."

"She did no such thing!" said Lucien.

The judge stood and glowered over the room. "You will sit quietly, Mr. Ashley, or I will have my bailiff escort you to a cell. You *are* willing to do that, Mr. Rivers, are you not?"

"With pleasure, Your Honor."

"I would be most happy to provide Sergeant Rivers assistance in that task, if necessary," said Lieutenant Stallings. Mrs. Morris suppressed a chuckle beside him.

Lucien sat. The judge held him in his iron glare before finding his chair. "Besides, we've no need for conjecture. Miss Ashley."

"Your Honor?"

Lucien whipped his head around and his jaw fell nearly to his chest. "Rosalyn! What in God's name . . ."

"Ashley!" The judge's shout drew Lucien's attention again. "This is your final warning. Explore your silence or become one with a cell."

Lucien slumped in his seat with arms crossed and brow collapsing.

Kingman nodded. "Now, Miss Ashley. Is Mr. Paynter's testimony accurate as best you recall?"

"Yes, sir."

"You gave him the key and the ledger?"

"Yes, sir."

"From *your* desk."

"Yes, Your Honor."

"Very well. The ledger is permissible as evidence of Mr. Ketchum's wrongdoing. And let me tell you, it paints quite the sordid picture. Murder, mayhem, grift, bribery, extortion. I've seen some of the worst this nation has to offer, and this ledger competes for a position in that dismal company. Which brings me back to you, Mr. Ashley."

Lucien straightened. Light from the adjacent window sparkled from the sweat beginning to dot his brow. Kingman steepled his fingers and tapped his toe while scrutinizing Lucien.

"Mr. Ketchum is . . . was your right-hand man. Do you deny it?"

"No."

"No, *Your Honor*. Say it before I hold you in contempt."

"No, Your Honor."

"Very good. Now, regarding the events captured by this record, did Mr. Ketchum take his orders from you?"

"No . . . Your Honor."

"Care to amend that statement?"

In the space of a heartbeat, Lucien's demeanor transformed. His scowl spread into a pleasant smile and his brow lifted to reveal the sparkle of his eyes. "Why, no, Your Honor." His voice became the same honey trap that had convinced dozens of settlers to follow him along the Oregon

432

Trail. "If I'd known of Mr. Ketchum's dastardly dealings, I would have dealt with him personally. I cannot have anyone drag the name of a United States senator's son through the muck without repercussions."

The judge worked his jaw to one side. "So you claim no responsibility?"

"No, Your Honor."

"And the fire?"

"I had no knowledge of that either." He put a hand to his chest. "Why, the very thought of such an atrocity sickens me."

Jake agreed. Lucien's one-man play had him near vomiting. He'd seen better performances from traveling road shows. Judge Kingman seemed not to believe him either but lacked the proof Jake had hoped to find.

"Rumor has it," the judge said, "that Dutch van Zandt's miscreants were involved in the setting of the near-fatal prairie fire. Do you know anything about that?"

Lucien's smile grew wider. "I believe the rumor. Van Zandt is a despicable specimen of humanity capable of most any barbarity. I would suggest you turn your attention his way. However, a word of warning. The last judge who did so slipped in his bathroom and accidentally cut his own throat."

Kingman lifted an eyebrow. "Good thing I rely on a barber."

"Indeed."

In the silence that followed, Spraggs leaped up from his chair. "What about me? What's to become of me?"

Kingman waved a hand toward him without looking away from Lucien. "You'll face a jury of your peers on Monday. They will most likely find you guilty, and you will hang on Tuesday. Miss Blue."

"Your Honor?"

"Return the marshal to his public accommodations. If he tries anything foolish, shoot him."

"Yes, sir."

As Stacy walked a rubber-legged Spraggs from the courthouse, Jake pondered the mixed bag of justice and injustice. Spraggs would pay for what he did. Ketchum was dead and buried, along with many of the others who had tried to burn the miners. Some, though, remained at large and seemingly out of reach. And the whole mess had cost Lucien nothing.

"May I address the court, Your Honor?"

The question from Lucien broke a stretching silence marred only by the music of creaking benches. Kingman frowned before nodding. "Make it brief."

"What about Paynter? He is under a federal sentence. The lieutenant must return him to Fort Bridger for immediate hanging or risk dereliction of duty."

Jake watched Kingman for what seemed several hours while the judge tapped his forefingers together in thought. "What you say is true."

Rosalyn inhaled an audible gasp, and Esther Morris began mumbling to Stallings. Gus dropped a hand on Jake's shoulder and gave it a firm squeeze. Lucien, on the other hand, struck a heroic Greek pose, chin lifted and lips curled in a coy smile. All he lacked was a laurel wreath. The murmuring ceased and Lucien's grin faded when Kingman raised a deliberate hand.

"However, I have one other document to consider."

Jake leaned forward in his chair to scrutinize the paper that had appeared from beneath the ledger. He couldn't make out what it was from where he sat. The judge tapped the document.

"As you know, I am new to this circuit, having been appointed by President Grant just this past March shortly after his inauguration. What you may not know is that the president and I go back a ways, before the war. I consider him a friend and I believe he returns the sentiment. And so, when I explained in a telegraph the circumstances of Mr. Paynter's conviction, I hoped he might offer some advice, given his military experience."

Jake glanced at Rosalyn to find her gripping the back of the bench in front of her, clutching elusive hope. He'd be doing the same but could only wait as the rest of his life was explained, brief though it might be.

"He offered no advice," said the judge. "But he did send me this document on the train from Washington, delivered to me not one hour ago all the way from Laramie by mounted courier. A full pardon, signed by the president of the United States. Any further advice is now moot."

Lucien shot to his feet and shook a finger at the judge. "This is beyond an outrage! Unacceptable!" He swung the finger toward Jake. "This man is a soulless killer. A cold-blooded murderer. He deserves to swing, yet you set him free? How dare you make such a mockery of the law."

Kingman slapped his gavel against the bench as his cheeks shot through with red. "No, sir! How dare *you*. The president of the United States has spared a man's life after considering *all* the testimony, and yet you dishonor my court by rejecting his mercy at the top of your lungs? You will stand down before I find you in contempt and lock you in a cell."

Jake was sure Lucien would press his luck, but the man surprised him for once. He lowered his finger and glared at Jake with seething hatred in his eyes. "Stay away from my sister, Paynter, or I will dispense the justice the court appears unable to. Mark my words."

Lucien glared at a defiant Rosalyn before

shoving his hat on his head and striding from the courtroom with hostile footfalls. Stacy passed him on the way in.

"What'd I miss, besides the death threat?"

"Nothing much," drawled Gus. "Just a presidential pardon for Paynter."

Her eyes nearly fell from her skull. "Really!"

Kingman's gavel slapped the desk again. "Order! For the love of Bess!"

Stacy slid in beside Rosalyn and they hugged each other, smiles as wide as a Wyoming sky.

The judge raised a finger toward Jake. "This pardon is yours, but with a caveat."

Jake creased his brow. There was always a catch. "Tell me."

"This town needs a marshal. A man that cannot be corrupted. I'd appreciate it if you'd consider the job."

Jake shook his head. "I am already corrupt, Your Honor."

Kingman smiled softly. "Not in the ways that truly matter."

"And if I decline?"

"I was joking about the caveat. The pardon is yours regardless. But I'd still appreciate the consideration. I figure you owe me at least that for removing the rope from your neck."

Jake stood as Gus unlocked his irons. "I will think on it, sir."

CHAPTER FIFTY-THREE

Jake spent the first five minutes of his newfound freedom warding off well-wishers and enduring inconvenient emotions. Judge Kingman started the uncomfortable parade.

"Keep this close to your person, Mr. Paynter." He extended the trifolded presidential pardon and left his hand out for a handshake after Jake accepted the paper. Jake stuffed the document into his shirt and shook the judge's hand.

"Thank you, Your Honor."

"My pleasure. Now, don't take too long considering my request."

Lieutenant Stallings replaced Kingman, offered a salute, and then begged another handshake. Jake obliged, although averting his eyes. He didn't want his former subordinate to notice his discomfort. "Will you return south tomorrow, Lieutenant?"

"The day is still young. We'll get a jump on the ride. Try to make twenty miles before nightfall."

"Good luck, then, Stallings."

"And to you, Paynter."

Jake moved one step away from the chair before Mrs. Morris corralled him. Her typically stormy demeanor wore a thin-lipped smile.

"Congratulations, Mr. Paynter. For what it's worth, I believe you'd make an excellent marshal."

He dipped his chin. "I could say the same of you."

"Now, you spin yarns. See you around."

Stacy waited for her to clear out before way-laying Jake with the hug of a bear. A smallish bear, anyway. He awkwardly returned the embrace before prying her away. She grinned foolishly at him. "You're free, ya big chucklehead. You gonna just stand here actin' all grim and chuffy?"

"No. I will leave presently and act all grim and chuffy out of doors."

She punched his shoulder before dragging a loitering Rosalyn in front of Jake like some burnt offering atop an altar. Rosalyn lifted demure eyes to meet his.

"I'm happy for you, Mr. Paynter. You deserve this." A stray lock of mahogany hair fell across one eye as she extended a white-gloved hand to him. "My congratulations."

He stared at the hand as if considering a coiled rattlesnake before gently squeezing it. When he tried to let go, his hand wouldn't break loose. With a herculean force of will, he released his grip. "Thank you, Miss Ashley."

She swayed in place and stared at the wall past his shoulder, as if finding it of acute interest. Her eyes flickered back to engage him again. "What will you do now that you're a free man?"

A dozen answers flooded his brain, detailed and glorious and mostly contradictory of one another. He inhaled deeply through his nose. "I haven't the foggiest notion. But . . ."

"Yes?"

"But I'll let you know when I think of something."

A tremor passed through her smile. "That's all I ask. Good day, Mr. Paynter."

"And to you, Miss Ashley."

Gus stood by Jake, watching Rosalyn and Stacy leave the courthouse. He shoved Jake's shoulder. "You're five dollars short of stupid. Lettin' her walk out with no more assurance than a sinner on Sunday."

"Pardon?"

"You heard me. She likes you, for reasons that remain mysterious to me."

"She's too good for me, Gus."

"Got that right. But last I checked, every woman is too good for us."

Jake shook his head and made for the exit. "She deserves better."

Gus followed him without invitation. "I'd knock you silly right now if I thought it'd help, but I know better. So take this instead." He pressed a coin into Jake's palm. A quarter.

"What's this for?"

"Two bits will buy you three beers at the Red

Hen. You need at least that many to clear your head."

Jake couldn't disagree. He hadn't drunk a saloon beer in nearly two years. "Join me, then."

"Can't. The saloon owner's a world-champion son of a bitch. He don't allow negroes, natives, Chinese, Irishmen, or women to cross his threshold. You ain't Irish, are ya?"

"No."

"You're from Texas. Got any Comanche or Kiowa blood?"

"Not that I know of."

"Then go drink yer beers and have one for me. Meanwhile, I'll go visit with the boys of the Tenth before they hit the trail. Try not to cause trouble."

Jake nodded. "What makes you think I'd cause trouble?"

"You're awake, ain't ya?" He slapped Jake's shoulder once more for good measure and sauntered away.

As he watched Gus go, Jake wondered why the man hadn't washed his hands of him long ago. Such were the mysteries of brotherhood and unlikely to be solved anytime soon. He walked three blocks to the Red Hen and eased through the swinging doors. Several rounds of conversation quieted as he approached the bar. The aproned man cleaning glasses sported long

442

sideburns and a mustache that framed impressive jowls. He frowned at Jake.

"Can I help you?"

"You the saloon owner?"

"Nope. I just keep the bar."

Instead of punching the man's eye as he'd intended, Jake plunked down the quarter. "In that case, bring as much beer as this'll buy."

Behind him, the conversations started up again, but more constrained. Presently, three beers appeared before Jake on the bar top. He was well into the second when the devil arrived.

"I was gonna kill you for bounty but just heard you're a free man."

The saloon fell silent again. The achingly familiar voice at Jake's back brought him slowly around, mug in hand. Ambrose Blackburn stood ten feet away, hand on his revolver grip. Jake recalled that his Kerr was still locked up in the marshal's office. That was unfortunate.

"What do you want, Blackburn?"

"What? No greetings for your oldest friend after all we been through together?" Blackburn's grin hardened, deepening the scar along his jawline Jake had given him last time they tangled. "Maybe I'll just kill you anyhow. My ankle still aches where you stomped it."

One of the patrons stood. Jake blinked when he recognized Francisco Aguilar. "I wouldn't do that, mister. He's one of us."

"Is that a fact?" said Blackburn. "Don't you know who this man is? What he's done?" When Aguilar fell silent, Blackburn laughed. "No? Well, let me tell you about ol' Jake Paynter here. He rode with us in '61 and '62, killin', lootin', burnin'. He was the coldest of a heartless lot and gunned down soldiers and civilians alike. Why, he burned people alive in a shed, though I tried to stop him. Then, he turned coat and joined the Union, where he killed a lot more men. Two years ago, he shot his commanding officer in the forehead rather than follow orders. So tell me. Is this the kind of man you want to claim as 'one of us'?"

Aguilar cut anxious eyes at Jake and slowly lowered himself to his chair.

Blackburn chuckled darkly. "Didn't think so. You'll not mind, then, if I administer a little vigilante justice." He scanned the room for resistance and, finding none, peered again at Jake. "Seems you got no friends, Paynter."

Jake spread his arms wide. "Do what you must, Ambrose."

When Blackburn's fingers curled around his revolver's grip, Jake flung the mug at the man's head. It struck a glancing blow but proved enough to allow Jake inside Blackburn's aim. He drove his nemesis onto the floor as the revolver clattered away. Bodies leaped from chairs and scattered to the edges of the room. Blackburn

444

pressed a thumb into Jake's eye and rolled free. They clambered to their feet and circled each other in the narrow space.

"Been waiting nigh on a decade for this," said Blackburn.

"The same."

Jake's response released the spring holding them apart, and they collapsed into one another like colliding planets. They went to the floor immediately, punching, gouging, and rolling about in a death struggle. Jake broke a choke hold only to meet Blackburn's fist, followed by a knee to his groin. In reply, he belted Blackburn with his forehead and slammed the man's head against the wooden floor three times. He only stopped when Blackburn's hidden blade found Jake's thigh. Jake rolled away and hobbled to his feet. Blackburn shot him a bloodstained grin.

"Gonna slice me some venison."

The red haze had already begun descending when Blackburn lunged. Jake blocked the blade by allowing the point to sink into his forearm and then belted his attacker with the back of his fist. He yanked the knife from his arm and flung it away before lifting Blackburn off his feet and slamming him again to the floor. Jake swung astride his opponent and began alternating hammer blows of his fists upside Blackburn's head. After half a dozen swings, he slid off the man's chest, hoisted him onto his shoulders, and began careening toward the window. A gunshot halted his progress. He turned his head to find the heavy-jowled barkeeper scowling at him with a smoking shotgun still aimed at the ceiling and debris falling around his shoulders.

"Do not throw him through the dang window! Don't ya know how much it costs to replace plate glass in these parts? God made doors for that. Throw the varmint through the dang door, by Harry."

Jake nodded and hurled Blackburn through the door with such force that the man bounced off the boardwalk and landed sprawled on his back in the muddy street. Jake watched him lie moaning in the muck. His soul waged a brutal war against itself, with grand plans of how to kill Blackburn and equally grand ideas about sparing the man's life. He maintained the waffling vigil even as Aguilar appeared at his side and began wrapping Jake's forearm and thigh with what looked like strips of curtain from the aforementioned plate-glass window. Perhaps it was that quiet act of kindness that helped Jake decide. The haze lifted. With new clarity, he saw the unconscious Blackburn for who he was. Not the man who'd won Jake's loyalty with stirring words and a killer's confidence. Not the demon who'd tried to shape Jake in his morally derelict image. Not the surrogate father whose hold had bound Jake to a wheel of guilt for years.

No.

As he studied Blackburn anew, Jake saw only a simpering bully, a shell of a human being who filled the hollows of his decay with the agony of innocents. A man with no rights to Jake's soul. He hurled a glob of mucus onto Blackburn's cheek.

"You can't touch me. You're a ghost."

The approach of six men drew Jake's eyes from the dirt. Lucien Ashley leaned over Blackburn and slapped his cheek, drawing a moan. He jerked his head at his men. "Get him up. He's going with us."

Jake and Lucien exchanged glares that might've melted lesser men.

"What're you doin', Ashley?"

Lucien smiled coolly. "I need a replacement for Ketchum, given that you put him in a grave. Mr. Blackburn will do nicely. I suspect he and Mr. Sweeney will get along famously. They both hate you with impressive fury."

"Sweeney?" Jake narrowed his eyes. "He still here?"

Lucien chuckled. "Oh, Mr. Paynter. You should know by now that I never throw away anything useful, no matter how vile. I even had use for *you* once."

With that, Lucien turned away to follow his men and the groaning Blackburn. A dismal vision formed in Jake's head—of Lucien, Sweeney, and Blackburn and what they'd do to the town if left unchecked. He turned to his benefactor, who'd just finished wrapping his arm. "Thanks, Francisco."

As he began to shuffle up the street, Aguilar called out. "Where you goin', Paynter?"

Jake continued limping along. "To see a man about a job."

CHAPTER FIFTY-FOUR

Judge Kingman adjusted his eyeglasses when Jake darkened the door of his chambers.

"What in God's green acres happened to you, son?"

Jake curled a hand around his forearm to cover the stain of blood spreading on Aguilar's makeshift tourniquet. "I had to wrestle a demon."

Kingman perused Jake's various wounds a few seconds longer. "Looks like you lost."

"Not this time," Jake said. "I left him in the street."

"Dead?"

"Still breathin'. I may come to regret that decision, but too late now. And speaking of regret, I accept your offer."

The judge bounced up from his chair. "Why, that's wonderful . . ."

Jake silenced him with an extended forefinger. "But with conditions."

Wariness invaded the judge's expression. He crossed his arms and frowned. "Right, then. Give me your list."

"I can resign whenever I like. No contract."

"Granted."

"And I won't evict anyone from their home.

You'll need to find someone else to do the bank's dirty work."

"Also granted. I wouldn't expect otherwise from you." The judge's frown melted into a wry grin. "Any more stipulations?"

"A couple. I won't hang a man." He paused to exhale. "I'm killer enough without adding 'executioner' to my gravestone."

"Agreed. There's a fella out of Denver who does that sort of work on contract. Should we need to hang someone, I'll send for him. And the last stipulation?"

Despite his aching thigh, Jake straightened and threw his shoulders back. "I require two deputies. Gus Rivers and Stacy Blue."

Kingman's eyes grew wide. "A black man and a woman?"

"Yep."

The judge rubbed his chin. "That sort of thing isn't done, you know. A lot of folks would be unhappy about it."

"Just because it ain't done doesn't mean it ain't right. And if I gotta walk on the shadow side of some folks to right a wrong, then I'll be sure to carry a big lantern."

Kingman lowered his hand and nodded. "You argue a good case, sir. Can we do it off the books, though?"

"So long as they get paid."

"Agreed. Miss Blue and Mr. Rivers will make

fine deputies, I'm sure. Do you think they'll accept the position?"

Good question, Jake thought. But he knew the answer in his gut. "They will, if nothing other than to keep me out of trouble."

"Right, then." Kingman shuffled through a desk drawer and came away with three badges. He pressed them into Jake's bloodstained hand. "One for each of you. I'll let you do the honors of notifying your new deputies. Now, git. Let Maddie Dunbar stitch up those wounds, for God's sake. I don't want my new marshal bleeding to death in my chambers."

"Yes, Your Honor."

Jake limped away from the judge and through the courthouse door. The Dunbar smithy was no more than a hundred feet away, and his wounds cried for relief. However, he paused on the porch to survey the street. Folks moved in both directions, going about their business. A few nodded to him as they passed by.

He suppressed a smile. These were his folks. For now, anyway.

Jake peered toward the high end of the street to where he knew the Morris family lived. Somewhere in that direction, Rosalyn was probably speculating about what came next. He wondered the same. But he knew instinctively that a dark day was coming when he'd lock horns with her brother, and one of them would not survive the encounter. It was only a matter of time, particularly given the badges clutched in his hand. Could he protect Rosalyn from Lucien? More importantly, could he save her from himself? The gradual taming of his inner demons left both questions hanging in doubt. Regardless, he hoped to become more the man she saw and less the man he was.

He pinned one of the star-shaped badges to his shirt and pocketed the others. With more pride than he'd felt in years, Jake turned up the street toward the smithy. He had work to do, but not before attending to open wounds—of many kinds.

ACKNOWLEDGMENTS

I owe an immense debt of gratitude to the four women who made this series possible: author Ann Aguirre who recommended me, editor Christa Désir who championed and guided the story, Dr. Aldora White Eagle who imbued the story with truth, and my true love, Karen Nix, who lent a supporting arm every step of the way.

I would also like to acknowledge those who populated the West but whose stories have not been told nearly enough: the indigenous tribes of the Great Plains and Rocky Mountains, the buffalo soldiers of the Plains Army, and the immigrants from outside of Western Europe who joined the mosaic of this nation. They are all still here in some form or another. They are us and we are them.

ABOUT THE AUTHOR

When I was eight, my adventurous parents hauled our young family from the West Coast to a Wyoming mountain town perched on the border of the Wind River reservation. That magical landscape infused my formative years with a wonder of local lore that was both historical and present and revealed to me that often the greatest stories have been all but forgotten or were never told. After publishing science fiction and historical romance for ten years, it seemed a matter of destiny that I'd eventually return to the tales of my youth. The Jake Paynter series brings together fact and fiction to explore places, people, and themes precious to me. I've called Austin home since 1998 with my wife and three children. The kids are grown now but remain in and around the heart of Texas and consider themselves honorary Wyomingites. I've been away from that mountain town for a long time now but never really left the place.

Center Point Large Print
600 Brooks Road / PO Box 1
Thorndike, ME 04986-0001 USA

(207) 568-3717

US & Canada:
1 800 929-9108
www.centerpointlargeprint.com